KU-134-668

THE
TEMPLE
OF SKULLS

ANDY McDERMOTT

THE TEMPLE OF SKULLS

HEADLINE

First published in 2022 by
HEADLINE PUBLISHING GROUP

1

Cataloguing in Publication Data is available from the British Library

Hardback ISBN 978 1 4722 8497 6
Trade paperback ISBN 978 1 4722 8498 3

Typeset in Aldine 401 BT by Avon DataSet Ltd, Alcester, Warwickshire

Printed and bound in Great Britain by Clays Ltd, Elcograf S.p.A.

HEADLINE PUBLISHING GROUP
An Hachette UK Company
Carmelite House
50 Victoria Embankment
London EC4Y 0DZ

www.headline.co.uk
www.hachette.co.uk

For Kat and Sebastian

Prologue

Teotihuacán, Mesoamerica: AD 550

The stone altar had been warmed for centuries by the blood of human sacrifices. Tonight, there would be one more.

Aratu gazed over his domain from the summit of the colossal Pyramid of the Sun. A swell of pride at the sight of the great city below stretching to the jungle horizon, aglow in the sunset. The young king ruled over the most powerful civilisation these lands had ever known.

Pride gave way to concern. History held an unwelcome truth: every empire falls. Those conquered by Aratu's ancestors had all once believed themselves invincible, eternal. Now, the people of Tekuazotl, the Jaguar God, faced a devastating threat to their own existence.

Had that threat been an invader, Aratu would not have been concerned. At his command was an immeasurably powerful army, so vast in number the ground would tremble if its soldiers marched in unison.

But that very vastness might become its downfall. Aratu's enemy was no warrior. It was hunger. A volcano had erupted a year earlier, its smoke and ash obscuring the sun. And without sunlight, there could be no crops. The sky had eventually cleared, but by then the growing season was gone. There would be no harvest.

1

Animals were slaughtered, soldiers and bearers sent across the empire to bring food to the capital. But it was not enough. The people were starving. Some were despairing.

Others were angry.

Aratu slowly turned, seeing his audience of thousands: almost all dead. The altar was flanked by dozens of stone racks, each holding several long metal rods. Upon them were impaled the skulls of all those who had died here. Row upon row of empty eye sockets regarded him in silence.

His gaze reached the wide staircase ascending the pyramid's western face. Four of his priests, aided by burly soldiers, were dragging a struggling man to the temple atop the great structure. More soldiers held back a growing mob at its foot. Their fury was understandable. The prisoner, Esatl, had been a popular civic figure before the famine. Now he was a threat to Aratu's rule.

The time had come to remove that threat, and remind the people of the true power of Tekuazotl – and his king.

A glance at the water clock beside the altar. The lower receptacle was almost full, each drip from the higher bowl bringing the moment of sacrifice ever closer. His timing had to be perfect. But he had faith in his ally, Tekuni, to be equally precise.

He stepped back as the men reached the summit. Esatl had tried to resist; his face was bloodied, lips split and swollen. But he was still conscious despite the beating, aware of what was soon to come. The flash of fear as he saw the waiting altar proved that.

'Esatl,' said Aratu. 'You are here.'

'Not through choice, *majesty*,' came the rasping reply. Esatl had once been almost in awe of his ruler. Now the honorific was practically spat at Aratu's feet.

'You know *why* you are here.'

'Yes. To take the blame for your failings,' Esatl replied. 'To show the people their fate if they dare speak against you!'

2

A priest struck him with the hilt of his obsidian dagger. 'Be silent! Do not disrespect your king!'

Esatl's head briefly lolled before he recovered. 'You deserve no respect. Your people are starving, and you have done nothing. No, worse – you have *let* them starve while those around you grow fat! Food comes into the city from all across the empire, but only the chosen few receive it – everyone else gets mere scraps! They will not take it any more. And killing me will only make them more angry. When I die, ten others will take my place.'

'No,' Aratu said firmly, controlling his displeasure at being challenged. 'Your sacrifice will change *everything*. Tekuazotl will affirm my right to rule.' He pointed to the altar. 'Bring him!'

Protesting, Esatl was hauled to the raised stone slab. The priests held down his limbs, pinning him in place. Aratu checked the water clock again. It was almost time.

'Summon the witnesses,' he ordered. 'It is time to perform the sacrifice.'

Directly below, deep beneath the Pyramid of the Sun, was a hidden chamber. The room was lit only by torches burning glutinous pitch, the air heavy with smoke. But Tekuni could see a second water clock clearly enough. Its lower bowl was nearly full. When the last drop fell into it . . .

Earthbreaker would strike.

The old man turned from the clock. Before him spread a landscape in miniature. Mountains and valleys, plains and coastlines were carved upon an oval slab of deep green stone, jade-like except for the glinting flecks within it. Shallow pools of mercury represented the oceans on each side of the landscape, tiny drops of the liquid metal filling in lakes on the land.

Tekuni regarded one particular lake. It was a useful landmark, the city above not far from it. He looked further afield. He needed a target close enough for the people to witness what happened, but not so close that the city – or the underground chamber he was in – would be damaged.

One of the volcanoes to the south, he and Aratu had already decided. It was over a day's travel away, but still clearly visible. An eruption would be a sign seen, heard and felt. The people would fall in line when Aratu's supposed power was confirmed.

The *real* power, Tekuni knew, was his. Aratu's rule came from lineage and politics. But it would be worthless without Earthbreaker to back it. It was the empire's greatest secret. The imperial army could besiege a city for weeks before destroying it; Earthbreaker could smash it in moments. Every conquest had been won with its aid. And only a select few could wield it.

Tekuni was one of those few.

'It is time,' he called to those in an adjoining chamber. 'Bring my sacred robes.'

Several younger men entered the map room. They carried elaborate clothing, a long, multi-layered cape made of jaguar pelts and decorated with brightly coloured feathers. Tekuni waited for his acolytes to place the robes upon him. Then he turned to receive the final item. The headdress was heavy, made from the skull of another jaguar and draped with more spotted animal hide. The beast's features were preserved in a snarl, its eyes replaced by unblinking black orbs of polished obsidian. Tekuni's face was half hidden behind a golden mask, also resembling the terrifying visage of an angry big cat.

He raised his head as the other men knelt before him. 'I act as the living vessel of Tekuazotl,' he intoned. 'My words are his words. My will is his will.'

'We are your loyal servants,' the priests replied. 'We follow you, Tekuni – Lord of the Dead.'

Even after decades in the role, he still felt a thrill of power. 'Tekuni' was a title bestowed upon the high priest, given only to those who could use Earthbreaker. But it had been so long since he had used his birth name that without a conscious effort of recall it was forgotten. He *was* the Lord of the Dead; guardian of the Underworld, arbiter of death and rebirth . . .

And bringer of earthquakes.

He gestured for his followers to rise. 'Ometian. Fetch Earthbreaker.'

One of the priests bowed and retreated into the adjoining chamber. He soon returned, bearing a long rectangular box of polished mahogany. 'Here, Tekuni,' he said, opening the lid.

Inside was an object wrapped in black cloth. Carefully, reverently, Tekuni took it out and began to remove the covering.

Earthbreaker was revealed inside.

To the uninitiated, it was nothing more than a dagger. The length of a man's forearm, carved from the same green stone as the map. A circular hole had been cut through the bulbous end of its hilt, several small notches around its edge. The weapon was sharp enough to cut flesh, but other than its unusual colour, it seemed little different from the obsidian knives and swords used by the empire's forces.

Tekuni and his acolytes knew otherwise. Earthbreaker was the most destructive weapon in existence, given to them by their god. And they alone controlled it.

He slipped the last wrap of cloth from the hilt and took hold of it. A crawling electric tingle ran through him as he felt its power. A power that could obliterate any enemy. But today, the enemy was within the city itself.

He nodded to another acolyte. 'Ixati, give the signal. Let Aratu know we are ready.' The man hurried into the tunnel to the surface.

Tekuni raised the dagger, admiring it in the flickering torch-light. All he had to do was touch the map at the precise moment . . .

'Are . . . are we doing the right thing?'

The hesitant voice belonged to the youngest acolyte, Narutetl. Tekuni turned towards him, expression dark. 'What do you mean?'

Narutetl licked dry lips before replying. 'I've known Esatl since I was a child. He helped my family, he helped a lot of people. And he is a loyal follower of Tekuazotl. Why must he be sacrificed?'

'Because that is the will of your king!' Tekuni snapped. 'And it is also *my* will. I speak for the Jaguar God. Do you challenge me?'

'No, of course not!' Narutetl bowed his head, unable to meet the high priest's stern gaze. Tekuni was about to look away when the younger man spoke again, almost in a whisper. 'But . . . Esatl is a good man.'

'If he were a good man, he would not oppose his betters.' Tekuni turned his back on the acolyte, watching the water clock as the last few drops ran out.

High above, Aratu went to the top of the staircase. The crowd below had grown, individual voices reduced to a garbled roar by distance. Were there enough soldiers to hold them back?

It wouldn't matter. The time had come. Off to the south, beyond the grand houses of the city's elite, he saw a torch flare in a specific spot. The entrance to the secret chamber was hidden there. Tekuni's signal: all was prepared.

He returned to the altar, passing a small group of men and women. They were witnesses, respected by the population, whose words would not be doubted. They would confirm to the masses below that the king had used Esatl's sacrifice to call upon their god – and that his call had been answered in no uncertain manner. His authority and right of rule would be fully restored. That a troublesome citizen would be removed in the process was a useful bonus.

Esatl was still pinned on the altar. He struggled as Aratu lifted a long, serrated ceremonial dagger. 'No!' he yelled as the king approached. 'I've done nothing wrong – all I want is for the people to have food!' He looked to the others around him. 'You can't let him do this!'

None responded to his pleas. Aratu gave the water clock a final glance. One last drop sent a ripple across the lower bowl, then the surface was still.

'It is time,' he announced. A gesture, and a young woman hurried to him, bearing a golden half-face mask in the form of a jaguar. She placed it carefully upon him, then retreated.

The blood-red light of the setting sun glinting off Aratu's mask, he raised the blade high above his head. 'In the name of Tekuazotl, the great Jaguar God, I offer this sacrifice. Through his death, we shall find new life. By the spilling of his blood . . . our blood will be saved!'

He plunged the dagger down into Esatl's chest.

Esatl screamed, convulsing with such force that one priest almost lost his hold on his thrashing leg. Blood spurted from the wound. Aratu felt the hot liquid splash his lower face, but pressed down harder. Bone and cartilage cracked as he sawed at the man's sternum. A final gurgling cry escaped Esatl's mouth, then he fell silent.

His death did not end the king's work. Aratu pressed on, forcing open Esatl's ribcage to expose the organs within. 'I free this man's spirit,' he chanted. 'May it travel swiftly to the Under-world to face the challenges of the Jaguar God, then be reborn!'

The blade carved through blood vessels, separating the heart from the rest of the body. More liquid gushed out, splattering Aratu's hands. He pulled the organ from the chest cavity, raising it above his head for all to see. One witness looked as if she was about to faint. 'His strength becomes my strength,' the king intoned. 'My strength becomes your strength!'

What was Tekuni waiting for? Alarming thoughts arose. Was this treachery? Had the priest deliberately not acted, to harm Aratu's standing? If so, it was a game that might prove fatal to both of them . . .

The witnesses' expressions were changing. Becoming uncertain – suspicious. Aratu gestured with both hands towards the volcano. 'The power of the Jaguar God arises!' he cried, improvising to buy time. Tekuni *couldn't* have betrayed him, he was sure. Their positions were symbiotic, each dependent on the other. There had simply been some unexpected delay, that was all. It had to be! 'Watch as he brings fire to the mountain!'

But there was no flame from the distant peak. Despite his kingship, despite his ceremonial trappings, Aratu suddenly felt very aware that he was just a man. A man with his arms out like a fool, awaiting something that was not going to happen.

And the others saw that feeling upon his face. He hastily lowered his hands, standing tall and commanding – but it was too late. They had witnessed not a reaffirmation of his power, but the impotence behind his mask.

'Nothing is happening,' said one of the witnesses, an older man. The hesitancy in his voice at challenging his king was quickly replaced by the confidence of the righteous. 'Tekuazotl has not spoken.'

'He will!' Aratu protested. 'Watch, wait! He *will* show you my power!' But still the volcano stood unchanging against the darkening sky.

The woman who had seemed about to faint spoke, anger behind her words. 'You killed Esatl for nothing! He . . . he was not sacrificed. He was murdered!'

Aratu flared with anger of his own. He turned to the soldiers. 'Kill her,' he snapped. 'Kill them all!'

But even his own warriors hesitated – and that was enough for some of the witnesses to break through the shock of his

9

command and flee. The soldiers pursued them, swords slashing, hacking them down. More blood spilled across the pyramid's summit. But the older man reached the staircase and raced down it, shouting as he went. 'The king is a liar! Tekuazotl has turned against him! He killed Esatl to protect himself while we starve—'

A soldier thrust his sword into the man's back with such force that the tip burst out through his chest. The witness crumpled, his body tumbling down the stairs.

But his words had been heard – and a new fire ignited.

Fury swept through the crowd. The soldiers blocking their way, massively outnumbered, had already backed into a tight phalanx. The front rank raised their weapons as the enraged mob surged towards them, cutting down the leaders – but more followed, dragging them down by weight of numbers.

The phalanx broke. Some soldiers tried to escape around the pyramid's foot, but were quickly caught and trampled to death. The others rushed up the stairs, a few braver ones trying to hold back their pursuers before they too were overcome.

Aratu watched in horror as the human wave swept towards him. He was trapped. The staircase was the only way up or down, the pyramid's sloping walls too steep to traverse safely. 'Protect me!' he cried to his remaining guards. 'They must not reach the temple!'

His men moved to act as a wall between him and the approaching mob. The yells from below grew louder, angrier. Aratu reclaimed his dagger from beside Esatl's corpse. If he was to die, he would die fighting. But he still looked towards the distant volcano with a last spark of hope that the peak would erupt with thunderous flames . . .

The spark died. The fires did not come. Aratu knew in that moment that his reign was over.

Fear rising, he clutched the dagger more tightly. Screams came from the staircase as the crowd met the defenders. More noises of pain and death followed, louder, closer . . .

Here.

The first of the mob swept on to the pyramid's summit. Aratu's soldiers attacked, weapons swinging, blood splattering over the stones. But they were too few, their opponents driven by rage. They had gone hungry while the elite stayed fat, their leader killed for a display of power that had failed miserably.

Now it was time for brutal retribution.

Aratu backed against the altar as his protectors were slain. Three left, two – then almost before he could take in the carnage, none. His people dragged him onto the altar beside Esatl. The dagger was ripped from his hands. He watched in terror as it was raised above his chest—

Then plunged into it.

Narutetl scrambled out into the open. The tunnel entrance was hidden in a small outbuilding beside a mansion. This part of the city was normally quiet, an exclusive enclave reserved for nobility and the richest of the empire's rich.

Now, it was engulfed in chaos.

The young priest heard shouting all around – and screams. He realised what had happened. Without Earthbreaker, Tekuni had been unable to bring about the display of power that would secure the king's position. Esatl's sacrifice had been for nothing, and the people had risen up in revolt.

He heard footsteps in the tunnel and ran, vaulting a wall. If the other acolytes caught him, they would kill him for his treachery. He had to get clear—

He rounded a corner – and found himself facing an angry mob.

Some of the crowd had stormed the Pyramid of the Sun. Narutetl could see people climbing the great stairway to the summit. But the rest had found another target for their anger, sweeping into the nearby enclave. Any guards had either fled or been killed. But the crowd's bloodlust was far from sated. The men leading the mob were armed, their weapons ranging from stolen swords to improvised clubs and even simple hunks of stone. Fires swelled in the houses behind them, spreading rapidly.

Explaining what he had done wouldn't save him. Narutetl hurriedly turned back—

A knife stabbed deep into his stomach.

'Traitor!' hissed Ometian, twisting the blade. 'You have betrayed Tekuazotl – betrayed Tekuni!'

'I . . .' Narutetl gasped, but the rest of his words caught in his throat. His legs gave way. Ometian kept hold of the knife as he fell, forcing it deeper before yanking it out with a savage slash. Narutetl collapsed in the dirt, Earthbreaker slipping from his numbing fingers.

His killer picked up the green dagger. He twitched as a residual ripple of power crackled through his hand, then raced back to the tunnel entrance.

The other acolytes had split up to hunt for Narutetl. The only person Ometian saw was Tekuni, the older man short of breath as he emerged from the outbuilding. Relief filled the high priest's face. 'You have Earthbreaker,' he gasped.

'We must return to the map chamber, quickly,' said Ometian. 'The people are rioting.'

'I know,' Tekuni replied, watching flames rise from a nearby building. 'They will be here soon. Listen, Ometian – you must run. Get away from here, and protect your knowledge of Earthbreaker. I will try to use it to scare the rabble back under control. But if I fail . . . you must become the new Tekuni.'

'Me?' Ometian said, shocked. 'But – I am not ready to—'

'Nor was I when I took the title. But you will manage. You *must* manage! Now go. If I do not succeed, you must return later and find Earthbreaker. Even if the map here is destroyed, there is still the other in the Underworld.' He clapped Ometian firmly on his shoulder, then pushed him away. 'May Tekuazotl watch over you. Now, run. Run! Before they catch you!'

Ometian reluctantly hurried off. Tekuni watched him round a corner, then returned to the tunnel entrance—

'There! A priest, there! *Kill him!*'

Several men barged through a gate. Filled with fear, Tekuni rushed into the tunnel, shutting its wooden cover. He pulled a beam across to seal it, but knew it would not last long. Shouts echoed behind him as he ran down the dimly lit passage. He was barely a quarter of the way along when he heard planks smash and splinter.

Earthbreaker was now his only hope. The dagger clutched tightly in his hand, he pounded onwards, breath rasping with every gasp of smoky, stagnant air.

Brighter light ahead. The map chamber. Nearly there – but his pursuers were closing.

He ran in, going to the map. A symbolic use of Earthbreaker would not be enough now. He had to strike the city itself, to terrify its rebellious citizens into surrender. The risk was huge, but he had no choice.

He found the dot of mercury representing the lake to the south. Readying himself, he raised the dagger. There was no time for ritual: the Jaguar God would understand, he was sure. He brought the blade's tip down, towards the miniature landscape . . .

Resistance grew the closer it got, as if the map itself were forcing Earthbreaker away, fearful of what would happen when it touched. Tekuni was prepared for the sensation. He pushed harder, feeling the weapon squirm in his hands. The tingle of power running through it grew stronger—

The rioters were upon him.

Someone tackled him, slamming him down onto the map.

He kicked out, knocking his attacker back. Earthbreaker was still in his hand. He tried to stab it down against the stone landscape, but someone else grabbed his arm. He swung the blade at their face. A shriek as the tip caught flesh, then Tekuni himself roared as teeth sank into his forearm. Earthbreaker clattered to the floor.

A new fear rose, more than primal self-preservation. Nobody else could be allowed to claim the dagger! There was a chance, however small, that one of them might be able to use it – and that would mean the end of centuries of rule by the followers of Tekuazotl.

A sudden strength filled him, as if sent by the god himself. He clawed at the eyes of the man biting him. His opponent fell back. Tekuni rolled from the map, splashing a mercury sea. He saw Earthbreaker and snatched it up. If he could touch it to the landscape—

More people rushed into the chamber. Tekuni knew he was out of time. All he could do now was run. Beyond the map room were catacombs, a web of tunnels dug long ago. He knew them better than anyone. He could lose the mob in the darkness, then slip back to complete his task.

He rushed into the adjoining chamber. A dark opening led into the catacombs. He ran towards it—

But didn't make it.

Hands caught his cape, yanking him to a stop as the ceremonial robes pulled tight around his neck. He fell backwards. Screaming faces loomed nightmarishly over him, fists and feet pounding his body. Beyond, the gods watched judgementally from the elaborate murals on the walls. He had failed them, failed the Jaguar God.

And now he had lost Earthbreaker. The green dagger was torn from his hand. He cried out for mercy – but could only stare in horror as it was thrust into his heart.

★ ★ ★

'Ometian!'

Ometian looked around in alarm at the call, seeing one of the other acolytes peering nervously around a corner. He had fled at full pelt through the city, finding breathless shelter on a smaller ziggurat south of the Pyramid of the Sun. From there, he could see what was happening in his wake.

The sight filled him with dismay and fear. Fires burned throughout the elite's enclave. Even as he watched, a roof collapsed, spewing out a cloud of smoke and sizzling embers. The riot had spread into other parts of the city. The broad Avenue of the Dead, stretching all the way through the capital's heart, swarmed with people, running and milling about like panicked ants. With the king dead, his soldiers overwhelmed, everything was falling into chaos.

The other priest called out quietly. Two more acolytes emerged from hiding. 'Where are the others?' Ometian asked.

'Dead,' came the shaken reply from the first man. 'The people caught them, and . . .' A heavy breath. 'What happened to you? Did you find Earthbreaker?'

'I did,' Ometian told him. 'I killed Narutetl and gave it back to Tekuni.'

'So where is Tekuni?'

'He went back to the map chamber. But . . .' He pointed towards the house concealing the tunnel entrance. It too was in flames.

The other man understood at once. He sagged in defeat. 'Then everything is lost.'

'No,' Ometian said firmly. He stood facing his companions. 'Tekuni gave me instructions. If he failed, I am to become the new Tekuni. We are to protect the knowledge of the Jaguar God – to find safety until the chaos is over.'

'And then what?'

'Then we return. We find Earthbreaker. We use it – either

here or in the Underworld.' His voice rose, filled with a new determination. Tekuni had entrusted him with a great challenge. It was one he would achieve, however long it took. 'And we will restore the followers of Tekuazotl to power!'

* * *

The ruins were lit only by burning torches, shadows dancing across the crumbling walls. But beneath his jaguar headdress, Tekuni could see everything he needed to see.

The altar was makeshift, a simple slab atop a brick plinth. It would have to do. The followers of the Jaguar God were persecuted, hunted. As much as he wanted to build a permanent temple, it was too dangerous. They had to conceal themselves amongst the masses, only assembling for rituals.

Tonight, it was time for one. For a sacrifice.

The victim was a wanderer, enticed and befriended by one of the Dispossessed with promises of drink and food. The alcohol had been drugged to pacify him. The man now lay bare-chested upon the slab, held by Tekuni's priests. He seemed unaware of what was going on, glassy-eyed and bovine. Human trash, barely better than an animal. Again, it would have to do. Finding more worthy subjects would draw unwanted attention.

Tekuni stepped up to the altar, raising the ritual blade. 'In the name of Tekuazotl, the great Jaguar God, I offer this sacrifice. Through his death, we shall find new life. By the spilling of his blood, our blood shall be saved.'

He drove the dagger into the man's chest.

In his drugged state, the victim's reaction was little more than a gasp. The priests barely needed to exert themselves to hold him. Tekuni worked the blade, expertly cutting him open. It did not take long before his heart was exposed. 'I free this man's spirit,' Tekuni said, carving the organ from its place. 'May it travel swiftly to the Underworld to face the Jaguar God, before being reborn.'

His followers echoed his words as he held the heart aloft. 'His strength becomes my strength. My strength becomes your strength.' He bit a bloody piece from the heart, then waited for the men and women to close around him before handing it to the nearest. One by one, each took a bite, sharing the flesh in a timeless, sacred ritual—

Tekuni's mobile rang.

Everyone froze, startled. Tekuni himself was momentarily taken aback. Few people had the number for this particular phone; all knew that calling him during a sacrifice was forbidden. There was only one exception to the rule . . .

With sudden excitement, he took the phone from beneath his robes and answered. 'Yes?'

The call was brief. Tekuni stayed silent for a moment after it ended, his followers watching expectantly. Then a smile of triumph formed beneath his half-mask. 'Earthbreaker has been found,' announced the latest in the long line of high priests of the Jaguar God. 'Lost for over a thousand years . . . but now, it has been found.' His voice rose to an exultant roar. 'After all this time, we *will* retake the blade. And we *will* return to power!'

1

New York City

'It's been a while,' said Eddie Chase.

'Yeah,' agreed Nina Wilde. 'I never thought we'd be here again, but . . .' She sighed, regarding the apartment door with trepidation. 'Olivia's just that stubborn.'

Eddie nodded. 'Have to admire her for that. Deciding you're not going to end your days in some hospital and arguing with your doctors about it while you're hooked up to half a dozen machines is pretty impressive. Especially when you're a hundred and one years old.'

'True. What worries me is that now, she *isn't* in a hospital. I know she can afford her own nurses, but . . .'

'It's her choice,' said the Englishman. 'It's what she wants. She's said that all along.'

'I know.' Nina sighed again. 'I'm just acutely aware that this might be the last time we ever see her.' She looked back towards the elevators. 'Speaking of "we", where's Macy?'

'Macy!' Eddie called. 'Hurry up, love.'

Macy Wilde Chase emerged from around a corner, phone in hand. 'I just had to answer a message,' said the teenager.

'Who from?' asked Nina.

Macy frowned – an expression her parents saw far too frequently. 'It's private.'

'You're not going skateboarding with that boy with the nose rings, are you?' Eddie rumbled.

'Tchuh, *no*,' came the huffy reply. '*So* past him.'

'Well, whoever it is, turn off your phone while we're seeing your great-grandmother,' said Nina. Macy huffed again and put the phone in her bag – without powering it down. Nina kept an exasperated growl inside her head, then knocked on the door.

Olivia's nurse opened it. 'Yes?'

'I'm Mrs Garde's granddaughter,' Nina replied. 'She's expecting us.'

'Oh yes – Professor Wilde. Please, come in.' The nurse ushered them inside.

It was two years since Nina had visited her grandmother at home. Her health had started to deteriorate before her ninety-ninth birthday, requiring increasingly long stays in hospital. Nina had suggested she move into an assisted living facility – an idea that had, inevitably, been rejected. Olivia Garde valued her independence more than anything.

But not even she could fend off the inevitable for ever. The nurse led them to the master bedroom. Macy let out a shocked little gasp as they entered. Olivia seemed shrunken, tiny amidst an expanse of crisp white bedding. Her face bore a line for each of her years. Even her eyes, once lively and sharp, now appeared tired and dimmed. The wires of several monitoring devices ran to machines around her.

'Olivia?' Nina said quietly. 'We're here.'

Olivia turned her head, even that small movement an effort. 'Nina,' she said, managing a smile. 'So glad you made it. I'm happy to see you all. Even Eddie.'

'Just making sure you're not giving the nurses a hard time,' Eddie fired back with a grin.

'Oh, they're paid enough. They can put up with it. It won't be for much longer, anyway.'

19

'Don't say that,' Nina and Macy said, almost simultaneously. They gave each other a faintly awkward look, before Nina continued: 'How are you feeling?'

'Lousy,' said Olivia. 'Even with whatever drugs they're filling me with, it's a struggle to do anything more than lie in bed. And I do hate lying in bed. It feels like a waste of what little time I have left. There's so much I still wanted to do.'

'Like what?' Macy asked.

'Well, I always had a secret desire to go . . .' she waited for her family to lean closer before completing the sentence, with a wink, 'waterskiing.'

'I can arrange it,' said Eddie. 'Might have to gaffer-tape your hands to the handle, though.'

'Thank you, but I'll pass. It's a bit too cold at this time of year.' Olivia smiled again, then looked back at Nina. 'I know you're going to Mexico in a few days. I wanted to see you now so . . . so I could tell you how proud I am. You've achieved so much – you would have made your mother proud too.'

Nina felt her eyes welling. 'Thank you.'

'I'm sorry I spent so long away from you. That I abandoned you, and Laura. All that time, I could have . . .' Olivia paused, brushing away a tear of her own. 'They say it's best to live life without any regrets, but that's one I can't deny. I'm not sure I can apologise enough.'

'It's okay,' Nina assured her, holding her hand. It felt cold, almost nothing beneath the skin but bone. 'I forgave you a long time ago. You're here with us now.'

'For however much longer.'

'Grams, stop saying things like that,' said Macy, going to the opposite side of the bed. 'My great-grandma never gives up, ever.'

'I'm glad you think so highly of me, Macy,' said Olivia, smiling. 'And I'm glad you came today. I understand you have quite the busy social life.'

Macy shot a sharp glance at Nina. 'Is that what you've heard?'

'Oh, don't blame your mother. You're a fifteen-year-old girl – astonishing as it may seem, I was once a teenager myself. And I had a daughter who was that age too. I know what it's like.' Another smile. 'But I wanted to see you again, and to let you know that even after I'm gone, everything will be all right for you. I've taken care of it.'

Macy blinked, confused. 'What do you mean?'

'Yes, what *do* you mean?' Nina asked pointedly, already knowing.

'The trust fund, of course,' Olivia replied.

Macy's bewilderment grew. 'What trust fund?'

Eddie grimaced. 'Oh boy. This'll be fun.'

Olivia turned back to her granddaughter. 'You haven't told her about it? What, at all?'

Nina's expression was a frozen mask. 'This would have been good to discuss *before* it became an issue, Olivia.'

'What haven't I been told about?' Macy demanded.

Nina was trying to think of a nuanced explanation when Olivia, to her dismay, got straight to the point. 'I set up a trust fund for you, Macy,' she said. 'When you were three or so. It'll become yours on your eighteenth birthday. I don't know the exact current value, but it's several million dollars.'

Macy's eyes went wide. '*What?*'

'All my other assets will be transferred to it per the terms of my will, as well,' Olivia went on.

'You're leaving everything to *me*?'

'Your mother and I discussed this, several years ago. She was adamant that she didn't want to inherit anything from me. So, as my only other living blood relative, everything will go to you instead.'

Macy stared at Nina in disbelief. 'You didn't want to be Grams' inheritor? Why?'

Nina had her reasons, but decided this was not the moment to explain them. Instead she rounded angrily on Olivia. 'You really thought *this* was the best time to tell Macy?'

'If not now, then when?' Olivia countered.

'You should have talked to me first! Dammit, Olivia, you *knew* I wasn't happy about the situation.'

'Macy is my great-granddaughter,' the old woman snapped. 'It's entirely my right to make her my beneficiary.'

'Yeah, but she's *my daughter*. Which means that while she's still a child, I have a say in anything that affects her life. And your casually announcing that she'll become a multimillionaire on her eighteenth birthday counts!' Nina raised her hands in exasperation. 'What if she decides "I don't need to work hard on my grades, I know I'll be rich"?'

'Mom!' Macy cut in, voice cold. 'The *child* is standing *right here*. You want to talk about me? Then talk *to* me.'

Nina held back an angry reply, knowing her daughter was right. 'Yes, I'm sorry. I shouldn't have done that. But this is not how you should have found out about it.'

'Then how should I have? When I turn eighteen and Grams' lawyer walks in and presents me with a giant novelty cheque?'

'All right, maybe this isn't the right time for a big argument,' said Eddie. 'Let's not make any of these machines start beeping, okay?'

Nina was annoyed, but nodded. 'Yeah. You're right. We'll talk about this later, Macy.' Her daughter's expression promised that said talk would not be amicable.

Under Nina's glower, Olivia also changed the subject, but an edge of tension underpinned the rest of the visit. However, Nina's anger was gradually overcome by sadness as she watched Olivia become increasingly tired, the old woman struggling to concentrate. The nurse came in every so often to check on her

22

patient; eventually she said, 'I'm sorry, but I think you should go now. Mrs Garde needs to rest.'

'We'll come back tomorrow, Olivia,' said Nina.

Olivia's eyes had almost closed, but she managed to open them, giving Nina a small smile. 'I'd like that.'

Macy held her hand. 'I'll see you then, Grams.'

A little laugh. 'I'm glad you could find a space in your busy calendar.'

'For you? Always.' Macy kissed Olivia's cheek, then stood, giving her parents an unhappy look.

The cab ride home was uncomfortably silent. It wasn't until the family returned to their apartment on East 78th Street that conversation resumed – with considerable intensity. 'So,' said Macy, almost before Nina had taken off her coat, 'why didn't you tell me about this trust fund?'

'For exactly the reasons I told Olivia,' Nina replied. 'I didn't want it to affect your childhood.'

'Will you *stop* calling me a child? I'm fifteen! And the cat's out of the bag, so now what happens?'

'I don't know. I really don't. I'm still angry with Olivia for telling you without discussing it with me first, but . . .' Nina exhaled heavily. 'I hope it doesn't change any decisions you've already made about your future. About going to college, what degree you might want to study . . .'

'Well, I don't know, do I?' Macy said sarcastically. 'I haven't had a chance to think about it yet. I'm still in shock! Are there any other secrets you've lied to me about? Like I'm adopted, or I have a brother you never mentioned?'

'No, there aren't,' Nina told her firmly. 'And I *haven't* lied to you. I just . . . kept something from you that you didn't need to know about.'

'It's the same thing. It's still . . .' Macy paused, searching

23

for the right – the most cutting – word. 'A *betrayal*. That's what it is, Mom. You hid something huge from me because you didn't trust me to handle it. I don't know if I can forgive you for that.'

Nina felt as if an icicle had been thrust into her heart. It took her a moment to speak again. 'Macy—'

But her daughter had already turned her back and stalked away. Her bedroom door slammed behind her.

Nina sagged, deflated – and hurt. 'Shit.'

'Well, Christ,' Eddie said, putting a hand on his wife's shoulder. 'She really is growing up, isn't she? Too bloody fast.'

'I don't . . .' Nina shook her head, lost. 'I don't know what to do. I was never like this with my mom when I was fifteen.'

'She's not you,' he pointed out. 'She's herself.'

'I know, but . . . this wasn't how I wanted it to be unequivocally confirmed!'

Eddie smiled. 'She'll be all right. Just give her some time.'

That time proved longer than the rest of the day, though. Macy only emerged from her room for dinner, treating both parents – but her mother in particular – with sullen, taciturn disdain before disappearing again the moment she'd finished. Nina felt too mentally drained to call her on it. It was far from the first time Macy had given her a sulky cold shoulder . . . but on this occasion, it was justified. *Should* she have been told about the trust fund? Even by the time she and Eddie went to bed, Nina had reached no conclusion.

★ ★ ★

Nina was woken by her phone in the early hours of the morning. She was immediately afraid. There was only one reason anyone would call her at this time.

Eddie sat up beside her as she answered. 'Yes?'

'Professor Wilde?' A woman's voice, familiar from the previous day. 'It's Helena, Mrs Garde's nurse. I'm sorry, but . . . I'm afraid I have some bad news. Your grandmother passed away in her sleep.'

'I . . . I see,' Nina replied, numb. Even expecting the news, it was still a shock.

'It was peaceful,' the nurse added. 'She wasn't in any pain.'

'Okay. Thank you for telling me.'

Helena waited for Nina to say something more. When she didn't, she continued: 'I'll call you again later. About the . . . arrangements. Again, I'm very sorry.'

'Thank you,' Nina repeated. She ended the call.

Eddie moved closer. 'Was that . . . ?'

'Yeah.' She sat silently for a long moment, then a shudder of emotion ran through her. 'My grandma just died,' she managed to say before her voice cracked. Sobbing, she curled into a ball as her husband held her.

2

The funeral was a larger event than Nina had expected. While she and Macy were Olivia's only living relatives, her grandmother had been prominent in the social circles of New York and New England for decades. At least a hundred people attended the service.

She didn't know any of them, though, and had no desire for interaction beyond exchanging condolences and superficial pleasantries. The throng gradually dispersed, leaving her alone with her family at the grave. Nina regarded the headstone. Olivia had been born in the year of the first Wall Street Crash – so long ago, it felt almost as ancient as the lost civilisations Nina had spent her career uncovering. A whole century of life, of experiences. How long would her own life be? She was now fifty, practically half her grandmother's age. How much more did *she* have left to experience?

She pushed aside the maudlin thought at a muffled sob. 'It's okay,' she told Macy, moving closer. 'We all miss her.'

Macy, eyes red from crying, looked down at her. Even not yet fully grown, she was already two inches taller than her mother. 'Can we go?' she whispered. 'I want to go home.'

Nina nodded sympathetically. 'Yeah, honey. We can.'

The funeral had been held in New Haven, Connecticut. Nina imagined the city had sentimental meaning to Olivia; she had lived there when her daughter Laura – Nina's mother – was young. Eddie took the wheel of the rental car to drive them back to New York. The mood was sombre, hardly a word exchanged.

It wasn't until Manhattan's skyscrapers were visible that Macy spoke. 'Mom? Why did you tell Grams you didn't want to inherit anything from her?'

It was an explanation Nina had hoped to avoid giving. 'Because Olivia's family's money came from . . . something dirty,' she said. 'Her family was part of what they called the Midas Legacy. They had a fortune in gold, but . . . it didn't belong to them. It was stolen by their ancestors. And when one of the other families in the Legacy decided they wanted more, they almost killed us for it.'

Macy frowned faintly as her mother's words sparked a memory. 'I remember . . . being with Aunt Holly, after kindergarten? Then there was a man, who . . .'

'He tried to kidnap you,' Nina said grimly. In a life containing too many terrifying moments, it had been one of the very worst.

'So that was *real?* Wow. I was only little; I'd always assumed that was just a wrong memory.' Macy's tone abruptly became more accusatory. 'Wait – and then someone *else* kidnapped me, like two years later?'

'He was a British spy,' said Eddie. 'We tried to stop him from blowing up Big Ben, in London. He went after you to get revenge on us.'

'You didn't stop him, though, did you? I mean, it's ten years on, and they still haven't finished rebuilding it. And then after *that*, first you involved me in a plot to kidnap someone else in Venice, and then I got kidnapped *again* and had an entire Chinese city blow up around me!' Her voice grew louder. 'Why not just put a handle on my back to make it easier for the bad guys to take me away? You're supposed to *protect* me, not put me in danger!'

'Macy.' There was a warning note in Eddie's voice.

'It's okay,' Nina insisted, knowing Macy's rising emotions were fuelled as much by grief as anger. 'We *did* protect you; we did everything we possibly could to keep you safe.'

He bit deeply into the heart, teeth tearing through the outer sac and into the muscle within. Blood sluiced down his chin. He ripped out a chunk of meat and chewed it, then swallowed. 'Through the blood of this man, I speak with the voice of Tekuazotl!' he proclaimed. He stepped away from the altar, pointing at the distant peak to the south-east. 'And now, the Jaguar God will show you the power I command – the power with which I rule!'

Tekuni stood at the map, the stone dagger in his hand. Under his breath he recited the words of the ritual going on above. '. . . the power with which I rule,' he murmured, bringing Earthbreaker's point towards the carved summit—

'This is wrong,' came a whisper from behind. Tekuni glanced back in surprise at the blasphemy – as Narutetl suddenly charged at him. 'No!'

The impact sent Tekuni staggering. He grabbed the map's edge to keep himself from falling. Mercury splashed, a powerful shock making him flinch. Before he could recover, Narutetl wrenched Earthbreaker from his hand – and ran.

The other acolytes were stunned by the unexpected assault. By the time they reacted, Narutetl had fled into the tunnel. 'Get him!' Tekuni roared. 'He has stolen Earthbreaker – bring it back!' Ometian led the hunt, the priests racing after their quarry.

Tekuni looked up in alarm towards the temple above. Aratu would have finished the ritual by now, and called upon the Jaguar God to deliver a sign. If that sign did not arrive . . .

Aratu stared eagerly at the horizon. At any moment, he would see the eruption, feel the earth tremble. When the quake came, the shouts of anger from below would be replaced by terror – then awe at his power. Any moment . . .

Nothing happened.

8

'And is that what you were doing by hiding Grams' trust fund from me?' Macy shot back. 'Keeping me safe – what, from money? Or were you ashamed that the family did something bad in the past, and you wanted to keep it secret to protect your reputation?'

'Macy, that's *enough*.' Eddie rarely raised his voice to his daughter; the mere emphasis was enough to startle her into silence. 'Your great-grandma wouldn't want this. Not today.' Macy shifted across the rear seat to avoid his gaze in the mirror.

The rest of the journey was deeply uncomfortable, nobody wanting to talk. Eddie dropped Nina and Macy outside their building so he could return the car; once inside, Macy immediately disappeared into her room.

Demoralised, Nina waited for Eddie to come home. 'Ay up,' he said, having received only one response to his called-out greeting. 'Going to guess you haven't had a big heart-to-heart and hugged things out.'

'What gave you that idea?' Nina replied with a weary, humourless smile. 'The metaphorical "go away" sign on our daughter's door?'

'If it only said "go away", I'd be amazed at her restraint.' Eddie sat with her on the sofa. 'You okay?'

'Yeah. I guess. Considering.' She sighed. 'Had a cry while you were out. Not as much as I'd expected, though. I guess funerals act as a kind of closure.'

'They do. Been to enough of them to know that, unfortunately.'

'Me too. Although . . .' Another sigh. 'I didn't get any closure at my parents' funeral. There were no bodies. Not until ten years later.' Nina felt a sudden rush of anger. 'And Olivia didn't even come to her own daughter's funeral!'

'She didn't?'

'Mom had told me she was dead, remember? Their stupid

28

goddamn feud over her marrying my father meant they cut themselves off from each other. Even for that!'

'Maybe Olivia was trying to protect you,' Eddie suggested. 'It wouldn't have been right for her to turn up and say, "Hi, I'm your lost-long grandma. Your mum lied to you by saying I was dead!"'

'Maybe not, but . . . God. We're one fucked-up family. All the women on my side are the same – stubborn to the point of stupidity. Olivia, Mom, me . . . Macy. You don't need to keep scaring off her potential boyfriends. I'm sure she'll terrify them all on her own.'

'I'm just watching out for my little girl.'

'As she keeps pointing out, she's not so little any more. She's already bigger than me; she'll probably top out above you at the rate she's growing.'

'It's all the bloody growth hormones you Yanks shove in your food,' Eddie said with a crooked smile. He ran his fingertips across his bald head. 'Shame they don't work on hair.'

The joke coaxed a small chuckle from Nina. 'Thanks.'

'For what?'

'Making me laugh for the first time since Olivia died.'

'Always here to help, love. Speaking of which, what are we doing about going to Mexico? We already postponed once for the funeral; are we going tomorrow, or rescheduling again?'

'To be honest,' said Nina, 'I'm considering cancelling it entirely. It's a nice gesture by the Mexicans, but there's no official need for me to see this thing. I think it'd be better for Macy if she had some time to herself to help her get through what's happened.'

'Or a trip abroad might be exactly what she needs to take her mind off it,' Eddie countered. 'Why don't you ask her?'

'I'm the last person she wants to talk to right now. You should do it. You were going training with her this afternoon, weren't you?'

'If she still wants to come. Why don't you come an' all? That way, we can both ask her. Plus, it's been a while since you've done much exercise. It might do you good – I mean, Mexico City's over seven thousand feet up. You'll probably pass out from lack of oxygen just walking around.'

'Thanks for that vote of confidence in my physical fitness,' Nina said, giving him a half-smile. 'But if I went, you'd both leave me for dust. Besides, it'd still be better if you ask her. She actually listens to you.'

'Except about her boyfriends. Okay,' he said. 'If Macy's still up for training, I'll see what she wants to do. If she says she still wants to go, are we flying out tomorrow?'

Nina thought for a moment. 'Why not?' she replied. 'I have to admit, I'm intrigued about what the Mexicans want to show me.'

It was a chilly day, but both Eddie and Macy were hot by the time they'd completed their run around Central Park. They stopped at Conservatory Water, a pond on the park's eastern side. Eddie checked his watch. Not his best time, but he hadn't been pushing. Still, not bad for a fifty-five-year-old. The former SAS soldier had been determined not to let his fitness slide after entering middle age, and so far his physical regimen had kept him in shape.

He was more impressed by Macy. It had taken some coaxing for her to join him, but once outside the apartment's four walls, her mood visibly brightened. The young redhead had little of her father's muscular stockiness, yet she had easily kept pace with him, occasionally even getting ahead and then – inevitably – challenging him to a race. She won a couple of the short sprints. 'I'm gonna start outpacing you soon,' she told him with a smile.

'Wouldn't surprise me,' he replied. 'You the fastest in your year at school yet?'

'Ah . . . *nearly*,' she reluctantly admitted. 'Second fastest. On a good day.'

'Keep at it, you'll get there. You're just like your mum; once you decide you're going to do something, it gets done.'

The mention of Nina darkened her expression. Eddie changed tack. 'So, Mexico,' he said. 'What do you want to do?'

'What do you mean?'

'Do you still want to go? If you don't feel up to it, that's absolutely fine. We can postpone it again, or call it off altogether. It's up to you.'

Macy eyed him warily. 'What does Mom want to do?'

'She's letting you decide.'

'Really?'

'Yeah.'

'But I thought it was a big archaeological deal. She never turns those down. Even if it means leaving me behind.' A hint of bitterness at that last statement.

'Either we all go, or none of us go. That's what your mum and I agreed.'

'Mom,' the young New Yorker corrected. 'And you know, there's a third option.'

Eddie grinned. 'Nice try, but we're not leaving you home alone.'

'But it's not like I'm going to hold a house party or anything!'

'That was a suspiciously specific denial,' he said with a laugh. 'So what's it going to be? Go, or stay?'

She considered the question. 'Well . . . it'll be warmer in Mexico. And we've already paid for the tickets, haven't we? I don't want to waste the money.'

'You can tell you're a Yorkshireman's daughter – watching every penny,' said Eddie.

'I won't need to when I turn eighteen.' A flare of resentment – but it quickly passed, to his relief. 'You know what?

Let's go to Mexico. It's been a bad few days. Maybe a trip will take everybody's minds off it.'

'I'm sure it will. Come here.' Eddie hugged her; she returned the gesture with a warm squeeze. 'We're going south of the border.'

3

Mexico City

An underlying tension remained between mother and daughter, Nina mused, but at least now there was something to distract from it. She hadn't visited Mexico for a long time, and Macy had never been, so novelty overcame disagreements – however temporarily.

Mexico City offered an appealing blend of the familiar and the alien. The country's proximity to the United States inevitably meant surface similarities: the same kinds of cars, billboards advertising familiar brands. Yet differences quickly became apparent. Buildings were more colourful, a kaleidoscopic montage of hot pinks, sunrise oranges and sea-foam greens rather than the pale pastels and raw brick and concrete predominating across the border. Nina had lived in New York City her entire life, and the two metropolises were comparable in population, but there was another energy here, the notorious outta-my-way rudeness of New Yorkers replaced by a more relaxed and open air.

But other differences were revealed as the pink-and-white taxi carried them through the city. A few enclaves of privilege aside, behind the vivid paint many buildings had crumbling facades, sidewalks and roads cracked and poorly patched. Not from decay, but simply finances stretched too far to cope with the wear and tear of almost nine million people. Mexico might adjoin the wealthiest nation in history, but little of that money made its way across the border by osmosis. It was hardly surprising so many wanted to cross that boundary in the hopes of finding a share of the riches beyond – by legal means or otherwise.

Mexico's present wasn't why Nina was here, though. The taxi headed north-east out of the city, travelling some thirty miles to the town of Teotihuacán. Beyond the modern municipality was its ancient eponym, a great expanse of ruins dating back at least fifteen centuries, and in parts many more.

For now, though, all she could see of them were tantalising glimpses beyond trees. The taxi brought them to Teotihuacán's archaeological headquarters, a walled compound in the site's south-western corner. Two armed guards regarded the arriving cab with suspicion. Nina understood their wariness. This was both Mexico's greatest historical landmark and one of its biggest tourist attractions, as important as the Pyramids and the Sphinx were to Egypt, and new treasures were still being unearthed, even now. Security was necessary to protect the tourists from criminals – and the relics from both.

Nina and her family exited the car. It was warmer than in New York, but at high altitude the sun provided less heat than she'd expected. She only had a light jacket, and she gave Eddie's heavier leather garment a jealous look. '*Hola*,' she said to the nearest guard. '*Mi nombre es Profesora Nina Wilde. Doctor Maldonado me*, uh . . . *expectora?*'

The man reacted with confusion, then amusement. 'Mom,' said Macy with disdain. 'You just told him Dr Maldonado is a cough syrup!' She corrected her mother in fluent Spanish, and with no small amount of smugness.

The guard chuckled. '*Sí, sí. Por aquí por favor. Te llevaré con él.*'

'He'll take us to him,' Macy translated.

'Yeah, yeah, I got that much,' said Nina, faintly irritated. She was sure her grasp of Spanish had once been better. Macy's smirk wasn't helping, either.

Eddie paid the driver, then collected their luggage. The guard opened the gate and led them inside. Run-down stone and pre-fabricated buildings surrounded a dusty red courtyard. A pickup truck was parked nearby, a couple of men unloading large plastic jugs of water. The guard brought them into one of the larger structures. '*Encontraré al doctor*,' he said. '*Espere aquí, por favor.*'

'*Gracias*,' Nina replied, hoping he'd said what she thought. Luckily, he had indeed gone to find their host. He soon returned with another man and a woman, both in hard-wearing and dusty clothing.

'Professor Wilde!' said the man, extending his hand to Nina. He was jovial, balding, head slightly hunched as if most of his time were spent staring down at the ground – which considering his occupation was perhaps the case. 'I am Gregorio, Gregorio Maldonado. We have spoken by phone, but it is a big pleasure to meet you in person.'

'Dr Maldonado, hi,' Nina replied, shaking his hand.

'Call me Gregorio, please, Professor Wilde.'

'Nina,' she said with a smile. 'A pleasure for me too. Thank you for inviting me and my family.' She introduced them.

'Good to meet you all,' said Maldonado. He gestured for his companion to step forward. 'And this is Dr Rosamaria Rendón. She is my deputy here, but in a few years I am sure she will be running the place!'

The woman laughed faintly. 'I am in no rush. Professor Wilde, hello. It is an honour. You've done so much for women in archaeology. I hope I can discover even one thing as important as your finds.'

'She is too modest,' said Maldonado. 'I think she has already! But you can judge that for yourself tomorrow.'

'We're not seeing the site today?' Nina asked.

'It is a little late. I want to give you the grand tour of the city before I show you what we have found under it. Besides,' a smile, 'I have booked a table at the best restaurant in town for this evening.'

'Great,' said Eddie. 'I love Mexican food. Although you probably just call it "food".'

'Eddie,' said Nina, rolling her eyes at the joke.

'Dad,' said Macy, doing the same.

Maldonado chuckled. 'Then you will be very happy tonight.' He glanced past his guests at a noise from the entrance. '*Oh, hola.*'

Rosamaria smiled. 'Professor Wilde, Mr Chase, Macy – this is my son, Diego.'

They turned to greet the new arrival. In the doorway, a five-gallon water jug on each shoulder, was a young man of around seventeen. Despite the cool air, his shirt was open, revealing a tanned, muscular chest. Shaggy black hair hung down to his shoulders.

'Oh. Hello!' said Macy, with considerable enthusiasm.

A little taken aback, Diego grinned. 'Hi.' Recognition in his eyes as he saw Nina. 'Professor Wilde! My mom said you were coming.'

'Yes, hi,' said Nina, aware that Macy was giving her a sidelong glare for drawing the handsome youth's attention. 'I'm looking forward to visiting the dig tomorrow.'

'I'll help show you around.'

'Diego joins in with our work when he can,' said Rosamaria. 'He has even made some discoveries of his own. I think he will make a great archaeologist some day.'

'Or a musician,' Diego replied, grinning again. 'I play guitar,' he added to Macy. From his mother's faint sigh, it was a potential career choice with which he enjoyed taunting her.

'Wow, that's so cool,' said Macy. 'Are you in a band, or . . .'

'No, I'm solo,' he told her. 'Just me and my songs.'

'You write your own songs? That's so amazing.'

Nina decided to leave them to it. 'By the way,' she said, turning back to Maldonado, 'I want to apologise for postponing our visit.'

He shook his head. 'It is not a problem. It must have been a difficult time for you.'

'Thank you.'

'Besides, the delay may be to your benefit. We have found something new – something remarkable. But,' he smiled again, 'you will see tomorrow.'

'I'm looking forward to it,' she said.

The Mexican glanced at their bags. 'Have you not been to your hotel yet? Okay, I will have someone drive you there. The restaurant is not far from it. We will see you there at . . . seven? Is that too early?'

'That'll be fine,' Nina assured him.

'Are you coming too?' Macy asked Diego. He nodded. 'Oh, cool.' She gave him the widest smile Nina had seen from her in some time.

'Then,' said Maldonado, 'let me be the first to say: welcome to Mexico!'

The restaurant was quiet, with few diners other than Maldonado's party. Nina didn't mind. The lack of noise made it easier to hear what the others were saying, and she was sure Maldonado and Rosamaria had plenty of interest to relate.

At the moment, though, she was the one talking. The Mexicans were making the most of having the world's most famous archaeologist as their guest. 'So then, after you left the IHA,' said Maldonado, 'you discovered the Hebrew Tabernacle and the Ark of the Covenant? By *chance*?'

'It wasn't quite by chance,' Nina corrected. 'We were

following the trail of another artefact – it just happened to be in the same place as the Ark.'

'Well, a bit more than that,' said Eddie. 'It was *in* the Ark.'

'Along with the original tablets of the Ten Commandments,' said Rosamaria. 'Incredible. You found what others have searched for their whole lifetimes, and you were not even looking for them!'

'I think that sums up archaeology as a whole,' Nina said. 'You can have all the knowledge, and expertise, and equipment you need to find what you're searching for. But sometimes, everything hinges on luck.'

Maldonado nodded. 'That is true. Even here at Teotihuacán. One of our greatest finds was made by chance. Sergio Gómez saw a sinkhole near the Temple of the Plumed Serpent after a flood, and wondered what was at the bottom. It was a whole complex of tunnels and ritual chambers. They are still being excavated even now, nearly thirty years later.'

'But what you've found under the Pyramid of the Sun could be even bigger?' said Nina, wanting to move the subject away from herself.

Maldonado gave a modest shrug. 'Perhaps, perhaps. But you will see for yourself in the morning. As for you, will you ever go back to the International Heritage Agency?'

'I've still got friends at the IHA, and the United Nations,' Nina told him, 'but I left over fifteen years ago. I think I'd suffer culture shock if I went back after so long. Besides, I'm happy doing what I do now. I enjoy teaching – more than I expected, actually. I'd thought I'd spend a lot more time on research and fieldwork, but . . . well, things change as you get older.'

'They do,' Rosamaria agreed. 'Sometimes for the better, sometimes . . . not. I am very sorry about your recent loss.'

'Thank you,' replied Nina, with a twinge of sadness – and guilt. Even only a day after Olivia's funeral, the journey to

Mexico had been enough to push it from her mind. She looked at Macy to see if she was all right. Her daughter, however, was preoccupied by a conversation with Diego in quiet Spanish.

Rosamaria nodded. 'My husband, Diego's father, died several years ago.' Diego looked around at the sound of his name, drawing Macy's attention to what the adults were saying. 'It was . . . a terrible time. I was very close to falling completely into despair. Especially when I was given platitudes about it being "God's will". How could God want such a good man to die?' Her face briefly tightened with restrained emotion. Diego put his hand on her arm, gently squeezing it.

'But,' she went on, brightening, 'then I found the light, and my faith was reborn. And so was my passion for archaeology. I was determined to find the truth about the history of Teotihuacán.'

'And she did,' said Maldonado. 'It was Rosamaria who discovered the hidden chambers beneath the Pyramid of the Sun.'

'How did you find them?' Nina asked.

Rosamaria smiled, somewhat shyly. 'I can only call it . . . divine help.'

'She had a theory,' Maldonado continued, 'and she pushed and she pushed, until eventually I gave in and permitted a survey. And she was right! There was a tunnel. So we opened it up, and found . . .' his eyes sparkled with enthusiasm, 'wonders.'

'Loads of impressive Aztec stuff, right?' said Eddie.

'*Dad*,' Macy scoffed. 'The Aztecs didn't build Teotihuacán.'

The Englishman was surprised. 'They didn't? I thought they had a big empire in Mexico.'

'They did,' said Maldonado, 'but long after Teotihuacán was built. Long after Teotihuacán was abandoned, in fact! The Aztecs ruled from the fourteenth century until the Spanish conquest in 1521. But the city has been here for at least two thousand years.'

'Who built it?'

'Nobody knows,' said Nina.

Maldonado nodded. 'We know very little about the civilisation that founded Teotihuacán. They did not have a written language, so the only records belong to the other cultures they contacted – or conquered. We know the names of a few of their kings and warriors that way: Fire Is Born, Spearthrower Owl. But we do not even know what they called their own city. Teotihuacán is a Nahuatl word, spoken by the Aztecs. It can mean "city of the gods". Or "the place where men become gods". The Aztecs found the city centuries after it was abandoned. They were so astounded by its scale, they believed only gods could have built it.'

'Why'd they abandon it?' asked Eddie.

'We do not know. We have found the remains of buildings that suggest a large fire in a part of the city where the nobility lived. There may have been an accident, like your Great Fire of London. Or there was an internal uprising against the ruling classes. This was in the mid sixth century, and the city never recovered. Nobody knows what happened. There are many theories, but,' he gave Rosamaria an approving smile, 'perhaps soon we will know which one is true, thanks to Rosamaria.'

'I'm more keen than ever to see what you've found,' said Nina.

Diego leaned forward to address her. 'Professor Wilde, can I ask you something?'

'Of course,' she replied.

The young man produced a satchel from under the table. 'It's such a great honour to meet you – the discoverer of Atlantis.' He took out a book. Nina immediately recognised it as one of her own: the Spanish-language edition of *In Search of History*, her account of finding the lost civilisation. 'I wondered if you could sign this for me?'

Nina smiled. 'I can, no problem. And I like that you brought the book rather than the movie based on it. It's . . . not one of my favourites.'

'Ah, stop moaning,' said Eddie. 'You're always complaining, "Oh, it's not historically accurate!" It's an action movie, not a documentary. What would you rather watch, someone using a little diddy brush to get dust off a stone, or somebody running along the top of an exploding train?'

'Ignore my husband, please,' Nina told her hosts as she signed the book. 'He thinks that just because we've had some, ah, *incidents*, archaeology always involves gunfights and car chases and collapsing buildings. Now, me? I'm happy that the counter in my office saying "days without being shot at" is currently on one thousand eight hundred and twenty-five, and climbing.' Eddie gave her a puzzled look. 'Five years, honey,' she added.

Maldonado laughed. 'I am very glad to say I have never once been shot at – in *thirty* years. Long may that continue!' He made the sign of the cross.

Nina returned the book to Diego. 'Thank you so much,' he said. 'I've got some of your other books as well.'

She smiled. 'Only some?'

'I'll get straight to the bookstore tomorrow!'

Everyone at the table laughed – except Macy, who was giving her mother an irritated look. 'You know,' she said loudly, '*I* have a theory about who built Teotihuacán.'

All eyes went to her. 'You do?' Diego asked. 'What is it?'

'I am always interested to hear such theories,' said Maldonado politely. 'Did you work on it with your mother?'

'Oh, no,' Macy insisted. 'Mom's kind of . . . set in her ways. She doesn't like to challenge the orthodoxy.'

'Excuse me? I discovered *Atlantis*!' Nina protested. 'The place everyone else dismissed as *mythical*?'

Macy ignored her. 'I know there's an official story about

41

Teotihuacán being founded by the Zapotecs and Totonacs.'
Maldonado's expression suggested that this was news to him, but
he let her continue. 'But I think my theory's pretty solid. Have
you heard of the Madrid Codex?'

The archaeologists exchanged amused glances. 'The *Códices
Matritenses de la Real Biblioteca*, by Bernardino de Sahagún?' said
Maldonado.

'Oh, so . . . you *have* heard of it,' Macy said, with a momentary
deer-in-headlights look. 'Okay, that's good, I don't need to
explain that part.'

'I haven't heard of it,' said Eddie.

'Bernardino de Sahagún was a Spanish missionary,' explained
Nina, wondering what Macy was going to say – and how deep
she would dig her own hole. 'He was also arguably the world's
first anthropologist. Once he came here, he devoted his life to
recording the history and culture of the native Mesoamericans.
He learned Nahuatl, and wrote what's known as *The General
History of the Things of New Spain* – that's the title's literal English
translation; it doesn't sound quite so odd in Spanish. It was a
colossal amount of work, split into numerous books – the various
codices. The Madrid Codex is one of them. It's called that
because, well, the original's in Madrid.'

Eddie grinned. 'Wouldn't be so impressive if it was in
Bognor.'

'Anyway,' Macy said impatiently, 'there's a part in the Madrid
Codex where Bernardino was told the history of the people. It
says that long ago, lots of ships came from across the ocean, and
the wise men, the priests, leading them went looking for smoky
mountains – which have to be volcanoes, right? Eventually they
found what they were after and went home, but they'd settled
long enough to pass down their knowledge – and the people who
stayed behind built Teotihuacán using that knowledge. Now, *I*
think . . .' she paused to make sure everyone was paying full

attention, 'the people who arrived in the ships were from . . . Atlantis.'

The revelation was greeted with silence. 'Interesting,' Maldonado said at last.

'Interesting good, or interesting crazy?' Macy asked hopefully.

'Oh, I would not be rude by calling you crazy. Although I have read the entire *Historia General* and do not recall such a passage. Perhaps you saw a non-standard translation?' he offered.

'I'm sure it's accurate,' Macy insisted. 'There's a whole website about it. Why would anyone make up something like that? People would be able to check.'

'Did *you* check?' Nina asked.

She hadn't intended it as a criticism, at least not consciously, but Macy still bristled. 'You of all people should be open to the idea that people came here from Atlantis, Mom,' she said. 'What are you saying – that they reached the middle of the Amazon jungle, that they reached *Tibet*, but them getting to Mexico is a step too far?'

'But *their* getting to Mexico,' Nina corrected.

'Dad says "them"!'

'He's from Yorkshire, he says a lot of strange things.'

Eddie nodded. 'Ay up, by 'eck.'

Macy huffed loudly. 'You always think you're right and you know everything!'

'So do you,' said Nina. 'The difference is, I'm a professor with over twenty years of field experience.'

Her daughter glared at her, unable to think of a comeback. Instead she snapped, 'God!' and stood, storming from the table.

'Macy, sit down,' Nina called after her. 'Macy!' But all she saw was the teenager's back disappearing through a door.

Diego got up. 'I'll make sure she's okay.'

'Will you now?' said Eddie, about to rise himself.

Nina touched his arm for him to stay put as Diego left the room. 'I am *so* sorry,' she said to her hosts.

Maldonado gave an amused shrug. 'I have three nieces. I know what girls are like at that age.'

'Unless you have to live with them? Really, you don't.'

Eddie leaned closer. 'You shut her down pretty hard,' he said in a low, gently chiding voice. 'You did kind of trigger her.'

'She's fifteen, and I'm her mother,' Nina reminded him. 'My *existence* triggers her!'

'All the same, I should probably go and find her.'

'Diego will look after her,' said Rosamaria. 'He is a good boy.' Eddie made a faint grumbling sound, but stayed seated.

'He and Macy seem to have a lot in common,' said Maldonado. 'They are both very interested in archaeology. You should be happy your daughter wants to do the same thing as you.'

Nina sighed. 'I think it's more that she wants to prove me wrong.'

Macy left the restaurant by a rear exit, finding herself in a narrow alley strewn with garbage. It was dark, the only illumination a single bulb above the door. Dogs barked somewhere nearby. Anger replaced by unease, she was about to turn reluctantly back when the door opened again. She started, relaxing when she saw Diego. 'Oh!' she said. 'Hi.'

'Hi,' he replied. 'Are you okay?'

'I'm fine. Thanks. It was just – ugh. My mom drives me *mad* sometimes. Yeah, she found Atlantis, but that doesn't mean she's right about *everything*.'

'She also found El Dorado and Paititi,' Diego noted. 'And the tomb of Hercules, and a lost Egyptian pyramid, and—'

'Okay, yeah, whose side are you on?' But it was said with humour.

The young man gave her a smile. 'Actually, yours. I thought your theory was interesting.'

Her heart jumped a little. 'You did?'

'Yeah. I mean, we know the Atlanteans went all over the world, thousands of years ago. Like you said, if they could reach Brazil or Tibet, why not Mexico? There have been civilisations here for a really long time. Maybe people from Atlantis founded some of them.'

She giggled. 'Wow. It's so good to meet someone who actually listens to me.'

'I'm a good listener. That's what I hear, anyway.' He paused expectantly, then, when Macy gave him a somewhat questioning look, went on: 'That was a joke. Maybe it works better in Spanish.'

'Oh, no, it was good!' Macy said hurriedly, laughing too loudly. 'Sorry, it took me a second. Your English is really good, by the way.'

'Thanks. I speak French, too – my dad was Canadian.'

She instantly felt guilty for laughing. 'I was really sorry to hear about your dad.'

'It happened a long time ago. I was only a kid.' He sighed. 'It was tough, especially for Mom. But . . . she moved on. We both did. Anyway,' he said, his tone lightening, 'tell me more about you. You must have done some amazing stuff. Did you go with your mom and dad on any of their expeditions?'

Macy was caught between being flattered by his interest and irked that he considered her an adjunct of her parents. She decided to give him the benefit of the doubt. 'Some of them. I've been to a lot of places. Iceland, England, Spain, Italy, Australia . . . Not so much in the last few years, though. I've been busy with school, and Mom hasn't gone into the field so much. This is the first trip I've had in a while.'

'Do you miss the travelling?'

'Some of it. I can manage without being shot at and kidnapped, though.'

Diego laughed, trailing off when she didn't join in. 'You're not joking?'

'I wish! I can't remember how many times I've almost died.'

His eyes went wide. 'Things were dangerous, and your mom and dad took you *with* them?'

'They didn't put me in danger on purpose!' Macy said, instinctively defensive – until she remembered she was supposed to be mad at her parents. 'It was more like . . . they're disaster magnets. They go on a cruise ship? Mom gets framed for robbery and goes on the run. Dad goes into a skyscraper? It blows up. I had to zipline from one building to another, thirty storeys in the air!'

'Wow. I thought I'd done some extreme things, but you've got me beat.'

'What kind of things?'

'I've been cave diving in the cenotes in Quintana Roo – some of the underwater tunnel systems are kilometres long. And I've done trail-bike riding, rock climbing, skydiving . . .'

Macy was impressed. 'You're right, those are extreme. No wonder you've got such a good shape. Are in such good shape,' she hastily corrected. 'I'd love to try skydiving, but I'd have to persuade my dad to prise open his wallet first. It must be expensive. I didn't know archaeologists were so well paid in Mexico!'

'They're not,' he admitted. 'But my mom's boyfriend is pretty rich. He pays for stuff like that. He's not my dad, but . . . he's cool.'

'I'm glad your mom found someone.'

'So am I.' They shared a smile. Then the dogs began barking again, closer than before. 'Probably strays,' Diego said, seeing Macy react. 'There's a lot of them around here.'

A lifelong Manhattanite, the only encounters Macy could recall with unleashed dogs were on morning runs in Central Park. 'Are they dangerous? I mean, do they have rabies or anything?'

'Probably not. But they might have ticks and fleas.' He took in her uncomfortable expression. 'You want to go back inside?'

She nodded. 'Uh huh.'

Diego laughed, then opened the door and ushered her in.

'They all seemed like a nice lot,' said Eddie as he led his family into their hotel room. 'Food was good, too.'

'It was,' Nina agreed. 'Although the evening could have gone a little less fractiously . . .'

'Don't even start, Mom.' Macy slipped between her parents to enter the bathroom.

Nina glared at her. 'Macy, you were so rude tonight. Dr Maldonado's spent his whole career excavating Teotihuacán, and you basically told him you thought his knowledge was worthless because you read somebody's mistranslation of Bernardino de Sahagún and jumped to seventeen paces beyond conclusions.'

'No, you know why I think you're so mad?' Macy replied. 'Because you thought I was saying *your* knowledge was worthless. Anything about Atlantis, that's your department, and nobody else is allowed to have any ideas. Isn't that right?'

'No, that's *not* right,' said Nina, feeling her hackles rise. 'What you don't seem to realise is—'

'All right, okay,' Eddie cut in, standing between them. 'Let's not end the day with a big fight. How about we all just agree you both acted like bell-ends, and leave it at that?'

'Eddie!' said Nina.

'Dad!' said Macy.

He grinned. 'See? Now you both agree about something.'

'*You're* a bell-end,' muttered his daughter.

'Whaddya know – we *do* agree about something,' Nina added.

Eddie gave a mock bow. 'All part of the service. So, we going to get some kip without any more fights?'

'I'm sure we can manage it. What do you say, Macy?'

'I suppose,' came the sullen reply.

Eddie shrugged. 'I'll take what I can get.'

4

The previous day, Nina had caught glimpses of Teotihuacán. Today, she and her family would see its wonders in full.

Maldonado had arranged a taxi from their hotel. He met them at the archaeological compound's gate. 'Good morning!' he said brightly. It was again sunny, if not especially warm. 'Did you sleep well?'

'Yes, thanks,' Nina replied. 'Although I woke up early – I couldn't wait to get here.'

'I hope Teotihuacán will live up to your expectations.'

Macy peered past him. 'Will Diego be here today?' she asked hopefully.

'He is with Rosamaria at the dig,' he said. 'I will show you the city, then you can see our latest discovery.'

They boarded a white pickup truck and set off. 'I will take you to the north end of the city, then we will walk back,' said Maldonado. 'The Avenue of the Dead is two kilometres long, and there is a lot to see; this will save time.'

'No problem,' said Nina. She had hoped to explore on foot at her leisure, but understood Maldonado's reasoning. Besides, there would be the rest of the day to experience the ancient city.

The pickup drove past several busy parking lots. Even early in the day, tourists were already arriving. 'Teotihuacán is one of Mexico's biggest tourist attractions,' Maldonado said with pride. 'That is good – it brings lots of money. But it makes our job harder. Everyone wants to climb the pyramids, but the more people do, the more damage they cause. There is as much

49

maintenance as archaeology going on. And,' a sarcastic snort, 'the land is valuable, so the government keeps selling pieces. The town of San Martín has grown to only a hundred metres from the Pyramid of the Moon. If some politicians had their way, they would put a shopping mall on the Avenue of the Dead.'

'It's the same the world over,' sighed Nina. 'When it comes to history versus money, there's only one winner.'

'And never the right one, eh?' The Mexican turned down a dirt track. 'We have to protect what we can, for as long as we can.' He stopped behind a long, low building. 'Stores selling tourist souvenirs,' he said dismissively. 'But the first site is just past it.' They got out, joining a paved footpath crowded with visitors.

Beyond was a complex of ancient structures. Most were ruined, but the tallest still rose a couple of storeys high. 'The Palace of Quetzalpapálotl,' Maldonado announced. 'The buildings you see date to about AD 450. They were built on top of much older ones.' He indicated an excavated area, the buried remains of walls exposed. 'I will show you the temple.'

He led them through the ruins to a relatively intact section. Wide steps to a building were fenced off, a security guard keeping watch, but he waved the head archaeologist and his guests past. They ascended and passed through a rectangular doorway into a courtyard.

Nina stopped and turned to take it in. She knew the building from pictures, but the reality was even more impressive. Hefty pillars supported capstones painted a vivid red, their surfaces carved with murals of birds and intricate geometric patterns. 'This is amazing,' she said, awed. 'Look at the detail!' She moved towards a pillar, then looked back at Maldonado. 'If I may?'

'Of course,' he replied. 'I trust you not to damage anything.'

Eddie laughed faintly. 'Well, that's tempting fate.'

'Nothing's going to get wrecked today,' Nina insisted, taking in the ancient artworks. 'What do you think, Macy?'

Macy's continuing frosty antipathy towards her mother was overcome by her admiration. 'Wow. This is so cool! And it's in amazing condition.'

Maldonado smiled. 'I almost do not want to disappoint you, but it has been restored – hopefully to its original beauty. But most of the city is as we found it. Or, when we are lucky, as its builders left it.'

'Like the underground chambers?' said Nina.

'Yes. And I can tell you are impatient to see them, so we shall move on.'

As they turned to exit, Eddie paused, regarding the red stones. 'It's weird, but . . . I'm sure I've been here before.' His voice took on a mystical tone, as though reliving a half-forgotten dream.

Nina knew him better than that. 'Is that right?'

'Yeah.' He grinned broadly, exposing the gap between his front teeth. 'In *Tomb Raider*.'

'Oh, be quiet,' she chided as they followed Maldonado out. 'You know Lara Croft is a terrible archaeologist, right? I mean, she's a tomb *raider*. A thief. It's right there in her job description.'

'Tchah. You'll be telling me Indiana Jones is a bad role model next.'

'Don't even get me started! "It belongs in a museum", my ass. What he means is "It belongs in an *American* museum". It's amazing how many students I have to deprogramme from that "we take whatever we find" mindset.'

'Aren't a lot of Atlantean artefacts that you found now in American museums?' Macy asked pointedly.

'And other museums all around the world. It would be great if people could see them in their original context, but Atlantis is eight hundred feet under the ocean. It's not exactly on the tourist bus route.'

'Whatever you say, Mom,' came the caustic reply. 'And you

should both update your cultural references. The twentieth century ended thirty years ago, you know.' Nina glanced at Eddie and mimed strangulation.

Maldonado led them past a four-tiered ziggurat to a broad plaza. 'This is the Avenue of the Dead,' he explained. 'And there . . . is the Pyramid of the Moon.'

He pointed north, revealing a larger pyramid at the avenue's end. *Much* larger, Nina saw. The great monolith rose in several tiers to its summit, each step taller than the entire height of its neighbours.

'How big is it?' asked Macy, impressed.

'Forty-three metres,' Maldonado replied.

Nina made an instant mental conversion. 'About a hundred and forty feet.'

'For the ancient world, a giant,' said Maldonado. 'It took centuries to build.'

'What was it for?' Eddie asked. 'Is it like the pyramids in Egypt?'

'There are tombs, yes,' the Mexican told him. 'But not for one ruler. There are burial complexes in some of the tiers. We think sacrificial victims were placed in them as part of religious rituals. That was the main purpose of the pyramid – to carry out human sacrifices. Perhaps in gigantic numbers – we have found many, many remains. Sometimes defeated enemies were killed. But we believe many victims went willingly to their deaths. Being sacrificed to serve your god and your people was considered a great honour.'

'Okay, glad I didn't live here back then,' said Macy.

Nina examined the pyramid more closely. A smaller ziggurat abutted the southern face, people heading up stone stairs to its top. Nobody was visible on the main structure, though. She realised why: the pyramid's summit was irregular, crumbling. 'It looks like the top's partly collapsed.'

'Yes, unfortunately,' said Maldonado. 'It was the last level built, and the quality was not as high as the rest. It is not safe to go up there now.'

'Wasn't too safe back then either,' Eddie joked.

'But the top of another pyramid is still intact,' Maldonado continued. He led them around another smaller ziggurat. 'That is where we are going: the Pyramid of the Sun.'

To the south, another huge structure rose above the surrounding ruins. Even from over a quarter of a mile away, it was instantly clear that, like their astronomical namesakes, the great Pyramid of the Sun was far bigger than the Moon. In shape, it closely matched the distant volcanic hills beyond.

'It is over sixty-five metres high,' proclaimed Maldonado as they walked down the busy Avenue of the Dead. 'Half as big again as the Pyramid of the Moon. Over two million tonnes of stone and rock. The only taller ancient buildings of its kind are in Egypt.'

The long avenue stretched away to the south, ending at a complex Nina knew to be called the Temple of Quetzalcóatl. More low ziggurats lined either side of the open boulevard. But her attention was dominated by the giant pyramid. She knew the basics of what had been recently discovered beneath it: tunnels leading to apparent ritual chambers. As Maldonado had reminded her the previous evening, similar subterranean features had been found under other temples in the ancient city. But the Mexican archaeologists were keeping the details close to their chests. That was normal; they were being diligent and cautious, properly excavating and cataloguing their find rather than rushing to reveal it to the world.

So why had they asked *her* to come and see it now?

Nina was sure it wasn't just because of her reputation. Her fame as an archaeologist didn't necessarily translate into eminence; in fact, there were certain elders of the profession who actively resented her media profile. (She was also certain that sexism was a major factor; some things never changed.) But since the Mexicans didn't seem ready to announce their discoveries, they hadn't brought her here to help with publicity. So, what?

They reached the Pyramid of the Sun. Rather than join the crowds heading for the steps at its base, however, Maldonado continued past. The Avenue of the Dead was broken up by a large sunken plaza; he brought them out of its eastern side and through more low ruins. Buildings gave way to trees and dusty grass, the number of tourists falling almost to nothing.

A section of open ground was cordoned off, a square of chain-link fencing covered in plastic sheeting to conceal whatever was inside. 'We believe this was part of the city reserved for the nobility,' said Maldonado as he neared the fence. A security guard sat under a shade at a gate; he stood as they approached, but relaxed when he saw who was leading the group. 'Most of the buildings here were burned down.'

'The fire you mentioned last night?' asked Nina.

'It would seem so, yes.' They reached the gate. A brief exchange, and the guard opened it. Another man was inside; both were armed. Within the fence was a wooden hut. A portable generator thrummed away beside it.

Maldonado opened the hut's door. 'Come in. Be careful, it is quite dark.'

Nina blinked as she went from bright daylight into shadow, letting her eyes adjust. There was little unexpected about the hut's contents: banks of shelving filled with excavation equipment and safety gear, a rack of hard hats, flashlights. The only things standing out as unusual were several full-face respirators.

Maldonado pulled open a large wooden hatch in the floor, revealing a shaft angling steeply downwards. A ladder descended to the bottom. 'Here,' he said, handing each of his guests a hard hat. 'Put these on, please.'

Eddie had also noticed the respirators. 'Anything we need to worry about down there?'

'Not any more.'

'Just checking. 'Cause you've got two blokes with guns outside.'

'Normal security, unfortunately,' said Maldonado. 'We have to guard against thieves and treasure hunters.' He collected a flashlight, then started down the ladder. 'Okay, follow me.'

Nina paused to tie her hair back into a ponytail, then followed him down, her family descending after her. Lights were dotted along the dark, musty tunnel they entered. Maldonado shone his flashlight at the ceiling, revealing wooden beams. Some were new, but others were clearly ancient – and darkened by soot. 'The original entrance was about twenty metres behind us,' he said. Nina looked, seeing that the passage was completely blocked by dirt and debris. 'The fire on the surface spread down into the tunnel, and caused it to collapse. Other parts of the tunnel have also been damaged, probably by earthquakes. We had to spend some time making them stronger.' He thumped a clenched fist against one of the new props. To everyone's relief, it held firm. 'This way.'

'Looks like there was a lot of smoke down here,' said Nina. 'Was that what the respirators were for?'

'No, worse than that,' said Maldonado. 'The air was full of mercury vapour.'

'Mercury?' said Eddie. 'Definitely don't want to be breathing that in.'

'It has all been made safe. But again, it took time. For the first few weeks, we had to wear masks while working.'

'Why was there so much mercury down here?' asked Macy.

Maldonado glanced back to give her a smile. 'You will soon see.'

The tunnel sloped downwards, taking the visitors ever deeper.

In places, the wooden props supporting the ceiling were assisted by metal scaffolding. The passage weaved enough to block direct sight of what lay ahead, making it impossible to judge its length. But Nina guessed that the hut had been about a hundred metres from the pyramid's base. If wherever they were going was directly beneath the centre of the monolith, the tunnel would stretch over two hundred metres: almost seven hundred feet. A long way underground, especially with two million tons of stone above her head . . .

She shook off the unnerving thought. Brighter lights eventually became visible. 'We are almost there,' Maldonado said. A dramatic tone entered his voice. 'Now you will see why we asked you here, Professor Wilde.'

They entered a well-lit chamber – and Nina's eyes widened as she saw what awaited her.

5

The room was rectangular, thick decorated pillars much like those in the Palace of Quetzalpapálotl supporting the ceiling. These had retained most of their original paint, reliefs of people and animals standing out in vivid green and red and blue.

But Nina's attention instantly went to the object between the pillars. Roughly oval, it stood at waist height, dominating the chamber.

A map.

But this was no mere chart on paper. It was carved from a single slab of a deep green stone, a landscape reproduced in miniature. The vista seemed familiar – then she realised it was a representation of part of Central America. Flat, undetailed areas marking the sea flanked the coastlines. The area it covered stretched from northern Mexico down through the narrow isthmus of Panama, and into the north-western corner of Colombia.

Maldonado had an expectant grin. 'What do you think?'

'This is incredible!' Nina replied. The detail was such that individual mountains could be seen. As far as she could tell, the topography was reasonably accurate. Its makers, whoever they were, had possessed both great stone-working skill and detailed geographical knowledge. 'When does it date from?'

'The tunnel was blocked in the mid sixth century,' said Maldonado. 'But the map may be much older. We can't carbon-date stone, of course, but we found residue of soot. Some was at least two thousand years old.'

Nina crouched to examine the map's underside. It was a ragged cone resembling an inverted volcano – or, more unsettlingly, the root of a tooth. 'It looks like it's been carved out of something larger.'

'We think so, yes.' Rosamaria entered from an adjoining room, followed by Diego. 'But we do not know what, or where it came from. We have not yet identified the type of stone.'

'Looks like jade,' Eddie offered.

Maldonado shook his head. 'It is much harder. And it has a high metal content.'

'I can see it,' said Nina. Tiny silver flecks were embedded beneath the stone's outer sheen.

Macy's only interest was now one of the new arrivals. 'Hi,' she said to Diego, with a coy smile. He grinned and returned the greeting. Eddie gave the young man a stern look.

Nina took in the whole of the map. Two thin threads had been stretched across it, meeting in Mexico. 'Is that where we are?' she asked.

'Yes,' replied Rosamaria. 'The map is very accurate. More than anything known from the Aztecs or the Maya.'

'Or even the people of Teotihuacán,' added Maldonado.

'You don't think it was made by them?' said Nina.

'Perhaps you can tell me.' He gestured at the map's curved edge. 'Look.'

Cut into the rim of the stone were small symbols. She recognised them instantly – and was shocked to see them there. 'These look like Olmec characters!'

'They are,' Maldonado confirmed. 'Perhaps even proto-Olmec. Or . . . the civilisation that came before them,' he added meaningfully.

Eddie frowned. 'Which lot are the Olmecs again?'

Macy broke off from a muted conversation with Diego to answer him. 'Come on, Dad, you know this one. They're the first Mesoamerican civilisation – and they were descended from the Atlanteans.'

'Their written language is very similar to the one used in Atlantis,' Nina added. She peered at the little symbols. 'Actually . . . these look closer to Atlantean than Olmec.'

'Do you think they could actually date back to the time of Atlantis?' asked Maldonado.

'I don't know. But . . . it's a definite possibility.'

Macy made a sound of triumph. 'I'm ready for my apology now, thank you.'

Nina looked at her in confusion. 'For what?'

'For totally dissing my theory about the link between Teotihuacán and Atlantis, duh! Wise men arriving from the sea, remember? You just said people from Atlantis were here, so guess what? I was right.'

'Let's not jump to conclusions,' Nina told her. 'There's still a lot of work needed to confirm anything.'

Macy let out an irritated breath. 'God! You can't ever let me win, can you?'

'It's not *about* winning. This isn't a competition.'

'Macy,' Eddie said, placating. 'Let's argue about this later, okay?'

Nina nodded. 'Yeah. There's a lot to unpack here.' She surveyed the rest of the chamber. Even though the LED lights were white, there was an orange cast to the illumination. Looking up, she saw why. The glow was reflected by gleaming golden spots in the ceiling. 'Is that gold?'

'Fool's gold,' said Maldonado. 'Pyrite. It helps brighten the light. The tunnels under the other temples are the same, and they also contained mercury. We used a robot to enter this one when it was first opened. A good thing, too – the air was toxic.' He pointed at one of the map's empty areas of ocean. 'See how the edge is raised? It makes a bowl – to hold mercury. It was used to represent water. Most had evaporated, but there was enough left to be dangerous. It took some time to decontaminate.'

'There was a whole river of mercury under the Temple of the Feathered Serpent,' said Diego. 'We think it was used in rituals.'

'But why would they use it if it was dangerous?' Macy asked him.

'They didn't know it was dangerous. Or at least they didn't know *how* dangerous.'

She regarded the empty seas with trepidation. 'Wow. Imagine breathing that stuff in the whole time you were down here.'

'They only used these chambers for rituals,' said Rosamaria. 'They would not have been exposed for long. And the mercury vapour was trapped here for centuries – there would have been more fresh air then.'

'You've found information about the rituals?' Nina asked her.

'Yes. In the next room.'

'We have more to show you,' said Maldonado. 'Come and see.'

Nina followed him to the entrance. 'So, you asked me to come here so I could confirm that the text on the map was Atlantean, huh?'

'Am I that transparent, Professor Wilde?' he said with a smile.

She grinned. 'See-through. But I can't complain – I've done things like that myself!'

'What, you've broken the rules?' muttered Macy. 'Hypocrite.'

Nina decided to ignore her in favour of seeing what else the underground chambers contained. A short passage led into the next. It was smaller and darker, and had suffered damage. One of its supporting columns had collapsed, scaffolding now bracing the ceiling. Much of the floor was littered with piled dirt and rubble. A tunnel mouth was visible across the room, but it was almost totally blocked by debris. A squat box on caterpillar tracks waited in front of it.

'Is that your robot?' said Eddie.

'We call it Elektra,' said Diego proudly. 'I usually operate it.' He picked up a remote control with a small built-in screen. 'We've been digging further into the tunnel.' He worked a little lever with his thumb, and a mechanical arm unfolded from the robot's side and waved at the onlookers. Macy giggled.

'Diego,' chided Rosamaria. He smirked and put the controller back down.

'It will take some time to open up the passage,' said Maldonado. 'But there is still plenty to occupy us in here.'

'I'll say,' Nina replied. Elaborate murals adorned the walls, but her gaze went first to the work in progress at floor level. 'Look at this! *Real* archaeology. Hands-on, careful, diligent. And yes, using little diddy brushes.' She gave Eddie a mocking look.

'Whatever turns you on,' he said. 'Me? I'd rather have fun with the robot.'

'Whatever turns *you* on,' she echoed.

The room was in the process of being excavated, divided into squares by taut strings. The archaeologists would work on each area in turn, painstakingly removing the detritus of ages to catalogue whatever lay beneath. From the look of it, much of what *did* lie beneath was human remains. A desiccated body was partially exposed in one square, its shrivelled face distorted where a heavy stone had crushed the skull.

Eddie moved to block Macy's view. 'Don't look at that, love.'

'Dad!' she protested. 'It's basically a mummy. I've seen them before. No big deal.'

'Your job's warped my little girl,' the Yorkshireman told Nina, only half jokingly.

'We found many others already,' said Maldonado. 'The ceiling collapsed long after they died. They were almost all killed by breathing smoke from the fire.'

'Almost all?' said Nina.

'One was murdered.' He led Nina to another partially excavated square.

A male figure was half exposed, lying on its back. 'Well, yeah,' said Eddie. 'You don't have to be Sherlock Holmes to work out he didn't die of natural causes.' A dagger was buried in the corpse's chest.

Nina peered at the green weapon. 'Looks like the same stone as the map.'

'We think so,' said Maldonado. 'But we will wait until he is fully exhumed before doing any tests.'

'This guy must have been somebody special.' The murder victim wore an ornate headdress. It had been rotted by time, but the remains of a large animal skull were still intact.

'A jaguar,' Maldonado said. 'He was a high priest.'

'He was called Tekuni,' said Rosamaria. 'The Lord of the Dead – the avatar on earth of Tekuazotl, the Teotihuacano god of death, rebirth and earthquakes.'

Eddie twitched an eyebrow. 'The last one seems a bit random.'

'One of these things is not like the others . . .' Macy said in a sing-song voice.

'I don't know,' said Nina, indicating the collapsed pillar. 'This was caused by an earthquake. With all the volcanoes in this part of the world, it was probably a pretty common way to die back in those days.'

'It still is,' Maldonado pointed out. 'But look at these.'

He went to one of the murals, shining his flashlight over it. A colourful stylised figure was revealed: a humanoid with the head of a jaguar, holding a long green blade. The big cat's mouth was open, dripping with blood. Its feet were spread wide, almost as if it were dancing. Various small symbols were marked nearby.

'It's the same knife,' said Macy, looking back at the body in the corner. As well as the distinctive colour, both shared another common feature – a circular hole in the end of the hilt.

Nina regarded the other murals. One was a large coiled snake, another a second humanoid – this one female, with the face of a bright green bird. Long intertwining feathers radiated outwards from her head. The last picture, though, was something more alarming. 'I guess that confirms what this pyramid was used for,' she said, eyeing a depiction of human sacrifice on a massive scale. The image was clearly a representation of the Pyramid of the Sun, topped by a structure built entirely from human skulls. Figures in ceremonial clothing stood within, arms held high, while below, the pyramid was strewn with bodies, the stairs running red.

Maldonado nodded grimly. 'The cult of the Jaguar God. No, not even a cult – it appears it was the city's dominant religion.'

'You've found written records?'

'Unfortunately, no. Only the Olmec text on the map. The Teotihuacanos had a numerical system and advanced visual arts, but not a written language.'

'So how did you find out about the jaguar cult?' asked Macy.

'My mom figured it out,' Diego said proudly.

Rosamaria blushed a little. 'It was a team effort.'

'She is too modest,' said Maldonado. 'When we first entered the chambers, she spent days photographing and analysing these pictures and the carvings in the map room – while wearing a gas mask! That is dedication to your work. Everything we know about the jaguar cult, the followers of Tekuni the high priest, comes from her.'

Macy's face took on a faint quizzical frown. 'How do you know his name if there isn't a written language?'

Rosamaria composed herself before explaining. 'Some of the symbols are similar to ones used by the Aztecs. In Nahuatl, *tekuani* means a jaguar, but also a feared and powerful person. The symbols here were not quite the same, so I made a translation that was also not quite the same.'

'Linguistic drift. But the name fits what we have found,' said Maldonado approvingly.

'It's all stunning,' Nina told him. 'An amazing find. You've filled in an enormous gap in Mesoamerican history.'

'Bigger than we first thought, if the connection to Atlantis is real. Would you be willing to help us investigate it further?'

'Of course – Macy, what are you doing?' Her daughter had taken out her phone.

'Selfie,' Macy replied, as if the answer was obvious. She stood beside Diego and angled her phone to capture some of the murals in the background, then took a picture.

Nina's jaw clenched with pent-up tension. 'Really? We're at one of the most incredible finds of the past decade, and all you can think about is updating your social media?'

'It is okay,' Maldonado insisted. 'But Macy, please do not make any pictures public before our discoveries are officially announced. We do not want uninvited visitors breaking in to see for themselves.'

'Okay, okay,' Macy said with reluctance. 'I'll keep it private.'

'Thank you.' He started back towards the exit. 'Now, Nina, there are other Olmec – or Atlantean – symbols on the map. If you are willing to translate them, maybe we will discover something new.'

'Happy to help,' Nina replied. The group filed back into the map chamber, leaving the room of corpses silent and still.

The security guard at the fence turned as a white pickup truck bumped over the rough ground and stopped by the gate. Three men wearing overalls got out. Some of the vast historical site's numerous maintenance workers, at first glance – but something triggered a faint warning in the guard's mind. The truck, maybe? It didn't have any logos identifying it as an official vehicle. And the trio's overalls were clean, new.

He stood to meet them. 'Hey. Can I help you?'

The group's leader, a tall man with deep-set blue eyes, regarded him with an unsettling stare. 'I thought this dig site was meant to have two guards.'

'It does. Hey, Jesús!'

His companion opened the gate. 'What is it?'

'I was just checking,' said the newcomer. He sidestepped—

The man behind him raised a gun, a fat suppressor attached to its muzzle. Before either guard could react, he fired. Multiple bullets slammed into each guard's chest, blood bursting from ragged wounds. They fell to the dusty ground, dead.

The leader regarded the twitching bodies with dispassion. 'Put them in the truck. Cover them up – we don't want some passing tourist to raise the alarm.'

'Of course, Tekuni,' said the gunman. He and his other companion dragged the corpses into the pickup.

Tekuni surveyed his surroundings. The massive Pyramid of the Sun was a looming presence to the north, tourists tiny dots on its summit, but there was nobody nearby. Had there been, they would have met the same fate as the security guards.

He started towards the hut. 'We've waited long enough. Let's get Earthbreaker.'

6

'Well?' said Maldonado expectantly. 'What do you think?'

Nina completed her slow circuit of the map. The symbols cut into the green stone were small, and in some cases hard to pick out. 'There are a few words I can't read. A couple are damaged, and there are others I don't know. Either they're Atlantean words that haven't been encountered before, or, like you said, there's been some linguistic drift. I could translate most of them, though.'

'And what do they say?'

'They're names – of animals, creatures. I'm wondering if the ones I didn't recognise are native to this region. The Atlanteans of the era I'm familiar with might never have seen them, so didn't have names for them. But I know things like "spider", "hummingbird", "lizard" – this one is "snake".' She indicated the nearest word.

'So what are they for?' Eddie asked.

She shrugged. 'You got me. Do you have any ideas, Gregorio?'

'I wish I did,' said Maldonado. 'When I thought the symbols were possibly Atlantean, I had someone translate them. They did not identify as many as you, but yes, they were all animals. I had hoped you might know if they had some significance.'

'Nothing that I can tell. Sorry.'

'Ah, well. A mystery for another time. But at least now we know . . .' He fell silent, frowning as he turned towards the tunnel to the surface. Footsteps echoed from it. '*Hola? Quién está ahí?*'

Eddie picked up on his surprise, subtly moving to place himself between the entrance and his family. 'What is it?'

'Someone is coming – but I told the other archaeologists who work in here to take the morning off.' The scuffle of footsteps echoed from the passage.

'Maybe there is an emergency,' said Rosamaria. 'Nobody can phone us down here.'

Maldonado was unconvinced, peering into the passage. '*Hola?*' he called again. Three men in overalls came into view—

Two of them raised guns.

'Back! Get back!' Eddie barked, pushing his family towards the other chamber.

Too late. The newcomers rushed into the map room. Nina jumped back as a gun was thrust at her. Her heel caught the protruding edge of a flagstone. She stumbled, catching herself on the map—

And gasped, jerking her hand away as what felt like a static shock cracked through it. The third man's intense eyes snapped towards her. But she had no time to think about it as the two armed men continued their advance. '*No te muevas! No te muevas!*' they shouted, gesturing towards a corner. '*Ve allá!*'

Eddie raised his hands to shoulder height, shielding Macy. He could tell the gunmen were professionals, probably ex-military. Their commands were controlled, just the right amount of aggression to intimidate into obedience rather than terrify into panic. The movements of their weapons were as precise. 'Do as they say,' he warned the others. They slowly backed towards the corner.

The third man lacked the same training, yet he appeared to be the leader. He regarded the map with greedy delight while his companions corralled their prisoners. Then his expression darkened. '*Dónde está la daga?*' he demanded. '*Dónde está Rompetierra?*'

Nina didn't know the last word, but it was clearly meant as a name. A portmanteau, maybe: *tierra* – earth? *Daga* was easy enough to translate, though. 'They want the dagger,' she whispered.

'He said "Earthbreaker",' Macy told her quietly. 'That must be what the dagger's called.'

'How does he know?' Eddie asked.

A sharp order from one gunman silenced any further discussion. The leader gave Eddie, Nina and Macy a vaguely puzzled look, as if he hadn't expected them to be present, before turning to the Mexicans. He stared unreadably at the Rendóns for a moment, then faced Maldonado. *'La daga verde. Dónde está?'*

Maldonado gestured hesitantly towards the adjoining chamber. *'Ahí.'*

The leader signalled for everyone to enter it. *'Vamos.'* At gunpoint, Maldonado led his charges into the other room. The tall man followed.

His excitement at first seeing the map was nothing to his reaction when he spotted the dagger. His expression became one of pure awe. He crouched beside the body, whispering reverentially. Then he reached out – and took hold of the dagger's hilt. His whole body twitched at the contact.

'No, no lo toques,' Maldonado protested – but the man tightened his grip and ripped the dagger from the desiccated flesh. He held it up to a light, admiring it. Nina noticed markings inscribed into the green stone blade, but they were too small for her to make out.

The man finally lowered his prize. *'Mantenerlos aquí,'* he ordered one of the gunmen: *keep them in here*. He and his other companion returned to the map room. The remaining man stood near the entrance, gun covering the prisoners.

'Everyone okay?' Eddie asked, cautiously eyeing the guard. No objections were raised to his talking; he risked moving closer to the Mexicans. The gunman watched, but didn't order him to stop. In a room with no other exits, there was nowhere his captives could go.

'Yes, but – what is happening?' said Maldonado, distraught. 'Who are these men? How did they know about the dagger?'

'It's what they want with it that worries me,' said Nina quietly.

'What do you mean?'

'When I fell against the map, I got what felt like an electric shock.'

He reacted with surprise. 'But it is just stone.'

'Maybe,' she replied. 'But when that guy touched the dagger, he seemed to react in the same way. There's something unusual about that material.'

'Oh, bollocks,' said Eddie, dismayed. 'Sounds like something we've seen before.'

'It's not the same. The things we've seen in the past, the stones and crystals that channel the earth's energy – I could *feel* the flow by touching them, like I'd gained an extra sense. This was different, just . . . raw power. Like sticking a finger in an electrical socket.'

'I do not know what you mean,' said Maldonado. 'An . . . energy? You can sense it through stones and crystals? You never said anything about this in your work.'

'It was classified by the IHA,' Nina told him. 'And I had reasons of my own for keeping it quiet. Various artefacts from Atlantis, and other ancient cultures, allow certain people to control this power. People who are directly descended from a particular group of Atlanteans.' She paused, then admitted: 'I'm one of those people.'

Rosamaria regarded her owlishly. 'Your ancestors were from Atlantis?'

'Yeah. And the same is probably true of the guy who took the dagger.'

'Which is never bloody good,' growled Eddie. 'Every time we

find some old relic that can channel earth energy, there's always some arsehole who wants to use it to take over the world. What did you say he called that dagger?' he asked Macy.

'Earthbreaker,' she replied.

'There you go. The clue's in the name. Great, another bloody ancient WMD.'

'We don't know that,' said Nina. 'But whatever it is, I think we should do everything we can to keep it out of the wrong hands.'

'It's a bit late for that,' Macy said snippily.

Eddie lowered his voice further, not knowing if their guard could speak English. 'First thing we need to do is get out of this room. Which means dealing with Charlie Cheesebits over there.' He moved a few steps to glance into the map room. Both the other intruders were occupied with the map itself. The leader was crouched, examining the miniature landscape. The other man had stretched a string from one side of the map to the other, and was carefully drawing another line taut.

The guard noticed Eddie's attention and waved the gun for him to move back. Eddie obeyed; he had seen what he needed. 'The other two blokes are busy doing something with the map,' he muttered. 'So if we can take this guy down quietly and get his gun, we can surprise them.'

'How are we going to do that?' asked Maldonado.

Eddie surveyed the chamber – and spotted something potentially useful. 'Macy,' he said, 'if you—'

The guard's tolerance finally reached its end. 'Hey, hey!' he snapped, stepping closer. '*Basta de hablar! Apartaos y collate.*'

Eddie raised his hands defensively. '*No hablo español.*' He actually knew enough Spanish to understand the order, but decided feigning ignorance might work to his advantage.

'He said stop talking, and move apart,' Macy translated for him.

'Okay, okay.' The group divided, the Mexicans reluctantly backing away from their guests. The guard returned to his position.

'Now what?' Nina whispered.

Eddie half turned so his right hand was hidden from the gunman. 'Macy.' He made a series of subtle signals with his fingers. Nina watched in confusion, but Macy nodded, replying with signs of her own. Eddie grinned. 'Good lass.'

'You're not doing anything that'll get Macy hurt, are you?' said Nina.

'If anyone gets hurt, it'll be me,' he replied.

'Yeah, that's not the reassurance I'd hoped for . . .'

But her husband and daughter were already moving. Macy sidled slowly towards one of the excavation areas, while Eddie approached the guard, hands raised. 'You speak English at all?' The man glared at him, gun rising. Eddie stopped. 'We've got money. Dollars? I mean, not actually on us – I don't carry fifty grand in my wallet. But we can get it for you.' He glanced towards Macy, seeing she was nearing her objective. 'If you let us go, you could have a nice wodge, no questions asked.'

The man stared at him, uncomprehending – then his gaze flicked towards Macy. Eddie immediately stepped closer—

One of two responses was inevitable. The Englishman gambled it would be the less lethal one. He was lucky, at least in a relative sense. The guard lunged and struck Eddie's head with his gun. The blow knocked him to the floor.

'Dad!' Macy cried, horrified.

'I'm okay,' he groaned. 'You just wait for the right moment, love.' Nina gave them both another look of alarm. They were planning something – but what?

The guard spoke in rapid Spanish, gesturing for Eddie to retreat. 'Hold on, hold on,' said the Yorkshireman. 'You just bloody clouted me, give me a minute.' Impatient, the intruder stepped closer, aiming his gun down at the fallen man—

Macy grabbed the archaeological robot's remote – and pushed the controls.

The machine jerked to life, clattering backwards on its tracks. The guard looked around in surprise—

Giving Eddie his opening.

He had deliberately drawn the other man closer – within reach of his legs. In a rapid, forceful move, he clamped the guard's ankles between his own and rolled hard to one side.

The man staggered and fell, slamming down on his side – and Eddie pounded his head face-first against the uneven floor. A wet crack as his nose broke was followed by the snap of teeth hitting stone as another strike pounded him unconscious.

The violence was over so quickly the onlookers took a few seconds to absorb what had happened. 'Did – did you kill him?' said Rosamaria in a shaky whisper.

'No, he's not dead,' Eddie replied, as Nina helped him stand. 'Hope Mexico has decent dentists, though. Otherwise he'll have a hard time eating apples.'

'You okay?' Nina asked. Blood was running from a cut on his temple.

'I'll need a whole box of Anadin, but I'll be fine. Everyone else all right?'

'Yes, yes,' said Maldonado, regarding the unmoving intruder with wide eyes. 'Rosamaria?'

She was equally stunned. 'I am good, yes.'

Diego's expression was part shock, part admiration. 'That was . . . pretty cool, Mr Chase,' he said to Eddie. 'You were fast!'

'My dad was in the SAS,' Macy told him proudly. 'He taught me all the hand signals they use. Never imagined I'd need them, though.'

'When did you do that?' Nina asked Eddie.

'We don't just go running together,' he replied with a crooked grin. 'I want my little girl to be able to look after herself.'

Nina was less than impressed. 'Well, maybe *tell* me before you give my daughter combat training?'

'Not the time, Mom,' Macy hissed. Nina glowered, but fell silent.

Eddie collected the downed guard's gun, then crept to the exit. Nina went with him, peering into the next room. The other men were still occupied with the map. The man with the dagger was bent low over the carved stone landscape, peering intently through the hole in the weapon's grip. Strings were stretched across the map; she saw they were attached to its edge in places inscribed with Atlantean text.

She realised what he was doing. Searching for something – or *somewhere*. The strings marked a particular location. Somehow he was using the dagger to take a sighting. What he was trying to find, though, she couldn't tell. From her vantage point, only part of the map was visible. And exactly how he was using the dagger was a mystery . . .

She put the questions aside as Eddie spoke. 'All right, everyone stay behind me,' he whispered, raising the gun.

'Are you going to kill them?' Rosamaria asked, alarmed.

'Only if I have to. Hopefully they won't do anything stupid. That's my job.' Before anyone could say more, he rushed into the map chamber.

Both men reacted with shock. The leader hadn't appeared to be armed, making the other gunman Eddie's primary target. The latter fumbled for his gun – but Eddie's weapon was already locked onto him. 'Drop it!' he barked. '*Suelta el arma!*'

A split second's hesitation – then the man raised his pistol. Eddie fired. The bullet clipped his target's right upper arm, blood spraying from the torn sleeve. It was a harder shot than simply plugging him in the chest, but with Macy there, Eddie didn't want to kill anyone unless absolutely necessary.

It did the job, though. The man lurched back, his gun spinning away. He slumped against the map, clutching the wound.

Eddie had already found another target. The leader had the green dagger in one hand, his other snatching for something—

Not a gun. The strings. He plucked them loose, and they fell in a tangled knot across the jade landscape.

Eddie fixed the gun upon him. 'Don't move,' he growled. '*No muevas.* Put down the knife.'

'Never,' came the reply, in English. The leader's jaw was clenched tight, seething anger in his deep-set eyes. 'I have waited my whole life to hold Earthbreaker! You will have to kill me to take it.'

'If you want,' was Eddie's even reply. 'You've got until I count to three. One—'

'Holy shit, Dad!' Macy said behind him as the others entered. 'You shot that guy!'

'I'll shoot this one an' all if he doesn't drop the knife. And mind your language—'

The brief distraction gave the leader a chance to move. But he didn't attack – or run. Instead, he darted forward, holding the dagger just above the map – where the two threads intersected over Teotihuacán. 'Put down your gun!' he commanded. 'Or I will use this.'

Eddie laughed sarcastically. 'Right, you stab the big lump of stone. I'm scared. Now, where was I? Oh yeah. Two.'

'Eddie, wait,' said Nina. The man's expression was one she had seen before. It was that of a true believer, willing to do anything for his cause – including dying. The face of a fanatic, a suicide bomber. Whatever he planned to do, he was convinced it would kill them all.

But Eddie was right. Stabbing the map would do nothing. Unless . . .

Unless the power she had felt was more than a mere static shock.

Her gaze went from the leader's face to his hand. It was trembling faintly, but not with the effort of holding the dagger's tip above the map. It was almost the opposite – that he was having to hold it *down*. As if the carved stone were somehow forcing the point away . . .

She'd seen something similar before. Diamagnetism: magnetic attraction or repulsion in materials that were not normally magnetic. It required extremely high voltages—

Or earth energy.

The green stone was charged with it, both the map and the dagger. She didn't know what it would do. But as Eddie had said, the clue was in the name . . .

Earthbreaker.

The leader somehow recognised her realisation. A hint of triumph appeared on his face. 'Eddie,' she said, urgent. 'I think he's serious. Let him go.'

'Are you bloody joking?' Eddie replied in disbelief. 'These arseholes pointed guns at my daughter! *And* my wife.' His finger tightened on the trigger. 'Last chance. Three—'

The man braced himself – and forced the dagger downwards.

The very air seemed to vibrate in the instant before the tip of the blade landed. A subsonic thrum ran through the room. Eddie hesitated, surprised—

Dust kicked up from the floor, the sound rising – then everyone was thrown off their feet as the entire chamber jolted as if struck by a colossal hammer.

7

Nina landed on her back, her hard hat bowling across the floor. Dust streamed from the ceiling as cracks opened in the stonework. 'It's an earthquake!' yelled Eddie. He hauled her beneath the map's overhanging lip. 'Macy, get under cover!'

Macy had also been knocked down. Diego pulled her into shelter beside Nina. '*Todos salgan!*' Maldonado cried. 'Get out!'

The leader of the intruders had expected the quake, already back on his feet. He shouted to his wounded companion. The other man scrambled up, grabbing his gun. They both ran for the tunnel.

The shaking eased – but didn't stop. Eddie rolled out from cover, Nina following. 'Macy, come on!' she called. The two teenagers scrambled out from beneath the map after them.

Maldonado was about to join them – then hesitated, looking into the next room. 'That man is still in there—'

Another ground-shaking impact – this from the other chamber as its ceiling collapsed. A deafening boom sent the Mexican reeling. Choking dust exploded from the opening. 'Jesus!' Eddie gasped, covering his mouth and nose. 'Move it!' He pushed Nina in front of him as they ran into the tunnel. 'Macy!'

'I'm here!' she said, catching up. 'Diego, come on!'

'*Mamá!*' Diego yelled, ducking back into the swirling cloud. He seized the coughing Rosamaria's hand and pulled her after him. Maldonado recovered and entered the tunnel's mouth – just as a support column broke apart. Tons of dirt and stone plunged down, the map room's ceiling disintegrating and sealing the chamber for ever.

But the danger was far from over. Nina led the way, hurrying up the winding passage. The lights danced and jittered as the ground shuddered. The props supporting the roof creaked and strained. She briefly glimpsed the two escaping men ahead, but then they vanished beyond a kink in the tunnel. By the time she reached it, they were gone.

She looked back. Eddie and Macy were with her, Diego and his mother not far behind. Maldonado, though, was falling back. 'Gregorio!' she shouted. 'Hurry!'

Eddie slowed. 'I'll get him.'

'No, I'll do it!' said Diego, pushing his mother onwards as he reversed direction. 'Get Macy out!' He rushed back to help Maldonado.

A wooden support prop ahead of Nina splintered explosively, soil gushing down from above. She shielded her eyes as she swerved past. 'The whole tunnel's going to come down!'

'How much further?' Eddie demanded.

'Not far,' Rosamaria said, panting. 'About fifty—'

The passage was suddenly plunged into darkness as the lights went out. 'Shit!' gasped Nina, stumbling to a halt. She stretched out her arms to feel for the tunnel's sides – then realised she could still see something ahead. A faint glow.

Daylight.

'I can see the exit!' she cried, moving again as quickly as she dared. The floor was still trembling underfoot. A normal earthquake would have been over by now, the initial tremor lasting perhaps thirty seconds – but this was clearly no ordinary quake. 'Come on!'

Traversing the final stretch felt like a nightmare, the ground bucking and the walls seeming to warp around her. But now she could see the ladder. Forty feet, thirty, almost there—

A *crack* of breaking stone – and something struck her unprotected head. She fell, dazed.

'Macy, keep going!' Eddie shouted. His daughter ran on as he stopped to aid Nina. The three Mexicans passed them. 'Get up the ladder!'

Macy stopped just short of it, looking back for her parents – as a huge lump of stone broke from the ceiling above her—

Diego threw himself into a dive, knocking her breathlessly to the floor. The heavy rock slammed down behind him. 'Are you okay?' he gasped.

'Yeah,' Macy managed to squeak. 'You saved my life!'

'Thank me at the top.' She took the hint and started up the ladder.

Eddie brought Nina upright, and they ran after the others. By the time they reached the ladder, Macy was out of sight above, Rosamaria climbing as Diego urged Maldonado after her. A thunderous boom rolled up the tunnel as an entire section of ceiling gave way. Displaced air rushed at them like an oncoming locomotive. 'Go go *go!*' the Englishman shouted. Everyone scrambled upwards, Eddie the last to start climbing. Another deep thud from below, bigger and louder. 'The whole lot's falling—'

A gritty wind blasted past him. Maldonado jumped clear of the ladder's top, but Eddie, Nina and Diego were still inside the shaft. The rush of air rose to hurricane force—

The shock wave hit, hurling them upwards. Eddie collided with Nina, the couple flying out of the shaft as Diego dived clear. The wooden hut was blown apart by the air-cannon blast. Debris rained around it.

Nina crashed down amongst the wreckage. Stunned, in pain, she opened her eyes – to see a broken plank spearing down at her. She jerked her head sideways. It hit the wooden floor beside her ear. 'Jesus!' she gasped.

The hut's ceiling was gone, leaving her looking up at open sky. She stared into the blue for a moment before her senses struggled back. 'Macy? Eddie!'

'I'm here,' Eddie groaned from nearby. 'Ow, balls. That hurt. The hard hat was a lot of bloody use.'

Nina sat up. 'Oh my God, where's Macy? Macy!'

'She's here,' said Diego. He had thrown himself on top of Macy to protect her from falling debris. A shard of corrugated metal had slashed his shoulder. He sat up, wincing. Rosamaria and Maldonado also stirred under broken wood.

Macy shook splinters from her hair. 'I'm okay. I think. What the hell happened?'

'I think,' Nina replied, standing unsteadily, 'Earthbreaker happened.' The ground was still trembling, a low-frequency judder interspersed with irregular harder jolts.

Eddie looked around. 'Where are the arseholes who took it?'

Beyond the damaged fence, Nina saw an overturned pickup truck. The raiders' vehicle – but they couldn't use it to escape. So they had to be on foot . . .

She staggered to the open gate. The trees swayed, shouts and shrieks from frightened tourists reaching her. Nobody in sight to the west, towards the Avenue of the Dead. She turned—

And froze.

The colossal Pyramid of the Sun loomed to the north – but its shape changed as she watched, the sharp, angled edges of the ziggurat's tiers crumbling. Dust trails raced down its flank as huge stones broke loose and tumbled towards the ground. Helpless horror rose: there were still people on the summit. As she watched, a chunk of the upper tier sheared away. Screaming tourists were swallowed by churning rubble or flung into the air before spinning back into the swelling cloud.

'Oh fuck,' gasped Eddie, joining her. 'Jesus Christ.'

Nina said nothing, overpowered by horror. All she could do

was stare in sickened disbelief as the pyramid's entire south-western corner gave way, a stone avalanche sweeping more people towards the crowded Avenue of the Dead. Then the carnage was blotted out by an eruption of dust.

She turned away – and saw the man who had caused the devastation. The leader of the raiders stood amongst undergrowth a hundred metres to the east, staring at the terrifying spectacle.

Sunlight shimmered off something green in his hand. The dagger.

'Eddie!' she cried. 'He's over there!'

Eddie's expression changed from dismay to a promise of brutal retribution. 'Let's get the fucker,' he growled.

'Mom! Dad!' Macy shouted from the wrecked hut.

'Stay there!' Eddie yelled back as he and Nina ran towards the raider. 'Make sure the others are okay!' Macy hesitated, but then moved to help Diego.

Even over the roar of collapsing masonry, the leader heard their shouts. He sprinted east to catch up with his wounded companion.

Tourists fled from a nearby modern building as its roof collapsed. The raiders passed the chaos, Eddie and Nina in pursuit. Nina already felt exhausted after the race through the tunnel. But she couldn't stop. The man responsible had to be caught.

Before he could use Earthbreaker again.

A parking lot lay beyond the wrecked building. People milled about in panic, not knowing what to do. The leader ran past the vehicles, seeing a red Toyota Corolla with its front doors open. Two people stood beside it, gawping at the collapsing monolith. The driver belatedly realised someone was rushing at him – only to fall with a cry as the polished stone blade was driven into his stomach. The female passenger screamed, but was knocked down by the wounded raider. Both attackers leapt into the car. It surged away in a spray of gravel, leaving its bloodied driver writhing on the ground.

Eddie was torn between helping him and catching his assailant. The latter won out. He searched for a way to pursue. 'Get into that truck!' he barked. An old GMC K-series pickup waited ahead, brown and bronze with jacked-up suspension and oversized tyres. Its baseball-hatted owner was at its front, transfixed by the destruction of the Pyramid of the Sun.

'*Disculpe*, mate,' Eddie said as he jumped up into the cab. Nina clambered in on the other side. By the time the owner overcame his shock, the Yorkshireman had started the engine and selected reverse. He stamped on the accelerator, throwing the pickup backwards into a skidding J-turn. A spin of the wheel, and the truck lurched about to follow the fleeing Corolla.

Nina spotted the red car peeling out of the lot's exit. It sped off beyond a chain-link fence. 'There they go!'

Eddie gripped the wheel. 'They're not getting away. Hold on!'

'You're not going to—' The fence rushed at them. 'Oh goddammit, you *are*!'

They both braced as the GMC smashed through the fence. It vaulted over a verge and slammed down on the road a few car-lengths behind the Toyota.

The chase had begun.

8

Eddie closed the gap to the Toyota, seeing one of the silhouettes inside change position. He immediately recognised the threat. 'Gun!' he snapped. Nina ducked as he swung across the road—

Muzzle flash – and the Toyota's rear window exploded. The bullet clanked against the GMC's front wing.

Eddie swept to the Corolla's left and accelerated. 'What are you doing?' demanded Nina. 'He's got a gun – and you're getting closer!'

'He's shooting left-handed 'cause I shot him, and his mate's in the driving seat,' Eddie replied. The pickup drew alongside the Corolla's tail. 'If he shoots at us, he'll deafen him – or blow his head off.'

'So again: what are you doing?'

'Trying to spin him out. Hold tight!' He turned to clip the Toyota's rear—

The driver anticipated the attack, braking and swerving hard to his left. The vehicles collided. The pickup was bigger and heavier, but the Corolla hit its front wheel, forcing it back across the street. 'Eddie, look out!' Nina cried. Shin-high concrete pyramids divided the road from the sidewalk, and the truck was heading right for them—

Eddie yanked the wheel. Too late. The front-left wheel hit a bollard, kicking the GMC's nose into the air. The truck flattened a chain-link fence. The Toyota sped ahead.

He regained control and swung the pickup back onto the road, accelerating again. The Corolla's passenger took another shot, cracking the windscreen. 'He's got ten rounds left,' said Eddie.

'Great,' said Nina. 'He can still kill us five times over.'

The pickup quickly gained on the Corolla. Eddie angled to overtake it. This time, he would ram the smaller vehicle off the road into a tree—

The Toyota suddenly veered sharply to the right. A dust cloud erupted behind it as it sped onto a dirt track. Eddie slowed, but the truck was already past the exit. 'Bollocks!' he barked. Braking and making a half-turn to return to the track would cost him valuable time.

He needed to make his own shortcut.

To his right was grassy open ground. He turned hard – and leapt the GMC over the kerb into the field.

Nina yelped as the landing almost tossed her from her seat. A stand of prickly pear cacti was splattered into spiky mulch by the truck's flat nose. Chunks of succulent hit the windscreen, damaging it still further. Eddie squinted through the prismatic haze. The Toyota was at the head of a dust trail ahead. Buildings were visible beyond the waste ground; the dirt track joined another road running past them.

'Okay, get ready for another bump,' he warned Nina. The Corolla fishtailed off the end of the track and headed east. Eddie swerved around more cacti, crashing through bushes before vaulting back onto tarmac—

The truck landed – then lurched violently. Nina gasped. 'That was more than a bump!'

Parked cars jolted, overhead power lines whipping madly. 'It's an aftershock,' Eddie realised, battling to hold the GMC on a straight course. Ahead, the Toyota struggled to do the same, almost hitting one of the high walls penning in the road. 'They're lighter than us – they're being thrown around more. We can catch up!' He accelerated again.

The lines spanning the street were decorated with dozens of blue and white paper pompoms. Eddie didn't know what they were for, but they gave him a handy visual reading of the aftershock's strength. They danced again, another blow kicking up through the pickup's suspension. Part of a wall toppled and fell, broken bricks scattering across the road. He jinked to avoid them, but debris still pounded the truck's flank.

'They've slowed down,' Nina reported. The road was obstructed by a larger pile of collapsed brickwork, forcing the red car onto the pavement. Eddie accelerated. This was his chance to catch up—

The overhead lines leapt once more, some snapping from their poles. A parked car was bowled onto its side – and beyond it, the road surface split open, shattered asphalt dropping into a chasm spanning the entire street. The overturned car slithered into the newly opened gap.

A gap at least five feet across – with the Toyota on the far side. If the pickup tried to cross it, it would end up nose-down in the crevasse. Eddie would either have to stop, or do something crazy.

He opted for the latter. 'Hang on!' he yelled, jamming his foot to the floor and swerving left—

The GMC hit the pile of bricks, flinging it upwards. It vaulted diagonally over the sidewalk and sideswiped the stone wall beyond, screeching along it before slamming down on the rift's far side.

Nina looked back in shock. 'Oh my God, we actually made it!'

'Think I saw the Fall Guy do that once,' he replied, as amazed as his wife that the stunt had actually worked. He saw the Corolla fifty yards ahead. 'We're catching up.'

The raiders had realised they were still being pursued, the passenger twisting in his seat again. 'And they're catching on!'

They both hunched down as more gunshots cracked from the

car. This time, one struck the windscreen squarely. 'Shit!' Eddie gasped as the glass shattered, showering him with crystalline fragments.

'At least you can see now,' Nina pointed out. The Toyota made a skidding turn to head north at an intersection. Eddie sent the GMC in pursuit.

The chase weaved through the narrow streets of San Martín. The quake had brought the town to a standstill, people fleeing buildings as the ongoing aftershocks brought down more walls. An overturned eighteen-wheeler blocked the road ahead, forcing the Toyota to swerve into a gas station's forecourt. Eddie followed—

Another shock pounded the pickup. The Corolla weaved – then turned hard under the canopy to avoid a large sign as it toppled like a tree. It smashed down onto a rank of pumps. Gasoline fountained from the wreckage.

The gunman fired several rounds into the spewing liquid as the Toyota whipped past. Hot lead hit flammable fuel – and a smashed pump exploded.

A fireball erupted behind the speeding Corolla. A support leg of the canopy had already been weakened by the quakes. The blast took it out entirely, the whole structure keeling over behind the fleeing raiders with a thunderous bang. More explosions sent a wall of liquid fire across the forecourt.

'Jesus!' cried Nina, cringing as the heat reached her through the broken windshield. 'We can't get round that.'

Eddie set his jaw. 'So we'll have to go over it.'

She gave him a disbelieving look. 'Oh my God, I married a maniac!'

'It took you nineteen years to realise?'

Nina braced herself as Eddie sent the truck racing towards the sloping roof of the fallen canopy—

It hit the makeshift ramp, shock absorbers compressing with

a bang, and powered up it – leaping over the roiling flames beyond.

Nina and Eddie both screamed as the GMC went airborne, tongues of fire lashing through the broken glass. The heavy-duty suspension barely survived the impact as it pounded down on the far side, metal groaning in protest. But the pickup was still in the chase, however battered and scorched.

Eddie forced it back after the Toyota, which had rejoined the road beyond the crashed tractor-trailer. 'You okay?'

Nina had ended up in the footwell. 'Apart from the terror? Yeah,' was her dazed reply.

'Great. This is just like old times, eh?'

'Yeah, I've really missed having everything explode around me.' Angry exasperation returned to her voice. 'Five years I've managed to go without any near-death experiences. *Five years!* But no, some asshole decides to raid an ancient tomb and cause a goddamn earthquake! Why is it always *me* who gets caught up in this shit? What did *I* do in a previous life to deserve this?'

'Maybe you were Hitler,' Eddie suggested with a grin. She returned to her seat and gave him as dirty a glare as she could manage.

The fleeing Toyota turned down a side street. Eddie wrestled the wounded pickup after it. This part of San Martín was run-down, most buildings raw brick and cinderblock rather than the usual cheery colours. The raiders were forced to slow to round debris from a fallen wall. The GMC, though, powered right over the rubble. 'We're catching them,' said Nina. 'How many bullets do they have left?'

'Enough,' Eddie replied.

The gunman was waiting for his pursuers to draw closer, not wanting to waste his remaining rounds. The street was a narrow channel. Once they got nearer, it would be much harder to weave and throw off their opponent's aim—

The problem suddenly became academic. A building ahead abruptly succumbed to the quake and collapsed into the road. Eddie braked hard, skidding to a stop. The way ahead was completely blocked – and the Toyota was on the far side of the piled debris.

'Buggeration and fuckery!' he growled. Even with its raised suspension, there was no way the truck could clear the blockage. The raiders were getting away—

A gate to the right revealed a yard beyond, a light industrial business. The workers had fled. He turned, using the truck's nose to barge the gate open. Beyond the yard was an empty plot strewn with broken bricks and scrubby cacti. 'Might be able to get through here.'

'And if we can't?' Nina asked.

'Then those arseholes get away with the earthquake-causing dagger. So no pressure.' He brought the truck over a low berm and accelerated. 'Might want to put your seat belt on.' Nina hurriedly buckled up.

Buildings ran across the far end of the wasteland. 'I can see a road,' said Nina, pointing at a space between the structures. Whatever stood there had been demolished, a low chain-link fence separating it from the street beyond. 'We should be able to—' She broke off at a flash of red between other buildings. 'They're coming along it!'

Eddie glimpsed the Toyota. He judged its speed – and floored the accelerator. 'We can catch them!'

The fence was directly ahead. He aimed for a small mound just before it, hoping it would act as a ramp. If the Corolla was maintaining pace, it would appear in seconds. He readied himself for the jump. Any moment—

There! The speeding Toyota came into view from his left. Eddie held his course. The pickup would land just ahead of it . . .

The car's occupants reacted to the sight of the onrushing

GMC – and the Corolla sped up. 'Eddie,' Nina said in alarm, realising the two vehicles were now on a collision course. 'Eddie!'

'Duck!' he told her, bracing himself. The gunman aimed through the car's passenger window as the distance between the two vehicles shrank—

The pickup hit the dirt mound – and hurtled into the air, smashing through the fence.

The gunman fired. The bullet punched through the door beside Eddie.

A moment later, Eddie's much larger projectile hit the Toyota.

The flying GMC's front bumper smashed through the side windows, crushing the gunman's skull. The force of the impact flipped the Corolla onto its roof. The truck tore free and made a nose-heavy landing beyond it. Front suspension wrecked, it slewed around and crashed sidelong into a wall.

Even with her belt on, Nina had been slammed against her door. Arm aching, she woozily looked around. Her husband was sprawled over the steering wheel, blood oozing from his nose. 'Oh my God,' she said, alarm overpowering dizziness. 'Eddie! Are you okay?' She clawed at the seat-belt buckle and slid over to him.

'Yeah, yeah,' came the pained reply. 'I braced for the airbag – then realised this thing doesn't have one!'

Nina let out a relieved breath, only to see they weren't out of danger. The Corolla lay on its back nearby like a flipped turtle. Smoke rose from its rear wheel arches. 'Oh shit. I think the car's on fire.'

'Time to go,' Eddie said, painfully pushing himself upright.

Nina pulled at her door handle. The door released – but wouldn't open, blocked by the wall. 'I can't get out!'

He struggled to open his own door. The various impacts during the chase had buckled the metal. 'Go through the windscreen.' Nina scrambled over the dashboard through the hole in the glass. Eddie followed, sliding over the truck's hood to the ground.

The inverted Toyota's passenger side faced them. The gunman was dead, his face looking as if it had been hit by a sledgehammer. 'Jesus,' said Nina, repulsed. It had been a long time since she'd seen the horrors of death close up.

Eddie's attention was on the car. Fire flickered inside its tail end, and he could smell the harsh tang of petrol. 'Fuel's leaking. We've got to get clear before it goes up.'

'Wait, what about the other guy?' she protested. The lead raider was visible past the crumpled corpse. His arm moved weakly. 'He's still alive! We've got to get him out of there.'

'Why? He caused a fucking earthquake – killed a lot of people! Let the bastard fry.'

'We need to know *how* he did it – to make sure nobody else can do it again. Come on!' She hurried around the car. Eddie made a disgruntled sound, but followed.

The survivor was sprawled against the driver's door. Nina and Eddie grabbed him through the broken window and drew him out head-first. They had just managed to get his waist clear when the *whumph* of igniting fuel came from the back of the car. 'If he's not out in five seconds, he's fucking staying,' Eddie warned.

Nina tugged the man's leg to twist his foot clear of the steering wheel. 'Got him – pull, pull!' They dragged the driver out. 'Get him clear – oh shit!' She darted back to the car. 'Where is it?'

Eddie hauled the limp raider away. 'Where's what?'

'The dagger!' She knelt to peer into the cabin.

'Nina, the fucking car's going to blow up any second!'

She ignored him, looking frantically around the upside-down Corolla's interior. The dagger wasn't on the ceiling, so it had to be stuck somewhere above. She twisted to look up—

The green blade was wedged between the driver's seat and the centre console. She stretched an arm, but couldn't reach. The crackle of fire grew louder, but she squirmed further through the window and reached up again. Her fingertips brushed the hilt's end, but couldn't quite find a hold. Just another inch . . .

The cabin's interior suddenly lit up in flickering orange and yellow as flames rippled up the rear seat. 'Nina!' Eddie shouted, dumping the raider and running towards her. 'Get out of there!'

'No, wait, I've almost—' One final stretch – and she hooked her index finger through the hole in the hilt. An electric tingle ran through her. A moment later, Eddie yanked her back out by her legs. The dagger jerked free, coming with her.

'Come on, *run!*' he yelled, pulling her away from the Toyota. A fireball gushed through the overturned car's cabin. Eddie and Nina ran – then dived to the ground as the Corolla's fuel tank exploded. Debris and shrapnel clanged down around them.

The couple looked back at the blazing wreck. 'That was *way* too close,' Nina gasped.

'It was almost bloody closer,' Eddie complained, kicking away a piece of flaming scrap before standing. 'What the hell did you go back in for?'

She showed him the dagger. 'For this.'

'Might have been better if you'd let it get blown up.' He helped her up, then went to the raider, crouching to examine him. 'Just think of the times we'd have avoided trouble if—'

The man's eyes flicked open.

His fist struck Eddie's jaw. The Yorkshireman fell with a startled grunt of pain. The man jumped upright and rushed at Nina. 'Earthbreaker is *mine!*' he snarled.

She backed away in fright, wielding the dagger. He hesitated, watching its sharp point warily. 'I am Tekuni, Lord of the Dead – high priest of Tekuazotl, the Jaguar God,' he told her. 'You have seen my power.' He made an attempt to snatch the

90

blade, jerking back as Nina slashed it at him. 'Give me Earth-breaker, or—'

'Oi!'

The man turned – and Eddie's balled fist slammed into his face. The raider crumpled unconscious to the ground. 'How about a fucking *nose*breaker?'

'Thanks, hon,' Nina said with relief. She regarded the downed man, then the object he had been so determined to obtain. 'I guess Earthbreaker lives up to its name. The question is: what the hell do we do with it now?'

9

The green dagger lay upon a table, the archaeologists gazing thoughtfully at it. 'So, we know this is called Earthbreaker,' said Nina. 'And we know what it can do. But what *is* it? How does it work? And most importantly, how do we stop anyone from using it again?'

'Smash the bloody thing with a hammer,' Eddie suggested from across the room. The couple had returned to the archaeologists' compound at Teotihuacán, after phoning Maldonado and through him contacting the authorities. The discovery of the dead security guards had helped convince the overwhelmed local police to arrest the mysterious raider.

Maldonado himself was distraught, pacing in agitation. Understandably, thought Nina: the historic site to which he had dedicated his career had been smashed by the earthquake. The Pyramid of the Sun was now a misshapen pile of rubble, through which rescuers were picking in the hope of finding survivors. The Pyramid of the Moon had fared only slightly better, one face having collapsed, while most of the smaller buildings had also suffered damage. The cultural loss was incalculable.

But the loss of life was even more horrific. As well as the tourists who died when the pyramid fell, the surrounding towns had been hit hard by the quake. Columns of smoke from countless fires rose into the sky for miles around. The zone of destruction reached as far as Mexico City. A death toll of thousands seemed inevitable.

And it had all been caused by one man, with an ancient stone dagger. How?

'It is a priceless artefact,' Rosamaria Rendón replied to Eddie, beating Nina to the objection. 'And it belongs to Mexico. What happens to it must be decided by its true owners, not outsiders.' Eddie said nothing, but his disapproval was plain.

Maldonado lifted the blade. 'I still do not understand. How could this cause an earthquake? It is just stone.'

'I've seen similar things before,' said Nina.

He looked at her in surprise. 'You have?'

'Yeah. Ancient weapons, with . . . well, I won't say *supernatural* powers, because I don't believe they are. But powers that go beyond conventional science, and which still haven't been fully explained.'

'Such as?'

'The Shamir, or the Horn of Jericho – it destroyed Big Ben in London ten years ago. It emitted a focused sonic pulse that could shatter stone. The Angels of Revelation – four statues containing meteorite fragments that when exposed to air produced an enormous amount of deadly gas. One of them killed everybody on a Caribbean island. The tidal wave in the Persian Gulf, eight years ago? That was caused by the Spear of Atlantis – a crystal that trapped and contained positrons. It was essentially an antimatter bomb created by the Atlanteans.'

Maldonado's eyes widened as she reeled off the list. 'All those disasters . . . they were caused by ancient weapons?'

'Yes.'

'And you were involved? You found them?' She nodded. His voice rose. 'Why did you not *warn* anyone?'

'They were classified,' said Nina, with sympathy; had their positions been reversed, she would have felt the same distress and sense of betrayal. 'The IHA's entire purpose was to contain knowledge of dangerous discoveries – first from Atlantis, but later from other civilisations as well. Even after I left, I still worked with them to make sure these finds didn't fall into the wrong hands. Unfortunately,' she indicated the weapon he was holding, 'this guy Tekuni got *his* hands on Earthbreaker before we knew the danger it posed.'

Maldonado was mollified by her explanation, even if he had not necessarily forgiven her. 'It would seem you are the expert,' he said. 'So what do we do now?'

'We find out as much as we can about Earthbreaker.' She had noticed inscriptions on the blade in the map room; now she could see them more clearly. 'Let's take a closer look.'

The Mexican placed Earthbreaker back on the table. Nina examined the carved symbols. 'Okay, that looks like Atlantean text, just like on the map. It's the same variant, so presumably they were inscribed around the same time.'

Macy had been hanging back, quietly talking to Diego, but now she piped up. 'So I was totally right about the connection to Atlantis. Still waiting for my apology, Mom.'

'This really isn't the time to gloat,' Nina said sharply. Macy had a retort on her tongue, but held it there. Instead she turned back to Diego, muttering. Her mother guessed she was the subject.

But she had bigger concerns. 'What do the inscriptions say?' asked Rosamaria.

'It's a puzzle, I think,' Nina replied, translating the symbols. 'Let me see . . . "Where jaguar and snake meet and hummingbird and lizard meet, through my eye see . . ." two names, I think, but I don't know them – some of the symbols aren't the same as the Atlantean ones. "Where the two . . . stand in line, you will find the gate to . . ."' She looked up, startled. 'The gate to the Underworld.'

'The Underworld?' echoed Maldonado. 'Is there an Underworld in the mythology of Atlantis?'

'Yes – it's more or less the same as the Ancient Greek concept. Most of Greek mythology was based on the Atlantean, from what we've discovered. The Underworld is where souls go after death, usually facing various threats and challenges on their way to judgement.'

'Just like the Mesoamerican cultures,' Diego remarked.

'That's right. The big difference is that in the Greek version, once the dead enter the Underworld, they don't come back out. But if I remember, the Mesoamerican take was more like the Egyptian one. The dead are judged, and then reborn in a new cycle of life. Is that right?'

Rosamaria nodded. 'In the Maya and Aztec cultures, yes. The religion of Teotihuacán seems to be the same. Their gods have different names, but all have the same roles.'

'They probably descend from the same source. Like the Roman gods being directly analogous to the Greek.'

Maldonado had another question. 'Which version of the Underworld myth was used in Atlantis? Were the dead trapped there, or were they reborn?'

'They played it both ways,' said Nina, with a faint smile. 'Most of the souls that entered the Underworld stayed there, but the strongest were able to overcome challenges and be judged worthy of rebirth. So their myth could have been the basis of the Underworld on both sides of the Atlantic. The European civilisations kept the dead below ground for ever, which in time led to the Christian concept of hell – its other name, Hades, comes directly from the Greek. But the African and Mesoamerican civilisations allowed for the dead to come back in a new form.'

Rosamaria took a closer look at the dagger. 'Then this tells us where to find the entrance to the Underworld.'

'So it's a real thing?' Eddie asked. 'I mean, we've been to enough places that were only supposed to be legends. Atlantis, Valhalla, El Dorado . . .'

'This "Lord of the Dead" seemed to think it was real,' said Nina. 'He was using Earthbreaker with the map to try to find it.' She thought back to the encounter in the underground chamber. 'Maybe he succeeded. He was pretty quick to knock those strings away so we couldn't see what he'd found.'

'Then he might know where it is?' said Diego.

'He might.'

'So he could tell someone else how to get there,' Eddie pointed out. 'Should have let the bastard burn in his car.' Rosamaria looked shocked at the suggestion.

'Even if the map survived two million tons of pyramid collapsing on top of it, it's buried,' Nina added gloomily. 'It'll be decades before those tunnels are opened again, if they ever are. There's no way we can find out what he discovered.'

The Mexicans exchanged glances. 'Actually,' said Maldonado, with unexpected optimism, 'there is.'

At Maldonado's instruction, Diego and Eddie cleared a space in the centre of the room. 'Because of the mercury contamination,' the senior archaeologist explained, 'we did not want to spend long periods in the map room, even wearing masks. So we used augmented reality technology to scan the entire chamber – including the map. That way, we could examine it on our computers.'

'You made an AR copy of the map?' Macy asked.

'Yeah,' Diego told her. He took out his phone. 'We didn't even need to bring in any expensive gear. A modern phone's good enough to do the whole thing.'

'My phone can't do anything like that,' said Eddie, nonplussed.

'Dad, your phone's *ancient*,' Macy scoffed. 'It's, like, steam-powered or something. And it can't even get a signal when it rains.'

'She's right,' said Nina. 'You still think Siri's some kind of witchcraft.' She turned to Diego. 'So you have the map room on your phone?'

He started the relevant app. 'Here. Take a look,' he said, aiming the phone at the room's centre.

Nina's eyes went wide as she saw the image on screen. Overlaid on the empty floor was the map from the subterranean chamber, looking as real as if it were actually there. 'Wow. That's impressive.' Phones had incorporated AR systems for several years – she was sure her own had one – but it was something she'd dismissed as a gimmick. She was clearly some way behind the technological curve. 'Last time I saw anyone use AR for anything, they were hunting Pokémon.'

Macy sighed. 'God, Mom. You're as bad as Dad. We use AR in school now. Like history – you can explore a site the way it was hundreds of years ago without having to go there.'

Nina arched an eyebrow. 'Where's the fun in that?'

'Or I can try out make-up and clothes,' Macy went on, 'or smash up the city with my own giant monster . . .' She trailed off, giving Maldonado and Rosamaria an embarrassed look. 'Although maybe now's not the most appropriate time to talk about that.'

Nina ignored her, watching the screen as Diego advanced. The digital replica of the map grew larger, perfectly anchored to the floor despite the phone's movement. 'Can I try?' she asked.

'Sure.' Diego handed it to her.

'Do I need to do anything to control it?'

'Just walk around. We scanned the whole map chamber. Whatever was in there, you'll see.'

Nina hesitantly brought the phone closer to the digital mirage, sidestepping to circle it. More detail was revealed as the parallax shift brought new areas into view from behind the sculpted mountains. She brought the phone to within inches of the non-existent object. At such close range, glitches started to appear.

The numerous still frames that had been stitched together to provide photorealism began to warp and smear, the seams blending them becoming obvious. But the model of the map itself remained solid beneath the images projected onto it. The phone's high-resolution LiDAR scanner had recorded it in extreme three-dimensional detail.

'Okay,' she admitted, 'you might have found a convert. I had no idea the tech had gotten this good.' Eddie peered over her shoulder to see for himself. 'I can get in really close before it starts going blurry . . .' A thought – and she whipped the phone back, finding a particular spot on the map's edge. 'Oh my God. It's so clear, I can read the inscriptions! This one says "jaguar" – so if we—'

Mind working faster than she could speak, Nina quickly circled the virtual map. 'Here, here,' she said excitedly. 'This is "snake", which is one of the clues on the dagger. I think I know what that guy was doing! If he ran a string between them . . .' She darted back to examine Earthbreaker. 'Okay, from jaguar to snake gives one line.' She rounded the map again, finding more inscriptions. 'And if you put another line between the second two creatures, where they meet gives you a point on the map!'

'The entrance to the Underworld?' said Maldonado.

'Maybe. Although there's more to it than that. There was something else written on the dagger, about things standing in line. But we can start by finding the coordinates. Have you got any string?'

Rosamaria searched a drawer, producing a ball of twine and some scissors. 'Here.'

'Great, thanks. Eddie, can you stand here, at "snake"?'

Her husband took her place. 'What am I doing?'

'Holding a piece of string. I know archaeology isn't your thing, but I'm sure you can manage that.' She handed him one end of the twine. 'Okay, now if I go back to where it said "jaguar" . . .' She backed away from him. The image on the screen resembled a low-altitude flight in a jet fighter, whipping over the digitised landscape as she passed through the map. She stopped, finding the inscription. 'All right, here it is.'

'Let me help,' said Maldonado. He took hold of the string as Nina cut it, then positioned it where a small virtual notch was visible above the ancient text.

'Thanks,' said Nina. 'So the other inscriptions were "hummingbird" and "lizard" . . .' She circled the map again, finding the correct spots. Rosamaria and Diego held a second length of twine between them.

The two lines formed a cross. 'Okay!' Nina said excitedly. 'So, they meet . . .' she went to the point of intersection, holding out the phone, 'at a big mountain. Or a volcano, from the shape.'

Maldonado peered at the screen. 'In Guatemala.' Like Nina, his voice became more animated. 'I think it is Tajumulco!'

'What's that?' Eddie asked.

'The tallest mountain in Central America. An extinct volcano. Or sleeping, at least. I don't think it has erupted in recent history.'

'So that's where the entrance to the Underworld is?'

'Somewhere,' said Nina. 'The inscription on Earthbreaker says that once you get there, you have to use it to put what I assume are landmarks in line. Macy, can you pass it to me?'

Macy picked up the green blade – and yipped in surprise, dropping it. 'Are you okay?' Diego asked urgently.

'Yeah, yeah, I'm fine,' she replied, composing herself. 'It just zapped me.' She picked it up again, her face wrinkling. 'That's . . . yeah, touching it feels weird. Like licking a battery.'

Diego gave her a teasing look. 'You lick batteries?'

'Not on a regular basis!' She passed the ancient weapon to her mother.

Now it was Nina's turn to flinch. Contact with the dagger produced a brief tingling sensation – slight, but enough to be unpleasant. It remained even after the initial shock, albeit at a lower intensity. It felt stronger than when she'd recovered it from the burning car.

'What is it?' asked Maldonado.

'Macy's right. It feels as if it's charged with energy. Or *channelling* it,' she added, with a glance at Eddie. He reacted with dismay.

'Just like you said about the map under the Pyramid of the Sun,' said Rosamaria.

'Yeah. And you can use the inscriptions on this,' Nina held up the dagger, 'to find the Underworld.'

'I suppose you're going to jet off and look for it,' Macy said. There was more of an edge to her words than her normal teenage sarcasm.

But Nina surprised her. 'No.'

Eddie was taken aback as well. 'Really?'

'Considering what's happened, I think this is something that should stay buried. Yes, the guy might tell someone else what he discovered in the map room – unless he's kept in solitary confinement for the rest of his life, there isn't really any way to prevent it. But,' she indicated the dagger, 'they can't find the Underworld's exact location without this. And I very much doubt the Mexican authorities will let it out of their hands.'

Maldonado nodded. 'I have already told the Secretariat of Culture that we have recovered it from the thieves. I will deliver it to them in Mexico City later today. They will keep it under high security.'

'Good. It might be worth contacting the IHA in New York as well. They have experience of protecting these kinds of artefacts.'

'A good idea.' Maldonado returned the phone to Diego, and was about to say more when his own phone rang. 'Excuse me.' He answered, holding a muted conversation in Spanish. His expression grew increasingly concerned, his gaze flicking repeatedly towards Nina.

'What is it?' she asked, handing Earthbreaker back to Macy before going to him. Macy put the dagger on the table – then, her expression suddenly thoughtful, took out her phone and opened its augmented reality app.

Everyone else's attention was on Maldonado. '*Sí, adiós,*' he said, ending the call.

'What happened?' said Nina.

'The man you caught,' he replied uncomfortably, 'the federal police have him. Some investigators from the government arrived, but he will not talk to them. He says he will only talk to one person.'

'And who would that be?' she asked, with a feeling of dread inevitability.

The answer was what she expected. 'You.'

10

'You want me to come in with you?' Eddie asked as he and Nina were escorted through the federal police station in San Martín.

'He said he'll only talk to me,' she replied unhappily. 'And he's chained up – he shouldn't be a threat.'

'Unless he can do a Harry Houdini.'

'Let's hope he doesn't have that on his résumé along with "can cause earthquakes".'

The cops leading them stopped outside an interview room. '*Aquí adentro,*' one of them said.

Nina and Eddie exchanged grim looks. 'I'll be right outside,' he assured her. 'That arsehole tries anything, the door'll be off its fucking hinges in two seconds flat.'

'Thanks.' She took a deep breath as the other officer unlocked the room. 'Okay, here I go.' She entered. The door closed behind her.

The room was small, the only furniture a plain table and chairs. The man she and Eddie had captured was seated, hands cuffed and chained to an eyebolt. He looked up at her, deep-set eyes widening with a predatory look. Even though he was shackled, Nina felt a chill. He had an aura of threat. She had seen it in others: the air of someone who had killed before, and would not hesitate to do so again. The Lord of the Dead, he had called himself.

But now she knew his real name. She held up the printouts she'd been given by the police. 'So,' she said, steeling herself as she sat facing him, 'you wanted to talk to me – Señor Corazón.'

The man gave her a sardonic smile. 'So they told you who I am.'

'Yeah. Ciro Corazón, age forty-three, resident of Mexico City. But here's the big surprise – also the owner of Corazón Productos de Carne. A major slaughterhouse business, from what I've read. Your family's been very rich for generations. So my question is: how does a multimillionaire businessman know about an ancient dagger that can cause earthquakes?'

Corazón leaned closer. 'Because it belongs to me. To my people.'

'And who are your people?'

'I am the leader of the Dispossessed.'

'A cult?'

He frowned. 'We are called a cult by those who rule now, to diminish us. But we are the *true* rulers of these lands, and far beyond. Centuries ago, Teotihuacán was our city, the heart of our empire. But we were cast out by the rabble, and overthrown. Without us, the empire collapsed. We survived in the shadows, hiding, hunted . . . until we were eventually forgotten. But *we* never forgot.'

'About Earthbreaker? And the map room?'

'Yes. We knew that some day it would be found. That day has come.'

'And gone,' Nina pointed out. 'The map room – the whole Pyramid of the Sun – has been destroyed, thanks to you. It survived for centuries after the city fell, until you brought it down in minutes.'

'When we reclaim what is ours, we will rebuild it,' Corazón insisted. 'Greater and higher than before. The Dispossessed will take back control. And I shall lead them.'

'You seem remarkably confident about that, considering you're chained up in a police cell.'

'I will not be in chains for long. And when I am free, we will overthrow those who overthrew us. I am the direct descendant of Tekuni, the high priest of Tekuazotl, the Jaguar God – the Lord of the Dead. I now hold his title. And,' he added with dark emphasis, 'I also possess his power.'

'The power to use Earthbreaker?'

He nodded. 'You saw it happen. The dagger's power was long dismissed as myth, as fantasy. But I have *believed*, all my life, just like those who came before me. We knew that one day, a Lord of the Dead would reclaim Earthbreaker. He would prove its power was real. And through that power, we will rule again.'

Nina would have dismissed his words as the megalomaniacal ravings of a lunatic – if not for what she had witnessed. 'But you can't use it again without the map, can you?' she said warily. 'And that's buried under two million tons of stone.'

Corazón let out a mocking laugh. 'There is another map. And now I know where it is.'

'In the Underworld?'

A flash of shock in the intense eyes. 'How do you know about the Underworld?'

'I read the inscriptions on the dagger.'

His expression changed to one of suspicion – and calculation. 'Who *are* you?'

It was Nina's turn to be surprised. 'You don't know? I thought that was why you wanted to talk to me.'

'No, that was because . . .' He paused. 'You know my name. It is only polite that I know yours.'

Nina hesitated, but then decided she would not be intimidated. Besides, if Corazón clammed up, she would have no way of finding out more about his goals. 'My name's Nina Wilde.'

A moment of thought – then recognition. 'Ah. The famous archaeologist,' he said, nodding. 'You discovered Atlantis.' A mocking smile. 'You look older than in your photographs.'

'I've been busy,' Nina shot back. 'Get to the point. You wanted to talk to me about something. What?'

Corazón regarded her probingly. 'You saw me use the power of Tekuazotl. When I touched Earthbreaker to the map, that power was released. But . . . you have felt that power too. I saw it.' Nina said nothing, suddenly uncomfortable. 'You felt the shock, the energy running through you. You are like me.'

'I don't think so,' she said firmly.

'No, you are. In every generation, a chosen few have the bloodline. They can feel the power . . . *use* the power. I can use Earthbreaker. And so can you.'

Nina tried to hide her unease. Corazón was right: there was a strong possibility that they were both distant descendants of the Atlantean priesthood, able to channel the lines of energy flowing through the earth itself. The most deadly use of such power she had previously encountered had destroyed cities through an explosive release of pent-up force. Earthbreaker, however, had the potential to flatten whole *countries*. If Corazón's followers got hold of it . . .

'You can't use it without the other map,' she said, covering her concern. 'So where is the Underworld?'

'Do you think I would tell you?'

'Why not? It's not as if you'll be able to find it from prison.'

'I will never go to prison.' The words came with the smug arrogance of the lifelong wealthy.

'The police found the bodies of the two security guards from Teotihuacán. You shot them.'

'I shot nobody. They have already tested my hands for gunpowder. There was none.'

'You may not have pulled the trigger, but you gave the order. I don't care how much money you have. It won't get you off a murder charge.'

A smirk. 'That is not true even in America. And it is definitely not true in Mexico. Once I am free, I will recover Earthbreaker and find the Underworld. Then you will see the full power I control.'

'Or maybe the power *I* control,' Nina retorted.

He did not like the suggestion. 'Earthbreaker is *mine*,' he hissed, suddenly angry. 'I am Tekuni, the Lord of the Dead. I serve the Jaguar God. Only *I* can control it!' The last words were almost shouted.

'Nina!' came another near-shout, from beyond the door. 'You okay?' Keys rattled in the lock.

'Yeah, I'm fine, it's all right!' she called back. The metallic clatter ceased. She knew that Eddie was poised in the corridor outside, ready to take violent action to protect her. He wouldn't have been joking about kicking the door down.

She looked back at Corazón. His surge of fury had subsided, but its embers were still hot. 'You may have the power,' he growled, 'but you do not have the *strength*. That comes from the blood of others.' His gaze flicked to one corner of the room. A small black object was mounted high on the wall, a camera or microphone. He knew he was being recorded. 'We have followed the old, true ways for centuries. Our ceremonies have kept us strong, given us the willpower we needed to keep going through the dark times.'

'What ceremonies?'

'Those of our ancestors. Here – at Teotihuacán. The great pyramids were temples, places of worship . . . and sacrifice.'

He did not need to elaborate for her to understand – and be appalled. 'You've *sacrificed* people?' she gasped. He said nothing, but his faint smile said everything. 'Oh my God. You own slaughterhouses! Is that how you got rid of the bodies?'

Another glance towards the monitoring device. 'You said that, not me. I admit to nothing.' He looked back at her, his face cold and threatening. 'Perhaps soon you will see the truth in person. *Very* soon.'

Nina stood. 'Okay, we're done,' she said as dismissively as she could, to conceal her fear. She went to the door and rapped sharply on it.

The keys rattled again. 'I *will* reclaim Earthbreaker,' said Corazón. 'And I *will* find the Underworld.'

'Not if I find it first,' Nina fired back as the door opened. 'And I have a pretty good track record at that kind of thing.' Anger returned to his face, but she turned her back and exited.

Eddie was right there. 'You okay?'

'Yeah, yeah,' she assured him, finding herself breathing heavily. 'Glad to be out of there, though. Jesus. He is one sick son of a bitch.' She started quickly back down the corridor.

'What did he say?'

'If he was telling the truth, and I think he was, he's the leader of some sort of cult. Claims to be a direct descendant of the former rulers of Teotihuacán. Normally I'd dismiss that as the kind of crap every cult leader says about themselves, but in his case . . . Well, you saw what he did.'

They reached the room where Macy and Maldonado were waiting. 'What about this Underworld place?' Eddie asked. 'Did he tell you where it was?'

'No.'

'But when you came out, you told him you were going to find it before he did.'

'You're going looking for it?' said Macy, jumping up. 'After you said you wouldn't?'

'I only said that to get the last word on him,' Nina assured her. 'No, I'm not going looking for the Underworld.'

Maldonado joined the discussion. 'Did he tell you anything else about it?'

'Not about how to find it, no. But he did say there's another map there.'

The Mexican's face fell. 'Like the one under the pyramid?

107

But if he finds it, and he has the dagger—'

'He won't find it,' she insisted. 'You have the dagger, right there.' She indicated the polycarbonate case under his seat. 'It's going to a secure location, and he's going to jail. Even if he tells his followers that the Underworld's entrance is somewhere on Mount Tajumulco, they can't find exactly where without Earth-breaker. And I looked at the area on my phone on the drive over. It's like thirty square miles of jungle. I've *explored* jungles, and I can tell you that unless you have a pretty solid idea of precisely where to look, you won't find squat. And even if by some miracle they *do* find the entrance? They still won't have the dagger. All they have is another map. There's no threat.'

'That is like saying a bomb with no fuse, but which is still full of gunpowder, is no threat. These people are dangerous!' Maldonado paced in exasperation, before turning sharply back to her. 'When you were head of the IHA, your job was to prevent archaeological wonders from being misused. Would you have refused to help find the Underworld if *America* were in danger?'

Eddie gave him a cold look. 'You saying Nina's racist?'

'Eddie, he's not,' Nina said quickly, but an awkward moment followed. The silence was broken when a police officer entered and spoke to Maldonado. The archaeologist nodded, then turned back to his visitors. 'They are taking him to the federal police headquarters in Mexico City to be interrogated. They want me to bring the dagger.'

'You're not taking it to the ministry?' asked Nina.

'The police want to examine it as evidence. They need to question all of you as well. You were witnesses.'

Macy made an irritated sound. 'Great. How long'll that take?'

'You got somewhere to go?' said Eddie.

'Well, yeah – I was kind of planning to see Diego again.'

'I don't think we'll be doing any more socialising,' Nina told her. 'Once we're finished with the police, as soon as the airport reopens, we're going home.'

Maldonado looked pained. 'But we need your help to find the Underworld. You are the expert on Atlantis – you have more chance of locating it than anyone else.'

'I'm sorry, Gregorio,' she said. 'There are people at the IHA who can translate Atlantean text as well as me, if not better. I'll put you in contact with them.'

'I am not talking about translating texts. You have *experience*, Nina. That is worth more than any amount of learning from books. You said you have explored jungles before. We will need someone who knows what they are doing in the field.'

'It's not my job any more,' Nina insisted. 'I'll do everything I can to help locate the Underworld, but I'm not leading an expedition into the middle of a jungle halfway up a volcano. I'm sorry.'

The Mexican was unhappy, but acquiesced. 'Whatever you say,' he replied, deflated.

The policeman spoke again. Maldonado collected the case containing Earthbreaker. 'It is time to go,' he announced.

'Do you have Diego's phone number?' Macy asked hopefully.

'No, sorry.'

Her face fell.

'Come on, then,' said Nina. 'The sooner we get this over with, the sooner we can go home.'

11

The quake had caused considerable damage and disruption to Mexico City, Nina saw as the police convoy entered the capital. Numerous roads were closed, causing jams, and the emergency services were badly overstretched.

The federal police were using three vehicles to transport everyone. A prisoner transfer van was followed by a pair of dark-blue and white Dodge Chargers. Maldonado was in the first of these with the dagger; the second carried Nina, Eddie and Macy. Macy had called shotgun, to the amusement of the young Federale driving them.

Even with strobe lights on to clear the way, the convoy kept getting caught in gridlock. 'This'll take all day,' Macy complained. Her initial excitement at riding in the front of the powerful police cruiser had long faded.

'The place *was* just hit by an earthquake,' Nina pointed out. 'We're lucky anything's moving at all.'

The driver, who had told them his name was Miguel, glanced back. 'We try to go other ways,' he said, in laboured English. 'Some roads closed so ambulances can use them. We get to one soon. We go faster then.'

'Oh, good,' said Macy. She was silent for a moment, then: 'So, Miguel. What's it like being a cop?'

Miguel grinned, pleased at the attention. 'It's cool.' He checked out his front-seat passenger. 'So, you at university, or—'

'She's *fifteen*,' Eddie rumbled pointedly from behind him.

'Okay, okay, okay,' the cop said, quickly turning his attention

110

back to the street. Macy shot her father an irked look.

The radio bleeped, a man's voice issuing instructions. Miguel responded, then spoke to his passengers. 'We turn soon. They open a road for us.'

'Great,' said Nina. Ahead, a stationary police car, a green and white Dodge Avenger, blocked the intersection with a side road. The traffic was so knotted that it took a few minutes to reach it. The Avenger backed up as the convoy arrived, the Mexico City cop inside waving his federal counterparts through.

Miguel brought the Charger onto the new route. It was a two-lane street, the buildings along it mostly small factories or workshops. 'This take us past a hospital,' he told them. 'After that, *pfft* – back into jam. But now we go faster.'

'I'll take what we can get,' said Nina. A glance back. The police car had returned to its original position to stop opportunistic motorists from following.

She looked away, not seeing the cop raise his phone to make a call – or two men leave the shadows of a doorway to climb into his car.

The convoy cruised down the empty road. Even here, thirty miles from the quake's epicentre, there was damage: broken windows, cracked walls, rubble on the sidewalks. Almost all the businesses had been hastily closed. Nina watched the deserted buildings roll by. Without the omnipresent Mexico City traffic, the lack of activity felt almost spooky.

The radio gabbled again, Miguel responding. 'A kilometre to the hospital,' he said, looking over his shoulder at Nina. 'Then we—'

A long-nosed box truck burst from a side alley ahead – and ploughed into the prisoner transport van, sending it spinning onto the sidewalk.

'*Mierda!*' Miguel gasped, braking hard. The Charger ahead did the same, barely avoiding a collision with the van. A Chevrolet Onix sedan sped from the alley in the truck's wake, skidding to a stop beside it. Two men leapt out – carrying Kalashnikov rifles.

One aimed at the van's cab and opened up on full auto. The windows exploded, rounds tearing through glass and metal and the men within. His companion swept his own stream of fire at the first Charger. The two cops in the front twitched and spasmed as bullets ripped into their bodies. Maldonado, in the rear, was hit and fell out of sight.

'Macy, get down!' Eddie roared. 'Miguel! Get us out of here!'

Another car, a BMW, emerged from the alley and stopped to block the street ahead. Miguel hurriedly shoved the gear selector into reverse and stamped on the accelerator as Macy hunched down. The Charger leapt backwards, engine roaring.

'Give me your gun!' Eddie shouted to the young cop. 'You drive, I'll shoot!' Miguel fumbled with his holster. Nina glimpsed a man running to the van's rear door as she ducked—

A car smashed into the Charger, throwing everyone back in their seats. The police Avenger from the intersection had followed to block their escape. Miguel's pistol clunked into his footwell. Both cars slewed around, the Charger's nose ending up on the sidewalk.

Nina straightened. 'Is everyone okay? Macy!'

'I'm fine, Mom,' came the shaken response from the seat in front of her. The airbags had fired, leaving Macy and Miguel dazed.

Eddie looked around in alarm. The Avenger was behind them to the left, its three occupants recovering. 'Come on, go, *go*!' he barked as the other car's doors opened.

Miguel pushed the deflated airbag aside to retake the wheel. His foot returned to the accelerator—

Too late.

His window shattered, blood spraying the windscreen as a

bullet smashed through his shoulder. He screamed. 'Shit!' Eddie yelped. The shooter was out of the Avenger, starting towards them. Another man exited the car's rear. 'Miguel, go!'

But pain had overpowered the Mexican. He clutched at his wound, letting out a shrill keen of agony. Eddie hit his seat belt release and stretched over the injured cop to grab the steering wheel. 'Macy! Push the accelerator!'

Macy stared at him, wide-eyed with fear. 'What?'

'If we don't move, we're going to *die*! Do it!'

Despite her terror, Macy flattened herself across the centre console. She groped for the larger of the two pedals and pressed it down, hard.

Tyres screeching, the Charger lunged backwards. Eddie jerked the wheel to send the car at the oncoming gunmen. They leapt clear, the first man twisting to track the vehicle as it passed. He fired. Eddie's window burst apart. The round clipped his back, tearing a ragged strip out of his leather jacket below his left shoulder. He yelled in pain. 'Eddie!' Nina cried.

'I'm okay,' he grunted. 'Keep down!' He dropped as low as he could. The man fired another shot, striking the car's front. Then the attackers raced back to their own vehicle and pursued.

Nina risked raising her head. The man she'd seen nearing the prisoner van was now hurrying from it—

A sharp *bang* and a gush of smoke, and the van's back door swung open, a hole blown through its lock.

'They're rescuing Corazón!' she shouted. But the cult leader was not their only goal. An armed man ran to Maldonado's vehicle and withdrew the case. 'And they've got Earthbreaker too!'

Eddie had other concerns. A Nissan Sentra rushed from an alley, falling in behind the Avenger. He needed to spin his vehicle around and head forwards, but his awkward position badly limited any manoeuvres. 'Hang on!' He turned the wheel, skittering the Charger backwards through an intersection. The new road was almost empty, the only thing moving a panel van heading towards police barriers a couple of blocks away.

Both pursuing cars swept around the corner, rapidly closing the gap.

Ciro Corazón staggered from the van. He'd expected a rescue attempt, but hadn't known when or how it would come. The crash had left him shaken, the explosion opening the door hitting him like a stun grenade.

But he was free, helped by two of his closest acolytes. Cruz was a former Mexican army commando, Garza an enforcer for the feared Sinaloa drug cartel. Natural enemies – now united in the service of the Jaguar God as his priests. Another man opened a case and held up Earthbreaker in triumph. 'We've got it!'

'Good,' said Corazón. 'Give it to me!' He was still shackled, his rescuers bearing him towards the BMW as the other man brought the dagger to him. The shrill of tyres caught his attention, more cars rounding a corner at speed. 'Who is escaping? Police?'

'The Americans.'

Corazón stopped short of the car. 'Nina Wilde was *here*? And she *escaped*?' The others flinched at his sudden anger. 'She's the only person who can find the Underworld before us! *Kill her!*'

'They're catching up!' said Nina. Peering over Macy's seat, she saw the two pursuing cars growing larger through the Charger's windscreen. A glance at the dashboard revealed they were moving at fifty kilometres per hour – thirty m.p.h. 'Macy, push that pedal down all the way!'

'It *is* down all the way!' Macy shouted back over the shrilling transmission. 'We can't go fast in reverse! God, don't you know anything?'

Nina seethed. 'This is *not the time*, Macy!'

The Avenger pulled out to overtake, giving the gunman in its front passenger seat a clear line of fire. Nina hurriedly ducked. A moment later her window shattered, glass hailing over her back.

The car drew level as they neared the panel van. The gunman extended his arm from his window, lining up another shot. Eddie jerked the steering wheel. The Charger sideswiped the other Dodge with a crash of buckling metal.

He'd hoped to crush the gunman's arm between the two vehicles, but by a fluke it had come through both windows, the gun just inches from Eddie's head. The other man overcame his surprise and pulled the trigger—

Nina shoved his arm upwards. The bullet punched through the roof directly above Eddie. Macy screamed. The man started to withdraw – but Nina grabbed his wrist, trying to wrest the gun from his hand. 'Macy!' Eddie shouted. 'Hit the brake!'

'I can't reach it!' she protested—

The attacking driver swung his own wheel. The Avenger bashed into the other police car, forcing it against the van's flank. Nina was thrown sideways. Eddie struggled to retaliate, but the Charger was now sandwiched between the two other vehicles.

The gunman broke Nina's hold. He cracked his automatic's grip against her forehead. She fell back with a cry.

The gun snapped back at Eddie—

Macy had been tossed further across the cabin. She could now reach the other pedal – and shoved it down.

The Charger's tyres screeched as it braked – and the gunman's arm was guillotined off above the elbow by the door pillars as the two cars ripped apart. The severed limb landed on Nina's lap. 'Jesus Christ!' she shrieked.

The van braked and swerved away. The police car reeled drunkenly as it suddenly broke free. Eddie almost lost his hold on the wheel. 'Macy, go again!' he said, seeing a second gunman in the Avenger's rear readying his weapon. 'Nina, get the gun!'

'Are you fucking kidding me?' his wife wailed, gingerly picking up the twitching arm. She tried to take the automatic, but the fingers remained firmly clenched around it.

'*Nina!*' The Charger accelerated, but the second Dodge was alongside again. The gunman took aim—

Nina flipped the entire arm around – and tugged its dead trigger finger.

The gunman jerked back as blood burst from a chest wound. The cop driving the Avenger realised he was just as vulnerable and hurriedly swung the car away.

'Nina, switch,' said Eddie.

She regarded him in confusion. 'What?'

'Give me Charlton Heston, and you drive. Come on, quick!'

'Charlton Hest— *Oh*, I get it,' said Nina, managing to roll her eyes despite the situation. She passed the severed arm to her husband, then leaned between the front seats to take the wheel from him. Not having to reach over Miguel, she was able to get a better grip on it, even though she had to put an elbow on Macy's back to support herself. 'Are you okay?' she asked her.

'Yeah, yeah,' Macy replied. 'Who's Charlton Heston?'

'Your dad'll explain his dumbass joke later – if we get out of this.' Nina looked back up. The Avenger was closing again – about to ram them. More pursuing cars were in sight behind it. 'Eddie!'

The Yorkshireman wrenched open the cold, dead hand. 'At least I didn't do the "farewell to arms" joke,' he said, taking the gun. 'Okay, duck!'

His wife and daughter did so. Eddie snapped up the automatic and fired three shots.

The first round broke the Charger's windscreen. The second punched a hole in the Avenger's – and the third hit its driver in the face.

The other police car abruptly swerved and smashed into a wall. Flaming debris sprayed across the street as it flipped over and exploded. The second car, the Sentra, braked hard to avoid the fireball.

'Okay, one down,' said Eddie. But the Sentra was already speeding up again as the explosion dissipated. 'Nina, Macy, I need you to do a J-turn – we've got to get this thing pointing forwards. When I tell you: Nina, give the wheel a hard half-turn to the right. Macy, you jam on the brake. The car'll skid around. Halfway through, switch it from reverse to drive. Then go again, full speed. Can you do that?'

'I think so,' Macy said, somewhat hesitantly. Nina's elbow was pressing against her spine; she changed position to relieve the discomfort.

'I know you can do it, love. Okay, ready?' They were closing on the police barriers, but the road was still empty of other traffic. 'Now!'

Nina yanked the wheel. The car's front end slewed around with a shriek from the tyres. Macy pushed down the brake pedal—

But not hard enough.

Her shift of position had cost her leverage. The car slowed, but rather than complete its half-spin, it reeled backwards and bounded over a kerb, coming to an abrupt stop against a wall.

'Oh no, no!' wailed Macy. 'I'm sorry, I'm sorry!'

'Just get us going again!' Eddie told her. 'Nina, get in the front! I need room to shoot!'

Nina clambered awkwardly over the front passenger seat. 'Macy, move over.'

'To where?' her daughter demanded. 'Miguel's taking up all the space!'

The Mexican had passed out. 'He won't mind – slide the seat back and get into the footwell!'

Macy reluctantly scrambled across the cabin as Nina thudded down onto her seat and put the car in drive. The Sentra was coming straight at them. Eddie fired, blowing a fist-sized hole through its windscreen between its occupants. The driver veered sharply away. 'Macy, put your foot – I mean *hand* down!'

Macy was sprawled over the unconscious cop's lap, head in the footwell and feet flailing over his shoulder. She found the accelerator. The Charger jumped forward. Nina retook the wheel. 'Where are we going?'

Eddie lined up another shot at the Sentra. 'Get onto the—'

The driver's seat suddenly slid backwards as Macy pulled the release lever and shoved. It clanked against the end of its rails, hitting Eddie as he fired and throwing his aim askew. '*Macy!*'

'Sorry, Dad!' But she finally had enough room to drop down into the footwell. Curled tightly, legs sticking up over the centre console, she kept her hand on the accelerator.

Even with a better hold on the wheel, Nina still found it difficult to steer from the wrong seat. She tried to bring them back along the street, but couldn't turn the rapidly accelerating Dodge sharply enough. The arc it was following would send them straight into a wall. 'Macy, slow down!'

Macy hit the brake again – this time, too hard. The Charger skidded, threatening to spin out once more. Nina gasped and hauled the wheel back to catch it. The entrance to a narrower side street loomed ahead; she jinked to send the police car into it, the rear wing clipping the corner.

The path ahead was clear for a hundred metres. Beyond that, traffic crossed a barricaded intersection. 'Okay, go again!' she told Macy.

'Make up your mind!' came the frantic response from the footwell. The police car surged onwards.

Eddie squirmed out from behind the seat and looked back. The Sentra had followed them around the corner, the BMW and

Onix now also in pursuit. A man leaned from the Nissan's passenger side and raised a gun. 'Incoming!' Eddie warned, ducking. Several shots echoed down the street – and the rear window blew apart.

A bullet smacked into Nina's headrest. She yelped and hunched as low as she could, peering over the dash at the road ahead. 'Shit, there are people!' Pedestrians were crossing on both sides of the barriers, a man with a little roadside stall sitting on the far side of one.

Panic entered Macy's voice. 'What do I do?'

'Brake when I tell you – but not so hard this time.'

'It wasn't my fault! I've never done this before!'

'*Nobody's* done this before!' Eddie pointed out. He returned fire, but the Charger hit a bump, sending his shot high. 'Bollocks!'

The car rushed towards the intersection. Nina was about to sound the horn, then spotted the switch to turn on the siren. The people ahead hurriedly ran clear – but the sitting man didn't move. 'Oh shit!' she said. 'Macy, slow down!'

Macy did so, this time more smoothly. The Charger shed speed. Nina swung the wheel to avoid the man, the car demolishing a barrier. Pedestrians screamed and dived clear as the Dodge vaulted the kerb at the corner and slammed down amidst the traffic beyond. Brakes screeched, cars skidding and swerving.

Nina swerved back and forth to avoid them, cringing at every near-miss. She saw a space and swung into it. The road ahead was clear for a short way – but she was on the wrong side, heading into oncoming traffic. 'Now speed up again!' she cried. 'Eddie, where are they?'

'Right behind us!' he replied. The gunman leaned from the Sentra again. More gunshots cracked after the fleeing Charger.

Nina jinked as rounds thunked into the police car's tail, but she was rapidly running out of room to manoeuvre. A large van was parked half on the sidewalk ahead – and a truck was heading straight at her in the remaining open lane. She glanced back, seeing the Sentra swing out to draw level on their left. 'Macy, *brake!*'

Mother and daughter worked in unison. The Charger abruptly lost speed and swerved to ram the Nissan's flank. The lighter car was thrown off course. Its driver braked, sawing at his wheel – but too late. The Sentra smashed head-on into the stationary van, demolishing both vehicles in a mass of mangled metal.

The oncoming truck also slammed on its brakes, juddering to a halt. Nina saw a narrow gap open on the other side of the road as a rubbernecker slowed to gape at the crash. 'Macy, go!' she said, aiming for the opening. The Dodge jumped into the space, whipping past the truck.

Another intersection ahead, the road to the right less crowded. 'I'm gonna turn hard in a few seconds,' she said. 'Macy, brake when I say.'

'The other two are still coming,' Eddie warned. The Onix led the BMW through the traffic after them.

Nina judged the turn. 'Okay, Macy – brake!'

She turned as the Charger lost speed – and kept losing it, Macy again pushing the brake too hard. The police car's tail slid wide. Panicking, Macy hit the accelerator once more. The tyres clawed at asphalt – and the car spun out in a cloud of acrid smoke. Nina was thrown against the centre console, one of Macy's flailing feet catching her in the face. 'Goddammit!' she yelled. The car had missed the turning, and was now pointing in completely the wrong direction.

'Go through there!' Eddie barked. Ahead was an auto mechanic's workshop, a roller door open. Daylight was visible through another opening on the building's far side.

Not knowing what lay beyond, Nina didn't like the idea – but

Macy had already shoved the pedal back down. All she could do was guide the Dodge through the doorway. The Onix made a high-speed turn to follow them.

The business was still open despite the recent earthquake, a man working under a car on a hydraulic lift. He ran in fright as the two vehicles powered into the workshop, dropping his welding torch. The intense flame shut off as he released the trigger.

But it was still connected to the oxygen and acetylene tanks on a small trolley. Eddie emptied his gun into the cylinders as the Charger shot past—

Shattering a pressure regulator.

The acetylene cylinder leapt from the trolley as highly pressurised gas blasted from the broken valve. It rebounded off the floor and shot across the workshop like a rocket – punching through the Onix's windscreen. The cylinder's blunt end smashed into the driver's face, pulverising bone and spraying blood. The Chevrolet veered madly and crashed into the lift. The car above toppled off and crushed its roof.

Only one hunter remaining – but they had nowhere left to run. The door at the workshop's rear led into an enclosed yard filled with piles of scrap. 'Macy, *stop!*' Nina screamed—

Her terror told Macy to hit the brake with full force. The police car shot out into the open, juddering as its anti-lock brakes activated – and ploughed into a large mound of old tyres. Flying rubber rained down on the roof and hood.

Eddie dragged himself upright. He could see through the workshop to the street – where the BMW had stopped at the roller door. Corazón glared at him from the front passenger seat. If the cultists came for them now, they were trapped—

The BMW abruptly sped away. A moment later, he realised why. Sirens rapidly grew louder. The federal police vehicles had GPS trackers, and someone at their headquarters had seen that the convoy had stopped moving. 'They've gone,' he said in relief. 'We're okay.'

Nina struggled up, seeing Macy clumsily extricating herself from the footwell. She made sure her daughter was unharmed before replying. 'Yeah, but Corazón escaped. And he's got Earthbreaker.'

12

Nina waited nervously outside the door of the hospital room. Through its little window she could see Rosamaria Rendón talking to the man in the bed: Gregorio Maldonado.

All she knew about the archaeologist's condition was that he'd been badly wounded in the convoy attack. After the police arrived at the workshop, Miguel, their driver, was rushed away in an ambulance while she, Eddie and Macy faced angry Mexico City cops and Federales. Macy had used her fluency in Spanish to explain what had happened – saving them from being immediately arrested.

Following that, the family had effectively been taken into protective custody by the federal police while they gave statements. It wasn't until the next morning that they were allowed to leave. Even then, they were under escort, a pair of armed officers driving them to the hospital. Maldonado had asked to see Nina; considering the circumstances, the Mexican authorities were keen to find out why.

So was Nina. She waited for Rosamaria to emerge. 'How is he?'

The other woman's grim expression said everything. 'Not good,' she replied.

'I'm sorry.'

Rosamaria blinked away tears. 'He . . . he is waiting for you.' She turned and walked away. Nina drew in a deep breath, then entered.

Maldonado was not alone. A nurse was in attendance – more

worryingly, so was a black-clad priest. 'Gregorio?' said Nina. 'I'm here.'

'Nina . . .' Maldonado's reply was barely audible. He exchanged whispered words with the priest, who backed away respectfully. Nina took his place at the bedside. Maldonado's face was ashen, covered in a sheen of sweat. Bandages covered his shoulder and part of his neck. An intravenous drip was hooked to his arm. 'You . . . are okay. Good.'

'I'm okay,' Nina confirmed. 'And I'm sure you will be too.'

Maldonado glanced at the priest, who had retreated to a corner, filling it like a shadow. 'He would not be here.' He closed his eyes, as if building up strength, before speaking again. 'They took the dagger. The men who shot me, they took Earthbreaker. That man, Corazón. He has it.'

'I know. He got away.'

'The earthquake . . . they tell me hundreds of people are dead. Perhaps even thousands.' His eyes opened, locking onto Nina's with a desperate intensity. 'Corazón caused it. And he can do it again. If he finds the Underworld, if he finds the other map . . .'

'The police are looking for him. He won't be able to get into Guatemala.'

Maldonado managed a feeble laugh. 'You have never seen the border, have you? There is no fence, no wall. There are a million places he can just walk across it. If he can get out of Mexico City, he can get into Guatemala. And then he can reach Tajumulco . . . and find the Underworld.'

'We'll warn the Guatemalan government. They can watch out for him on the roads to the volcano.'

'The Guatemalan government has bigger problems. A corruption scandal, drug cartels at war, left-wing rebels, threats of a military coup . . .' A weary, pained shake of his head. 'I could try to warn them. But would they believe me? Probably not. But you . . .'

'You want me to warn them?' said Nina. 'I can do that. If I go through the IHA and the United Nations, it would have more weight—'

He gripped her wrist with a trembling hand. 'Yes. Do that. But – you have to do more. Only you can find the Underworld before they do. Only you can stop Corazón.'

'I don't think I can,' she replied unhappily. 'Not without Earthbreaker.'

'We still have the map, the virtual map. Use that. You have to find exactly where they are going – find the Underworld.'

She nodded with reluctance. 'I'll do what I can.'

'You must.' His grip tightened. 'You have seen what Earthbreaker can do. If Corazón finds the map and uses the dagger again, it would be a catastrophe. For Mexico – for all the countries on the map. Millions of people are depending on you. They are—'

Maldonado's eyes suddenly went wide with pain. His hand became a claw, nails digging into Nina's wrist. 'Nurse!' she cried. '*Enfermera!*'

The nurse rushed to the bedside. Nina pulled free of Maldonado's hold to let her reach him. She hurriedly checked his pulse – then darted to the door and called for assistance.

None came. The hospital was beyond full capacity, overloaded by quake victims. The nurse rushed back to the bed.

Eddie ran in, Macy following him. 'What's happening?' he asked.

'I don't know,' Nina told him, feeling useless.

Macy nervously retreated to the door. 'I'll go find a doctor.'

'I don't think there's much point, love,' Eddie said softly. The nurse straightened with a low sigh of failure. She whispered to the priest. The man in black bowed his head, then stepped up to the bed and began reciting a prayer.

'Oh my God,' gasped Macy, hands going to her mouth. 'Is he . . .'

Nina put a hand on her shoulder. 'I'm afraid so.'

'Oh God.' Macy froze, unable to turn away despite her horror at witnessing death for the first time.

Eddie gently ushered her to the doorway. 'Come on. Let's wait outside.'

Nina gave Maldonado a last anguished look before going with them. 'Oh, damn. Poor Gregorio . . .'

'Did you manage to talk to him?' Eddie asked.

'Yes. He wanted me to find the Underworld and stop Corazón from using Earthbreaker again.'

'What did you tell him?'

'I told him I would. I couldn't say no, could I?'

'How are you going to find it?'

A helpless shrug. 'I have absolutely no idea.'

They turned at racing footsteps. Rosamaria hurried up, accompanied by her son. 'Diego!' said Macy.

Rosamaria came to Nina. 'I heard the nurse call out. How is . . .' She peered into the room, face falling as she saw the unmoving figure on the bed. 'Oh . . . Gregorio. *Lo siento mucho . . .*' She closed her eyes, leaning against Diego for support.

'I'm sorry,' said Nina. 'He asked me to help find the Underworld, and the other map. To make sure Ciro Corazón doesn't get to it first.'

Neither mother nor son responded for a long moment. Finally, Rosamaria wiped away a tear and looked up. 'What did you say?'

'I said yes.'

'You did?' She sounded surprised. 'I spoke to Gregorio on the phone after he left the police station, before he . . .' A glance towards the hospital room. 'He said you did not want to help, that you were going back to New York.'

'I changed my mind,' said Nina. 'Corazón's free, *and* he has the dagger. And Gregorio was right. I probably am the best person to help find the Underworld.'

'But how?' Diego asked. 'We don't have Earthbreaker any more.'

Macy let out a sudden squeak. Everyone turned towards her. Nina was about to chide her for inappropriate behaviour when she recognised the look on her daughter's face. It was *excitement*; the thrill of realisation, of discovery. It was an expression she was sure she herself had worn on numerous occasions. 'What is it?' she asked instead.

'We don't have Earthbreaker any more,' Macy said eagerly. 'But we've got something nearly as good!'

Two hours later, the group was in a meeting room at the Secretaría de Cultura in Mexico City. They were not there to discuss matters with ministry officials, though. Instead, Eddie and Diego moved furniture to create an open space. 'All right, so what now?' Eddie asked. 'Indoor picnic?'

'Now,' said Nina, 'we have another look at the map. Diego?'

Diego took out his phone and brought up the augmented reality app. 'Ready.'

'And Macy,' Nina went on, 'do *your* thing.'

Beaming, Macy brought up her own phone. On the screen was an image of Earthbreaker – which changed perspective as she moved. 'It's working!' she said.

'When did you take that?' Eddie asked.

'After you put the strings across the map to find the Underworld, I scanned the dagger in my AR app,' she told him. 'Thought it might be useful. I didn't know *how* useful, though.'

'You should really have asked before doing it,' said Nina. 'In terms of professional ethics, making a copy of an artefact, even a digital one, without permission from . . .' Both her husband and daughter rolled their eyes. 'All right, on *this* occasion it turned out to be a good thing. But my point still stands!' She went to Diego. 'Can I use your phone?'

The young man gave it to her. Nina walked towards the empty space, seeing the recreation of the map overlaid upon it on the screen. 'So, Tajumulco is . . . here,' she said, homing in on a particular part of the landscape. The volcanic cone stood out clearly. Macy, can you show me Earthbreaker?'

Macy touched the on-screen controls to freeze the virtual dagger, then went to Nina. Another tap, and it released, now seeming to float in one spot as the phone moved.

Nina looked between the screens. 'Okay, this is like trying to watch two different TV shows at once,' she complained. 'Macy, how much detail is there on the dagger? Can you get closer to it?'

'Sure,' Macy replied. She slowly brought the phone forward, the image of Earthbreaker enlarging to reveal more detail. 'The LiDAR scanner's got an HD mode for small objects. It should be able to show stuff less than a millimetre across. See – you can read the text on the dagger.'

'You can,' said Nina, genuinely impressed. 'Can you look through the hole in the end of the hilt?' Macy lifted her phone. The circular opening in Earthbreaker's grip slid into view – the room beyond visible through it. 'Wow, you really can. Is that in full 3D?'

'Yeah,' said Macy. To prove it, she rotated the phone around the dagger, revealing its other face. 'I scanned both sides. The computer figured out what it was looking at and combined them.'

Nina raised her eyebrows. 'Eddie, I'm starting to think modern phones actually *are* witchcraft.'

'Give it another ten years, they'll be running the world for us,' Eddie quipped.

'Considering the state of things, that might be an improvement. Okay, Macy, move it over here. If we can figure out exactly what he was looking at in the map room, we might be able to narrow down the location.'

Nina and Macy shifted positions, trying to reproduce what they had previously seen. Unfortunately, it proved easier said than done. They were treating the phones as if they were transparent, little frames through which they could view a seemingly three-dimensional object. The phones, however, considered each other to be solid. Trying to align the virtual dagger with the equally hallucinatory Tajumulco merely resulted in, from Nina's point of view, Macy's phone obscuring the map – with the empty void of the meeting room behind the dagger on its screen.

'It's not working,' she said, frustrated. 'I guess I prefer *actual* reality. I need something solid to work with.'

'So you can't do it?' asked Rosamaria. 'You cannot find the Underworld?'

'Not like this.'

'Then there is nothing else we can do.'

'I didn't say that.' Nina regarded the floor thoughtfully before turning to Rosamaria again. 'You got your friends at the ministry to let us use this room. Could you persuade them to let us raid their office supplies?'

Eddie gave the pile of assorted cardboard items a dubious look. 'Don't know about finding the Underworld, but you might get a Blue Peter badge for using this lot.'

Macy frowned. 'Obscure twentieth-century reference?' she asked Nina.

'Obscure British reference,' came the reply. 'I have no idea what he's on about either.'

'Tchah,' Eddie scoffed. 'Not my fault if you Yanks don't understand the cultural importance of sticky-back plastic.'

Mother and daughter exchanged weary looks. 'I'm just gonna ignore him until he stops talking,' said Macy.

Nina nodded. 'That's usually wise.'

'*Tchah!*'

'I have to admit,' said Rosamaria, 'I am curious too. What are you going to do with all this junk?'

'It's not junk,' Nina replied, picking up a stack of disposable coffee cups. 'We're going to rebuild the map – in the real world, not the virtual. We'll use the phone to find all the landmarks in the area of Tajumulco, then build our own copies of them. That way, we can use Macy's scan of Earthbreaker to find the location of the Underworld. Once I work out the map's exact scale, I'll be able to pin it down more precisely. If we're lucky, I'll be able to find it to within a few hundred metres.'

Rosamaria nodded. 'That is very clever. I would not have thought of doing that.'

'I used to do a lot of arts and crafts with Macy,' Nina said with a smile. She looked towards her daughter in the hope of an appreciative response, but Macy was talking to Diego and hadn't heard. 'Okay, if we start by marking Tajumulco's position, we can build things up from there. Macy, can you give me a hand?'

'In a minute, Mom,' came the dismissive reply.

'Come on, love,' said Eddie. 'Help us out.'

With a huff, Macy broke off her conversation and stomped towards the piled materials. 'All right, then. Give me some string.'

Nina sighed, then set to work.

It took over an hour to cobble together the replica. Nina stood back to . . . *admire* her work was not the best term, she admitted. It looked like exactly what it was: cardboard and paper and plastic crudely taped together like a child's half-finished school project.

But it would do the job. Diego had sent the AR scan of the map chamber to her phone; she was surprised how quick and easy the process was, making her wonder if Luddism was an inevitable by-product of age. With her own copy of the map literally in hand, she set about finding each landmark peak around the Guatemalan volcano, then marking their positions in the physical world. Tajumulco was represented by a paper cone stuck to the top of a long cardboard tube; other mountains and hills were made from coffee cups and drinking straws. The makeshift topography was taped precariously in position atop chairs and boxes; one accidental knock could bring it all tumbling down.

For now, though, it was ready. A last check, comparing the virtual landscape to the model, and she stepped back. 'Okay, I think it's done.'

'Great.' Eddie was kneeling, securing one of the more ramshackle pieces with extra tape. 'I'm too old to be grovelling around like this.'

'You should have asked Macy.' Nina belatedly realised her daughter was no longer in the room. 'Where is Macy? I need her to send me her scan of Earthbreaker.'

'Said she was going to the loo a while ago.'

Rosamaria had also been preoccupied by the map. 'And where is Diego?'

Eddie got up and went to the door, peering into the corridor. 'Macy?' No answer. 'Where is she?'

'She can't have gone far,' said Nina. 'Surely?'

'That's the place,' said Diego, pointing through the taxi's window.

Macy saw the storefront ahead. It was a copy shop – but of a more advanced kind than those merely duplicating documents or printing envelopes. This offered while-you-wait 3D printing. There were several such businesses in the Mexican capital, but while some were closer to the Secretaría de Cultura, they were shut following the earthquake. This one, when Diego phoned to check, was still open, but had taken the pair a cab ride to reach.

131

Now that they were here, Macy was having second thoughts. Even on a normal day, the street would have made her uneasy. Some of the parked cars were practically wrecks, tyres flat or in one case missing entirely. The walls were splattered with crude graffitied tags, and there were an unsettling number of young men hanging around in groups, watching passing vehicles with predatory interest. The quake's effects had been felt here: some windows were broken, a couple of storefronts hastily boarded up, and those people who weren't loitering were moving in an anxious hurry. 'Are you sure this place is safe?'

'I have to admit . . . no,' Diego replied.

'That does *not* make me feel any better.'

'Sorry,' he said with a grin. He told the cab driver to halt as they reached the store, then reached into his pocket. 'Here. Just in case.' He handed Macy something.

She examined it: a small switchblade. 'You carry this around all the time?'

'It makes me feel safer. There's a lot of crime in the city. Here, I'll show you how to use—'

She snapped the weapon open in a single quick movement, exposing the glinting five-inch blade. 'Like that?'

'Uh, yeah,' said Diego, startled. 'You've used one before?'

'My dad showed me. He's taught me all kinds of stuff, actually. He's got a friend in the police who let us practise at an NYPD gun range once. Although don't tell my mom,' she added hastily. 'Dad told her we were going running.' She flicked the blade closed.

The driver heard the noise. 'Hey, hey! If you're going to screw around with knives, you can get the fuck out of my cab!'

'Sorry, sorry,' Macy said, belatedly registering that she'd spent the entire journey conversing in Spanish. She offered the knife back to Diego.

'No, no, you keep it,' he insisted. 'Just in case.'

'But what if you need it?'

A cocky smile. 'I can look after myself.'

'Yeah, I bet you can,' she replied, grinning. A moment's hesitation, then she pocketed the switchblade in her pink jeans. 'Don't tell my mom about this either.'

'Are you kidding? *My* mom'd go mad if she found out I had it!'

Diego paid the scowling driver, and they got out. As they started for the copy shop's entrance, Macy's phone rang. She answered. 'Dad?'

'Macy? Where are you?' Her father's voice had a sharpness that she knew meant she was in trouble.

'I'm okay. I'm with Diego,' she replied.

'That's not what I asked. Where've you gone?'

'We're at a copy shop.'

'Why? There's a machine just down the hall.'

'*Copy*, not coffee.'

'Where is she?' Nina said in the background.

'Somewhere in the city,' Eddie replied.

'*What?* Give me the phone.' Sounds of a hasty transfer, then: 'Macy, where are you?'

Macy gave Diego an exasperated look. 'I just told Dad, we're at a copy shop.'

'You went out for *coffee*?'

'Ugh! No, a *copy* shop. Cop. Pee.'

'Why?'

'You said yourself, you work better with physical objects. So we're going to use the scan on my phone to make a 3D print of Earthbreaker. That way, you can actually hold it instead of looking at a screen.'

Nina's reaction was not what she'd expected, or hoped for. 'Get your ass back here *right now*,' she said in a dangerously level voice.

'The cab just drove off,' Macy replied, watching the vehicle pull away. 'And we're here now, so we might as well do what we came for. They've got a high-speed printer; it should only take a half-hour, maybe forty minutes.'

'Macy! I want you back at the—'

She grimaced at her mother's rising anger. 'Sorry, you're breaking up, the phone network must be overloaded because of the quake. See you soon. Bye!' She ended the call. 'Oh boy. My mom is *pissed*.'

'Let's get into the store,' said Diego urgently. One of the nearer groups of young men had noticed the couple and were taking an interest – especially in Macy.

'Yep, yep,' she agreed. 'Let's do that!'

13

'Just remember,' said Eddie, 'if you kill her, we might find it a bit difficult to get out of the country.'

'Oh, I'm not going to kill her *here*,' Nina replied, fuming. 'I was going to wait until we reached thirty-six thousand feet, then kick her out of the plane!'

Rosamaria gave them a concerned look, perhaps wondering if they were serious. 'Here they are,' she said as the meeting room door opened.

Macy entered first, holding up her prize – a grey plastic replica of Earthbreaker – as a conciliatory offering. 'Look at this!' she said, too brightly. 'We got it.'

'Don't you go trying to pretend that nothing happened,' Nina growled, stepping right up to her. 'You do *not* take off on your own into a city you don't know – a city that was just hit by an earthquake! Anything could have happened to you!'

'I wasn't on my own,' Macy protested. 'I was with Diego!'

Nina was not mollified. 'He's still a kid – he's seventeen. And you're *fifteen*! Do you have *any idea* how worried I was?'

'But I'm okay. Nothing happened. And look, hey, important thing, right here.' She waggled the copy of Earthbreaker to draw her parents' attention. 'Take a look at it, Mom. It's perfect.'

'It does look like the real thing,' Rosamaria commented. 'Perhaps we should see if we can use it?'

Nina snatched it from her daughter. 'We are not done with you yet, Macy,' she said as she went to the cardboard assemblage. 'But okay. Let's see.'

She examined the dagger. It did indeed seem a perfect copy. An experimental touch showed that while the blade didn't have the original's razor sharpness, nor would she want to catch her skin on its edge. Macy had been right about her phone's accuracy; the inscribed characters were clearly defined. It was only when she looked extremely closely that she discerned a telltale blockiness to the fine details. 'So, it says that where the four animals meet,' she indicated the strings she had crossed over the paper Tajumulco, 'you look through the dagger's eye – which is presumably this hole. "Through my eye see" two names I haven't translated yet. "Where the two stand in line, you will find the gate to the Underworld."'

The others stood around her. 'So what could the names be?' asked Rosamaria.

Nina peered at the makeshift map, then took out her phone and brought up its AR counterpart. 'They have to be things that could be seen from a distance,' she said. 'The whole area's jungle, so they can't be small, local features – they'd be as hard to find as the Underworld itself in that kind of vegetation. So we're talking about large landmarks: mountains or hills, or some distinctive geological structure.'

Eddie examined where the strings met above the ersatz volcano. 'This is the west side, so that rules out anything to the east.'

Diego leaned closer to the map with a thoughtful expression. 'So if we work out those names, we'll be able to find the Underworld?' he asked.

Nina nodded. 'I'll have another look at the inscriptions.' She examined the replica dagger, regarding the tiny carved words intently. 'One of the names . . . if you directly transliterate the symbols, it could be read as similar to Tajumulco.'

'What *is* the name?' Rosamaria asked.

'It definitely begins with a "ta" sound. The next syllable

doesn't quite match the Atlantean, though. It's similar to the symbol of a hard "c", but—'

'Tacaná,' Rosamaria cut in, realisation dawning. 'Another volcano,' she added for the visitors' benefit.

'The second biggest after Tajumulco,' said Diego. 'It must be this one here.' He indicated the next-tallest of the conical cardboard peaks. It stood north-west of Tajumulco. 'It's on the border between Mexico and Guatemala. It's active – there were some small eruptions a couple of years ago. I was going to go hiking there last year, but the government said it was too dangerous.'

'That would be an easy landmark to spot from Tajumulco,' said Nina. She looked at her phone again, slowly sweeping it between the two volcanoes on the virtual map. Several smaller summits stood between them, parts of chains of hills descending towards the flat plain along the Pacific coast. She moved behind the taller cone. 'And if you were standing on its western flank, looking towards Tacaná . . . there's really only one other peak between them, on this ridge. That must be the second name.' She pointed out an inverted coffee cup topped by a drinking straw snipped to a point. 'What do you think, Rosamaria?'

The other woman shook her head. 'I don't know. Perhaps it is, but . . . I do not know,' she repeated. 'What if the other name is not even a mountain?'

'What else could it be?' Macy asked. There was no criticism in her voice, but Rosamaria reacted as if stung.

Nina's attention was on her map. 'Corazón used Earthbreaker to take a reverse sighting. He lined up the two landmarks from above, to look down at the map and pinpoint where you'd stand to take a sighting on the ground. But . . .' she raised the replica dagger, peering through the hole in its hilt, 'this is too big to do that. Even if you held it at arm's length, you'd see half the mountain.'

'That's not pinpointing anything,' said Eddie. 'I mean, we already know roughly where to look. That's making things worse.'

She nodded. 'So there must be something more to it . . .' She examined the dagger's finer details again. 'Look. There are little notches around the edge of the hole.'

Rosamaria pursed her lips. 'They might not have been there in the real Earthbreaker. This is not a perfect copy.' She indicated blemishes on the blade where glitches in Macy's scan or flaws in the printing process had left bumps and indentations.

'No,' said Macy. 'I'm pretty sure they were there on the real thing.'

'There were notches on the real map,' Eddie pointed out. 'You put the strings through them. Maybe you do something like that.'

'Maybe,' said Nina. 'Not with string, though. It's too thick. More like . . . a hair.' She carefully plucked a single red strand from her scalp.

She delicately wound it around the hilt, working it through the little notches around the hole. That gave her two horizontal lines running across it. Another pair of dents were positioned at the top and bottom; she brought the strand upwards over the space. 'Okay. What do we have here?'

'Congratulations, love,' said Eddie. 'You've just invented the cross hair.'

Nina smiled. 'Not me. Whoever made Earthbreaker.' She reread the text on the blade. 'So, you look through the hole, line up the two landmarks, and . . .' She frowned. 'There's one vertical cross hair, but *two* horizontal ones. Which do I use?'

'If it was a rifle scope, they'd be to adjust for range,' Eddie told her. 'They tell you where the round's going to hit when the target's further away.'

'I know the Atlanteans were advanced, but I don't think they invented bullets,' said Macy sceptically.

'With Earthbreaker, did they need to?' Nina retorted. She gazed at the map again – then the answer came to her. 'I've got it. When it said to line up the two landmarks, I thought it meant directly – as in, both peaks meet in exactly the same spot. But there are two lines. One for each landmark. You line them up against the vertical line, then when the highest peak is at the *top* cross hair and the second one the *bottom* . . .'

She brought the dagger back up, fixing the upper cross hair upon the very top of her improvised Tacaná. That immediately revealed something she hadn't previously considered. 'I just realised – whatever Corazón found, it won't be completely accurate.'

'Why not?' asked Rosamaria.

'Tacaná's taller – it's blocking my view of the smaller peak. He would have had the same problem with the real map. And it's not like he could just move a piece of the stonework out of the way.' There was sudden enthusiasm in her voice. 'Whereas we *can*! Macy, there's a pencil on the floor there. Can you get it and hold the point exactly on the top of Tacaná?' Macy did so. 'Okay, now keep it absolutely still, and move Tacaná clear.'

Macy cautiously tipped the cone sideways. The cup-and-straw hill behind it was revealed. Nina gingerly moved the dagger millimetre by millimetre until the straw's tip touched the lower cross hair, while the upper one remained fixed on the pencil. 'Eddie, get a Sharpie. You need to make a mark on the side of Tajumulco, right where I tell you. Just a really small dot.'

'Damn, I was going to draw a knob on it,' said Eddie as he collected the felt-tip pen. Rosamaria gave him an uncomprehending look, but Diego smirked.

'Dad,' Macy complained.

'All right, all right.' He hovered the tip over the cone's side. 'Tell me when.'

One eye closed, Nina guided him in. 'All right, left, a bit farther. Stop. Up a little, a bit more . . . *there*.'

Eddie touched the marker's nib against the paper, leaving a tiny dot. 'That okay?'

'That's perfect.' She lowered the dagger. 'I can align that mark with the virtual map on the phone, and then compare it to a *real* map. A dot that small will mean the coordinates are probably accurate to within fifty metres.' Her face lit up with excitement. 'Corazón won't have been able to be so precise. We can find it before him!'

Nina's first priority was to call a friend at the United Nations. Oswald Seretse was senior and influential enough to be listened to by officials of the UN's member nations; she was certain the combination of his connections and her name would get what she needed from the Guatemalan government. To wit: watching the border for Ciro Corazón, and for the military to secure the area of Tajumulco she had pinpointed.

Her faith was rewarded – in part. Seretse, however, revealed some unwelcome qualifications when he called back. 'The Guatemalans want you to lead the military expedition.'

'What?' Nina protested. 'Why do they need me? All they need to do is send soldiers to the coordinates, secure the area, and arrest Corazón's people if they turn up. Once they're in custody and Earthbreaker has been secured, they can get their own archaeologists to examine anything at the volcano.'

'Unfortunately, they insist,' the Gambian diplomat told her. 'A dagger that can cause earthquakes is, you must admit, a bizarre story. The only reason they gave it any credence is because it came from you. However, they are still not convinced – about either Earthbreaker or the existence of the Underworld of Mesoamerican myth on their soil. Since you are the expert in such matters, they want you there with their forces to find it.'

'So they won't do anything unless I put some skin in the game, is that it?'

'That is one way of putting it, yes. The Guatemalans have their own internal troubles; nobody in the government is willing to put their head above the parapet by taking responsibility for what they see as a distraction. However, if such an expedition were led by the world-famous archaeologist Nina Wilde . . .'

'If we don't find anything, they can blame me, right?' she said with a cynical laugh.

'In essence. Perhaps you should come back to the IHA, Nina. You certainly have the experience to navigate the political waters.'

'I like my current job, but thanks for the offer, Oswald. Okay, I need to discuss this with my family. I'll call you back.' She said goodbye, then turned to the others in the meeting room. 'Well, you probably heard most of that.'

Eddie nodded. 'They won't do anything unless you go with them.'

'Are you saying that if you do not lead an expedition, they would let Tekuni find the Underworld?' asked Rosamaria.

'Pretty much,' Nina replied. 'So the question is: what do I do?'

Eddie sighed. 'I'm not keen, but I think you'll have to do it, love. If that arsehole finds the other map, he can use the dagger to cause more earthquakes. A lot of people'll die. We can't let him.'

'We? You're coming too?'

He chuckled. 'Course I bloody am. You don't think I'd let you go off into the jungle on your own, do you?'

'I wouldn't be on my own. There'd be soldiers with me.'

'All the more reason for me to go. I used to be a soldier – I know what they're like!'

'If you are going, I should come too,' said Rosamaria.

'It might not be safe,' Eddie warned.

'You will be there to protect me – and soldiers, too! But I know more about the history and mythology of the Teotihuacanos than you, Nina. If the Underworld exists, I may be able to help you enter it. And,' her eyes lit up, 'it would be an incredible find. It would make up for the loss of everything under the Pyramid of the Sun.'

'It would,' Nina agreed. 'And yes, having your knowledge would be a huge help.'

'Then I'm coming too,' said Diego.

Rosamaria shook her head firmly. 'No. It is too dangerous.'

'If there's danger there, I'm not going to let my mom walk into it!' the young man insisted. 'There's no way you're going without me.'

'Same here,' said Macy. 'I'm coming as well.'

It was Eddie's turn to shake his head. 'Not a chance.'

'Absolutely not,' Nina said at the same moment. 'You're going back to New York.'

'*What!*' Macy protested. 'Are you kidding me?'

'You did want the apartment to yourself,' her father reminded her.

'No, that's not fair!'

'Actually,' Diego said, 'Macy can't go home yet. The airport's still closed because of the earthquake.'

Macy folded her arms in triumph. 'Ha!'

'Then you can stay in a hotel until it reopens,' Nina told her, annoyed.

Her daughter's expression became even more smug. 'What, you'd let a fifteen-year-old girl stay on her own in a city she doesn't know?'

Nina's jaw muscles clenched in exasperation. 'Macy, you are *not* coming.'

'Why not? You went on archaeological expeditions with *your* parents. It's where you got your necklace – I've lost count of how many times you told me the story.' Nina instinctively put a hand to her pendant, made from a tiny scrap of Atlantean alloy she had found as a child; it was such a part of her that she'd forgotten she was wearing it. 'If you're denying me something you did yourself, that's really hypocritical.'

Eddie stepped in before Nina could explode. 'Macy, we don't want you to come, because it's not safe.'

'It's not safe here either!' Macy countered. 'There's a lunatic cult leader who tried to kill us on the loose. What if he wants to finish the job? If I'm stuck in a hotel, I'm an easy target!'

Nina muttered an obscenity. Frustrating as it was to admit, that was true. Corazón knew she posed a threat to his plans. Sending his followers after Macy, whether to kill her or take her hostage, was an obvious way to counter that threat. 'All right,' she said, with great reluctance. 'You can come with us.'

'Awesome.' Macy flashed a broad smile at Diego, who returned it more subtly.

'But,' Nina went on firmly, 'this isn't a vacation. We'll be in a potentially dangerous situation. If we tell you to do something, then you *do* it, okay? No arguing, no messing around.'

'Yeah, okay.' The reply lacked conviction.

'Macy,' said Eddie with a warning tone.

'All right, okay!' she said, throwing up her hands. 'You're in charge, I get it.'

'Good.' Nina took out her phone. 'I guess I'd better tell Oswald we'll need a bigger Jeep.'

The Mexican government, keen to ensure that the events beneath the Pyramid of the Sun were not repeated, arranged a helicopter flight early next morning from the capital to a military airbase, where a business jet awaited. The two families were ushered aboard the aircraft, which quickly took off.

Nina glimpsed Teotihuacán in the distance as the plane turned to head south-east. The destruction there had been immense – but she couldn't shake the ominous feeling that it was only a fraction of the cataclysm possible if Corazón unleashed Earthbreaker's full force. The replica dagger was in her handbag; even knowing it was not the real thing, it still made her uneasy.

And Corazón himself had still not been found. If he were not already across the border in Guatemala, he could by now be well on the way. His cult had had enough members to attack the police convoy; Eddie made the worrying observation that their tactics suggested military training. The so-called Lord of the Dead might have plenty more followers, which made finding the Underworld before they did all the more imperative. Even if Corazón had been unable to pin down its position as accurately as Nina, once in the right general area, through weight of numbers, they would eventually find anything hidden there.

If they found the Underworld, and the map it supposedly contained . . .

The only way to prevent that, Nina knew, was to find it first. If she could.

The grim thought dominating her mind, she sat back as the jet carried her and her companions towards whatever awaited in Guatemala.

14

Guatemala

The man who met the new arrivals in Guatemala City made his antipathy towards his mission absolutely plain. 'I think this is a waste of time,' said Major Armando Mancillo once introductions had been made. The soldier was in his late thirties, the profile of his gaunt, narrow face putting Nina in mind of an axe-head. 'We should be fighting the drug gangs, the insurgents – but the civilian government,' a small curl of his lip, 'wants me out of the way for a while. So they make me babysit an archaeologist. Huh! Magic daggers that cause earthquakes? I have never heard anything so stupid.'

'Y'know, three days ago, I wouldn't have believed it either,' said Nina, trying not to be intimidated by his hostility. It was a hard task. Mancillo was considerably taller than her, with a recent scar running from above his left ear almost to his mouth, as if someone had tried to decapitate him with a machete. She couldn't help thinking he would have responded in kind.

'Mom,' Macy said quietly, 'you saw a lost race of Nephilim try to blow up New York with energy crystals from their secret temple underneath Uluru. Why was Earthbreaker such a big step?'

'I was just illustrating a point, honey,' Nina replied tartly.

'Doesn't really matter if you believe it,' Eddie said to Mancillo, stepping closer. The Guatemalan was taller than him too, but the

Englishman fixed him with a steady, unblinking gaze. 'You're a professional, you know the drill as well as I do. You get a job; you get it done.'

Mancillo narrowed his eyes. 'You are a soldier?'

'Was, yeah. 22nd Special Air Service.'

A brief twitch of an eyebrow. 'Rank?'

'Sergeant. For a while.'

'Ah, a grunt. No, wait – that is the American word. A *squaddie*, yes?' Mancillo grinned, but it was not the smile of a shared joke; rather, someone hoping to have found an insult.

Eddie shrugged. 'And proud of it.'

The taller man nodded dismissively. 'The SAS. Good fighters.'

'Best in the world.'

The unpleasant smile returned. 'No. They are not.' He indicated his headgear: a deep maroon beret bearing an oval patch depicting a flaming sword. '*We* are. The Kaibiles. We would take on any other special forces in the world, and win.'

'Sure, right,' said Eddie, with a slow, sarcastic nod of his own. 'I've heard about you. You've got a pretty good reputation—'

'Thank you.'

'—but your training sounds, how can I put it? Psychopathic.' Mancillo maintained his smile, but his eyes betrayed a flare of anger. 'You don't get the best results by torturing your recruits.'

'You call it training,' the major replied. 'We call it . . . *hell*. And if a man can survive hell, he can survive anything.' He tapped the patch on his beret. 'Do you know our motto? "If I advance, follow me. If I stop, urge me on. If I retreat, kill me." Words we live by. And easier to obey than "Who dares wins".'

'Ours is snappier, though,' Eddie retorted. 'So, you've got your orders – when do we get going?'

Mancillo grudgingly returned to the task at hand. 'A plane is on the way.' The travellers had met him at a hangar in Guatemala City's La Aurora airport, which as well as being the country's main international air terminal doubled as a military airbase. 'After it refuels, we will fly to an airstrip near Toquián Chico. From there, we drive to Tajumulco. An old mining road will get us part of the way, but then we will be on foot, through the jungle.' He gave his visitors another dismissive look. 'Can you manage that?'

'We can,' said Nina firmly, annoyed both by Mancillo's macho theatrics and the fact that he had dragged Eddie into his display of verbal chest-beating. 'Have you got all the gear we requested?'

'We have. As Mr Chase said, I am a professional. I get a job, I get it done.'

'Good. Then as soon as this plane arrives, let's get going.'

Said plane landed twenty minutes later, a Cessna Grand Caravan with a cargo pod fitted flush to its underbelly. To Eddie's slight surprise, it was a civilian aircraft rather than part of the Guatemalan Air Force, but Mancillo pointed out that all the military's planes were on assignment around the country. 'Like me, they have better things to do,' he said sardonically.

While they waited for the Cessna to refuel, Mancillo introduced them to his squad of seven. All were younger than their leader, in their twenties, brimming with the pushy arrogance of men who believed they were the best of the best and wanted everyone to know it. 'My second in command,' said Mancillo of a large, stubbled man, 'Lieutenant Juarez.' Juarez regarded the new arrivals dismissively – except for Macy, his lips curling with lecherous interest.

Eddie moved to block his view. 'Ay up. You're a big lad, aren't you? Eat a lot of beef? Must take you an hour to have a crap.' Nina would normally have chided him for his crudity, but on this occasion was more impressed by his restraint.

Juarez looked the smaller man over. 'Nice coat,' he said at

last, eyeing Eddie's leather jacket. 'I give you ten dollars for it.'

Eddie was unimpressed by the attempt at intimidation. 'Doubt it'd fit you, mate.' Juarez chuckled humourlessly.

At Mancillo's command, his men readied their equipment for inspection outside the hangar. Nina took some minor comfort from knowing that if they did encounter Corazón and his followers, the Guatemalans had both training and firepower on their side. Most of the Kaibiles were armed with assault rifles, backed by a couple of heavier machine guns. She also spotted a rotary grenade launcher and what she guessed to be a mortar amongst the gear.

The archaeology team's own equipment was delivered to the plane on an airport trolley. 'I will check it,' said Rosamaria. 'I made the list, I'll make sure everything is there.'

'Thanks,' Nina said absently. Guatemala City was at a lower altitude than Mexico City, making it warmer, but it was considerably more humid, and she was finding the change in climate unpleasant. The sky had also caught her attention, heavy clouds looming to the west – where they would be going. 'Are we in for a storm, you think?' she asked Eddie.

He surveyed the heavens. 'Probably. Hopefully not for a while, though. Just hope they've got enough tents.'

'Wait, we're camping?' said Macy.

'What did you think, we were going to book into a hotel?' Eddie replied. 'We'll be halfway up a mountain in the middle of the jungle! Be lucky if we can find six feet of halfway-flat ground to stick a tent on.'

Macy looked less than thrilled at the prospect. 'It'll be okay,' said Diego, coming to her. 'I've been camping in the jungle. It's cool! I can show you what to do.'

Her attitude immediately improved. 'I'd like that. Maybe we could share a tent?'

Diego's gaze flicked to her disapproving parents. 'I, ah . . . I don't think your mom and dad would like that. But I could pitch my tent right next to you.'

Eddie scowled. 'I'll be pitching my bloody *boot* against your—'

'Dad!' Macy snapped.

'Eddie, Eddie,' Nina added, turning him away from the young man. 'I don't think he was making a double entendre.'

'He's a teenage boy,' Eddie growled. '*Everything's* a double entendre for them.' He shot Diego another glare, but he was looking only at Macy as she hurriedly apologised in Spanish.

'I know you're only trying to protect Macy, but he seems absolutely fine. I like him.'

Eddie's only response was a low rumble. Nina grinned, looking back at the newly arrived equipment. Rosamaria spoke to the overalled delivery man, who handed something to her before indicating some of the cargo on the trolley: two large carryalls and a case. She nodded, then called out to Diego, who went to her and unloaded them.

Nina joined them as the man departed. 'You've got quite a lot of gear.'

'I wanted to be ready for anything,' said Rosamaria, picking up one of the carryalls. 'And I asked a friend for a camera and lights.' She nodded at the case Diego was holding. 'If we find the Underworld, I want to photograph everything inside.'

'Good thinking.' Nina turned at a call from the pilot. The airport worker fuelling the plane had withdrawn the hose.

Mancillo strode forward. 'We are ready to go,' he announced, barking orders to his men. They quickly carried their gear to the Cessna.

Most of the cargo, including the weapons, was loaded into the underbelly pod. There was a small amount of space behind the seats at the cabin's rear; Nina, Eddie and Macy squeezed their backpacks into it as they boarded.

'We'll sit up front,' said Nina, negotiating the narrow aisle.

The passenger seats were arranged with two to its right, one to its left.

Macy looked back. Diego and his mother were still outside. 'No, you go. I want to sit with Diego.'

Eddie ushered her after Nina. 'Come with us, love. It's only a short flight. You can spend an hour with your mum and dad, can't you?'

'Seriously?' Macy protested, but Eddie had already man-oeuvred her into the aisle. There was no way around him short of scrambling over the seats. 'Oh, come on!'

'Just sit down, Macy,' said Nina tiredly. She reached the front row, behind the pilot's position, and took the starboard window seat. Macy pointedly dropped into the lone port-side seat. Eddie sighed and sat across the aisle from her.

The Kaibiles filed aboard, filling the seats behind them. Nina looked back, seeing Rosamaria and Diego board last and secure their carryalls behind elastic webbing at the rear. The pilot, a civilian in a tatty baseball cap, closed the door, then clambered through a smaller hatch into his seat in front of Macy. Mancillo took the co-pilot's position beside him.

The engine started, the single propeller spinning up with a roar. A short radio exchange between the pilot and the control tower, then the Caravan made its way to the runway. It took off, heading west towards the volcanic peaks – and the darkening skies above them.

15

The flight was noisy and bumpy. The Cessna had to fly high to clear the mountains, but that left it susceptible to turbulence beneath the gathering clouds. The storm had not yet broken, but it seemed inevitable it would strike before the day ended. 'Thought I was done with yomping through jungles in the pouring rain,' said Eddie, regarding the weather front ahead.

'So did I,' Nina agreed. 'Oh well. Life's full of surprises.' Her nose wrinkled at the smell of tobacco smoke. New York had cracked down on smoking to such an extent that the acrid scent was almost shocking in a confined space. 'Jeez, speaking of surprises . . .'

She and Eddie turned to see the soldier behind Macy drawing deeply on a cigarette. The smoke wafted forward, making the teenager cough. 'Oi,' Eddie said to him. 'Do you mind?'

The soldier gave him a disdainful glance. Eddie stared back, annoyed – then reached across and squeezed the cigarette's end between his thumb and forefinger, pinching out the little fire. It hurt, but he ignored it. 'You should give up smoking. It's bad for your health.'

The Kaibile's face flushed with anger – then he smacked Eddie's hand and the extinguished cigarette away, starting to stand—

'Borrayo,' Mancillo snapped. The man hesitated, then sat again, glowering at Eddie.

Before anything else could be said, the plane lurched as it hit an air pocket. Muted sounds of alarm came from the soldiers, followed by laughter as they competed to be the least concerned.

The pilot spoke on the radio, then passed on information to Mancillo. 'Twenty minutes until we land,' the major told his passengers. 'There is Tajumulco.' He pointed ahead.

Nina looked over his shoulder. Their ultimate destination stood out clearly, a conical peak stabbing at the clouds just above. At this time of year, the mountain was capped with snow, a narrow band of bare brown rock below it before the verdant green of the jungle began. In the distance stood another tall cone, which she guessed was Tacaná. 'Will we get there before the rain starts?' she asked.

Mancillo shrugged. 'It doesn't matter. Rain, snow, heat – the Kaibiles are ready to fight in any weather.'

'I'm not,' Macy grumbled. 'I didn't know we'd be going into a storm.'

'You asked to come with us,' Nina reminded her.

Macy ignored her, turning to look down the aisle. She waved at Diego, but he was talking to his mother and didn't see. She sat back with a displeased huff, tapping her feet against the pilot's seat in boredom. 'Macy,' Eddie chided.

Another sulky huff, and she stopped, reaching into a pocket for her phone. Instead she found the knife Diego had given her and fished it out, irritably flicking it open and shut, open—

Eddie belatedly realised what she was holding. 'Where the bloody hell did you get that?'

Macy froze. 'Diego gave it to me?'

'Well, give it to *me*! Now!' She hesitantly held it out, and he snatched it away, closing it and shoving it into a jacket pocket. 'For f . . . God's sake. He gave you a bloody *flick knife*? I'm definitely having words with that lad when we land.' He turned to Nina, glowering. 'You sure you still like him?'

'I'm having second thoughts,' she admitted. 'Macy, what the

hell? You're carrying a knife? You'd be arrested for that in New York!'

'We're not in New York, are we?' Macy replied. 'Diego gave it to me so I could protect myself.' Behind, Diego looked up at the sound of his name.

'Protect yourself from what?' Eddie demanded.

'The 3D printing place was in a bad neighbourhood with some scary-looking gang guys hanging around, so he—'

'He took you somewhere with *street gangs*?' The Yorkshireman glared down the aisle at Diego. The young man hurriedly leaned out of sight behind a soldier.

'Oh my God!' said Nina. 'Macy, were you out of your mind? What were you *thinking*?'

'I just wanted to help,' Macy said angrily, not making eye contact as she hunched lower in her seat. 'I mean, I was the only person who thought to make a scan of the dagger. If I hadn't done that, we wouldn't be here, would we? Although I'm kinda wishing I hadn't come now.'

'We didn't *want* you to come!' The words emerged with more force than Nina had intended, propelled by pent-up exasperation.

Now Macy looked at her parents, albeit through scowling eyes. 'This is just because you don't want me to be with Diego, isn't it? For fuck's sake!'

'Macy, watch your language,' Eddie snapped.

'You swear all the time when you think I can't hear you! "Buggeration and fuckery" and all your other weird catchphrases. And you've been even worse than Mom about Diego. What, you think I'm going to elope with him and have six kids? He's cool, I really like him, but we only just met! I'm not an idiot, whatever you both apparently think.'

'It's nothing to do with Diego,' Nina insisted, aware that the soldiers were taking an amused interest. 'We almost got killed twice in Mexico – we're just trying to keep you safe!'

153

'And we're okay,' said Macy. 'We got through it! We always do. Why don't you believe I can take care of myself? I'm not a little girl any more. You're just being totally overprotective!'

'I got bloody *shot* protecting you,' Eddie rumbled, showing her the rip in his jacket. 'I'm not asking for gratitude, but you know, some bloody *acknowledgement* would be good.'

Nina could tell he was on the edge of fury, a place he had almost never gone with his daughter. 'You're damn right I'm overprotective, Macy!' she said. 'I would do whatever it takes to keep you safe. After what happened to the other—'

She halted mid sentence. Eddie whirled to give her a warning look. But it was too late.

'After what happened to *who*?' Macy asked, with deep suspicion. When there was no immediate answer, her anger rose again. 'What's going on? What are you hiding from me?'

'It's . . . Okay, I haven't told you this before,' Nina began, suddenly hesitant. 'We named you Macy after a friend of ours.'

Macy waited for her to elaborate, expression darkening as seconds ticked by. 'What friend? I mean, she must have been called Macy, obviously, but I don't know her.'

'Her name was Macy Sharif. She was an archaeologist – well, she was all kinds of things, but she was an archaeology student when we first met her.' Nina became horribly aware that she was prevaricating, and she could tell Macy knew it. 'She died before you were born. She died . . . because of me.'

'Nina,' said Eddie, putting his hand on hers.

'No, I have to tell her now,' Nina insisted, feeling her eyes prickle as long-buried emotions resurfaced.

'What do you mean?' Macy said. Her expression told Nina she was almost afraid to hear the answer.

'She was on an expedition with us, to find the Fountain of Youth.'

Her daughter's eyes went wide. 'The – the *what*? It's *real*?'

'Yeah. We found it.'

'You never told me about that!'

'We never told anyone. Some other people were trying to find it too. *Bad* people, the worst. They tried to force me to help them locate it. When I told them I wouldn't, they . . . they killed Macy. They murdered her – right in front of me.'

Macy stared at her in horror. Then another emotion formed – or rather, returned. She drew back from her parents, eyes narrowing with slow-burning anger. 'Your friend got killed because of something you did . . . so you named *me* after *her*? That's . . . Oh my God.' She was unable to speak for a moment – then the words exploded out of her. 'Oh my *God*! That is completely fucked up! Holy shit, Mom! I got my name – my whole identity – because you felt *guilty*?'

'That's not why I did it!' cried Nina, feeling guilty for another reason – she could no longer remember if that was the whole truth. She had spent months in therapy after Macy Sharif's death, trying to deal with the mental torment of knowing that the life of a young woman – a friend – had been brutally and callously ended because of her. Being pregnant at the same time had only added to the emotional tornado. 'I wanted to *honour* her, to remember her.'

'So if you hadn't named me after her, you would have *forgotten* her?' The accusation hit Nina like a punch to the heart. 'And you told me at home you weren't keeping any secrets from me. I guess that was a lie. Jesus Christ.' Macy unfastened her seat belt and stood.

'Where are you going?' demanded Eddie.

'I don't want to be with you two right now,' she fired back. 'You were right. I shouldn't have come. I want to go home. But I *can't*, unless I jump out that door,' she jabbed a finger at the hatch near Diego, 'so I'm just going as far away as I can.'

She started down the aisle. Eddie raised an arm to block her way. 'Eddie, don't,' Nina pleaded. He reluctantly withdrew.

Macy pushed by him, ignoring the soldiers' curious stares on the way to the back row of seats. One of the Kaibiles occupied the single port-side chair in front of the rear door; she asked in Spanish for him to move. He seemed about to refuse, but softened at the sight of her tearing eyes and quivering lips. With a grunt, he rose and let her take his seat, then squeezed forward to fill the place across from Eddie.

'Fuck's sake,' growled the Englishman, giving his new neighbour an irritated look before turning back to Nina. 'Are you okay?'

'No,' Nina admitted, wiping her eyes. 'Oh, God. I fucked up.'

'She would have found out about the other Macy eventually. I mean, we've got pictures of her – she would have asked who she was sooner or later.'

'That's not what I meant. She was right: I *did* lie to her by not telling her. And now she's found out in the worst possible way. Now she hates me even more.'

'She doesn't hate you. She's just angry.'

'And justifiably so.' Nina slumped back in her seat. 'I'm *tired*, Eddie. Tired of every single day being a fight. And now Macy's got something *real* to be angry at me about, not just teenage bullshit. I've just kicked the legs out from under her whole identity, right at the age when she's most desperate to be her own person.' She gave her husband a mournful look. 'Never mind therapy. We'll be lucky to keep her out of prison – probably for murdering me in my sleep.'

'She's stronger than that,' Eddie told her. 'You know that. She *will* be able to look after herself, when she's older. We just have to make sure she gets there.'

'If she lets us.' A deep, miserable sigh, then she peered ahead again. The snowy peak of Tajumulco was much closer, the plane angling to skirt its southern flank rather than climb into the heavy clouds. The Caravan was an older aircraft, lacking a radar. With the mountain stretching over four thousand metres into the air, the pilot was sensibly staying clear of the obstacle. 'At least we'll be landing soon. This is one flight I'd rather forget.'

'Are you okay?' Diego asked Macy. 'What happened?'

'I'm all right,' Macy said, swallowing hard as she tried to control her emotions. 'My mom and dad got mad because of that knife you gave me.'

Rosamaria, who had been looking out at the approaching mountain, reacted with alarm. 'What knife?'

'*Está bien, nada de qué preocuparse!*' Diego hastily assured her. 'Then what?'

'And then,' Macy went on, 'Mom dropped a bomb on my *entire life*. One of those "everything you thought you knew is wrong" moments. So I'm, I'm . . .' She trailed off. 'I don't know *what* I am.'

'I'm sorry,' said Diego softly. Beside him, his mother looked out at Tajumulco again, then took something from her coat pocket. Macy fleetingly registered it as resembling a small TV remote, but her attention was on the young man. 'Are you going to be okay?'

'I don't know,' Macy admitted. 'But . . . thanks for asking.'

Diego smiled. Rosamaria meanwhile pushed a button on the device, then returned it to her coat and nudged him. He looked momentarily startled, as if remembering an impending appointment, then stood so she could slide from her seat and go to the rear bulkhead.

Macy gave her a glance as she freed one of the carryalls from the webbing, then looked back at Diego. 'It's funny,' she said. 'Both our moms are archaeologists. But I bet your mom hasn't been like a tenth on your case about every little thing as mine. No, forget that – a *millionth*.'

He leaned across the aisle to whisper to her. 'Yeah, she's cool. Now, anyway. After my dad died, we were both in a pretty bad place. But then she met someone who changed everything for us.'

'Her boyfriend?' Diego nodded. 'Is he basically like your stepdad, then?'

'No – well, not yet. Maybe sometime, if everything works out. But he's in the middle of something big at the moment. I haven't seen him much recently.'

'That's a shame. He sounds interesting.' Macy gave Rosamaria a more curious look as she brought out the second of her two carryalls and opened it – to reveal a backpack with multiple harness straps inside.

Diego noticed her attention. 'Yeah, yeah, he is,' he said quickly. 'I'll see him again soon, which is good. But anyway, what about you? You must still be pretty upset about what just happened. Do you want to talk about it? I'm right here if you do.'

'Yeah, that'd be great,' she replied, but her interest was now well and truly piqued. Rosamaria donned the new pack, then opened the second carryall, removing another item identical to that in the first. 'Uh . . . are those *parachutes*?'

The word was similar enough in Spanish to be recognisable. Heads turned as the Kaibiles in the rearmost rows reacted to her question.

Rosamaria exchanged a worried look with Diego – then yanked a gun from her coat. '*Quedarse quieto!*' she shouted, jabbing the weapon at Juarez as he started to stand. '*Todos se sientan!*' The soldier dropped back into his seat, but remained coiled, ready to leap up in an instant.

Rosamaria sidestepped behind Macy's seat as Mancillo drew his own sidearm. 'Jesus!' Eddie yelled. 'Don't be a fucking idiot! You'll hit Macy! *No dispares, no dispares!*' he yelled to the other soldiers. 'Don't shoot!'

'Diego,' Rosamaria snapped, gesturing for her son to join her.

He hesitated, then moved behind the rear seats and took the second parachute.

Macy watched in disbelief. 'Diego, what's going on?'

'I'm sorry, Macy,' he said, the apology genuine. 'We were going to jump out before anyone realised what we were doing. But—'

Mancillo barked an order at the pilot: to change course and land at the nearest military airfield. The man nervously obeyed, putting the Caravan into a descent. 'No!' Rosamaria cried, sudden panic in her voice. '*Mantente por encima de los cuatro mil metros!*'

'What happens at four thousand metres?' Nina demanded. Rosamaria's reaction was more than fear of arrest when they landed.

'There is a bomb!' Even the Guatemalans who didn't speak English understood the word, alarm spreading through the cabin. 'It will explode when the plane goes below that height!'

Nina looked sharply at the altimeter. Thirteen and a half thousand feet: just over four thousand one hundred metres – and falling. 'Jesus, level out, level out!' she ordered.

'No!' Mancillo countered. 'Do you really believe there is a bomb?'

'*She* believes it! And she had a case at the airport – she said it was camera gear, but it could be anything!'

Mancillo glared at Rosamaria, barely visible in cover behind Macy's seat – then with a snarl of frustration snapped a command. The pilot grimaced, bringing the plane back into a climb.

Diego finished fastening his parachute straps. 'You didn't tell me there was a bomb!' he said to his mother, before looking at Macy. 'I didn't know, honest!'

Rosamaria called down the cabin to the pilot, issuing nervous instructions. 'She's telling him to fly over the west side of Tajumulco so they can jump out,' Macy translated for her parents.

Mancillo shook his head. 'They are not going anywhere.'

'Do it!' said Rosamaria. 'Or – or I will shoot Macy!' She reached around the rear seat's headrest to grab Macy by the hair, pushing the gun against her head. Macy screamed.

'*Mamá!*' Diego cried in appalled disbelief.

'No!' was Nina's equally horrified shout. She whirled to face Mancillo. 'Let them go, let them jump!' The pilot, his duty to protect his passengers overriding other concerns, changed course, curving the Cessna towards Tajumulco's jungle-covered western face.

Mancillo's face was pure stone. 'If they open that door, I will kill them.' He aimed his gun down the aisle, the other Kaibiles shifting sideways to give him a clear shot. Diego crouched fearfully behind the empty rear seats as Rosamaria pulled Macy higher to shield herself. Undeterred, the major shut one eye, lining up his sights—

Eddie grabbed his wrist. 'I will take your fucking arm off if you point that gun at my girl.'

The man in Macy's former seat snapped out his own sidearm and aimed it at Eddie, looking to Mancillo for orders. 'Jesus!' gasped Nina.

Mancillo glared at Eddie, who looked back unflinchingly. 'Okay,' the major finally growled. He tilted his gun hand upwards, giving the soldier a small shake of his head. The other man withdrew his weapon, but kept it pointed in Eddie's general direction. 'Let them go. It doesn't matter. I will call reinforcements to find them – or send an air strike if I have to.' He reached for the radio in the centre of the instrument panel—

'No!' said Rosamaria. She jumped up – and fired several shots down the aisle. Mancillo jerked his hand back as bullets smashed the radio, and other instruments around it. Some of the Kaibiles rose, drawing their pistols. But she had already ducked again, still using Macy as a shield. Mancillo angrily commanded his men to hold fire. 'Diego! We are going, now! Open the door!'

Diego looked helplessly between Macy and his mother, until parental authority won out. He scurried across the cabin and pulled the hatch release.

The rear door, designed as much for parachute jumps as cargo loading, was divided into two halves. A freezing wind roared in as he pushed the top section upwards, then swung the lower part out against the gale until it locked open. 'Diego, go!' said Rosamaria.

'Macy, I'm sorry,' said Diego – before propelling himself through the opening. Rosamaria released Macy and followed him out into the void.

Macy sprang from her seat and hurried up the aisle to Eddie, who clutched her tightly. 'Are you okay?' he asked.

'Yeah, yeah,' she gasped, shivering – not solely from the frigid air. 'What the hell's going on?'

'I think,' Nina said unhappily, 'Rosamaria is a member of Corazón's cult!'

Mancillo looked through the side windows, trying to track the departed Rendóns, but they had already fallen out of sight. 'Put us back on course.'

'*Y la bomba?*' the pilot protested.

Nina checked the altimeter again. They were at slightly below fourteen thousand feet – barely higher than Tajumulco's peak, and almost in the lowering clouds. 'If we drop another two hundred metres, the bomb will explode.'

Mancillo was still not convinced. 'If there *is* a bomb.'

'Only one way to find out,' said Eddie. 'Someone's got to go out there and look.'

16

Diego and Rosamaria Rendón descended towards Tajumulco, wind whistling through their parachute cords. The steep landscape below was blanketed by dense jungle, the nearest land cleared for farming kilometres away in the crumpled valley to the west. The only closer evidence of human incursion was a single track weaving part-way up the volcano's base.

They both pulled their toggle handles to aim for the twisting line. Rosamaria had been in surreptitious contact with other followers of Tekuni; the cult's influence spread beyond Mexico's borders into its Central American neighbours. Teotihuacán had once been the seat of power over a vast region – and there were those who wanted to see that power restored. They had successfully smuggled Tekuni out of Mexico and into Guatemala, where a group was assembling to locate the Underworld. When they arrived, they would have an experienced archaeologist to guide them to the map chamber.

Where Tekuni would use Earthbreaker to destroy their enemies.

The ground drew closer. Diego had made numerous parachute jumps with his new father-figure: Ciro Córazon. He easily controlled his descent, making a near-perfect landing in a clearing near the track. His mother was less experienced, coming in faster. She hit the ground hard and tumbled to a stop.

'Mom!' Diego cried, running to her. 'Are you okay?'

'Yes, I . . . I think so.' She sat up painfully, revealing a cut on her head.

'You're hurt!'

'I'll be okay.' She stood. 'We have to get to the road. Ciro and the others will be here soon.'

Diego looked up. The plane was visible high above, a tiny cross against the clouds looming over the volcano's snowy summit. 'Mom . . . would you really have shot Macy?'

She didn't quite make eye contact. 'No. Of course not.'

'And why didn't you tell me there was a bomb?'

'There isn't a bomb. I just needed to distract them, and stop them from shooting us. If Macy hadn't sat with you, we would have jumped out before they even realised what we were doing.' Again, she didn't quite meet his eyes.

Diego gave the plane another worried look, then sighed. 'Okay. Let's go and meet Ciro.'

'Tekuni,' she said firmly. 'Everything we do from now on is for the Jaguar God. From this moment, he's not Ciro Corazón. He is Tekuni – the avatar of Tekuazotl on earth. I know you haven't learned everything about our religion, but you have to remember that. He is more than a man. He is our leader.' Her eyes had a messianic gleam.

'I know, Mom,' said Diego. 'I know.' He helped her remove the empty parachute pack, then they started downhill.

The cargo pod beneath the Cessna's belly had four hatches in its port side. The latches of the front two were, with difficulty, accessible from the pilot's door.

The rearmost was, with more difficulty, within Eddie's reach as he inched from the Caravan's aft hatch. He lay on his front, two burly Kaibiles holding his legs. Even with the plane barely above stall speed, the wind and propeller wash lashed him with near-hurricane force.

He found the first latch and turned it. The second was further away, forcing him to squirm forward until his hips were out of the fuselage. If the soldiers lost their hold, he would fall out. Fingers numbing in the freezing air, he groped for the metal protrusion. He brushed it, but couldn't get a proper hold. Swearing into the gale, he edged further out, feeling the Kaibiles straining to keep their grip.

His fingertips found the latch, closed around it, pulled—

The hatch dropped open. He jerked back with a yelp as a loose pack fell out and was whipped away by the airstream. 'Pull me back!' he shouted. The soldiers hauled him into the cabin.

'What can you see?' called Mancillo from the front.

'Your gear, mostly,' Eddie replied breathlessly. 'No sign of Rosamaria's case. It must be on the other side of the pod.'

'I think it was one of the first things that was loaded,' Nina confirmed. 'So what do we do?'

'We'll have to start chucking stuff out to see what's behind.'

'No,' Mancillo said firmly. 'We need our weapons and equipment. You will have to bring them into the plane.'

'It was hard enough just turning the latches,' said Eddie. 'Start swinging heavy packs around, and I'll be getting a free trip to the volcano. And before you start with the macho bollocks, your guys wouldn't do any better either. Let 'em look; I guarantee you won't get any volunteers.'

His professional assessment didn't stop Mancillo from issuing an order to one of the men at the rear door. He dropped flat and leaned out, his companion holding him. It took only seconds before he returned, giving a negative report to his superior.

'Told you,' said Eddie. 'Either someone climbs out there and starts pulling things loose, or we shake the plane and try to make stuff fall out. We might get lucky and drop the bomb too.'

Nobody was keen on the first option. Mancillo reluctantly told the pilot to try the second. Everyone returned to their places. 'Fasten your seat belts,' Eddie warned Nina and Macy, who had retaken her original seat. 'Might be worth having some barf bags ready too.'

Nina hurriedly secured her belt. 'You know what? I'm never going to leave Manhattan again.'

'Yeah,' said her husband, 'but whenever you try something like that, trouble always comes to *us*.'

'Okay, then I'm never leaving the *apartment* again!'

The pilot called out a warning countdown. Everyone braced themselves – then he rolled the Cessna sharply on to its port side.

Nina clung to her seat as the aircraft tipped over. The horizon to her left lunged upwards, replaced by the verdant mountainside below. Bumps and rattles came from beneath the cabin. One of the Kaibiles shouted to Mancillo, and she glimpsed something spin away towards the ground. The man kept up his excited report as more items fell through the cargo pod's open hatches—

A squawk of alarm from the pilot, and he threw the plane back level, then raised the nose sharply to gain height. Nina realised why when she saw the altimeter. Four thousand metres was just over 13,100 feet – and the needle had dropped to barely above that fatal threshold.

Mancillo looked back. *'Puedes ver la bomba?'* he called to the rearmost soldier.

Macy translated his reply. 'He says most of the equipment and guns are gone . . . There's a box he doesn't recognise, but it's stuck.'

Eddie unfastened his belt and headed aft. 'Let me have a look.'

'Be careful!' Nina said in his wake.

He gave her a grin over his shoulder. 'If I fall out, I'll try to land on Rosamaria.'

'Dad, don't,' said Macy. 'I'm scared.'

He instantly became serious. 'Don't worry, love. We'll get down to the ground in one piece.' He reached the rear door, adding in a mutter, 'Might be doing terminal velocity at the time . . .'

The soldiers held his legs again as he leaned out. Macy's translation had been accurate: inside the pod was a black box, some sort of equipment case. It had only just fitted in through the hatches, and by accident or design, a folding handle on its top was standing upright, making it too tall to slide out.

But as well as the handle, it also had a strap – which was flapping in the wind through the third hatch. 'I can see it!' he shouted. 'Going to try to pull it loose!' He stretched out one arm, bracing himself against the pod with the other.

The strap flicked back and forth, just beyond his fingertips. Another movement brought him close enough to touch it. Acutely aware of his precarious position, he tried to grab the tough woven nylon. It flapped mockingly against his fingers. He risked advancing a few extra millimetres, then clutched at it again—

One finger hooked around it. He tugged his hand back, drawing it taut, but couldn't get his other fingers into the loop of fabric. 'Pull me in!' he yelled. The Kaibiles hauled at his legs. The strap strained, the case still wedged in place—

It suddenly jerked loose.

Eddie let out an involuntary cry as the strap abruptly went slack, making him lose his hold on the pod. Arms windmilling, he dropped—

The soldiers caught him. A moment to brace themselves, then they hauled him back up. One shouted to the pilot, who brought the plane into another climb.

The case slid towards the rearmost cargo hatch – which was also the smallest, its lower edge curving upwards to match the pod's streamlined shape. Eddie realised instantly that it wouldn't fit through. 'Go down, *down*!' he bellowed, bringing his right arm through the door to grab the base of the rear seat. 'Roll left and go down!'

Macy gave a frantic translation to the pilot. One eye on the altimeter, he obeyed, shoving the Cessna into a sharp, banking descent. The cabin echoed with shouts of alarm over the roaring wind.

One of the Kaibiles holding Eddie lost his balance and toppled into the aisle. Even with his grip on the seat, the Yorkshireman found himself sliding helplessly out into nothingness—

The other soldier desperately clawed at him. He caught Eddie's ankle, wedging his own legs against the door frame.

Hanging halfway from the hatch, Eddie swore, then checked the cargo pod. A box containing weapons was caught by the tearing wind and spun away towards the mountain below. But even though the case was part-way through the hatch, its handle still prevented it from falling free. 'Again!' he shouted. 'Go back up and try again!'

The Cessna was now below Tajumulco's snowy summit, the volcano topping out at 4,220 metres. The pilot needed no encouragement to gain altitude. He pulled back on the controls. The altimeter needle wavered just above the critical height, then rose again.

The fallen soldier recovered and helped drag Eddie into the cabin once more. The Yorkshireman waited for the plane to climb higher, then called out, 'Okay, we've almost shaken it loose – do it again!'

Macy relayed the instruction. The pilot threw the Cessna into another rolling dive. Eyes streaming in the freezing gale, Eddie looked outside again. Another piece of cargo tumbled away, but the box was still there. The handle was no longer standing vertically, though – it had caught the hatch's upper frame, just barely holding it inside. 'One more go!' he cried. 'Once more should do it!'

The plane swung into another roller-coaster climb, sending its passengers' stomachs churning. It levelled, giving them a moment of respite . . . then dropped again, banking hard to port. Eddie tightened his grip on the seat's frame as he leaned out. The case slid across the pod, the handle striking the hatch's frame—

And folding flat.

The case fell out, strap flapping behind it. 'Yes!' Eddie cried—

The strap caught on the port-side landing strut – and the case jerked to an abrupt halt. 'No!'

The pilot hastily hauled the aircraft back upwards. The case swung from its wheel like a demented pendulum. 'For fuck's sake!' Eddie roared, retreating into the cabin.

Nina looked through Macy's window to see with dismay that the situation had somehow worsened. 'Now what do we do?'

'Shoot the strap,' said Mancillo, drawing his sidearm.

'If you miss, you might shoot the bomb,' she pointed out. He scowled, but lowered the gun.

Eddie regarded the landing gear. It extended outwards from the fuselage's side above the cargo pod, slightly forward of the open lower door's leading edge. 'I can climb out and cut it loose.'

Nina gave him a look of disbelief. 'Are you out of your mind?'

'The cargo pod's empty – I can use it as a step. I won't have to go far to reach the wheel. If the pilot flies as slow as he can, I should be able to hold on against the wind.'

'Dad, that's crazy,' was Macy's assessment of his plan.

Mancillo was equally unconvinced. 'You won't make it.'

'I've got to live up to my old SAS motto, haven't I?' said Eddie.

A disdainful snort from the major. 'For every "Who dares wins" there is a "Who dares dies".'

'We can't bloody stay up here for ever! Someone give me a knife.' Mancillo unsheathed a combat knife and handed it to him. 'All right,' Eddie said, 'tell the pilot to keep it level, as slow as he can.'

Mancillo relayed the instruction. The pilot eased back on the throttle. The air-speed indicator dropped until it bobbed at around sixty-five knots. It was faster than Eddie had hoped, over seventy miles per hour. The wind would still be hitting him at motorway speeds. 'All right,' he said, 'here I go.'

'Don't fall, Dad,' Macy pleaded.

'Not part of my plan, love,' he assured her. With a last look at Nina, he clamped the knife between his teeth and manoeuvred himself through the door.

The airstream tore at his clothes. Even with his leather jacket zipped shut, it still flapped and rippled around him. He lowered a foot into the cargo pod's rearmost hatch, then gripped the lower half of the open door and sidestepped from the cabin. Aluminium creaked under his boots, but the pod had held all the team's equipment; it should take his weight.

He hoped.

More careful steps. The pilot was holding the plane level, but that did not mean it was moving smoothly. At speed, air acted like a fluid medium, as churned-up as a windswept sea. If anything, the Cessna's low velocity made things worse, its controls slow to respond to commands.

Eddie turned his head to check the landing gear. The case's strap had not gone over the wheel itself, but was snagged on its inner hub, held by a protruding bolt. He might not need to cut it. If he worked the knife underneath it, he could simply lever it loose . . .

A jolt made him clutch the door more tightly. He still had to *reach* the strap. Two more steps, watching where he put each foot. Tajumulco slid past below. The pilot was using the rudder to circle over its western flank. But the clouds now brushed its peak, getting lower. It wouldn't be long before they forced a choice between descending perilously close to the four-thousand-metre limit – or flying blind over mountains.

One last step, and he was at the landing gear's root. He

gripped it and twisted around. He would have to use the strut for support as he leaned across, but the wheel was just within reach—

The Cessna shook again – more violently. Warmer air from the coast was rising as it reached the mountains, forming the growing storm clouds above. The sudden lurch made Eddie's hand slip. An involuntary gasp – and the knife fell from his mouth, clanging off the strut—

It rebounded back at him.

The point stabbed into his left shin. He flinched at the sudden pain – and one foot slipped from the cargo pod. The wind hit him as he swayed, knocking him backwards.

His other boot was jarred from its foothold. He dropped, only his one-handed hold on the door stopping him from falling. The hinges creaked and strained as they took his weight—

One snapped.

The door swung downwards with a crack of breaking metal. The other hinge sheared apart. The panel fell away – taking Eddie with it.

17

Eddie grabbed desperately at the cargo pod as he dropped – one hand catching an open hatchway.

He jerked to a stop. The metal edge cut into his fingers, tendons searing as they took his weight. The broken door tumbled away below. He flailed his other arm, managing to grab the pod's rear hatch with his fingertips. Macy's scream reached him over the roar of the wind.

He tried to raise himself higher, but found no extra grip. All he could do was cling on with his rapidly numbing fingers. A soldier yelled from the rear doorway, stretching out an arm, but his hand was just out of reach . . .

Nina squeezed between Macy and the pilot's seat to look through the window. Her daughter's scream had terrified her, making her fear the worst. What she found wasn't far off. Pressing her face to the Plexiglas, she saw Eddie hanging from the plane's underside, legs swinging in the wind. 'Oh my God! Grab him, pull him up!'

'He can't reach!' cried Macy.

'Shit!' Nina looked desperately around the cabin. 'There must be a rope—'

'All our equipment was in the cargo pod,' Mancillo reminded her, grim-faced.

'There must be something we can do!' She darted back to the window. The mountain's white top rolled by—

Frantic inspiration struck. 'How deep is that snow?' she demanded.

'I don't know,' said the major. 'It doesn't often snow here, even on the mountains. A metre? Maybe two?'

'Deep enough to jump into?'

He stared at her. 'You are as crazy as your husband.'

'It's either that or land this thing on top of a volcano.' She looked back at Tajumulco. The summit, which would have offered the best chance – however slim – of landing, was now hidden by roiling cloud. But below, close to the snowline, was an area marginally less steep than the rest of the towering cone . . . 'There!' she said, pointing. 'We might be able to bail out there!'

Mancillo was unconvinced, but held a rapid discussion with the pilot. 'He says if we come in from the north, into the wind, he will be able to fly slower without stalling,' he reported. 'But that ground is only just above four thousand metres. If he goes too low, the bomb will explode. It might explode anyway,' he added. 'Altimeter fuses are not always accurate.'

'We've got to risk it,' Nina told him.

She was about to head aft when Macy grabbed her arm. 'Mom, are we gonna be okay?'

'Working on it, honey,' said Nina, kissing her cheek before hurrying to the door. She grabbed the rear seat and leaned out. Eddie was still hanging on – but his pained grimace warned her that his reserves of strength were fading fast. 'Eddie!' she called. He squinted up at her. 'We're going to fly over some thick snow so you can drop down!'

He turned his head to survey the mountain. 'Where's the thick snow?'

'Hopefully where you land!'

'Oh, fucking fantastic!'

'It's all we can do. Just hold on!'

She returned to the front of the cabin. 'Okay, he's ready,' she said. 'Just . . . take things nice and easy.' Macy translated for the pilot, then watched fearfully as he banked and descended towards the mountain.

Details on the ground came into view. To Nina's alarm, it was not as barren as it had seemed from a distance, vegetation poking through the snow at the lower end of the hoped-for landing zone. But it was the only possible option. Elsewhere, the snow would either be too thin to cushion Eddie's fall – or he would tumble helplessly down the steep mountainside to his death.

She peered through the window again. Her husband still clung to the cargo pod. How much longer could he last? 'Just stay with us, Eddie,' she whispered, holding Macy's hand. 'Stay with us . . .'

A change in the engine's rasp told Eddie the pilot was slowing still further. Flying into the wind would give extra lift, letting him reduce speed. But even so, the ground seemed to move faster as it neared. If the snow was too thin, he would die – there was only unyielding rock beneath the white covering.

The plane dropped still further, the mountainside blurring under him. Thirty feet, the plane wobbling as the pilot fought to hold it level. Twenty. Ten—

'*Mierda!*' gasped Mancillo. Nina followed his gaze – and saw that the altimeter needle was only just above 13,100 feet. They were scraping the four-thousand-metre barrier, and the bomb was hanging even lower from the wheel—

Eddie let go.

He crossed both arms in front of his face, chin down against his chest to protect his head—

Snow exploded around him. He carved through a drift, rolling as it compressed beneath him. A painful thump of impact as he hit solid ground below, then he bounced back into open air. The plane roared overhead. Another *whumph* of impact with piled snow . . . and he stopped.

His dizziness gradually subsided. He cautiously lifted his head. Resistance: he was inside a drift, the snow crumping as he moved. He tried to stand. Icy flakes dropped into his collar, making him shiver. The sudden coldness did nothing to numb the throbbing pain in his back.

But . . . he was alive.

He struggled upright, shaking off clods of snow. The slope was steeper than it looked from the air. The Cessna climbed again as it banked away from the mountain. He waved, hoping its occupants could see him.

'He's okay!' Nina cried, spotting the figure in the snow. 'He made it, he's okay!'

Macy released the breath she'd been holding since her father dropped from the plane. 'Oh, my God. I – I thought he was . . .'

'He isn't,' Nina assured her. 'And if he can do it, so can everyone else.'

Mancillo barked an order to his men, who started to leave their seats. The Kaibile who had swapped places with Macy glanced at the two women, asking a question. Mancillo frowned, but nodded. 'You go first,' he told the Americans.

'Gee, thanks,' said Macy as she stood. She added in a whisper to Nina, 'He only said it because the other guy called him on it.'

'At least he said it,' Nina replied. She shouldered her handbag, then they moved to the rear door. Freezing air gusted in. 'Okay, I'm having second thoughts about this plan.'

'We don't have much choice, Mom.'

'Yeah, I know.'

Mancillo moved up behind them. 'Have you made a jump like this before?'

'Surprisingly, yes,' said Nina. 'Curl up, protect my head, and hope I stop before I hit anything solid – or go over a cliff.'

A sardonic chuckle. 'Then there is not much else I can tell you.'

'*I* haven't done this before,' Macy said nervously.

'You've gotten through other things that were just as bad,' Nina reminded her. 'Like in China – you escaped from a collapsing skyscraper.'

'Yeah, but Dad was with me.'

'Well, *I'm* with you now.' She put her hands on Macy's shoulders, fixing her with a look of determination. 'Stay with me. *Trust* me. I'll get you through this. You're my daughter, and I love you, and you are going to be fine. Okay?'

Macy hesitated – then replied with new assurance, nodding. 'Okay. Yeah. We can do this.'

'Good.' Nina went back to the door. The plane had made its turn, lining up again with the stretch of snowy ground. She glimpsed Eddie watching its approach. 'I'll go first. You count to three, then follow me. Cross your arms in front of your face, like this.' She demonstrated. 'Curl up and hold your knees together. That'll give you the best chance of not getting hurt.' She knew the landing would be painful no matter what, but decided not to scare Macy still further. 'Let's get ready.' She took her daughter's hand again. 'We can do this. *You* can do this.'

Macy managed a weak smile. 'Okay, Mom.'

Nina took up position at the door. The Cessna descended towards the mountainside. The case swung from the landing gear. How close were they to its detonation point? One slip by the pilot, one unexpected air pocket, and they could find out . . .

Thirty feet. Steep, raw rock below was replaced by snow. A few skinny trees whipped past – then the slope ahead was clear. She saw Eddie's landing point, a ragged gouge in the pristine white. If he could survive his touchdown, so could she.

In theory . . .

Twenty feet, the plane pitching upwards to match the slope's angle – while still descending towards it. The dangling case drew dangerously close to the rushing snow. If it hit, would it act like a brake and drag the Cessna into a crash-landing?

The thought spurred her into action. 'Macy! Count to three, then jump!' she cried – then threw herself from the doorway before the fearful part of her mind could object.

She barely had time to bring up her arms before smacking into the snow. The impact knocked the breath from her lungs. Despite her best efforts to keep her knees together, her legs flailed as she rolled, one foot cracking hard against a buried rock. She gasped – only to take a mouthful of snow.

Spitting, she came to a stop. But even dazed, she forced herself to lift her head. 'Macy!' she gasped. *'Jump!'*

Macy saw Nina hit the slope in a burst of flying snow. The landing looked terrifying – but her father had survived the same impact. If her parents could do it, so could she. 'One, two – *three*,' she said—

And jumped.

Arms up, knees together—

She hit a mound of snow – and burst straight through it.

Macy shrieked as she landed hard on her side and rolled downhill. Panic rising, she threw her arms out to slow herself.

She stopped her tumble, now on her back – but was still sliding head-first down the steepening slope. She kicked her heels into the snow, trying to brake, but it barely slowed her descent.

If she couldn't stop, maybe she could turn—

She raised her right leg, driving her left foot down as hard as she could. Spicules spat into her face as the movement swung her around, now skittering feet-first. The landscape to the west came into view . . .

As did the edge of an abrupt drop.

She screamed as she careered towards it, heels hacking at the snow in a desperate attempt to find purchase. The valley opened out below her. Terror filled her heart—

A flash of movement to one side – and someone dived at her.

Eddie pounded down on his front, grabbing her arm. Boots carving through the snow to rasp against the rocky surface beneath, he dragged Macy to a standstill. She halted with both legs hanging over the edge of a fifty-foot drop.

He puffed out steaming breaths from his exhausting interception sprint. 'Ay up, love. You okay?'

'Daddy!' Macy cried, scrabbling back onto solid ground. She hugged him. 'Oh God, I thought I was going to die!'

'I've got you. We're all right. Let's find your mum.'

'M-mom,' she managed to say. Eddie grinned.

They started back up the slope. Macy was shaking, but only partially from the cold. He wrapped an arm around her as they headed for Nina's landing zone.

'There she is!' said Macy, spotting a figure rising from the snow. They yomped uphill towards her.

'Are you both okay?' Nina called as they approached. She took a few experimental steps to meet them, but winced whenever her right foot took her weight.

'Got bashed up, but I'm okay,' said Eddie. 'Macy had a bit of a slide. She's all right, though.'

'Apart from the mind-shredding trauma, but yeah, totally okay,' Macy said.

Eddie regarded Nina's leg. 'You hurt? Can you walk?'

'I'll have to,' she replied. 'I can't stay here and wait for someone to rescue us. The clouds are getting lower.' She indicated the summit. The peak had now been completely swallowed by the grey mass.

Eddie searched for the easiest way down, but his attention

was caught by the plane, coming back for a third pass. 'Christ, if he gets any lower, the bomb'll hit the ground.'

'We need to move out of the way, or the soldiers'll hit *us*!' Macy warned. The family hurriedly scuttled downhill, Eddie supporting the limping Nina.

The plane roared towards them. Figures piled from the rear door in rapid succession. Nina, Eddie and Macy ducked as the Caravan thundered by, dropping its payload of human bombs. The Kaibiles rolled and tumbled and flipped through the snow, two men colliding with a thud audible even over the engine noise. Eddie kept count of the Guatemalans as they landed. Five, six – there was Mancillo – seven . . . Where the hell was the last man – *there!*

The final Kaibile, the man who had changed places with Macy, made his jump. The pilot pulled up the moment he was clear. The soldier hit the snow, spinning over a rise . . .

And landing hard on the steeper ground beyond it.

'Shit!' Eddie watched in horror as the man picked up speed. He tried to arrest his descent, throwing all four limbs wide to catch as much snow as possible—

It didn't work. The soldier shot over the cliff edge, his scream echoing from the rocks – then abruptly ending.

Macy stared open-mouthed after him. 'Oh – oh!' she gasped, shocked. 'Did he just, did he . . .'

Nina held her, gently shielding her from the sight. 'I'm sorry, honey. I'm sorry.'

Eddie regarded the cliff for a grim moment, then turned away. 'We need to find the others.'

It didn't take long to round up the surviving Kaibiles. The two men who had collided were bloodied, one's nose smashed, but both could still walk, and they seemed almost proud of their injuries. Any humour vanished when they learned about their lost comrade, though. 'Miranda,' said Mancillo. 'A good soldier.

A good fighter.' He turned to his surviving troops. '*Será vengado.*' They echoed the words, some almost with relish.

'What did they say?' Nina asked, suspecting the answer wouldn't surprise her.

'He will be avenged,' Macy replied. Nina's suspicion was indeed correct.

'That's all great,' Eddie said loudly, 'but we've got to get off this bloody mountain first. We need to—'

A change in the Cessna's engine note drew everyone's attention. Rather than make another orbit, it had doubled back and was heading for the upper end of the slope. 'What's he doing?' asked Macy, confused.

'He can't be trying to land,' Mancillo insisted. 'The ground is too steep, he will crash.'

Nina saw the case swinging from the landing gear. 'He's trying to get rid of the bomb.'

Macy let out an excited gasp. 'If he can knock it loose, he'll be able to land and get help!'

'*If* he can knock it loose.'

Eddie watched the plane descend with growing concern. 'Even if he doesn't fuck up – sorry, Macy – he's going to come right through where we're standing.'

Mancillo nodded. '*Todos se mueven cuesta abajo. Con rapidez!*' His men hurriedly moved down the slope. Eddie, Nina and Macy followed.

The Cessna continued its descent. The case dropped lower – and clipped a ridge of snow. The impact knocked it wildly backwards, making the plane's port wing dip towards the ground. The pilot banked to compensate, but didn't climb, still trying to tear the bomb loose. Another strike as the case swung back down. The plane jolted again—

Its port wheel hit the snow.

The sudden drag threw the aircraft sharply to the left. The

pilot yanked back on the controls, trying to gain height, but centrifugal force had already flung it into a roll. The starboard wheel came down hard, slicing into the snow. The plane slewed around, kicking up white spray as it slithered almost sidelong down the hill – then the landing gear collapsed.

The Cessna slammed down hard on its belly, crushing the cargo pod. The whirling propeller hacked into the ground. The blades shattered, shrapnel flying as the fuselage thundered downhill. It bumped and slammed over the uneven surface, panels splitting open and a wing flap breaking free. The pilot struggled to bail out, but a violent jolt pitched him back into the cockpit.

'Oh, shit, *shit*!' Nina yelped – as she realised that the beached aircraft was sliding straight at its former passengers. '*Run!*'

Everyone scattered as the battered juggernaut hurtled towards them. Macy and Eddie ran – then he sharply reversed course as he realised Nina wasn't with him. He grabbed his limping wife's hand, but the Caravan was on them—

'Down!' he yelled, pulling her to the snowy ground. The Cessna's tail scythed over them.

They both raised their heads and watched as the aircraft continued downhill. The port landing strut had buckled, but remained attached at its root, dragging behind the fuselage like a bird with a broken leg – and the case was still caught on the wheel hub—

The plane finally dropped below four thousand metres – and the bomb went off.

The altimeter fuse didn't care whether the Cessna was in the air or on the ground. The detonator fired – followed a split second later by four slabs of plastic explosive.

The blast ripped the fuselage apart and ruptured the fuel tanks in the port wing – which also blew up. Nina and Eddie dropped flat again, the Yorkshireman shielding his wife's head as debris hailed down around them. An oily orange fireball roiled into the sky. Blazing wreckage bowled down the mountain to smash into the trees below.

Eddie waited for the echoes of destruction to die down before lifting his head. 'Jesus,' he said, panting. 'Guess there really was a bomb in that box.'

'The pilot didn't get out,' Nina said, stunned – before looking around in alarm. 'Where's Macy? Macy!'

'Mom! I'm here!' Macy clambered out of a mound of snow.

'Oh, thank God.' Nina rose and staggered to her.

Mancillo picked himself up, then called for his team to assemble. Nobody had suffered additional injuries. 'We are all okay,' he told Eddie. 'You?'

'We're fine,' Eddie replied.

'In relative terms,' Nina added.

Mancillo nodded. 'Good. I would not want to waste time carrying injured civilians down the mountain.'

'Glad to be of help,' said Eddie sarcastically. 'Come on, then. Let's get going.' He started to lead his family down the slope, glancing back when the soldiers didn't immediately follow. 'What're you waiting for, Christmas?'

Mancillo irritably barked an order to his men, then set off after them.

18

It did not take long to descend below the snowline. Mancillo pointedly overtook Eddie to lead the way, his men following in a line. High-altitude scrub gave way to taller trees: the jungle's upper reaches. The mountainside was steep, but the Kaibiles were clearly experienced in negotiating such terrain.

Nina was less assured in her steps. Her aching foot slowed her, and she slipped on more than one occasion. 'Dammit!' she snapped as she almost fell again.

Macy caught her. 'I've got you, Mom.'

'Thanks.' Nina sighed. 'Fifty years old, and I'm having to be helped to walk by my daughter like a little old lady.'

'You *did* just jump out of a plane without a parachute,' Macy reminded her. They both smiled.

Eddie stopped, waiting for them to catch up. 'You two all right?'

'Yeah, we're good,' Nina assured him. She took the opportunity for a rest, looking across the valley ahead. The cone of Tacaná rose in the distance, beyond a nearer ridge of peaks. 'Huh. We're pretty much heading for where we were going.' The volcano and the closer summit were almost exactly in alignment. She took the copy of Earthbreaker from her bag. It had survived the landing mostly intact, a couple of chips and notches in the blade. She aligned the cross hairs on the landmarks. The mountains were too widely separated vertically to meet them. 'The entrance must be a lot lower downhill, though.'

'Do you think the bad guys are heading there too?' Macy asked.

'Rosamaria and Diego wouldn't have bailed out if they didn't think somebody was going to meet them,' said Eddie. He looked back towards the summit. The smoke from the wrecked plane had dispersed, descending clouds almost completely blotting the snowcap from view. Southwards, a wall of much darker, heavier clouds was closing in. 'Let's keep moving. Looks like we're in for a storm.'

He set off again, Nina and Macy picking their way down after him. The soldiers were over a hundred metres ahead, showing no inclination to wait for them. They traversed some distance before Macy spoke again. 'Mom?'

'Yes?' Nina replied.

'I'm sorry.'

'For what?'

'For . . . for being an asshole. I've been so horrible to you, about everything. But you really were looking out for me, the whole time. Even if I didn't want to admit it.'

Nina had an admission of her own. 'I haven't exactly been the world's number one mom either. I know how much you want to do your own thing – to find out who you are. You probably won't believe me, but I was just the same when I was fifteen. I'm sure I drove my mom mad too. She had her way of doing things, and I had my own ideas. Sound familiar?'

'I may have heard of something like that, yeah,' Macy replied with a faint grin.

'And I should have listened to you more. I'm sorry. As you get older, you become set in your ways, even if you don't mean to – you start to resist change. Which when you've got a fifteen-year-old in the house is about the most futile position possible!' Nina stopped again, facing her daughter. 'I never wanted us to be on opposite sides, over anything. I love you, and I always will. And I'll always want to protect you, no matter what.'

For a moment she thought Macy was about to cry, but then

her face crinkled into an emotional smile. 'Thanks, Mom.' She hugged her. 'I love you.'

Nina returned the embrace. 'I love you too.'

'You okay?' Eddie asked as they separated.

'We are, Dad,' Macy told him. 'We are.' Nina smiled, and the family continued downwards.

Before long, the trees became tall and dense enough to block sight of the valley. Nina paused when they reached a clearing. The two peaks were still almost perfectly lined up, but the gap between their summits was smaller than before. They were nearing the supposed entrance to the Underworld.

The question was: would Corazón and his followers already be there?

As if reading her mind, Macy spoke again. 'I can't believe I was such an idiot.'

'About what?' Nina asked.

'About Diego. I thought he was such a great guy, really smart and nice, and, y'know . . .' a faint flush came to her cheeks, 'hot. But he was one of *them* all along – those psychos who tried to kill us! He tricked me, he lied to me.'

Nina put a comforting hand on her shoulder. 'If it means anything, I don't think he knew about the bomb. He seemed as shocked as us when Rosamaria warned us about it.'

'Doesn't make much difference, does it? He still played me for a fool.'

'Sometimes people aren't what they first seem. In good ways, as well as bad. The first time I saw your father, I thought he was stalking me!'

Macy was startled. 'Really?'

'Remind me to tell you about it sometime,' said Nina, grinning.

They followed the Kaibiles down the slope. The soldiers had drawn even further ahead, almost lost amongst the trees, but soon came back into view. 'Why've they stopped?' Macy asked.

The answer became clear as they emerged from vegetation to see the landscape open out before them. Mancillo's route came to a sudden stop at the edge of a near-vertical cliff. Without climbing gear, the way down was completely impassable. 'We will have to go around it,' said the major, annoyed.

Nina paused to take in the view. Far below, she picked out areas of cleared farmland around Tajumulco's base, a road winding between villages in the valley bottom. Above it was nothing except deep green jungle . . .

Almost nothing. Another track was visible, weaving upwards amongst the trees. 'Is that the mining road?' she asked.

Mancillo nodded. 'We can follow it to a village and find a phone.'

Eddie peered at the distant track. 'Looks like somebody's already using it.' He pointed. Two vehicles were visible, a 4x4 leading a colourful bus.

'It must be them,' said Mancillo. 'The mine is closed, so the road does not lead to anywhere.'

'Is that a bridge?' Eddie asked. The little convoy had slowed; ahead of it was a rift through the jungle, a sagging arc of wood crossing the gap.

'Yes,' Mancillo replied. 'There are rivers running down the volcano that cut canyons through the rock.' He surveyed the landscape below. 'Dr Wilde. Are we far from this . . . Underworld?' A faint curl of his lip; he still did not believe a word of it.

'No,' she replied. 'If we keep going downhill, we'll be in the right area. I'll be able to use the replica of Earthbreaker to pinpoint it using those mountains as landmarks.' She indicated the two distant peaks.

'Do *they* know how to find it?'

'Rosamaria knows as much as I do, and Corazón has the real dagger. I'd guess they do.'

Mancillo stared thoughtfully at the two vehicles amongst the oppressive green. 'If we are going down, and they are coming up . . . then we will meet,' he said, expression suddenly predatory. He repeated his deduction in Spanish. His men seemed enthused at the prospect, those soldiers who hadn't lost their sidearms while escaping from the plane drawing and checking them.

'You want a firefight?' said Eddie dubiously. 'They've got a bus – there could be thirty armed guys in it. There's seven of you, and some of you don't even have guns.'

'We are Kaibiles,' Mancillo scoffed. 'We do not *need* guns.'

'Well, just remember you've got civilians with you – who you're here to protect,' the Yorkshireman said pointedly.

Mancillo merely frowned, then turned to continue the trek down the mountain.

Ciro Corazón held his breath as the open-topped Jeep Wrangler scrabbled over the last few planks. The bridge spanning the ravine was old, wood rotten and gnawed by insects, supporting ropes frayed and mouldering. He'd led the way over on foot, acting as guide for the 4x4's driver. There had been some alarming moments as the Jeep skidded on the damp wood – but now it was across.

His second vehicle would be a far greater challenge. It was a 'chicken bus', an old thirty-five-foot school vehicle taken at the end of its working life in the United States to begin a new and even more stressful one in Guatemala. Functional yellow paint had been replaced by a gaudy multicoloured explosion of stripes and chevrons, the radiator grille re-chromed and polished to a mirror shine. The name 'Brujo' was emblazoned above the windscreen in rainbow-shaded script.

Corazón thought the vehicle was hideous, as artistic as vomit, but perversely it was the best way to move without attracting attention. Chicken buses were how most Guatemalans travelled for any distance, a common sight even on isolated roads. This one had an extra feature to minimise its chances of being stopped by the Guatemalan authorities – or anyone else. Several emoji-style faces were painted on it, giving onlookers fearsome rictus grins. His local follower who hired the bus had explained they were symbols of the region's gangs; a stamp to prove the owner had paid his protection money. Nobody, cop or criminal, should hassle it in transit.

Which suited Corazón. Not only was he a wanted man, but his followers in the bus were all armed. Rosamaria Rendón had managed to pass on word that the Guatemalans were sending soldiers to Tajumulco with the American. If they reached the mountain, he had to be prepared to fight.

Whether they would need to depended upon Rosamaria herself. Had she smuggled the bomb aboard the plane? Had she and Diego parachuted out? He hoped they were both safe on the ground. Rosamaria had been first his follower, then his lover, for several years now. He had initially seen her merely as a means to find the lost map chamber beneath Teotihuacán, but over time their relationship had become something more. And Diego . . . the boy felt almost like his own son. If things were different, then maybe . . .

No time for such thoughts, he chided himself. Not when his lifelong goal was so close. He turned to gaze at the towering mountain. The Underworld was so near he could almost feel it. When he brought Earthbreaker to the second map, he would have a power unmatched by any man in well over a thousand years!

But first he had to find it – and defend it. He looked back at the bus, calling for its passengers to disembark. If the worst happened and the bridge collapsed, he wanted his followers – and their firepower – to be on the right side of it.

His men filed out and started across. He had chosen them for their experience. Cops, soldiers, criminals, and men of simple anger and violence. Whatever their background, they knew how to use force . . . and were believers in the Jaguar God. All accepted him as Tekuni, their unchallenged leader.

The last man passed him. Now for the bus. He signalled for it to start the crossing. The Jeep's driver hopped out to help direct it. It was much wider than the Wrangler, barely enough room for a person to fit between it and the bridge's low guide ropes.

The front wheels rolled onto the first plank. The whole bridge strained, wood creaking. The bus inched forward, coughing black smoke from its exhaust. Its rear wheels reached the deck, the creaking growing louder. It advanced one plank at a time, the driver making minute steering adjustments to keep it centred—

A crack, loud as a gunshot. A plank broke under the bus's weight, pitching it to one side. The vehicle hit the guide rope and stretched it taut. 'Shit!' the Jeep's driver gasped. 'It's going to go over!'

'Stay calm,' Corazón ordered. His own confidence – his faith – was unbowed. The Jaguar God was with him. Earthbreaker had been found, the god's avatar rescued from captivity, the Underworld located. Every setback had been overcome. This would be no exception. 'He'll make it.'

His companion cringed as the deck tipped . . . then slowly stabilised. Corazón shot him a triumphant look, then shouted instructions to the bus's driver.

The front wheels turned back towards the bridge's centre line. Another growl from the engine, then the bus edged free of the broken plank. The deck tilted again, ropes moaning in protest, before easing back to something approximating level. The colourful vehicle slowly advanced. Another lurch as its rear wheels reached the damaged plank—

The wounded wood finally snapped and fell towards the river

below. The bus's back end dropped – then the large tyres caught on the neighbouring planks. The bridge bucked, a whip-crack wave running through its supporting ropes. The heavy logs around which they were wound, driven into the ground at each end of the crossing, jerked and creaked. Several cultists hurriedly backed clear, afraid that they were about to tear apart.

Again Corazón stood firm. The Jaguar God would not allow everything to end in disaster, not when they were so close. 'Keep going!' he shouted. 'Slowly, very slowly – ease it out!'

His confidence spurred the driver on. A moment of wheelspin – then the vehicle jolted free. The dilapidated structure rocked, the bus threatening to slide sideways again, but then it found grip and growled forward. Everyone watched, faces tense, until it finally reached the muddy track on the far side.

The Jeep's driver gasped in relief. 'He made it, Tekuni. I didn't think he would.'

'Tekuazotl is with us,' Corazón replied. 'All right! Everyone back in.'

The cultists reboarded their vehicles. Corazón took the Wrangler's front passenger seat, checking a GPS unit as the convoy set off. They were less than two kilometres from their target point. Nothing in normal circumstances – but in steep, dense jungle, with a storm brewing, there was no telling how long it would take to reach.

And once there, they had to find something concealed for nearly fifteen centuries. No, not just find it – they then had to survive the challenges of the Jaguar God . . .

His driver brought his attention back to the track. 'Tekuni – it's Rosamaria!'

Corazón looked ahead. Two figures waved from the side of the overgrown road. A moment of relief, and delight: both Rosamaria and Diego had made it safely. 'Pick them up,' he ordered.

The Jeep stopped. 'Tekuni!' cried Rosamaria, hurrying to it. She hugged the cult leader. 'You're here, you're okay!'

'And so are you,' he said with a smile. 'I'm glad. And Diego!' The smile broadened. 'How was your flight?'

'Short,' the young man replied, grinning.

Rosamaria whispered in her lover's ear: 'He thinks the bomb was just a bluff.'

Corazón nodded. 'We're all here now – and the entrance to the Underworld isn't far away.' He opened a satchel and took out the green stone dagger. 'I have Earthbreaker – the key that will let us inside.'

He stood in his seat, turning to address those in the bus. They had no trouble hearing him; many of its windows were open, the old vehicle lacking air conditioning. 'It is time!' he cried, raising the blade high above his head. 'Time for us to retake what belongs to us – time for us to reclaim our rule! And now that I have Earthbreaker, no one can stop us!'

His followers cheered. Corazón exulted in the sound, then sat again. 'Rosamaria, Diego, ride with me,' he said. They clambered into the rear seats. 'You found Earthbreaker and led us here – so now let's get what we came for.'

The Jeep set off, the bus following on the final leg of their journey.

19

'I'm okay, really,' Nina insisted as Eddie and Macy helped her down a slippery bank of earth. 'My foot's not hurting as much as it was.'

'That'll be the necrosis setting in,' said Macy, giving Eddie a devilish smile.

'Smartass,' Nina shot back, but with humour.

She looked ahead as her family released her. A gap in the trees revealed the distant peak of Tacaná, still rising above the nearer summit across the valley – but her descent had brought the two nearer together. 'We're getting close,' she called out.

Mancillo, a short way ahead with his men, stopped and looked back. 'Close to what?'

'The Underworld's entrance. Watch out for anything unusual.'

'Like what?'

'Like . . . anything that isn't a tree or a rock, I guess.' Nothing nearby qualified. The darkening sky sapped still more light from the green cloak shrouding everything; even if there *was* something unusual, it might easily be missed.

'All I am watching for are the people who stranded us here,' said Mancillo dismissively. He resumed his march downhill, the other Kaibiles following.

'We'll keep an eye out,' Eddie assured Nina as they set off again. 'But what *are* we looking for? It's the entrance to the Underworld, yeah – but if it was obvious, someone would have found it already.'

'I know,' she said. 'If it's some kind of gate, it might have collapsed over time, or been buried by a volcanic eruption a thousand years ago.'

'Well, that would be good, right?' Macy suggested. 'If it's buried, the bad guys won't be able to find it.'

'Maybe. But I'm worried that it *hasn't* been buried – just well hidden. And Corazón has Earthbreaker to guide him. Once he gets to the right area, given time . . . he *will* find it.'

'Then we have to find it first,' said Macy.

'Or stop him,' Eddie added.

Nina nodded. 'Yeah. I just have a horrible feeling that both options'll be harder than we think.'

'Is it here?' demanded Corazón.

Beyond the bridge, the mining track had run parallel to the canyon before twice bending back on itself, zigzagging higher up the volcano's side. The cultists had reached the spot where both peaks to the north-west were in alignment – meaning the Underworld's entrance was uphill in the opposite direction. They left their vehicles and began the trek up Tajumulco's flank. The jungle was dense enough to prevent them from taking a sighting on the landmarks from the ground. Instead, Diego volunteered to scale a tree to look through gaps in the canopy.

Rosamaria watched nervously as her son clung to a high branch with one hand, Earthbreaker in the other. 'No,' he called down. 'The summits are too close together, so it's higher up. We need to keep going.' He held the blade between his teeth and quickly descended the tree.

Corazón used his GPS to take a bearing. 'That way,' he said, pointing. The group followed him up the slope.

Before long, a rumbling noise became audible. The source was a waterfall, gushing from an opening in sheer rocks into an oval pool. A stream ran from it, winding downhill towards the river. Rosamaria paused to gaze at the beautiful sight, but Corazón regarded it with annoyance. 'We'll have to go around it.'

'Could the entrance be here?' asked Rosamaria.

Diego took another reading. 'No, we're still too low.'

Corazón looked uphill past the waterfall. All he could see was a shadowy wall of trees and undergrowth. 'Then let's find it,' he ordered, starting around the pool.

A gust of wind set the foliage swaying. Birds took flight, chattering in alarm. 'Winds of change,' Eddie warned, peering southwards. What was visible of the sky through the trees was now a menacing slate-grey. 'That storm's coming in.'

'Great,' said Macy. 'And all our wet-weather gear was in the plane.'

'It's on the ground now,' he pointed out. 'You never know; if we're lucky, we'll find it.'

'When are we *ever* lucky?' Nina said sardonically.

'Still alive, aren't we?'

'I'll give you that.' Not far below, the soldiers had stopped for a brief rest. She followed their example, sitting on a moss-covered rock. Similar stones were scattered amongst the trees downhill. She glimpsed Tacaná through the rustling canopy. 'If the Underworld still exists, the entrance can't be far from here,' she realised. 'Look – the mountains are lined up pretty much as I saw them. It's probably within a couple of hundred metres.'

'No sign of anything, though,' said Eddie. Only trees and rocks were visible at ground level.

Macy had taken out her phone, hoping to get cellular reception, but saw only a NO SIGNAL warning. She put it back in her pocket. 'Should we look for it?' she asked. 'I mean, we're right here.'

'I think you'd have to convince Major Mancillo,' said Nina. The Guatemalan was getting ready to move out—

He suddenly dropped to a crouch, hissing a sharp command. His men immediately followed suit, those who were armed drawing their weapons. 'What's going on?' Macy asked.

Eddie pulled her behind a bush. 'Dunno, but I think we should take the hint.'

Nina hurriedly scrambled behind the rock, listening. At first she heard nothing but the rising hiss of the wind – then, somewhere distant, a voice. 'It's them,' she whispered. 'The cultists – they're here!'

'I can't hear anything,' Eddie grumbled.

'Just wait, they're getting closer.' Her husband's hearing had been affected by close exposure to far too many gunshots and explosions over the years.

'I can,' Macy said, suddenly afraid. 'Oh God, they've found us!'

'They don't know we're here,' Eddie assured her. A peek around the bush revealed that the Kaibiles had spread out, hiding behind trees and rocks, or using their camouflaged fatigues to blend into the undergrowth.

He looked downslope beyond the Guatemalans – glimpsing a flicker of colour between the trunks, off to his left. Sixty to seventy metres away, but moving slowly uphill.

The Kaibiles had also noticed the approaching intruder, a soldier pointing him out to Mancillo. Then another man spotted a second, off to the right. From his slightly higher position, Eddie picked out others advancing up the slope, further away. At least one carried a rifle. 'Wait here,' he whispered to Macy and Nina, before crawling the short distance to the nearest group of Mancillo's men.

The major glanced around as he arrived. 'What do you want?'

'Thought you might like an extra pair of eyes. There's at least seven men coming this way, probably armed. About sixty metres off.'

Mancillo nodded. 'They are spread out, searching for

something. Maybe they also think this Underworld is here.' He listened as a soldier several metres away made a quiet report. 'The main group is below us, at least ten men. Others have moved out on each side.'

Eddie looked for himself. Mancillo's estimate was correct – though probably an understatement. There were stragglers behind the group moving up the centre, a second rank of searchers watching for anything the first line might have missed. 'What're you going to do?'

'If we shoot, we alert them. We do not have any suppressors. We will have to kill them silently.' A narrow smile. 'But that is what we are trained to do. Do you have any objections?'

'Nope,' said Eddie. 'They tried to kill us. Fuck 'em.'

The smile broadened. 'Perhaps you are okay after all, Chase.' Mancillo indicated a small rise topped by boulders not far to their right. 'Get the women into cover over there. I will join you in a minute.'

He issued commands as Eddie returned to Nina and Macy. 'What's going on?' the latter asked.

'They're going to take 'em out stealthily,' Eddie replied. 'Stay low and follow me to those rocks over there.'

'Take them out – what, you mean *kill* them?'

'I think it's best that we stay out of the way, honey,' Nina said softly. 'Come on.' Eddie leading, she ushered Macy after him.

They reached the boulders, Mancillo and a couple of Kaibiles soon joining them. The other soldiers slipped away in different directions, vanishing into the jungle.

'What's the plan?' Eddie asked.

'We will pick off the men on their flanks,' said Mancillo, 'and take their weapons.'

'Won't take 'em long to realise something's wrong.' The approaching cultists were calling out to each other at semi-regular intervals, someone – Corazón? – in the central group wanting to know if anyone had found anything. So far, all replies were in the negative.

That would soon change.

Eddie peered cautiously over the boulders. The nearest cult member was still over fifty metres away, a half-seen form in the deepening shadows between trees to the left. Even knowing what to look for, though, he had lost all sight of the Kaibiles. This was their environment, the place where they were meant to fight. He had trained for jungle combat in the SAS, but still wouldn't want to face them on their home turf.

He tracked the slowly moving figure. Someone else shouted off to the right, momentarily drawing his attention. Then he looked back to reacquire the walking man—

He was gone.

A brief flurry of movement, a bush shuddering as something moved – or was dragged – through it. Then the only motion was branches swaying in the wind.

A new sound. Eddie would have dismissed it as a bird call, if not for its coming from the direction of the vanished cultist. His suspicion was confirmed by Mancillo's approving expression. 'We got one,' the leader reported with triumph.

The oncoming visitors remained unaware that their numbers had just been reduced. They continued their plodding survey. Eddie tried to count how many enemies they were facing. Fifteen, at least—

Another trill, this time to the right. There was no sign of anything having happened, but Mancillo nodded again. 'Now two,' he said. 'My men will have taken their guns. If these people keep coming, they will be boxed in. We will be able to cut them down.'

Macy's reaction to the prospect of imminent bloodshed was one of fear. 'It's all right, love,' Eddie told her. 'Just keep down behind these rocks and nobody'll be able to shoot at you.' She nodded and hunched lower, still frightened.

Nina, though, now wore an expression he knew all too well: the kind of curiosity that inevitably led to trouble. 'What is it?' he asked.

'These rocks . . .' she said, gently running her fingers along one.

'What about them?'

She fixed him with a look of excited discovery. 'They're not rocks. They're *blocks* – they've been *carved*. Somebody made these!' She pointed out a straight edge half hidden by moss and dirt. 'It might be part of the Underworld's entrance—' She stopped abruptly, looking down at the ground. 'It might *be* the Underworld's entrance. We're right on top of it!'

Another bird call from the flanking trees – but Corazón's followers were starting to realise that something was amiss. A man kept calling another's name, becoming increasingly alarmed by the lack of a reply. Other voices rose, trying to determine if anyone else was missing. 'They will realise what has happened soon,' warned Mancillo. He brought up his gun. 'We must be ready.' He whistled an avian warble of his own, getting echoing responses from amongst the trees.

Eddie checked the killing zone below. Some of the cultists were now in clear view, walking obliviously into the trap. He assessed them. Men with the rough, hardened features of those accustomed to violence. They carried a mix of rifles, mostly Kalashnikovs but also some American AR-15 derivatives. Any sympathy for what was about to happen to them vanished. They had come here armed and ready to kill—

Other figures caught his eye. One was Corazón, the cult leader marching at the centre of the group – but with him were Rosamaria and Diego Rendón. A flash of conflict. Rosamaria had planted the bomb on the plane, so was responsible for two deaths – but she was now unarmed. And Diego was just a boy, one who'd seemed shocked by his mother's actions . . .

The trio halted, Corazón surveying his surroundings before saying something to Diego. The young man took Earthbreaker from him and hurried to a nearby tree. He held the green dagger between his teeth and scaled the trunk with athletic ease. Rosamaria watched him ascend, her nervousness clear even from a distance.

Corazón, meanwhile, spoke to one of his men. Gesticulation towards the trees to the left – then the cult leader shouted a name. There was no reply.

'They know something is wrong,' Mancillo growled. A brusque command to the two soldiers with him, who readied their weapons. Mancillo himself took aim – at the youth climbing the tree.

'What the fuck are you doing?' Eddie demanded.

'If he looks round, he will see us,' said Mancillo impatiently.

'He's just a kid!'

'He is a *threat*.'

Macy reacted to Eddie's remark, realising he could only be talking about one person. She peered over the blocks – and gasped as she saw that Diego was Mancillo's target. 'No! Don't shoot him!' she said in alarm.

'Shut up!' Mancillo growled at her.

'Don't you fucking tell my daughter to shut up,' Eddie snapped back. 'And you can't shoot a kid in the back, you psycho.'

Before the Guatemalan could reply, Diego shouted from the tree. Eddie saw him hold out the dagger to line up the two peaks. 'He says they're in the right place,' said Macy as the young man excitedly told Corazón what he had discovered. 'They're at the entrance to the Underworld!'

'Then they won't leave until they find it,' said Mancillo. 'My orders are to *stop* them finding it, yes? Let me carry them out.' He gave another sharp bird-like whistle, its meaning obvious: *get ready*.

Diego's revelation had distracted the cultists, but now their concern returned. Corazón called out into the trees, still receiving no answer. Diego began to descend, turning towards the group in hiding as he came down the trunk.

Mancillo locked his gun onto him, trigger finger tightening—

'No!' Macy cried, lunging past Eddie to hit the major's gun arm as he fired. The bullet cracked past the youth into the trees. 'Diego, *run!*'

The cultists were momentarily frozen in surprise. Then they moved, those with military training diving for cover and bringing up their weapons as the others scattered. Diego dropped to the ground and rolled behind the trunk. '*Mamá!*' he cried, gesturing frantically for his mother to seek shelter.

Mancillo rounded on Macy in fury, a fist raised as if to hit her. Eddie's own angry look deterred him. '*Abran fuego!*' he shouted instead. The Kaibiles opened fire, the men with Mancillo sending pistol shots down at their targets while those off to each side let rip with their newly acquired weapons. One cultist fell immediately, bullets tearing bloodily into his chest.

The others retaliated. Rifle fire sprayed through the jungle. Eddie shoved Macy down as rounds smacked against the blocks shielding them. Nina also ducked, stone chips spitting over her.

Mancillo scrambled along the line of rocks to take up a new position at one end, shouting orders. A scream from below as another cultist's abdomen was torn open by a burst of bullets. But his companions had by now reached whatever cover they could find. Corazón and Rosamaria ducked behind a boulder, Diego hurling himself over a smaller rock. A bullet smacked off the stone in his wake.

Corazón's followers returned fire as their leader bellowed commands. 'What did he say?' said Eddie, only partially catching the Spanish. 'Did he tell them to throw grenades?'

'Not grenades,' Macy said in alarm. '*Dynamite!*'

Mancillo heard and shouted orders of his own. The Kaibiles' fire slowed as they hunted for anyone about to throw explosives – which emboldened the cultists. Nina ducked again as more gunfire pounded the stone barrier.

A yell from below. 'Oh crap!' gasped Macy. 'I think that means "fire in the hole"!'

Eddie risked looking over the stone. The cultists had spread out, hunched behind trees and rocks, but were still contained in a relatively small area.

That could soon change. He spotted a telltale sputter of light: a lit fuse. 'On the left, fifty metres!' he shouted to Mancillo.

The major saw the threat, commanding his troops to concentrate their fire on the target—

Too late. The cultist made his throw, a stick of dynamite arcing through the air on a spiralling trail of smoke as he ducked behind a trunk. It landed amidst a clump of trees. Bushes suddenly flailed as a camouflaged Kaibile burst from them—

The dynamite exploded.

The blast disintegrated a tree's base. The running man was hit by flying shrapnel and tumbled bloodily to the ground. The shattered tree fell, sweeping downwards like a colossal fly swatter. Juarez was on the ground below; he tried to dive clear, but was knocked flat and pinned by the swathe of branches.

The opening on one flank let several cultists break from their positions. Mancillo and the soldiers with him tracked them, but failed to bring anyone down. Then they were forced to duck behind the blocks as other opponents concentrated automatic fire on their position.

Eddie dropped too – but glimpsed a second fuse being lit, closer than the first. 'Another one coming!' he warned. 'Nina, Macy, we might have to run!'

The cultist darted out from behind a tree, arm drawn back to fling the explosive—

Mancillo's gun found him – and fired. The man was hit in the chest and fell backwards with a choked scream . . .

But he had already thrown the dynamite.

Nina heard a swooshing, fizzing sound grow louder – then her eyes went wide as the dirty red stick landed with a plop between her and the nearest Kaibile. '*Shit!*' she cried. The fuse had already almost burned down. '*Run!*'

She leapt up and sprinted away from it, Eddie and Macy scrambling with her. The soldiers also broke from their cover and ran – except for the closest Kaibile. He darted to snatch up the dynamite, about to toss it back over the line of rocks—

The sizzling spark reached the fuse's end – and the explosive detonated.

The man vanished in a wet shower of red. The blast smashed the blocks beside him, sending ragged chunks of stone bowling down the slope.

Those fleeing were knocked down by the explosion and left dazed and half deafened. Eddie, shielding Macy, took the brunt of the shockwave. He collided with his daughter as he fell—

Bowling her over the edge of the little rise.

Macy rolled down the slope, crashing through undergrowth. Her painful journey came to a sudden stop as she hit the foot of a tree. Dizzy, in pain, she raised her head – only to drop flat with a scream as bullets thudded into the trunk inches overhead.

She heard Diego shout over the rattle of gunfire. 'Macy! Stay down! I'll get you!'

'No!' Corazón said in Spanish. 'Diego, stay where you are! Cruz, Lopez, get that girl – bring her to me!'

Macy looked up, seeing two men running towards her. In panic, she jumped up and tried to climb back up the slope. It was too steep, vegetation tangling her legs. 'Dad!' she cried. 'Dad, help!'

'Macy!' Eddie shouted from above. She saw him stand – only

to dive behind a block as the cultists fired on him. 'Run, get out of here!'

But she had nowhere to go, the two men still charging at her. She made a desperate break sideways along the slope. They angled to intercept her. 'No, go away, get away!' she screamed as they closed in—

One man grabbed her clothing, pulling her back. She swung a balled fist at his head in both terror and anger. He wasn't expecting resistance from a teenage girl – much less a blow strong enough to break his nose. Blood spurted from his nostrils. He yelled and stumbled back, letting go.

But the other man overtook him. He caught Macy's hair rather than her clothing, and she screamed as he dragged her to the ground. She clawed at his eyes – but he jerked back, her nails only grazing his cheek. Then he punched her hard in the stomach. Macy folded in breathless pain. She was unable to fight back as the two men dragged her into the trees.

Eddie crawled behind the stones until he found a gap he could see through without drawing fire. What he saw chilled his blood. '*Macy!*' he roared, seeing his daughter disappear amongst the trunks. He looked around in desperation for help. Mancillo and his surviving companions had been knocked down by the explosion, only just recovering. He scuttled to them. 'Give me a gun!' One of the Kaibiles had dropped his sidearm; he snatched it up.

The soldier snapped to full awareness and grabbed for it, but Eddie had already pulled back. The man gave him a lethal glare. Mancillo brought up his own weapon, watching Eddie as much as the situation down the slope. 'What are you doing?'

'They've got Macy!'

A new bird call off to the right. Mancillo's concerned reaction told Eddie the signal was not good news. No shots had come from that direction for several seconds – the hidden Kaibile had probably run out of bullets. 'Give him his gun!' said the Guatemalan. 'They will get *us* if we don't fight!'

'What do you *think* I'm going to fucking do? I'm—'

Eddie broke off at a shout from below: Corazón. 'Mr Chase! I have Macy! Surrender – or I will kill her!'

Nina's cry of fear from along the ridge was echoed by a shocked yell of protest from Diego. Eddie peeked over the blocks to see his worst fears confirmed. Two men had dragged Macy to Corazón, who held a gun to her head, using her as a human shield. Another pair of his followers pushed the appalled Diego away as he tried to reach her. 'Come out and drop your guns!' the cult leader continued. 'You have ten seconds!'

Eddie turned back frantically to Mancillo. 'He's going to kill her!' he pleaded. 'Do what he says!'

The major's expression turned cold. 'The Kaibiles do not surrender. *Ever.*' He looked away, about to issue more orders—

Eddie snapped the gun up at Mancillo's head. 'Stand down. *Now!*'

The brief shock of the other soldiers was replaced by anger. The remaining armed man locked his weapon onto Eddie. The only thing stopping him from shooting, Eddie knew, was the risk of a muscle spasm when the Englishman was hit, causing his own gun to fire – and blowing his commander's head off.

Mancillo stared at the unwavering muzzle. Then his eyes met Eddie's once more. 'We. Never. Surrender.' Each word was delivered like a bullet.

None of the men moved for what seemed like an eternity, trapped in the stand-off. Then Eddie's eyes narrowed. The movement was almost imperceptible – but Mancillo knew what it meant. He opened his mouth, about to tell the soldier to fire before the Yorkshireman did—

Nina broke the impasse – by jumping onto the ragged row of blocks, hands raised high. 'Don't shoot!' she cried – as much to the Kaibiles as the cultists below. 'I'm coming down!'

'Nina, don't!' Eddie yelled, keeping his gun fixed on Mancillo.

'I have to! They've got Macy!' Arms still up, she picked her way unsteadily down the rise, terrifyingly aware that rifles were tracking her.

Corazón smiled. 'Chase, your time is almost up. If you want your wife and girl to live, show yourself – and the soldiers with you!'

Eddie gazed unblinkingly at Mancillo. 'You heard him. That's my wife and daughter down there. You'd do whatever it takes to protect your country? I'd do the same to protect my family. Now drop your fucking guns – before I drop *you*.'

The lack of any immediate reaction from the two soldiers told him they didn't speak English. The only person who understood his threat was Mancillo. How would he respond? Would he see this was a situation they currently couldn't win, or . . .

Mancillo didn't need to speak to repeat himself a third time. The words were clear in his eyes. *We never surrender.* He drew in a breath to give his order.

Eddie's finger curled more tightly around the trigger—

'No, no!' said the armed Kaibile, hurriedly turning his gun upwards. '*No dispares!*'

Mancillo's expression of cold determination was rapidly melted by fury. Eddie stood, keeping his gun on him and gesturing for the others to rise and drop their weapons. They did so, Mancillo with deep reluctance. 'Okay!' Eddie shouted to Corazón, discarding his own gun. 'We're coming down! Let her go!'

For a heart-freezing moment, he thought the cult leader was going to shoot Macy anyway, not moving the gun from her head. Then, almost with a shrug, he pushed her away. Macy nearly fell, but recovered. Diego started towards her, but she pointedly turned away and ran to meet Nina. Mother and daughter embraced tearfully, ignoring the weapons pointed at them.

Eddie raised his hands and started down the slope, followed by the Kaibiles. The other surviving soldiers reluctantly emerged from the surrounding trees, met at gunpoint by armed cultists. The major castigated his troops for their surrender, before turning his anger upon Eddie. 'Do you think they will let us live?' he hissed. 'You have killed us all!'

'They would have killed Macy,' Eddie growled.

'And they still will! All you have done is delay it. Now we will all die because you were afraid!'

'You're fucking right I was afraid – I was afraid they were going to kill my little girl!' he shot back. 'You're not a dad, are you? You don't have a fucking clue what that means.'

'I *do* have a child,' Mancillo fired back. 'And my son knows what it means to have a *real* soldier as a father. I would kill to protect him, yes – but if I had to choose between him, and my country? He knows I would sacrifice him for my country.'

Eddie regarded him in disbelief. 'Then you're a pretty shit dad, aren't you?'

Mancillo sneered. 'If the rest of the SAS are as weak as you, then your country is fucked if it ever has to fight.'

Eddie ignored him, joining Macy and Nina. 'Are you both okay?'

'Yeah,' said Nina. 'For now.'

Macy looked at him, eyes running with tears. 'What's going to happen now?'

Corazón signalled for his men to corral the Kaibiles at riflepoint before striding towards the reunited family. 'Now?' he said, with a triumphant smile. 'Now we are going to find the entrance to the Underworld. And open it.'

20

Finding the hidden entrance did not take long. Rosamaria reached the same conclusion as Nina: the boulders on the small ridge were actually carved blocks. Her probing excavation quickly revealed a sloping wall beneath them, buried beneath earth and vegetation.

The cultists had brought digging tools. The prisoners were pressed into service to clear away the undergrowth and soil. The only one not forced to dig was Macy, who was left with Diego as her guard. He tried a few times to talk to her, but met only angry silence as she turned her back to him.

The upper part of the wall was soon exposed. Set into it were decorated pillars, closely resembling those in the Palace of Quetzalpapálotl in Teotihuacán. Colourful paint was still discernible on the carved animals, even under the dirt.

But it was what stood between the pillars that raised excitement. 'It's a door,' Rosamaria proclaimed. It was the upper part of a single massive stone block, inscribed with elaborate patterns. 'We've found the way in!'

'Dig it out,' Corazón ordered as rain began to fall. 'Quickly!'

The reluctant workforce shovelled away the wet earth. Once cleared, the entrance's full scale was revealed. It stood twelve feet tall and six wide, the chiselled patterns surrounding an ornate representation of a giant jaguar at its centre. Corazón stared at the image with an almost ecstatic expression. 'All this time,' he said to Rosamaria. 'All these centuries, generation after generation of Tekuni keeping the faith alive . . . and we finally found it. *I* found it. The Underworld – the domain of Tekuazotl. It's real. It's here. And it's *mine!*'

Rosamaria squeezed his hand. 'I just hope everything inside has survived. It's been a long time; there have been earthquakes, volcanic eruptions . . .'

'It's all there. I know it. The Jaguar God wouldn't bring me this far and then take it from me. So now, we just have to get inside.' He switched from Spanish to English to address the captives scraping away the last of the soil. 'Professor Wilde! Your professional opinion?'

Nina clanked her shovel against the door. 'I'm hardly the expert. You should ask your pet archaeologist there.' She gave Rosamaria a harsh look.

'I am sorry,' said Rosamaria. 'None of this was supposed to happen. If you had come to Teotihuacán when originally planned, you would not have been there when Tekuni claimed Earthbreaker.'

'Apology *not* accepted, *Doctor.*' The Mexican appeared genuinely hurt by Nina's rejection. 'It wasn't your butcher boyfriend who planted a goddamn bomb in our plane. It was you!'

Diego, still guarding Macy, rounded on his mother. 'You said the bomb was just a bluff.'

'Yeah, when it exploded and killed the pilot, it went *ka-bluff*!' Macy said sarcastically. Rosamaria had no reply, not quite able to meet her son's gaze.

'Enough,' snapped Corazón, gesturing for his followers to move the prisoners away from the entrance. 'No, she stays,' he added as a man was about to push Nina with the others. The cult leader walked to the door, examining the carvings. 'Tekuazotl,' he said. 'You see? He left his symbol to show his followers they were in the right place. And now we are here.'

'So how do you get in?' Eddie asked. 'I don't see a doorbell.'

'Rosamaria,' said Corazón, summoning her. 'And Professor

Wilde. I am sure you do not want to help me, but I have my religion – and you have yours. An archaeological wonder from a lost civilisation. Can you resist such a find?'

'Sure I can,' Nina replied . . . but she was already looking at the door with a scientific eye. The design of the jaguar carving, long tail coiling around its curved body, formed a spiral, drawing attention inexorably to its face. Or more specifically, its *mouth*. There was a small slot in the stone, the right size to accept something flat, like the blade of a dagger . . .

But she said nothing. A lost wonder it might be, but she had no intention of assisting Corazón.

Not that it mattered. Rosamaria too had noticed the little opening. 'Tekuni, here!' she said, running a fingertip across the jaguar's mouth. 'Look. Is it the right size to fit Earthbreaker?'

The cult leader drew out the green stone dagger. 'Let us see.' He cautiously examined the slot, using Earthbreaker's tip to clear out loose soil. Then he stepped back, staring with reverence into the eyes of the carved cat as he chanted in the long-lost language of the Teotihuacanos. The cultists joined in, echoing his words.

'We should attack now,' Mancillo hissed to Eddie as the closest gunman accompanied the chant. 'While they are distracted.'

'They've got Nina,' the Yorkshireman growled back. '*And* Macy.'

'It is her fault we were captured! I should—'

'You should fucking shut up before you say something that pisses me off,' Eddie said firmly. By now, another guard had noticed the increasingly unsurreptitious exchange, a thrust of his rifle warning them to be quiet.

Corazón reached the end of his chant. He raised the dagger, then, gripping the hilt tightly, pushed it into the slot.

Nina saw him flinch as the blade's point made contact with something inside. A moment later, a deep thudding *boom* came from behind the great slab. The sound was followed by smaller, sharper bangs as if stacked stones were falling one by one . . . then, with a nerve-jarring scrape, the door began to swing slowly open.

Corazón hastily retreated, bringing Earthbreaker with him. Removing the dagger from the keyhole didn't affect the barrier's inexorable movement. It finally halted with an abrupt crunch, fully open.

A passage leading into the mountainside was revealed. Nina looked inside, but saw only darkness. Her gaze went to the door itself. It was a foot thick, probably weighing several tons, but it had been driven open smoothly even after well over a millennium.

A closer look as Corazón cautiously stepped over the threshold revealed how. A block of the same green stone as Earthbreaker was inset in the door's back, slightly below the slot, which cut all the way through the huge slab. It appeared to have been forced downwards, repelled by the dagger, by about half an inch. That small movement had been enough to move a metal lever, which in turn tripped a larger mechanism beside the door. A huge stone cylinder had been raised at one end of a teeter-totter arrangement; smaller blocks had been knocked away to release it, its weight as it descended acting on some mechanism in the giant door's hinge to force the barrier open. A fairly simple device, but cleverly engineered. And the presence of the green stone showed her there was more to it than met the eye . . .

One of Corazón's men brought him a powerful flashlight. The cult leader shone the beam into the passageway. Heavy stone blocks made up the walls. It led slightly upwards for fifty feet before angling away.

'So you found the Underworld,' said Nina acerbically. 'Congratulations. I don't suppose you'd consider letting us go now?'

Corazón gave her a brief mocking smile. 'I don't think so.'

'Yeah, I kinda guessed that. So, you're gonna make us wait in the rain without umbrellas?' Her flippancy was forced; she had a horrible feeling that Corazón intended to kill his prisoners. Her humour, however weak, was an attempt to connect to his humanity. His feelings for Rosamaria and Diego appeared genuine, so he wasn't a complete sociopath; perhaps he could still be appealed to on an empathetic level . . .

For a long, chilling moment, it seemed she had failed. Corazón's stare was emotionless – the look of a slaughterhouse worker facing the last calf of his shift. But then a new expression formed. It was no more welcome than the blankness it replaced: calculation, with a hint of cruel amusement. He had something more in mind than simple executions. 'No,' he said. 'That would not be fair, would it? Not after you have come all this way. No, you come with us. We will see what waits in the Underworld together.'

He gave orders to his followers. The Kaibiles and Eddie had their hands tied behind their backs. The Guatemalans did not submit willingly, two men being clubbed to the ground before being bound. Eddie only allowed himself to be restrained with great reluctance, aware that his family would suffer the consequences if he fought back. 'Hope we don't have to climb any ladders in there,' he said as the prisoners were pushed to the entrance. 'Be hard to hold on with my teeth.'

'Enough talking,' Corazón snapped. He had been speaking to Rosamaria, but now returned to the entrance. 'We are going in. Professor Wilde, I am sure you will be glad to get out of the rain.'

The downpour had worsened, the ever-darkening sky suggesting more was coming. 'I dunno,' Nina said. 'I'm starting to think staying outside's the better option.'

The Mexican's insulting smile returned. 'Where is your sense of adventure?'

'About a decade in the past, along with my interest in pop culture.'

Despite the situation, Eddie chuckled. 'More like three decades.'

'No, Dad, that's you,' Macy chipped in.

'*Vamos*,' Corazón commanded. He took the lead, Rosamaria beside him as they entered the tunnel. The others followed, Nina, Eddie and Macy accompanied by Diego and a couple of guards. The rest of the cultists kept a close watch on the soldiers behind them.

The procession soon reached a bend in the passage. Beyond, the tunnel walls were decorated with elaborate colourful reliefs. Rosamaria paused to examine them. 'Tekuni, look at this. It is the Pyramid of the Sun, but . . . it is not complete.' Corazón halted, telling a couple of his men to scout ahead before regarding the image with great interest.

Nina looked for herself. It was indeed the great pyramid of Teotihuacán – but missing its uppermost tiers. A large wooden structure topped it instead. 'This picture must have been made before it was completed.'

Rosamaria nodded. 'We think it took over a century to build.'

'Must be the same people they use to fill potholes in England,' Eddie quipped. Only Macy was amused.

'The last level could have been built as long as fifty years after the rest,' Rosamaria continued. 'So this picture shows the pyramid as it was in the first half of the second century.'

'So nobody's been down here for almost nineteen hundred years?' said Diego, awed. 'Ciro, do you know when this place was abandoned?'

'It was never *abandoned*,' Corazón replied. 'It was left waiting for us to return. But in the stories my father told me, nobody had travelled from Teotihuacán to the Underworld for hundreds of years. They did not need to. The map under the Pyramid of the Sun did the same as the one here.'

'What else was in these stories?' Nina demanded. 'How much do you know about what's down here?'

'Enough to know that the legends of the Underworld are true,' was his arrogant reply.

'Which legends? The challenges that the dead have to face to be reborn?'

'Yes. But as Tekuni, I will not have to face them. I will lead my followers through safely, and—'

He broke off at a shout from along the tunnel. 'Tekuni!' called one of the scouts. He continued in Spanish.

'What did he say?' Nina asked, only picking out a few words.

Macy had already made a translation. 'Basically, "I don't know what I've found, but it's fricking amazing!"'

The group set off again, rounding another corner. Ahead was something that immediately raised Nina's alert level: a tall cage-like metal gate blocking the way to a larger space beyond. The walls to each side were smooth stone, the ceiling rising in a carved arc to open out into the main chamber.

Rosamaria was also surprised by the sight, but for professional reasons. 'That looks like iron,' she said, shining a light at the obstacle's rust-flecked bars. 'But Mesoamerican cultures did not work in iron.'

'Atlantean ones did,' Nina said. The other woman was about to advance for a closer look, but she put a hand on her arm to stop her. 'Hold on.'

Her warning tone instantly caught Corazón's attention. 'What is it?'

'I think we just reached our first challenge. I wouldn't—'

'Tekuni!' the scout said in excitement. He moved forward, aiming his flashlight through the gate to illuminate what lay beyond – and above. '*Tienes que ver esto!*'

Gasps of amazement came from the observers as the beam swept over a giant statue: a blockily stylised jaguar, mouth open and fangs bared as if roaring. The figure was coated in gleaming gold, an auric glow reflecting back. Its eyes were formed from the sparkling green of numerous emeralds. It stood a good twenty feet tall, looming over the vestibule at the chamber's entrance.

Corazón stared up at it, astonished. 'Tekuazotl . . .' he whispered.

'You didn't expect to see it?' asked Nina.

'The stories said the Jaguar God was waiting for those who entered the Underworld. But I had no idea it would be so . . . *magnífico.*'

The scout went to the gate. '*Abriré esto,*' he said, putting down his light to take hold of the bars, '*y luego podemos—*'

A dull metallic *clunk* echoed through the space.

Nina reacted instantly. 'Back, get back!' she cried, quickly retreating. Eddie followed, extending an elbow to nudge the startled Macy with him. Everyone else scrambled backwards, the other scout yelling in fright as a second metal gate, which had lain flush with grooves cut into the floor, abruptly swung upwards under him like a drawbridge. He barely clambered over its top as it banged noisily to a stop in a vertical position, blocking the vestibule's entrance.

The man trapped between the two gates looked around in panic – as the jaguar statue moved.

21

The great head began to descend, the dust of ages spilling from it as it slowly swung towards the vestibule. Its lower jaw opened wider with the grinding growl of ancient mechanisms. The intent of the Jaguar God was clear.

To devour whoever stood before it.

'Sal de ahí!' Corazón shouted through the bars. 'Sube por la puerta!'

At the command, the cultist overcame his fear and turned to climb the inner gate – only to see that the gap above it, at the bottom of the curving ceiling, was too narrow to fit through. He spun and began to ascend the inner barrier instead. The jaguar rumbled remorselessly closer, but he would reach the top of the gate before it blocked him—

He screamed – and fell back into the vestibule, blood running from his hands. The gate's upper bars were topped with razor-sharp metal shards.

'Macy, don't look!' Eddie blocked his daughter's view as the jaguar's head, fanged mouth fully agape, entered the enclosed space. The man backed desperately into a corner, but there was no hiding place. The antechamber had been built to match the form of the descending statue. It steadily dropped the last few feet, its terrified prey scurrying on hands and knees from one side of the vestibule to the other. Then there was no more room to manoeuvre—

A final scream – which turned to a nerve-chilling shriek of agony. The wet crunch and snap of breaking bones replaced it.

The glow from the man's flashlight vanished as it too was flattened.

The machinery's rumble stopped, the silence almost startling. Then it began again as the jaguar's head rose, lower jaw closing and scraping up the crushed body of its victim. Blood dripping from its teeth, the statue returned to its original position. Its emerald eyes glared tauntingly at those below as the outer gate dropped back to its recess in the floor with a clang.

Nina moved to hug Macy, who had buried her face against Eddie's shoulder. 'It's okay,' she said. 'It's over.'

'*Madre de Dios!*' gasped Corazón, in his shock momentarily forgetting which deity he worshipped.

'You weren't expecting *that*, were you?' said Nina.

'No, I was not.' He composed himself, regarding the bloody mess on the vestibule's floor. 'So how do we get past it?'

She gave him a disbelieving look. 'You don't know?'

'My father told me the Tekuni could pass all the challenges without being harmed. But . . . he did not say *how*. That knowledge has been lost over time.'

'Well, that's a lot of bloody use, isn't it?' said Eddie. 'Maybe your ancestors should have spent less time ripping out hearts and more time inventing writing!'

Corazón controlled his anger, facing the two archaeologists. 'There must be a way through. We have to find it.' Taking care not to step on the lowered gate, he ran his torch beam systematically over one of the vestibule's walls.

Rosamaria did the same on the other side. 'Tekuni,' she said, spotting something. 'Look.' Several slots were set into the stonework at chest height, a couple of feet beyond the entrance.

'They're the same size as the one at the surface,' said Nina. 'Maybe you have to use Earthbreaker here too.'

Diego peered warily at the wall. 'So which slot do you put it in? Ciro, were you told how to open it?'

'No,' Corazón replied reluctantly. 'There was a part of the story: the dance of the jaguar. Something to do with where it placed its paws. But I was never told anything more.'

'A combination?' Nina wondered. 'You put the dagger into specific slots in turn?'

'I don't know,' was the irate reply.

'The dance of the jaguar,' Diego said thoughtfully. 'Where it puts its paws . . . I've seen this before,' he said with sudden excitement. 'This pattern, the slots – there are ten of them. A row of three, then four, and another three. I know I've seen it somewhere . . .' He stared intently at the openings – then whirled to face the others. 'I know where! The chamber under the Pyramid of the Sun, where we found Earthbreaker – it's on the picture of Tekuazotl!'

Rosamaria's face lit up in realisation. 'Yes, of course! On the picture,' she went on, explaining to both Corazón and Nina, 'there are markings at the bottom, and some have symbols of jaguar paws above them. It could be the jaguar dance, Tekuni – showing where to place Earthbreaker to open the gate.'

'So which are the right slots?' Corazón asked.

'I . . . don't remember.'

Anger clouded his face. 'You don't *remember*? But you are the archaeologist – you should know!'

'I don't remember either,' said Diego, stepping to his mother's defence. 'We didn't realise it was important!' He closed his eyes, struggling to draw the image from his memory. 'I think there were three groups of paws, but . . . I'm not sure exactly where they were.'

'Oh! Oh, hi,' Macy piped up. 'I think I might know.'

Corazón regarded her with contempt. 'How would *you* know?'

'Because I took a photo of it?' She reached into a pocket. A cultist snapped up his rifle. 'Ah! It's a phone, *teléfono*! Not a gun!'

Corazón gestured, and the man stood down.

Macy hurriedly swiped through her photos. 'Here, look!'

Nina saw for herself. It was the selfie she had taken in the partially excavated chamber adjoining the map room. The painted reliefs on the walls were visible behind her – and at the foot of the image of Tekuazotl, there was indeed a pattern marked with small paw prints. 'God, you're right. How far can you zoom in?'

Macy expanded the picture, the pattern pixelating as it filled the screen. Three tiers of vertical lines appeared – some with painted paw marks above them. 'Three, four, three, just like the slots here,' she confirmed. 'And look at the paw prints. There's one above this line, then two over this one. Maybe that's the right order.'

'There is only one way to find out,' Corazón said. 'We test it.'

'Rather you than me,' said Eddie.

The Mexican smiled malevolently. 'Actually, it *will* be you.'

'What?' said Nina in alarm.

'Yeah, what?' Eddie added.

'You will go in and test the dagger,' Corazón told him. 'If these markings are the dance of the jaguar, you will be okay. If they are not . . . then I will still be safe.'

'Hey!' Nina protested. 'What the hell happened to "Tekuni will pass without being harmed"? I thought you had faith in the Jaguar God?'

'I do,' the cult leader replied. 'But that,' he indicated the statue, 'is a machine. Machines are built by men. And men can make mistakes. I do not wish to die so close to my goal because of another man's mistake.'

'Oh, nice rationalisation,' Macy muttered.

'Enough,' Corazón snapped. 'Untie him. Professor Wilde, I assume you have the fake dagger. Give it to him.'

'What, I don't qualify for the real thing?' Eddie complained.

'He'll need the real Earthbreaker,' Nina insisted, producing the replica. 'That's the whole point of these traps – you can't get through them without it.'

The Mexican shook his head firmly. 'I would not trust him with it.' The cultist who had barely escaped the booby trap released Eddie's bound wrists. Eddie rubbed them, then took the 3D-printed blade with a scowl. 'Remember that I have your wife, and your daughter,' said Corazón. 'Do not do anything stupid.'

'So what *am* I supposed to do?' Eddie replied, before frowning. 'Wait, that didn't come out like I meant it to.'

'Here, Dad,' said Macy, showing him the enlarged image. 'That slot's got one paw, so I think it's first.'

'You *think?*' Eddie said, eyebrows rising. 'You're not sure?'

She pointed out the markings. 'One, two, three paw prints, so first, second, third. That's the only interpretation I can come up with.'

'She's right,' said Nina. Macy looked at her in surprise – and gratitude. 'I can't think of anything else it might be, even if the Teotihuacanos used the Atlantean numerical system.'

Macy nodded. 'Which was completely insane, with all the stuff about using the gaps between your fingers, but even they couldn't make counting to three *that* difficult.'

'You both know what you're doing,' Eddie told them. Macy beamed with pride. 'Okay, so let me see. That slot, then that one, and finally that one, right?' He indicated each hole in turn. 'Let's hope this jaguar's dance was the safety.' His daughter's expression was blank. 'The safety dance? Twentieth-century joke.'

Her look didn't change. 'Yes, Dad. I guessed.'

'Tchah!' Eddie took a breath, then moved towards the vestibule. 'All right, how about everyone holds this thing down so I can get out if Tibbles wants a snack?' He pointed at the gate set into the floor.

Corazón did not seem inclined to help, but Diego spoke up.

'We should do it. We don't want anyone else to get hurt. Do we?'

'Okay,' was the cult leader's less-than-enthusiastic response. He signalled for three of his followers to stand on the gate. Mancillo, still held prisoner with the surviving Kaibiles, reacted with new alertness as some of his guards were drawn away, but others moved to cover for them. The major said nothing, but kept watching for any opportunity to escape.

'Someone give me a light,' said Eddie. A torch was passed to him. He stepped cautiously over the vestibule's threshold. The chamber beyond remained silent, the jaguar statue unmoving.

'It didn't activate until that guy went to the inner gate,' Nina reminded him. 'Stay by the slots, and you might be safe.'

Eddie nodded, but still shone his light warily up at the golden beast before turning it to the slots. He crouched to peer into them. 'Can't see anything inside this one, or this one . . . Wait, this one's got something shiny at the back. Looks like a polished bit of stone.'

Nina checked Macy's phone. 'If we're reading this right, that's the last slot. It might be a trigger to open the gate.'

'So what are the first two for?'

'They could be a combination lock. You have to release the first two latches before you can trip the third.'

'And if they're not?' He swung the torch beam back up at the looming statue. 'I'm cat food.'

Corazón watched impatiently. 'Get on with it. Put the dagger in the first slot.' One of his companions aimed his gun at the Englishman for emphasis. Another did the same to Nina and Macy. With a muttered curse, Eddie turned and raised the blade.

A thought came to Nina. 'Eddie, wait, what colour was the stone?' she asked urgently – but her husband had already pushed the fake Earthbreaker into the opening.

A *clunk* from behind the wall – and the deep noise of shifting metal echoed through the chamber again. The lowered gate immediately began to rise, even with the men standing on it. Whatever counterweight was lifting it weighed more than all of them combined. Two cultists fell backwards, another jumping clear with a startled yell.

'Shit!' said Eddie, rushing back to the threshold – but even that short distance was too far. Before he had climbed even halfway up the gate, the gap above had narrowed too much to squeeze through. He whirled and aimed the light at the statue. The head of the Jaguar God, green eyes glinting greedily, was already descending towards him, bloodied mouth widening. 'All right, *now* what do I do?'

'The dagger!' Macy cried. 'Put it in the next slot!'

Eddie hurriedly yanked out the replica, finding the second slot in the sequence. He thrust it inside. Again it met resistance, another trigger being pushed. The third and final slot was next—

Nothing happened.

Eddie jiggled the dagger. Still no result. He snatched it out. The plastic tip was squashed and deformed. 'It won't reach!'

'It won't make any difference!' Nina said. She rounded on Corazón. 'I told you, only Earthbreaker'll work! Give it to him!'

His cold, frighteningly inhuman expression returned. 'Why?'

'If you don't, he'll die!' Macy pleaded.

Corazón did not reply, instead raising his head to watch the descending statue. 'You son of a *bitch*!' Nina screamed, lunging at him. One of his followers threw her back against the wall. The Mexican gave her only the briefest glance, then looked back expectantly at the imminent carnage—

'Ciro!' cried Diego, horrified. 'For God's sake, help him!'

His plea broke his mother's stunned paralysis. '*Ciro, por favor! No delante de su hija!*'

For a moment, it seemed their words had made no difference. Then, with visible irritation, Corazón raised Earthbreaker and went to the gate. 'Here!' he barked, slipping the dagger between the bars.

Eddie snatched it from him. 'Cheers,' he said with angry sarcasm as he jammed the real blade into the slot—

Nothing happened. The giant jaguar's head continued inexorably towards him. 'Buggeration and fuckery!' he said, pushing harder at the hilt. 'It's not bloody working!'

'But that was the right order,' Macy protested. 'It *has* to work!'

'It will – but not for Eddie,' Nina realised. She pushed past Corazón and reached through the gate, grasping for the dagger. It was just beyond her outstretched fingertips. 'Shit! Corazón, you'll have to do it!'

The cult leader looked up at the snarling animal as it descended into the vestibule. 'No! Give me the dagger before the statue breaks it!'

'Mom, move!' said Macy. She took Nina's place. 'I can reach it!' She forced her arm as far through the bars as she could, clawing for Earthbreaker's hilt.

Eddie ducked lower as the golden jaguar bore down upon him. 'Macy, get back!'

'No!' She drove her slim shoulder through the barrier. 'I'm not – gonna – leave you!'

Her fingers reached the dagger.

She yelped at the static-like shock as she made contact – but kept hold. A hollow *thunk* came from the wall, followed by the rattle of a mechanism.

But still the jaguar didn't slow, coming lower, lower, fangs stabbing at Eddie as he dropped flat to the floor . . .

A loud metallic bang rolled through the chamber – and the great beast jarred to a stop.

Eddie cautiously looked up. The big cat's malevolent emerald eye stared back from less than a foot above him. 'Macy, are you okay?'

The jaguar's head was pressed against her outstretched arm. 'Yeah, I – I think so,' was her quavering reply.

Another loud mechanical clatter. The jaguar jolted, then started back to its original position. Macy hesitantly eased her hold on the dagger. When nothing happened, she released it and withdrew her arm.

'What happened?' Eddie asked. 'Why didn't it work the first time?'

'The green stone inside the slot,' Nina explained, 'it's the same material as Earthbreaker – and the map under Teotihuacán. They repel each other, like magnets when you try to push matching poles together. I saw it when Corazón first used Earthbreaker in the map room. He had to physically push it down to make contact. And the door at the Underworld's entrance worked the same way – there was a piece of green stone inside the lock that triggered the mechanism when it slid away from the dagger.'

'So it didn't work for me because it's another earth energy thing?'

She nodded. 'Something similar. Only certain people have the right DNA to channel it. It must have been passed down through all the Tekunis,' she nodded towards Corazón, 'for centuries.'

Corazón regarded mother and daughter calculatingly. 'And through your bloodline as well.' Behind him, Mancillo listened with interest.

'All the way back from Atlantis, and beyond.'

Macy eyed their captor with distaste. 'So we're, like, distant cousins? Ew.'

Further discussion was cut off as the raised gate lowered. This time, the gate blocking the exit also swung downwards with a shrill of metal. Nina hurried in to help Eddie. 'Are you all right?'

'Yeah,' he replied – surreptitiously passing her the replica of Earthbreaker. 'Hide it, might be useful,' he whispered. She kept her back to the cultists as she slipped it into her bag.

Corazón advanced behind her. She tensed, but he was only interested in the real Earthbreaker, pulling the dagger from the slot. Nina cringed, looking up at the looming figure of the Jaguar God, but it remained still. 'Okay, so now we know what your stories meant,' she told him. 'Someone who can use the dagger can also deactivate the traps – the challenges.'

'Wait, *traps*, plural?' said Macy.

'These things never bloody come on their own,' Eddie said, standing. 'Trust me. They're like Pringles. Someone has one, they can't resist another.'

'It's true, unfortunately,' Nina confirmed. 'But at least we know we can get through them now. Corazón just has to solve the puzzles and then use Earthbreaker to open the exits.'

The cult leader gave her a humourless chuckle. 'Not quite, Professor Wilde. *You* will solve the puzzles. The stories did not tell me how to pass the challenges. That is your task.' He turned to Macy. 'And *yours* will be to open the way with Earthbreaker.'

Macy stared at him, wide-eyed. 'What? Why me?'

'Because with you and your father facing each challenge,' a cold smile, 'that will give your mother a very big incentive to find the right answers.'

22

Another tunnel led out of the chamber. Now forewarned about further traps ahead, everyone's movement was far more cautious. Corazón no longer led from the front, instead putting Nina, Eddie and Macy into the lead. Two armed men immediately behind them deterred any thoughts of flight.

Nina had no intention of running, though. Charging into the unknown was a sure-fire way of getting hurt – or killed. She maintained a steady pace, flashlight sweeping the walls, floor and ceiling. More reliefs adorned the passage. The images became increasingly disturbing. Scenes of conquest, slaughter . . . and mass human sacrifice. The empire of Teotihuacán had not taken control of new regions through reasoned debate. It had conquered, subjugated and killed. Anyone who resisted was either massacred in battle, or brought as a prisoner to the Pyramid of the Sun, there to be stabbed, gutted, dismembered – and devoured. The Jaguar God's ancient followers believed that by eating the flesh and organs of those they had defeated, they would gain new strength.

The same was true of their present-day descendants. The more gruesome and bloody the images became, the more enthused Corazón grew, stopping to point out particularly vivid scenes to his followers – who reacted with equal energy, their chants echoing through the tunnel.

'This is sick,' Macy whispered to her parents. 'What the hell is wrong with these people? Corazón was brought up with it his whole life, I can kind of get that. But Rosamaria? She's smart, she's educated, I'm guessing she used to be a pretty devout

Catholic. So how did she fall into this?'

'Loss and grief can really mess people up,' Nina said unhappily. Rosamaria was chanting with as much fervour as Corazón himself. 'Her husband died, leaving a huge void that I guess the Church didn't fill . . . and Corazón and his cult found her when she was at her most vulnerable.'

'Diego doesn't seem to be a part of it, though.' Macy watched the young Mexican. His expression was troubled, and he appeared to be miming, as if he didn't know the words.

'He's only a boy. And I think Rosamaria's protecting him to some extent,' said Nina thoughtfully. 'Maybe he hasn't been indoctrinated into the cult yet.'

'I really hope not.'

Corazón ended his ritual, turning to his unwilling scouts. 'Keep moving. The next challenge can't be far ahead.'

'It'd help if we had some idea what it might be,' Nina said as they set off. 'We've met the Jaguar God. Who else is there?'

'The closest allies of Tekuazotl are Mitlancali, the Bird Goddess, and Qu'kamotz, the Snake God,' he replied. 'The stories said we will face their challenges as well.'

'Qu'kamotz?' muttered Eddie. 'Sounds like Klingon.'

'Mitlancali is the real name of what most archaeologists who have studied Teotihuacán call the Great Goddess,' said Rosamaria. 'There are several frescoes of her in the city. She is also called the Spider Goddess, because there are spiders with her in the pictures. But Tekuni knows the truth, of course.'

'Of course,' was Nina's snippy reply. 'But the truth doesn't say how to get through their challenges, right?'

Macy hurriedly took out her phone. 'Wait, wait – bird and snake deities? There were pictures of them with the Jaguar God!' She brought up her selfie from beneath the Pyramid of the Sun. 'There!'

Nina stopped to see. Macy was right: two of the murals in the background were indeed a snake, and a woman in an elaborate bird-like headdress. 'Zoom in.'

The first image she enlarged was the snake. 'I'm not keen on that,' Eddie rumbled. It portrayed a giant stylised constrictor, its body surrounding a human figure with limbs protruding help-lessly from the crushing coils. 'What are those things around it? A zodiac or something?'

'Other gods of the Teotihuacanos,' said Rosamaria, indicating a circle of pictographs. There were twelve in all, each representing a different animal.

'Part of the challenge?' Nina wondered.

'Show me the Bird Goddess,' demanded Corazón.

Macy scrolled the picture. The figure that came into view was a sitting humanoid, bare-breasted, partially shrouded in a long cloak of green and red feathers. Her face, though, was a bird's, with a hooked yellow beak and round, staring eyes. Her tall headdress was also feathered, but with much longer plumage. The thick quills intertwined with each other to form a tangled, complex web. Not all of it was visible, however; Macy's head covered part of its right side.

'No extra markings,' said Nina, examining it. 'None that we can see, at least.' Macy gave her an apologetic look. She turned to Corazón. 'How are we supposed to figure out how to get through the challenges?'

'I'm sure survival instinct will concentrate your mind,' was his arrogant reply. 'Keep moving.'

The passage, which had run level for some way, began to slope gently downwards. Before long, it ended at a set of heavy stone pillars. Nina shone her flashlight over their carvings. 'Snakes,' she reported.

Eddie grinned. 'Why did it have to be—'

'Ah-ah.' Nina held up a finger. 'We don't want to violate anyone's copyright, do we?'

Macy sighed. 'I don't know what you two are talking about, and I probably won't want to.'

Corazón arrived behind them. 'It must be the challenge of Qu'kamotz,' he announced. 'Go in.'

'How about we see what we're dealing with before marching into a booby trap, huh?' Nina replied. She leaned through the opening, seeing only stone walls ahead before angling her beam downwards. 'Okay, there's a chamber below – it looks flooded, can't tell how deep the water is.' She crouched for a better view. The walls curved away from rungs carved into the wall directly below the entrance. 'It's circular or oval, not very big.' Something set into the stonework drew her gaze. 'And there's . . . I don't know, some kind of chains, perhaps? They're running around the wall.'

'Can't see a way out from here,' said Eddie.

'Then go down and look,' Corazón ordered coldly. 'You and the girl.'

'I'm not "the girl",' Macy snapped. 'I hate that. It's so reductive.'

'Move!' shouted Corazón. One of the guards jabbed his rifle at them.

'Give me the goddamn dagger, then!' she replied. 'I can't get through the challenge without it, can I?'

The cult leader's face was a portrait of barely restrained fury, but he handed Earthbreaker to her, hilt first. 'If it is damaged, I will kill you and your family,' he said with level menace.

'If it's damaged, it won't stop the trap, so I'll be dead before you get the chance,' Macy fired back.

'Give me your torch, love,' Eddie said to Nina.

She passed it over. 'I'd say be careful, but I know you will anyway.'

'With Macy with me? Bloody right I will.' He kissed her, then one of the cultists shoved them apart. 'All right, you twat, I'm going.' He and Macy went to the top of the shaft. 'I'll go first,' he told her. 'If it looks like I'm about to get shut in, you go back up, fast as you can.'

She gestured with Earthbreaker. 'But then you won't be able to get out.'

'Have to chance it. I'm not having anything happen to you.' He swept the torch around the space below, then warily descended the stone ladder.

Faint sounds reached him: the quiet tinkle of dripping water. He paused, twisting around to view the whole chamber. As Nina had thought, it was oval. 'There's a way out at the other end,' he reported. 'Can't get through it, though.' More carved rungs led to a second opening in the ceiling, but it was blocked by a metal grate.

Another feature in the roof caught his eye – and raised his alert level. Between the two vertical shafts was a concave indentation, a dark hole at its centre. The end of a chain ran from it to join near the second ladder with what Nina had seen. It was a long line of silvery metal rods, each around a foot in length and two inches thick, linked together at each end. They were marked with zigzag patterns. At first glance he thought there were several ranks of them around the chamber's perimeter, but then he realised there was only one, spiralling down from the ceiling to disappear into the water below. At numerous points, it passed through chunky metal rings set into the wall.

He relayed his findings. 'Part of the trap, you reckon?' he asked Nina.

'It has to be,' she replied. 'I've got no idea how it works, though.'

Macy did, however, and the thought made her nervous. 'It . . . kinda looks like a snake. Like the one in the photo, crushing that guy?'

Eddie took a closer look at the metal serpent. It was set into a groove carved in the wall. He cautiously hooked his little finger around the joint between two of the rods and gently pulled. They moved fairly easily. The channel in the stone behind them was smooth, almost polished, as if to let them slide easily. 'However it works, let's try not to set it off.' He continued his descent until he reached the final rung above the water.

'How deep is it?' Macy asked from above him.

'Not sure.' He aimed the light straight down. 'Have you got a coin or something?'

She put Earthbreaker inside a recess and held on with one hand, rooting through her pockets with the other. 'Yeah, a quarter.'

'Drop it into the water.' She did so. A faint silver reflection came back to him in the torch beam. 'It's not that deep. About a foot.'

'Careful,' Nina warned as he lowered one leg. 'Your weight might trigger it.'

'If it's going to, it's going to,' he said with resignation. 'Macy, get ready to climb back up.' He stepped off the ladder.

Cold water swilled into his boots, but nothing happened. All the same, he scanned his surroundings cautiously before risking any more movement. Whatever triggered the trap, he hadn't reached it – yet. 'Okay,' he said, slowly turning in place, 'now what?'

Macy retrieved the dagger and followed him down, stopping above the water. 'Let me have another look at the picture.' She switched the dagger awkwardly with her phone.

'Be easier if you stepped off there, love,' Eddie told her.

She looked unhappily at her canvas shoes. The expedition's gear had included sturdy walking boots, but Macy hadn't changed into hers before the ill-fated flight. 'Do I have to?'

'Unless you can walk on the ceiling, then yes.'

She cringed, then reluctantly stepped down. 'Ew, oh, it's freezing!'

'Could be worse; could be snake pee,' said Eddie. Macy gave him an annoyed frown. 'There, that took your mind off it. So what are we supposed to do in here?'

She brought up the picture on her phone. 'Okay, we've got the zodiac thing around the Snake God. But none of the animals are marked, so there must be some other clue.' She scrolled around the image. 'Oh, oh! Look! Across the bottom.' She pointed out a detail. 'A line of animal symbols – a fish, a lizard and a snake. They're in the zodiac as well.'

'If it works like the first challenge, maybe that's the order you have to put Earthbreaker into the slots,' Nina suggested from above.

'So where *are* the slots?' asked Eddie. He ran his torch around the room, but saw nothing.

Macy looked more closely at one of the duplicate icons. 'Actually . . . I don't think that is a lizard. Look at these frilly things behind its head. It's an axolotl!' She thought for a moment. 'Fish, axolotl, snake – they can all swim. Maybe the slots are in the water.'

Eddie looked down. 'They're in the pool? How are we supposed to see them?'

His daughter's gaze flicked between the screen and the chamber's wall. 'If this chain thing is the snake, then its head is . . . there.' She pointed to where the spiralling line of rods met the chain running from the hole above. The last segment had different markings to the others: the metal slightly flattened to resemble a head, circles suggesting eyes. 'So if that matches the position of the snake on the mural – we'll call it twelve o'clock – somewhere in line with it there should be a snake marking.'

Eddie aimed his light at the pool's surface, but the water's murkiness made it impossible to pick out anything below. 'Still can't see anything . . . Hang on, I've had an idea.'

'Did it hurt?'

He gave a tired smile at the much-overused joke. 'Is your phone waterproof?'

'Yes,' Macy replied, following with a suddenly wary, 'why?'

'Let me borrow it.'

'*Why?*' From her tone, it was as if he'd asked to borrow a limb.

'So I can use it to see what's down there.'

'Why can't you use *your* phone?'

'What, my steam-powered one that goes funny in the rain?'

She acknowledged his point with bad grace. 'Okay. But *I'll* do it, okay?'

'Why, you got something on there you don't want me to see?'

'No!' was the slightly too forceful reply.

Eddie grinned as Macy, scowling, activated the phone's camera and inverted it, dipping the lenses into the pool while keeping most of the screen above the surface.

The phone's view of the chamber floor was far clearer. Macy slowly swept it from side to side. 'Give me more light,' she said, taking a cautious step forward. Eddie moved the torch to comply. 'Yeah, look – there's something there!'

Revealed on the screen was a symbol carved into a flagstone: a stylised serpent. 'And there's where to put the dagger,' she added excitedly, picking out a slot cut into the floor beneath the image.

'Well, let's not rush into that,' said Eddie. He looked back up at the snake's head. 'So where are the things we need on the zodiac?'

Macy compared the line of three icons to the ring of symbols. 'Four o'clock, then nine, then twelve – which is the one we already found. That's assuming the order runs from left to right.'

'Do you know if it does?' said Eddie.

'Ah . . . nope.' She chewed her lip in concern.

'It probably does,' Nina called down to them. 'All the ancient cultures that worked right to left in their ideographies were in the Middle East or Asia. Everything known in the Americas worked left to right.'

'Everything *known*, eh?' Eddie echoed pointedly.

Rosamaria leaned around Nina. 'She is right. I have never seen anything to suggest the Teotihuacanos worked any other way.'

Corazón moved her aside to shout an impatient order. 'Find the right slots and use Earthbreaker. We are wasting time.'

'Okay, okay,' said Macy, adding under her breath, 'asshole.'

She and Eddie started the search of the oval room's four o'clock position. 'By the way,' Eddie said quietly, 'I was really proud of you when you stood up to him.'

Genuine delight blossomed on her face. 'You were? Oh, thanks!' She looked suddenly apprehensive. 'I was really scared right after I said it,' she admitted. 'He looked so mad, I thought he was going to kill me. Or you, or Mom.'

'Sometimes you just have to give dickheads like him some lip. They deserve it; knocks them down a peg. And occasionally they get angry enough to make mistakes. It's got me and your mum out of trouble a few times.'

'Really?'

'Got the crap kicked out of me a few other times as well,' he added with a shrug. 'But at least they didn't have it all their own way.' Father and daughter exchanged smiles. 'Ay up. Is that it?'

The screen revealed a carved fish beneath the water. 'That's it!' said Macy. 'That's where we start.'

'Good,' Corazón said. 'Now, use Earthbreaker.'

Nina gave him a scathing look. 'It might be a good idea if they found the other slot *before* activating the trap?'

'They know where to look. Do it! Now!'

Eddie faced Macy. 'Think you can find the last one?'

She drew in a breath. 'Yeah.'

'Okay. Let's do it.' More quietly, he added: 'If it all goes wrong, snap that fucking thing in half to stop him using it.'

'Dad, watch your language,' she said, managing a small smile. 'You find the axolotl. I'll put the dagger in.'

Eddie took the phone and reluctantly sloshed across the chamber to look for the axolotl carving. Macy probed with her free hand to find the slot under the fish, then readied Earthbreaker. A faint, vaguely uncomfortable feeling had run through her hand the whole time she'd held it, whatever power it channelled reaching her at a low level. She suspected it would become more intense when she made contact with the challenge's final lock.

But before then, she had to open the first one. She lowered the stone blade into the water and carefully slipped it into the slot—

A moment of resistance – then something moved beneath it.

A dull *thump* came from below the floor, a few escaping bubbles rising around her hand. Progressively louder and heavier noises followed, a domino effect of moving weights shifting others—

Metal screeched above – and a gate swung down from above the archway at the top of the ladder. Nina and the others at the entrance had barely a second's warning to jump back before it slammed shut. The redhead gasped, then pushed at the new barrier. It didn't move.

Macy hurriedly withdrew the dagger as the ominous sounds continued. 'Uh, Dad, you found that axolotl yet? Because I kinda think we need to hurry up . . .'

A new metallic rattle, directly above – and the snaking line of silver rods started to retract into the hole in the ceiling.

Eddie looked up in alarm as the chain disappeared, segment by segment. Below, the rest of the spiralling serpent scraped through the rings in the wall – pulling the uppermost one outwards. He snapped his torch beam onto it. The ring formed the end of a metal pole, gradually extending further from the wall. From the way it was resisting the chain's pull, there was a spring or counterweight trying to haul it back. As he watched, the tightening chain began to tug a second ring from its resting place.

He realised with a chill what was happening. The spiral formed by the snake would get tighter and tighter as more of it was drawn up through the ceiling – with him and Macy inside. And when it reached a certain point . . .

They would be crushed.

23

'kay,' Eddie said, hurriedly aiming his torch back at the water, 'better find that axolotl!'

Macy splashed towards him, watching fearfully as he dipped her phone below the surface. 'It's got to be there somewhere; it was definitely at nine o'clock on the mural – there, there! Go back!'

Eddie moved the device through the water. A carving on the stone floor came into view. 'Is that an axolotl? Looks more like a dinosaur with antlers.'

'That'd be a horned lizard, and they don't have them in Central America!' Macy replied, with a distinctly *ugh, Dad* under-tone. Above them, the silver constrictor continued to unwind from the wall. Horrible shrills of metal echoed through the confined space – which became more confining with every passing moment. 'Okay, where's the slot?'

'Here, it's here!' said Eddie, spotting the opening between the carved axolotl's feet.

Macy drove the dagger into it. She felt a vibration through the weapon's hilt as something jolted beneath it. The second lock releasing – if she was right about the combination. If not, at the rate the snake was tightening, she and her father had less than a minute to live . . .

Eddie was already moving back to the chamber's far end. 'I'll find the last one!'

Macy yanked Earthbreaker out and followed as he thrust the phone into the water. They had both been bending down to see what was under the surface – but now they had no choice. The chain pulled ever tighter above them, leaving no room to stand.

'Can you see it?' she asked.

'Not yet,' he replied. Their movements had churned up sediment in the water, the phone's view now obscured by a brown fog. 'Arse! We'll have to feel for it.' He gave the phone back to Macy and dropped both hands into the water, groping across the flagstones. 'Where is the bloody thing?'

'We had it a minute ago!' Macy cried. Another loop of the snake separated from the wall at her eye level, dragging a guide ring with it. The retracting chain formed a conical space, getting lower and narrower every second. 'Dad, we're running out of room!'

'We'll find it, love,' said Eddie, trying to sound confident. 'We'll find – wait, here!' His fingertips brushed over complex grooves in the stone. 'Got the snake!'

'Where's the slot?'

'Yeah, give me a second, I'm working on it.'

'We don't *have* a second!'

Eddie was forced to duck his head lower as the closing coil scraped against it. 'You sound just like your mum!'

'I'm gonna take that as a compliment.' She ran her own fingers across the floor – finding a straight line cut into it. 'I got it!'

Eddie tried to retreat, but found his path blocked by the tightening metal coils. 'Get that bloody knife in there,' he urged.

Macy bent lower and pushed Earthbreaker into the slot. It went in for several inches—

Then stopped.

She pushed harder. The blade sank a fraction lower, but there was a rasping resistance. 'It won't go in! Something's stuck in the slot!'

Eddie dropped to his knees as the chain spiralled tighter above his head. 'Then clear it out, love – sharpish!'

She withdrew the dagger slightly, then worked its point from side to side. It caught against something. A piece of grit was wedged inside; only small, but it was enough to block the blade.

Her panic rose as the snake wound ever more closely around them. The obstruction refused to shift. 'Oh shit, shit, it's not moving!'

Eddie extended his arms and grabbed the snake, trying to force the chain wider. It was no use. The weight pulling it tight was irresistible, too much to withstand using muscle power alone. 'You'll have to *make* it move!'

Teeth clenched, she desperately sawed at the stone, feeling Earthbreaker's edge grind against it. The coils finally reached her, forcing her to edge backwards – meeting Eddie as he was pushed forwards. 'Shit, *shit!*'

'Macy!' Nina screamed, beating her fists uselessly against the gate above. 'Eddie, *Macy!*'

The coils tightened around Macy's chest—

The pebble jolted loose.

She scraped it out of the slot – then thrust Earthbreaker back in as hard as she could.

Fear shot through her as she felt resistance again. The slot was still blocked! But this was different, as if something was pushing *back*—

Then contact was made.

An electric jolt of power hit her. Whatever was at the bottom gave way with a muffled *clonk*, the counter-pressure vanishing . . .

A louder noise somewhere above – and the silver snake clattered to a halt.

Macy drew in a relieved breath, only to find herself so constricted her inhalation was stopped halfway. Her father was squashed awkwardly against her back. Seconds passed, but their prison remained still. 'Okay,' she whispered, 'so did we beat it, or was the designer just a sadistic asshole?'

To their relief, a moment later a raucous metallic rattle echoed through the chamber. The pressure around them eased – and the metal poles bearing the guide rings slowly retracted into the wall, pulling the snaking chain with them. The segments that had disappeared through the hole in the ceiling scraped back into view as the trap gradually reset.

The gate barring the entrance swung back upwards – and its counterpart blocking the exit did the same. Eddie and Macy sloshed towards it. The moment the snake had withdrawn enough for them to reach the ladder, they scrambled up it. 'Are you okay?' Nina called, voice shaky.

'We're fine, Mom,' Macy replied as she clambered from the chamber. 'Just a bit fusilli-shaped.'

A low thump echoed through the underground space as the great chain stopped moving, back in its original position. Nina was about to descend when Corazón pushed in front of her. 'The way is clear,' he announced imperiously. 'We can move on.'

'You're welcome,' came Macy's deeply sarcastic voice from ahead.

The Mexican descended into the waterlogged room. Macy had left Earthbreaker in the slot. He retrieved it. The trap did not restart; Nina guessed a manual reset was needed to prime it again. She waited for Rosamaria and Diego to go down the ladder, then followed. Behind, she heard Mancillo protest to his captors. With their hands bound behind their backs, the Kaibiles couldn't negotiate the rungs. Corazón issued an obviously reluctant order to untie the prisoners.

If Mancillo and his men had hoped to take advantage of their freedom, they were disappointed. They were tracked by guns the whole time as they went through the chamber, only to be immediately restrained again at the top of the second ladder. The look Mancillo gave Nina, though, told her he was still waiting to pounce upon the slightest opportunity to strike back against their captors.

Once everyone was through, the expedition moved deeper into the mountain. Nina was reunited with her family at the front. Macy was subdued, still trying to process the ordeal she had just endured. 'Are you sure you're okay?' Nina asked.

'Yeah,' was the muted reply.

'Because I know what it's like to go through something like that. Oh God, do I know what it's like.'

Eddie nodded. 'I'd known your mum for about five minutes before we were going through booby traps in the middle of the bloody Amazon jungle.'

Macy gave Nina a half-hearted smile. 'I know, Mom. I've read your books.'

Nina squeezed her hand. 'Just remember that if you ever need my help, I'm always here for you. Always.'

The smile widened. 'I know.'

Eddie slowed. 'Ay up. Think we've reached the next challenge.'

Ahead, more elaborate pillars flanked another opening. Nina paused; the air felt subtly different, a faint breeze touching her face. But how? They were now some distance underground . . .

Corazón was impatient to find out. 'Keep moving,' he said. 'This must be the challenge of Mitlancali.'

'The Bird Goddess?' said Eddie. 'Macy, see if she's on Twitter.' Macy groaned, but took out her phone.

Nina examined the picture. The mural was furthest from the camera, partially obscured by her daughter's head. 'Let's hope there isn't a vital clue hidden behind your ear.'

Macy snorted. 'Did you know it's possible for family reconciliations to be undone? Just saying.'

'Let me see,' said Corazón, taking hold of her wrist to pull the phone closer. 'There are no symbols, no keys,' he noted after a moment. 'Rosamaria, do you remember anything else from the Pyramid of the Sun?'

'No, Tekuni,' Rosamaria replied apologetically. 'That picture was the only one of the Great Goddess in the room.'

The cult leader stared irritably at the looming portal. 'Then we will have to find the way through the challenge as we go.' He turned to Nina. 'Lead on, Professor Wilde.'

'Yeah, no pressure,' was Nina's sardonic reply. She approached the opening cautiously. The pillars suggested that Corazón's assumption about the challenge's nature was correct; they were adorned with carvings of brightly painted birds, posed as if ushering visitors into whatever lay beyond.

A change in the echo of the group's footsteps told her that the next chamber was large – perhaps very large. She slowed, angling her flashlight downwards. More colourful carvings appeared on the stone floor beyond the pillars. 'It's Mitlancali,' she said, seeing a much larger version of the bird-faced visage from the mural in Macy's selfie. 'The Bird Goddess.'

Corazón's reaction was reverential. 'The last guardian of the afterlife,' he said, stopping at the entrance to gaze at the image. 'The one who guides the dead to judgement at the Temple of Tekuazotl.'

'That's what's through here?' Nina asked. She raised the flashlight – and blinked at what it revealed. 'I guess it's on the other side of *that*.'

The Bird Goddess was carved into a ledge over a deep rift in the mountain's heart. Hanging on chains from the ceiling some forty feet above were numerous circular platforms. More chains ran horizontally across the gap; five radiated outwards from the ledge at the top of Mitlancali's head, extending to a wider landing on the chasm's far side. Three more lines arced between them, forming a curved grid with a platform at each intersection.

The pattern created by the chains made Nina think of a

spider's web, the thought becoming all the more uncomfortable as she realised she was effectively at its heart. 'Bird Goddess . . . or Spider Goddess, right?' Rosamaria nodded.

Eddie's response to the sight was more practical. 'Some of 'em are broken,' he observed. A few of the chains linking the hanging platforms dangled down into the abyss below. 'So how do we get across?'

'I don't know,' said Nina. 'The challenge might be purely physical, being able to climb across on the chains, but . . . that wouldn't really fit with the others. They needed the knowledge from the chamber under the Pyramid of the Sun – you *had* to be a part of the priesthood of Tekuazotl to have a chance of getting through them. If you hadn't seen the murals and understood the clues, you were almost certainly going to die.'

'But there *are* no clues,' said Diego. 'There weren't any symbols on the picture of the Bird Goddess.'

'Unless the clue *is* the picture,' Macy suggested.

Corazón stepped up behind her, impatient. 'We need to cross it. Get moving.'

Eddie exchanged looks with Nina, then cautiously advanced onto the ledge. 'Careful,' Macy warned.

'I think this part's safe,' said Nina. 'Unless the ancient Teotihuacanos were pissy about people stepping on the face of their goddess.'

Eddie stepped sharply sideways to avoid doing exactly that. Instead he peered over the edge. 'Long way down.'

Nina directed her light back across the cavern. Another passage led from the ledge opposite. 'That's where we have to reach . . .'

'So reach it,' said Corazón curtly. 'You, Chase – climb across.' The two guards aimed their guns at the Englishman.

'Yeah, I know the drill by now,' Eddie replied irritably. 'Do I get a rope or anything? Might be useful when everyone else follows me over.'

'If you make it across.' But the Mexican was forced to concede Eddie's point. One of his followers produced a coil of rope from a backpack.

Eddie took it, spotting a rock protruding upwards from the rear of the ledge. He secured the rope to it as best he could. 'Hope that'll hold,' he said as he looped the rest of the line around himself. 'Otherwise I'll be taking a trip to the under-Underworld.' He crouched to examine the central chain, taking an experimental tug at the links. They rattled, dust shaking loose. The hanging platform at the other end swung gently in response, the other chains connected to it clinking.

Nina shone her flashlight along them. 'Everything seems to be holding.'

'For now,' Eddie replied. A sour glance back at Corazón and his people, then: 'Better get moving, I suppose. Apparently taking over the world can't wait until after teatime.'

He lay down and took careful hold of the chain with both hands, pulling himself along, then rolled beneath it to wrap his legs over its top. The chain pulled taut under his weight, but held. The platform swung towards him until the other chains reached their limit and jerked it to a stop, clanging and clattering. Nina drew in a fearful breath, but the ancient metalwork held.

Eddie advanced slowly. The first length of chain was some twenty feet long. He was an experienced climber, and traversed the distance easily. He peered up at the platform as he neared it. 'You'll definitely need the rope to get across,' he reported. 'I'll be able to climb up there, but I'm not sure everyone else—'

The metal eye attaching the chain to the platform snapped – and he fell.

24

Eddie dropped helplessly into the dark chasm below—

He was still gripping the chain. It yanked taut, rasping painfully through his hands – until he lost his hold. But that was enough to slow him before the rope also jerked tight, swinging him back towards the wall.

He hit hard, pain driving through his left shoulder. The broken chain smacked against him like a whip. But he didn't fall.

'Eddie!' Nina cried above. He struggled to look up. The plunge had left him hanging inverted, the rope constricting his chest and waist. A torch beam dazzled him. 'Oh, Jesus! Eddie, are you okay?'

'Been better,' he rasped. 'Pull me up!'

A pause as Nina convinced Corazón to help – then the line juddered, hands taking hold. Straining for breath as the rope drew tighter, Eddie was hauled upwards. Someone grabbed his legs and dragged him back on to the ledge. He rolled over, seeing Diego helping Nina, Macy and a couple of reluctant-looking cultists bring him to safety. 'Thanks,' he gasped.

Nina loosened the rope. 'Are you all right?'

He gingerly raised his left arm. Pain crackled through the shoulder joint. But nothing was broken; he'd been lucky. 'Think so,' he said with a grimace. 'What happened?'

'The chain broke.'

'Yeah, I noticed. But why? It was absolutely fine until I was almost at the platform, everything was taking my weight, then suddenly – snap!'

Macy regarded the web of rattling chains. 'That must be the challenge – the trap. There's some secret way over, and if you don't know it . . .'

'You fall,' said Nina. 'Macy, let me see that picture again.' Macy showed her the phone. She zoomed in on the head of the Bird Goddess – specifically its top, where the long quills extended up from her headdress. 'Five feathers on her head,' she said, counting them, 'and five chains crossing the gap from this ledge where she's painted. I doubt that's a coincidence.'

'What does it mean?' Corazón demanded.

'I think it shows the way over – if you know how to follow it.' She examined the tangle of feathers more closely. Each was a different colour. They passed over and under each other . . . with one exception, pale yellow, which always crossed on top of the rest. 'It's like a maze. You follow the only unbroken path until you reach the end.'

'That's it?' Macy sounded almost disappointed. 'After all the stuff you've dealt with before, I was expecting to have to identify prime numbers or something.'

'A puzzle that might seem simple to us would be really difficult to a civilisation that didn't commonly use the symbology. Besides, the solution to this one was kept restricted; only the priests of Tekuazotl could see the mural containing it. Anyone else who got this far would have to use trial and error.'

'And they only got to make one error,' said Eddie. 'What's the right way over, then?'

Nina compared the image on the screen to what lay before them. 'We start at the far left chain. Then we go forward to the first platform, then right, forward again, then keep heading right until . . . ah.'

Macy winced. 'Oops. Sorry.' The rightmost side of the mural disappeared behind her grinning face in the selfie.

The yellow feather reappeared on the next line up, sweeping

all the way back across until turning upwards – and opening out in a peacock-like fan rather than clenching shut at the end like the others. 'There are only two vertical lines we can't see,' said Nina, scrutinising the picture. 'So you either go all the way to the right-hand side and then forward, or you go up the one before it. That narrows things down a lot.'

'But not enough,' said Diego, moving alongside Macy to look at the phone. 'If it's another trap, then you've got a fifty-fifty chance of setting it off.'

'I've had worse odds,' said Eddie. He went to the leftmost chain and gave it a firm pull. It held. 'So this is the way?'

'If my theory's correct, yes,' Nina told him.

'They usually are,' he said, managing a smile. She returned it. 'All right. Take two. But get ready to catch me a bit sooner, okay?'

Diego took hold of the rope behind him. Corazón glanced at him, then, with a dismissive nod, ordered the two cultists to join him.

Eddie began his traversal, more slowly than his first attempt. When he drew close to the platform, he paused to test the metal eye, then the wood into which it was driven, for signs of weakness. There were none that he could find. Holding his breath, he brought himself along the last length of the chain . . .

And reached the hanging platform.

He pulled himself onto it. 'One down,' he said. 'Only eight or nine to go.'

'Eight or ten,' Nina corrected.

'Be good if I knew whether it *was* eight or ten.'

'I know. Okay, go across to the right, then forward.'

'That makes it sound so bloody easy!' He carefully negotiated the circular platform to the next length of chain.

This too remained secure as he traversed it, as did the next. 'This is a bit too straightforward,' he told Nina. 'Where's the trap?'

'If you're on the right path, there isn't one,' she assured him. 'It's the part we couldn't see on the mural where it gets worrying. You should be okay until you get to the second-last platform. After that, you either go forward, or you go to the last platform and *then* go forward.'

'Let's hope I guess right, then.' He reached the penultimate platform, then knelt to check each possible route, shaking the chains. They held in place. 'They both seem solid. But one of 'em's *got* to be rigged to break. How do I work out which?'

Macy went to the ledge's lip, staring intently at the platform where the first chain had broken loose. 'Mom, can you give me your flashlight?'

'What is it?' Nina asked, handing it to her.

She directed the beam at the eye set into the wood across the gap. 'Look, it's broken underneath – like a piece got snapped off. The metal looks thick at the side, but gets thinner as it goes around to the bottom.'

Nina saw what she meant. The ring was not a complete circle, but more like a crescent, the points not quite meeting. 'It broke because it was deliberately designed to have a weak spot,' she realised.

'Yeah,' said Macy. 'When it's just hanging normally, the weight of the chain's being taken at the side, where it's thicker. But when someone climbs across, the closer they get to the platform, the more they pull the chain downwards – and that's when the ring breaks!'

'Well done,' Nina said to her daughter, not hiding her pride. Macy beamed at her. 'Eddie, we've figured it out – I mean, *Macy* figured it out. The booby-trapped rings aren't complete circles, but have a little gap on the underside.'

Macy aimed the flashlight at the rightmost platform on Eddie's row. The ring appeared to be complete. For comparison, she redirected the beam to a closer wooden disc – and saw a difference right away. 'That one's rigged!' she said. 'Look, there's a space at the bottom.'

'I see it,' Eddie told her. 'You say the first one's solid?'

'Yes.'

'Your mum's not the only person I trust to be right,' he said. Her smile returned. 'Okay, I'm going for it.'

He began the crossing. The chain clanked and shuddered with his weight – but held. He blew out a relieved breath as he clambered onto the wooden plate. 'You were right, love – thanks,' he said to Macy. 'I would've taken the shorter route if you hadn't told me. Good job my daughter's as smart as my wife.'

'Well, she had to get her brains from somewhere,' said Nina, grinning.

He mouthed something that she was certain was rude, then climbed across to the last row. From there he went back to the left, pausing to check the ring connecting the suspect chain to the earlier platform. It did indeed have a small gap on its underside, the metal tapering to nothing. Macy had been correct. He continued along until he reached the last of the five platforms, then – with a *hope you were right* look back at his family – traversed the final chain.

It held firm. He was soon on the far ledge. 'Thank fuck for that,' he said as he stood. 'All right, I'll tie the rope so everyone else can come across.'

He secured it to another protruding rock. Nina and Macy started to follow his path, but Corazón stopped them. 'My men first,' he said, '*then* you.'

'Still don't trust us, huh?' Nina retorted.

'The Dispossessed have been in hiding for fifteen centuries. We do not trust anyone.' He told the two guards to make the crossing. One kept his rifle trained on Eddie as his companion followed the rope, then made the journey himself.

Everyone else made their way over. Again the Kaibiles were

untied for the crossing, each man's bonds retied on the other side at the point of multiple guns.

Finally, the last cultist reached the far ledge. Corazón was already waiting impatiently near the exit. 'Now we will see what we have come for,' he told Nina.

'You're sure there aren't any more challenges?' she asked.

'We have faced everything from the stories passed down by the Tekuni before me. All that is left now is the temple of Tekuazotl – where I will reclaim my destiny.' He led the way into the new passage. 'Follow me, and you will be my witnesses!'

The cultists' cheers filled the tunnel as they forced their prisoners to march in their leader's wake.

25

The passage was not long, soon opening out into a larger space. Nina swept her flashlight beam around it. The chamber was a ragged teardrop within the rock, an opening high on its far side connecting to another void beyond. Again she felt a faint breeze on her face, air coming from the far side of the gap. She could also hear a low, echoing rumble – a waterfall.

But there was nothing here except a weaving pathway partially carved, partially worn from the stone floor – and at its end, a steep flight of stairs. They led to another tunnel. This was wider than the one they had just left, massive decorative pillars standing to each side.

'Tekuazotl,' said Corazón triumphantly. Oversized images of the Jaguar God adorned both hulking columns. 'This is his temple. We are here!'

He increased his pace. Everyone else hustled to keep up. Corazón took the stairs two at a time. He paused at the top to shout encouragement in Spanish to his followers. Even though she couldn't fully translate his words, Nina knew from his tone that he expected to reveal something incredible.

That turned out to be true. It was also something terrifying.

Corazón led the way into a new chamber. This was man-made, hewn from the mountain's innards. It was a broad rectangular space, the ceiling supported by rows of thick pillars much like those beneath the Pyramid of the Sun in shape.

In design, though, they were very different. Rather than stylised carvings of people and animals, these were covered in skulls.

Human skulls.

And they were not carvings. They were real.

Nina had seen displays of ancient bones before in her career, but the sheer scale of this made her briefly freeze with instinctual fear. There were hundreds of them – no, *thousands*, she realised as the flashlight beams probed deeper. Each pillar was completely covered in them, rank upon rank fixed in place with gritty mortar. The walls too were lined with the dead, rows of empty eye sockets staring across the room. Even some of the floor space was filled with the cult's victims; so-called 'skull racks' were common to several Mesoamerican cultures, stone pillars with metal rods running between them – upon which were impaled even more broken human heads. Each pillar was a blocky statue, savage animals devouring people. The entire chamber was a monument to violent, brutal death.

'Oh, Jesus,' Macy gasped as she saw the endless lines of remains. She clutched Nina's hand. 'Mom, I'm scared.'

'Yeah, honey,' Nina whispered. 'So am I.'

Corazón, though, was delighted by the horror before him. 'It's here!' he cried, looking back at Nina as he advanced into the room. 'The Temple of Tekuazotl – it is here! And it is intact!' He headed for the chamber's centre, where a feature rose from the floor. It was a ziggurat in miniature, a stepped ten-foot pyramid with a flat summit – upon which stood what Nina immediately guessed was a sacrificial altar. Skull-covered pillars rose to the ceiling at each corner of the rectangular platform. He climbed the steps, laying his hands upon the stone slab. 'Everything is exactly as my father told me, and his father told him. But I am the one who found it – I am the Tekuni who will bring my people back to power!'

'What're you going to do, throw skulls at everyone?' Eddie snarked.

'Dad,' Macy whispered, 'let's not antagonise the murderous

250

psychopath now he doesn't need us any more.'

Corazón responded with a malevolent smirk. 'I will show you. There is more to see than just the temple.' He ordered his followers to guard the Kaibiles, then gestured for Nina and her family to join him on the ziggurat. Their two armed guards came with them, as did Diego and Rosamaria.

The cult leader went to one of the pillars. Nina had by now noticed grooves cut into the floor; he moved to a sloping stone trough angling down from the pillar into one of them. At the trough's top, a stubby metal pipe protruded from between several skulls. 'Something else my father described,' said Corazón. He forced open a silver cap covering the pipe's end. A glutinous fluid ran out of it, flowing down the trough into the groove below, from where it began to follow the floor's gentle incline. He took out a lighter and clicked it on, holding it to the trough – and the liquid ignited with a dazzling flash, making everyone flinch back. It was oil, flickering orange flames rushing along the length of the ever-growing flow.

He called out to another cultist, who disappeared behind one of the larger pillars below. After a moment, more shimmering light began to fill the space. 'Oil reservoirs,' Corazón explained, indicating a large stone cistern set into the pillar's top. It disappeared into the ceiling, suggesting a larger reserve hidden above. 'The empire of Teotihuacán stretched into what is now Venezuela. My ancestors found deposits of oil so close to the surface it could be extracted by hand, and they brought it here to light the temple.' The man below lit a second trough of flowing oil, then another.

'Great, can't beat breathing in diesel fumes,' said Eddie.

Nina watched the smoke rise from the expanding fires – and saw it was not moving as she would have expected. 'I don't know – look, it's being drawn out through there.' There was another exit at the chamber's far end, a large opening flanked by more decorated pillars, and the swirling coils were moving towards it.

'Natural ventilation,' Corazón said. 'And it clears more than smoke. Come with me.' He sounded almost excited, as much wanting to share the revelation as gloat over it.

He lit a second oil cistern, then led them down the steps at the head of the ziggurat. More fires were lit below. Like the chambers beneath the Pyramid of the Sun in Mexico, the ceiling was coated with pyrites to reflect light. The glow from the lines of flames illuminated the entire room. There was not a single vertical surface not covered with skulls. The warmth of the fires did nothing to make the sight less chilling.

The exit to the next cavern was not far from the pyramid's base. Between the two was a large stone trough resembling an open sarcophagus. 'An offering trough,' said Rosamaria. 'The body parts of sacrificial victims were placed in it, so Tekuazotl's followers could eat them and gain their strength.' Macy made a retching sound.

The oil channels rounded the trough to reach each side of the exit, from where a flight of broad stone stairs led downwards. The slowly flowing liquid had not yet reached the steps, but was drawing closer. The noise of the waterfall was louder here, splashes echoing up from far below. 'This is what I came for,' said Corazón, stopping at the top. 'This is how I will restore my people to power.' The oil reached the incline and picked up speed, the travelling flames lighting up what lay below. 'I have Earthbreaker . . . and now I have *this*.'

Nina's eyes went wide as she saw what the fiery glow revealed.

It was a map, carved from green stone like the one beneath Teotihuacán – but larger. *Much* larger. That had been the size of a table. This would occupy a house, a sculpted landscape big enough to walk across. This time, she instantly recognised it as Central America – and beyond. Mercury seas marked the coasts of both North and South America, the former stretching well up the eastern and western seaboards, the latter reaching to what were now Ecuador and Guyana. Its sheer scope, well beyond anything previously known or even imagined for a Mesoamerican culture, immediately made her suspect it was of Atlantean origin; the Teotihuacanos had perhaps inherited it from their distant ancestors.

But there was even more to the map than she had first realised. As the burning oil descended, more of the new chamber was revealed. The map was merely the summit of something much bigger. An almost vertiginous feeling struck Nina as she looked down, as if she were standing at the top of a mountain – one of glistening green. A conical slope, hand-carved and polished higher up and rougher and raw some way below, descended into the depths of the towering void within the mountain. Somehow, she *felt* that it did not end there. It was merely the visible tip of a colossal mass, a stone iceberg extending deep into the earth . . .

Macy's fear was overcome by awe. 'Wow,' she said, astounded. 'What *is* this?'

'This,' said Rosamaria, 'is how the Teotihuacanos controlled their empire. They used Earthbreaker to cause earthquakes – anywhere on the map. Wherever the dagger touched, a quake would happen.'

A disbelieving frown formed on Eddie's face. 'Not wanting to say that's bollocks, because I've seen a lot of weird stuff in my life, but . . . *how?*'

'And if they could use the map under the pyramid,' Macy added, 'what was this one for?'

'They are connected – they are the *same*,' said Corazón. He pointed at the topographic expanse below. 'See there, in Mexico – where Teotihuacán would be?' Nina saw that a chunk had been removed from the giant map, leaving a roughly oval hole like the site of an extracted tooth. 'The other map was cut from this one and transported to the Pyramid of the Sun. But they are all still the same stone – linked on a quantum level.'

Nina raised an eyebrow. 'So you're a slaughterhouse owner with a sideline in quantum physics?'

He gave her a cold stare. 'People often make the mistake of thinking that because of my family's business, I am uneducated, or stupid. It is sometimes the last mistake they ever make. Remember that, Professor Wilde.' He turned back to the wonder below. 'It is the theory of quantum entanglement – that a part of something reacts to an event in the same way as the whole, even if it is separated.'

'Spooky action at a distance, Einstein called it,' Macy piped up. 'He was mocking the idea, but it turns out it was real. It happens instantly, no matter how far apart the two linked things are, even if that means breaking the speed of light.' Everyone looked at her. 'What? Hey, I'm not stupid either. I like finding out about crazy stuff.'

'So this,' said Nina, indicating the giant rock below, 'is a single object – and the map from Teotihuacán behaves as if it had never been removed?' The cult leader nodded. 'So how does Earthbreaker fit in? Is that part of the same whole too?'

'That, I don't know,' he admitted. 'The dagger is so old, even my people did not know its full history. It is the same substance as the map, but ... *inverted*. Something to do with the energy that flows through it, perhaps. When it is brought to the map – either map – it is pushed away. But when they finally touch ...'

'Boom,' Nina finished for him. 'The energy is channelled by the person holding it and focused on the point where Earthbreaker touches the map, and somehow that energy is ... magnified, I guess, and transmitted through the whole of the stone.'

'How does that work?' said Eddie, still dubious.

'Same way that every point on a map has an exact equivalent on the ground. But this particular map spans two continents.'

'So how big *is* the stone?' Diego asked.

'Huge,' Corazón replied. 'I have secretly paid for geological surveys – shear-wave analysis, gravimetric scans. We are standing on an object that descends hundreds of kilometres into the earth, and is *thousands* across. It may not even be from this world. One theory is that it is the remains of another planet that smashed into the earth early in its formation. That would account for what it can do.'

Nina nodded. 'We've seen meteorites with unusual properties before. Nothing on this scale, though.'

Corazón seemed surprised, but also pleased at her understanding. 'Touch Earthbreaker to a point at its top, and the effect travels through it to the same equivalent point at the bottom – growing in power as it goes. Then the energy is released on whatever is directly above.'

'Causing an earthquake,' said Nina.

'Earth energy again, eh?' Eddie said. 'You know, the world'd be a much safer place if the Atlanteans had never bloody discovered it. How many times have we found something powered by it that's almost got us killed?'

'I don't know, Five? Six?' Nina offered. 'I think we've had more trouble with evil billionaires. But this is more powerful than anything we've seen before, even what was hidden in Australia. It could destroy a whole *country*.'

'And it will – unless the governments surrender their power to me,' said Corazón, descending the stairs. The others followed him. The lines of burning oil had now reached the map, draining down channels cut into the sloping peak. 'I am Tekuni, heir to the empire of Teotihuacán – the true ruler of all these lands.' He swept out a hand to encompass the sculpted region below.

'Do you think they will just *give* power to you?' echoed

Mancillo's mocking voice. Corazón's followers were as eager to see the cavern's secrets as their leader, and had come to the entrance, bringing their captives with them.

Corazón's tone was equally sarcastic. 'No. I don't. So I will use this,' he held up Earthbreaker, 'to demonstrate what will happen if they do not obey me.'

'You already gave a demonstration,' Macy said, alarmed. 'In Mexico. You destroyed Teotihuacán – and killed thousands of people!' Diego seemed equally shocked by his father-figure's destructive plan.

'Nobody will believe I caused that earthquake.' Corazón reached the foot of the staircase, stepping onto the map. 'But if I tell them a quake will occur at an exact time and an exact place, and it then happens . . . they will not be able to deny it. They will *have* to give in to my demands. Because if they do not, I will destroy them.'

Nina halted on the steps, regarding the mercury pools warily. Natural evaporation over time had caused the quicksilver seas to retreat from the shorelines, but there was still a considerable amount remaining. Mercury vapour was heavier than air, so would have sunk to the bottom of the great chasm, and the ventilation to the surface, presumably via the channel through which the waterfall was flowing, would also help clear the atmosphere, but she still didn't like the idea of being in close proximity to the liquid metal. 'I don't think your job as the new ruler of Mexico will get off to a good start if you've just killed a lot of Mexicans.'

'Mexico?' he scoffed. 'I am not thinking so small, Professor Wilde.' He indicated various parts of the jade landscape. 'Venezuela. Colombia. Brazil. Even,' he gave her a nasty smile, 'the United States. I can use any of them to show Earthbreaker's power – *my* power.' He walked across the map, heading through Mexico towards the southern edge of North America. 'Geography is not my speciality, but I think this covers Los Angeles . . .

Miami . . . Washington.' The dagger pointed in the direction of each city in turn, before he aimed it at the map's very edge. 'Perhaps even New York. Any of those would make a good demonstration, don't you think?'

'You're crazy,' was all Nina could say in reply.

His face hardened. 'Thousands of years ago, the enemies of Teotihuacán all believed they could not be conquered. But they fell. It has happened before – it will happen again. The old ways, the *true* ways, will return. And *I* will bring them back.' He returned to the staircase, gesturing for those at its foot to head back upwards. The two guards forced Nina, Eddie and Macy to obey. 'Beginning now.'

'What do you mean?' Eddie demanded.

Corazón did not reply until the group was almost at the top of the stairs. 'My ancestors always held a ritual before using Earthbreaker,' he said. 'An offering to the Jaguar God.' The altar within the temple came into view as he spoke; Nina realised his meaning and whirled to face him. 'A *sacrifice*,' he said, in cruel triumph – before shouting a command.

Several cultists rushed to grab Nina and Eddie. Eddie resisted, smashing an elbow into one man's face. The man reeled backwards into a skull rack. Ancient bones smashed, pieces cascading across the floor. Eddie spun, punching another man – but then a rifle butt clubbed him savagely to the flagstones.

Two more men seized Macy. 'Mom! Dad!' she cried, struggling to break free. Her captors were too strong; instead she lashed out a foot, trying to catch one in the groin. The cultist twisted just in time to take the strike on his thigh, but still grunted in pain. The other man slapped her hard across the face and hissed an angry insult in Spanish.

'*No, que estas haciendo?*' shouted Diego, rushing to them. He tried to pull Macy away, but the first man shoved him back, making him fall.

'Diego!' Corazón barked. '*Aléjate de ella!*' He jabbed a finger, ordering him to retreat.

'Do it, Diego,' said Rosamaria, almost pleading. Her son looked up at her in disbelief.

Macy kicked and writhed, still trying to shake off the two men – but to no avail. 'Diego! Help me! Please!'

The young man looked for a moment as if he was about to charge at her attackers – then he lowered his head. 'I'm . . . I'm sorry,' he whispered, remaining still beside his mother.

The cult members guarding the Kaibiles drove the prisoners back towards the skull racks. Corazón pointed at the altar. '*Tomarla!*' The men holding Macy dragged her towards it.

By now, Nina and Eddie's hands had been bound behind their backs. Eddie kept fighting as he was hauled upright, even though every attempt to kick or headbutt the cultists was met with a brutal response. 'Let her go, you bastards!' he roared. 'I will fucking kill every one of you if you hurt her!' He managed to catch one man's kneecap with his boot, making him yell in pain – only for the cultist to snatch out a pistol and shove it against the Englishman's side—

'No!' snapped Corazón. His follower hesitated, then withdrew. 'I want you to witness my return to this place as Tekuni,' he told his prisoners, voice gloating. 'To witness the victory of the Dispossessed!'

He gave more commands. Four of the cultists left the main group and ascended the ziggurat to the altar, removing their backpacks and taking out the contents: ceremonial robes. One particularly elaborate garment was drawn out with special reverence and unwrapped to reveal something else within. A headdress, the skull of a jaguar nestled in the predator's pelt. The flames from the oil channels glinted off its dead obsidian eyes.

Corazón marched back to the altar and stood as the others

placed the robe and headpiece upon him. He spread his arms wide, beginning a chant as they stepped back. The two men holding Macy forced her up the steps towards him. She screamed, the sound echoing from the bone-covered walls.

Nina and Eddie's guards pulled them to join the other prisoners. Eddie made another furious attempt to break loose, but was thrown hard to the floor and kicked repeatedly. He folded as a boot slammed into his stomach, rolling on his side—

Something jabbed painfully into his wrist.

He forced himself into stillness as he realised what it was. A shard of bone; a piece from a broken skull. Its edge was sharp enough to cut his skin.

And other things.

He squirmed, shifting position to take hold of it – then one of his attackers delivered another brutal kick. Eddie convulsed, a choked groan escaping his mouth. There was nothing he could do to stop another blow . . .

None came. His tormentors were now more interested in what was happening on the altar.

Nina looked frantically around one of her captors at him. 'Eddie! My God, they've got Macy, they've got—'

He fixed his eyes upon hers. 'I'm okay,' he said, his voice unnaturally flat. She instantly recognised it as a signal and fell silent despite her desperation. Not knowing how many of the cultists spoke English, he could say no more without risking tipping them off.

Ribs aching, Eddie gingerly worked the piece of bone between his fingers. If he could position it properly, he would be able to start cutting through his bonds . . .

Another scream from Macy spurred him on. He had to do it, no matter what. If he didn't, he knew that the last thing he saw before his own life ended would be his daughter's murder.

★ ★ ★

The two men brought Macy to the top of the ziggurat. Her fear escalated as she saw what awaited her. The four cultists with Corazón had all now donned ceremonial robes, their clothing covered by elaborate arrangements of animal skins and feathers. But Corazón's was the most terrifying of all. Beneath the snarling head of the jaguar, a golden mask covered most of his face, only his cold eyes and unsmiling mouth exposed.

'Bring her here,' he said in Spanish. 'Hold her on the altar.'

The high priests took up positions at each corner of the rectangular slab. 'Get the fuck away from me!' she yelled, struggling harder against her captors. But it was no use. She was lifted bodily onto the altar and pinned down, a priest holding each of her limbs against the stone. The pair who had brought her withdrew to stand with Rosamaria and Diego by the offering trough. 'You psychos, let me go!'

Corazón moved closer, drawing Earthbreaker. 'You should be honoured,' he said. 'Your sacrifice will bring about the return of the true—'

Macy spat in his face. Gasps of outrage came from the observers below. 'Go fuck yourself,' she said, her New York accent never stronger.

The Mexican's face wrinkled in distaste. He wiped away the glob of spittle from his lips. 'There is only one punishment for blasphemy,' he growled. '*Death.*'

His priests pushed down harder on Macy's arms and legs. She cried out, desperately looking for help. But trapped on the elevated altar, she couldn't see anyone except the men who were about to kill her. 'Mom! Dad!' she screamed as Corazón lifted the dagger. '*Mom!*'

'Macy!' Nina wailed. She tried to run towards the ziggurat, but two cultists threw her hard to the floor beside her husband.

Eddie's eyes met hers. For a moment she felt a surge of hope;

whatever his plan, it was under way. But the feeling faded as she recognised the rising fear in his expression.

He knew he was out of time.

Corazón raised the dagger high above Macy's chest, beginning the ritual chant. For years he had carried it out as much out of duty as hope, almost afraid to dream that the day would come when it would take place in earnest.

But now that day was here. He had Earthbreaker; he had the map; soon he would have unlimited power over the lands that were his by birthright. 'In the name of Tekuazotl, the great Jaguar God, I offer this sacrifice,' he said, voice booming across the stone chamber. 'Through her death, we shall find new life . . .'

Shielding the bone shard from his guards, Eddie sawed away at his bonds, feeling them weaken.

But not fast enough.

He heard Corazón's voice rise towards a climax, the cultists surrounding him tensing in eager anticipation. The sacrifice was about to take place . . .

And there was nothing he could do to stop it.

26

Macy stared in horror at Earthbreaker. She was now too frightened to protest, to resist – all she could do was watch as Corazón lifted the ancient weapon higher, about to plunge it into her chest. 'By the spilling of her blood, our own blood shall be—'

'*No!*'

A shout – and Corazón turned in surprise as someone charged up the ziggurat at him.

Diego.

The young man ploughed into him, barging him into the man holding Macy's left leg. The priest fell. The other robed men reacted in shock at the blasphemous interruption.

Corazón recovered and rounded on Diego. 'You *shit!*' he snarled. 'I give you everything – and you do *this*?' He shouted to the two guards, who were already hurrying up the ziggurat to aid their leader. 'Get him!'

Diego turned to run, but they tackled him to the floor. Corazón scowled down at him. 'There will be more than one sacrifice today!'

Eddie couldn't make out what Corazón was saying, but Diego's actions – and his mother's appalled cry of '*No!*' – made it easy to guess.

The cultists were all looking up at the altar, momentarily distracted. No time left to conceal what he was doing. He rasped the bone harder against the cord.

262

One of the men beside him caught the movement. He shouted in alarm, fumbling to bring his rifle around—

The rope snapped.

Eddie rolled, driving the jagged shard into the cultist's calf – and twisting it. The man screeched and dropped to one knee, trigger finger clenching tight in his pain—

His gun barked, sending a three-round burst of bullets over Eddie into the back of his other guard. Bloody exit wounds exploded from the man's chest and stomach.

Eddie yanked out the shard. The man he'd stabbed screamed again – only for the sound to end abruptly as the Yorkshireman drove his makeshift weapon through his right eye socket and into his brain.

Mancillo was already responding as Eddie jumped to his feet. The major body-slammed the startled guard beside him, sending him into one of the oil channels and setting his legs aflame. The cultist shrieked and lurched back – convulsively firing his gun on full auto.

Nina started to run, only to find another cultist already lunging to grab her – and the burning man flailing in her direction. Arms still bound, all she could do was follow Mancillo's lead and fling herself at her would-be attacker. They crashed together, the surprised man stumbling backwards – into the line of uncontrolled fire. Bullets ripped into his torso.

Nina didn't emerge unscathed. A round clipped her upper right arm, searing pain slicing through her flesh. But she forced herself to keep moving as her unwitting human shield fell, throwing herself behind the nearest skull rack. She landed on her bag – feeling something sharp inside.

The replica of Earthbreaker.

Panic erupted as everyone tried to flee the gunfire. Mancillo and his men reacted far faster than their captors, the Guatemalan barking a command to run for cover and free each other. The soldiers split up, haring around the temple's pillars towards the entrance.

Corazón stared at the chaos below, briefly frozen – then whirled back to Macy. Three of the priests still held her down. She tried to kick him with her free leg, but he raised the dagger again, about to plunge it down—

Eddie snatched the AK from the man he'd impaled and flicked it to full auto – then fired up at the ziggurat's top. From below, Macy was shielded on the altar, but the men beside it were completely exposed. The two to her right fell dead, one slumping over her legs as the other crumpled bloodily to the floor. Corazón and the two priests on the other side hurriedly ducked behind the hefty dais. The men holding Diego scrambled for cover on the ziggurat's far side, dragging him with them and pinning him on the steps.

'Macy!' Eddie shouted. 'Get off there!' She kicked away the corpse and rolled over the altar's side, putting it between herself and the surviving priests.

The man on fire finally ran out of ammo, his screams replacing the pounding blasts of his rifle. One menace removed, the cultists began to fight back. A man sent a sweep of gunfire after the Kaibiles, hitting the rearmost soldier and sending him tumbling into a skull rack.

Another armed man swung his rifle towards Eddie. The Englishman's own gun was still aimed up at the altar; he dived behind a statue as the cultist opened fire. Bullets ricocheted noisily off the carved figure. Eddie darted around the statue's other side and shot back—

Only one round was unleashed before the Kalashnikov's bolt closed with a hollow *clack*. The magazine was empty; its former owner hadn't reloaded after the battle in the jungle. The lone bullet narrowly missed Eddie's target, who flinched before he too recognised the distinctive metallic sound. He let out a sharp exhalation – then advanced on the statue, weapon raised.

Corazón cautiously raised his head above the altar. Many of his followers had scattered in panic, the burning man screeching and flailing behind them. The surviving soldiers were running for the entrance, whether to flee or regroup he didn't know – but none were armed. His people could deal with them once the situation was back under control.

Wilde and her husband were his priority. He glimpsed the Englishman behind a statue, a follower – Fernandez, a former soldier – advancing on him. Where was the woman?

Movement behind a skull rack, a red-haired figure illuminated by a nearby oil channel. 'The American woman!' he said to one of the priests, Garza, crouched beside him. 'She's down there – kill her!'

'My pleasure, Tekuni,' Garza replied with a smile like a slit throat. He drew a knife from his robes and rounded the head of the altar to go after his target.

Fernandez advanced on the statue, rifle readied. There was no-where for his prey to go, and with an empty gun, no way for him to fight back . . .

Something appeared from behind the statue. Fernandez whipped his gun higher – but it was just a skull, tossed into the air. What—

Another movement – and the stolen Kalashnikov whirled into view, its stock striking the skull like a baseball bat and sending it flying at Fernandez's face.

It smashed into pieces as it delivered a bony headbutt. The cultist reeled, momentarily blinded. Then he opened his eyes again – to see the Kalashnikov rushing at him as Eddie charged out from behind the statue. Its grip struck his forehead with sledgehammer force, smashing him into unconsciousness.

Eddie dropped the empty AK and snatched up the fallen cultist's rifle. A glance at the altar to see Macy still lying flat alongside it, but he had lost track of Nina in the commotion.

The man on fire succumbed to agony and collapsed, flames still crackling around him. One of the priests hurried down from the altar. Eddie raised his new gun, but then saw other weapons turn towards him as the cult members began to regroup. He instead targeted the greater threat, sending a couple of rounds into the crowd. Someone screamed and fell, others scrambling clear. Eddie retreated into the cover of the hefty stone pillars.

Nina had managed to extract the replica dagger from her bag. She sawed it against the cord holding her wrists. Strands stretched and snapped as she wriggled her arms, but more needed to go before she could break loose—

Through the skull rack, she saw one of the priests heading straight for her. She rose with a strained gasp, backing away around the row of pillars as she kept slashing at her bonds. Heat rose behind her. She caught herself just before stepping into a channel of burning oil, angling towards the trough feeding it.

A final rasp – and the cord broke. She pulled her wrists apart and raised the dagger – finding to her alarm that the point had snapped off the plastic blade when she landed on it.

The priest came around the skull rack after her.

Nina dropped the useless weapon and vaulted over the oil channel, ducking under the sloping trough. There had to be some way to fight, to save Macy and Eddie as well as herself—

Skulls regarded her with dark, empty eyes from the pillar. The metal valve through which the oil flowed narrowed at its end, to prevent the fire from reaching the reservoir above. The approaching priest was obscured by the flames running down the trough.

Three things, suddenly coming together in her mind into a single whole—

She grabbed the valve's handle and shut off the flow. The fire oozed downwards, leaving a smoking residue behind. One skull, jawbone missing, was barely secured to the pillar by crumbling mortar. Nina grabbed it and pulled. It broke loose with a crunch. The priest increased his pace, realising she was doing something but unable to see exactly what through the flames.

She shoved the valve open again. More oil ran out. She scooped some up with the inverted skull – then splattered it on the floor. The man came around the trough, raising a knife—

The newly flowing oil caught up with the running fire below – and ignited.

A bright flare burst from the trough. The priest squinted at the sudden burst of light, but kept coming—

Briefly dazzled, he didn't see the spilled oil on the floor.

One foot slid from under him. He staggered, throwing out his arms for balance – putting a hand into the flaming trough. He jerked it back, instinctively pressing his burned palm between his other arm and his chest—

Nina lunged at him, swinging the skull. It smashed against his head. He stumbled sidelong into the trough. Flames rushed up his shoulder. His oily foot slipped again as he tried to push himself clear, and he fell – landing on his upturned knife.

The man spasmed as the blade drove between his ribs into his heart. He tried to rise . . . then collapsed, blood oozing in a pool around him.

Nina dropped the broken skull on his back. 'Don't touch my daughter.'

★ ★ ★

267

Corazón watched his followers pursue the Englishman as he ducked behind a pillar. 'Go after him!' he ordered the men pinning Diego down, before glancing back at his remaining priest, Cruz. 'Hold Diego.' Cruz drew a gun, pulling the young man upright and shoving the weapon against his side as the two guards hurried away.

Corazón and Diego stared at each other. 'I can't believe you betrayed me,' the former snarled as he slowly advanced, Earthbreaker in his hand. 'After everything I've done for you, everything I've given you and your mother – you turn against me? For some *American*?' He practically spat the word.

'I didn't know about . . . *this*,' Diego replied, gesturing at the walls of skulls watching them. 'I knew you led a religion, a cult – but I didn't know you were a fucking murderer!'

'It's not murder,' said Corazón. 'It's the old way – the *true* way.' He stopped in front of the young man. 'The will of Tekuazotl. And anyone who opposes him . . . must *die*!'

He whipped back his arm, about to stab Diego in the stomach—

Macy vaulted over the altar, swinging both legs around to kick Corazón hard in the back.

Corazón crashed against one of the oil troughs, outstretched arm going into the flames. He yelled in pain. The dagger flew from his burned hand as he jumped back. It went over the ziggurat's end and clattered down the steps towards the offering trough below.

Macy landed beside the altar. Cruz spun, gun coming up—

Diego whirled and drove an elbow into his stomach. The priest bent double, dropping his gun – and the young Mexican kneed him in the face, bowling him down the ziggurat's side.

Macy grabbed Diego's arm. 'Come on – we've got to get the dagger!' They both hurried down the steps after it, flanked by lines of burning oil.

Corazón swatted out flames on his sleeve. He looked around, realising the boy and the girl had fled – and Earthbreaker was nowhere in sight. He ran to snatch up the fallen gun.

Eddie backed against a pillar and thumbed the release to remove the Kalashnikov's magazine. It wasn't fully loaded, a little hole in its curved back revealing black metal rather than brass. The gun's previous user was again no professional, failing to reload after the firefight.

How many rounds left? Decades of experience gave him an answer from weight alone: less than half. Twelve shots, give or take. At least four armed opponents were coming after him directly, and there were more cultists still in the temple.

Not great odds. But he'd faced worse. And when his family's lives were at stake, odds meant nothing. Results were all that mattered.

He clicked the magazine back into place. The entire process of checking it had taken under two seconds. He didn't expect what happened next to take much longer – however it turned out.

He raised the rifle in his right hand, wrenching a skull from the pillar with the other and tossing it to his left. One of the approaching cultists reacted on adrenalin-pumped instinct to the movement, unleashing a burst of automatic fire. Another gun joined in the barking cacophony as a second man did the same—

Eddie swung out from the pillar's right. The closest of the cultists was less than twenty feet away – but looking in the wrong direction, at the thrown skull.

It was the last thing he ever saw. Eddie dropped him with a single shot to the chest, snapping his AK onto the next-nearest man and putting another two rounds into his torso. Both the cultists who had fired at his distraction were off to the left, turning back towards him—

Eddie swept the gun around, blasting out the remaining

rounds in a deadly arc. One man fell with a scream, clutching his abdomen. The other toppled backwards in a spray of blood, an uncontrolled burst from his own rifle ripping chunks of stone from the ceiling.

Another metallic *clack* from the AK as the bolt closed. Out of ammo. His estimate had been accurate: twelve shots. But another man was coming for him with a combat knife . . .

Eddie gambled with all he had and aimed the empty rifle at him. The man broke in panic and ran for cover.

None of the remaining cultists posed any immediate threat, either wounded or unarmed. 'Nina! Where are you?'

'I'm okay!' she replied, voice echoing from somewhere behind the large pillars. 'Get Macy!'

He looked up at the altar. No sign of his daughter – but he *could* see Corazón, moving away from him with clear purpose. Eddie pursued, taking the steps two at a time.

Macy and Diego reached the ziggurat's foot. 'Shit!' said Diego, glancing back to see Corazón above. 'He's got a gun!'

The oil channels curved to skirt around the offering trough. Diego angled as if to jump over the flames. Macy pulled him back. 'No, in there!' she cried instead.

They piled over the hulking trough's high side – as a bullet smacked into the stonework just behind them. Corazón swore and started down the steps in pursuit.

Macy landed inside on her back – with Diego on top of her, the pair ending up nose to nose. 'Ah! Sorry!' he yelped, pushing himself up off her. She yanked him back down – as another round hit the trough's inner lip where his head had just been. He gasped at the close call, then gave her a panicked look. 'We're stuck in here!'

'I know,' she said, worried. 'Just be ready to move when we get the chance.'

'How do you know we'll *have* the chance?'

'I don't – I'm just trying to be positive!'

But no amount of affirmative thinking could make Corazón retreat. Macy looked past Diego, seeing the jaguar-headed figure looming above them. His gun tilted down towards his trapped, helpless targets—

Rosamaria threw herself at him.

The archaeologist had hidden behind the trough when the shooting started. Now she rushed out to protect her son, knocking Corazón back and clawing at his face as she shouted for Diego to run. But the cult leader quickly overcame his surprise. He backhanded her in the face, sending her to the floor with a bloodied nose. 'You too?' he snarled. 'You bitch!'

He kicked her – then stepped back to the offering trough, gun raised.

Eddie reached the top of the ziggurat, finding only bodies by the altar. He ran to the other end. A priest lay sprawled senseless at the bottom of the structure to his right, but his sole concern was Corazón. The cult leader stood at the stone trough below, framed by lines of fire. Rosamaria lay curled in pain nearby – and inside the offering trough he glimpsed Diego.

He knew instantly that Macy was with him – and that Corazón was about to kill both teenagers.

No weapon, no way to reach him in time—

A dead priest was slumped against the altar. Eddie grabbed the body and hauled it upwards . . .

Then threw himself into a dive over the ziggurat's end.

The corpse landed in one of the channels flanking the steps with a great splash of burning oil. The Yorkshireman thumped down on top of it. He dropped as low as he could as his makeshift sled picked up speed down the steep slope, the dead man's face cutting through the oil like a snowplough and kicking up gouts of flaming spray. Eddie's leather jacket protected his body, but sizzling droplets caught his exposed hands and the back of his head. He let out a roar that was as much battle cry as pain.

Corazón turned – and froze in shock at the sight of a blazing body hurtling towards him. Before he could recover, the dead priest reached the bottom of the slope and hit the oil pooled there, hurling up a volcanic burst of fiery liquid. Rosamaria screamed as she was hit by several burning globs.

Corazón threw up both arms to shield his face from the flaming spatter and made a blind flying leap over the line of oil rounding the offering trough. Eddie rolled off the corpse, seeing Corazón and scrambling up to charge at him. The Mexican recovered and brought his gun to bear—

Eddie tackled him – bowling them both over the top of the slope to the huge chamber below.

27

Eddie and Corazón rolled down the steep incline. Eddie managed to flip onto his back, using his feet to slow himself – only for the Mexican to grab one ankle. The two men's eyes met – then Corazón swung his gun at him—

Eddie whipped his other foot across to kick him hard in the face. Corazón spat out teeth. He lost his hold, sliding sidelong towards the map below.

A fall to Eddie's left, fire on the right – and mercury ahead. He took the least-worst option, crossing his arms protectively in front of his face and throwing himself right.

Flames seared his skin as he rolled over the oil channel – then a different pain struck as he tumbled down the unyielding stone steps . . .

And abruptly thumped to a halt at the bottom.

Corazón was less lucky. He slithered onwards, hitting the raised lip at the map's edge – and was pitched over it to land in the quicksilver ocean with a heavy, ringing *splat*.

But he didn't sink, the human body far less dense than mercury. Instead, he bobbed helplessly on the surface. His gun floated in the middle of the sea, out of reach. He flailed his limbs, trying to swim to solid ground. The liquid metal resisted his efforts, but he made just enough headway to touch the edge with an outstretched hand. Relieved, he pulled himself closer, wallowing on the shimmering surface—

'Ay up.'

Corazón raised his head – and saw Eddie standing over him.

The Yorkshireman's boot heel smashed down on his fingers, breaking one. The cult leader screamed. Eddie didn't ease the pressure, mercilessly grinding his foot on the other man's hand. 'Going to kill my little girl, were you? You *fucking wanker*! Let's see how you fucking like it!'

Still crushing Corazón's fingers, he extended his other leg over the mercury pool – and stamped it down on the Mexican's head, driving his face into the thick liquid. Corazón thrashed, but Eddie didn't yield. Air bubbles blorped from the rippling mirror as the other man struggled to breathe—

'Eddie!'

He looked back. Nina was at the top of the great staircase, holding a cultist's rifle. His joy and relief were multiplied when Macy appeared behind her, Earthbreaker in her hand. 'Are you both okay?' he called.

'Yeah!' Nina replied. 'Ah . . . what are you doing?'

'Giving this dirty little bastard a bath.'

'Well, don't kill him!' Nina protested, descending the stairs with Macy. Diego appeared at the top, holding his bloodied mother.

'Why not? He deserves it!'

'I know, but I'd rather you didn't murder anyone in front of our daughter, okay? We're the good guys!'

'That's a pain in the bloody arse sometimes,' Eddie said, but he raised his foot. Corazón popped back up, gasping. 'All right, fuckwit. Get up here.' He stepped off the cult leader's hand, then dragged him to solid ground. Shiny beads rolled off Corazón's clothing and pooled around him. 'Bloody hell, he weighs a ton!'

'He must have swallowed some of the mercury,' said Nina.

'Guess we'll have to start calling him Freddie.'

'Why?' Macy asked, puzzled.

He sighed. 'And you call *me* uncultured.'

'No I don't! Well, not much.'

Eddie dropped Corazón, who vomited out a silver streak. 'This stuff won't kill us from being so close, will it?'

'No, as long as we don't stay near it for too long,' said Nina as she and Macy reached the bottom of the staircase. 'The vapour'll sink, so if we're above it, we should be fine.'

Eddie eyed his gasping captive. 'What about him?'

'I don't think the body absorbs elemental mercury, so it should pass through him pretty quickly. I wouldn't want to use the bathroom after it does, though.'

'Oh!' said Macy suddenly, with a small laugh. Her parents looked at her. 'Freddie Mercury. I just got it.'

'She *finally* appreciates one of my dad jokes,' Eddie said with a faint smile. 'So, we stopped the cult. Now what do we do?'

'Professor Wilde!' came another voice from the top of the stairs. 'Chase!' They turned to see Mancillo and two of his men, now bearing arms acquired from the cultists. Borrayo had already lit a cigarette. Juarez held Diego and his mother at gunpoint. 'Are you okay?'

'Yeah, we're fine,' Eddie shouted back, adding with cutting sarcasm: 'Thanks for turning up *after* the nick of time. What happened to "If I retreat, kill me"?'

Mancillo started down the steps. 'We had to find cover so we could untie the ropes. Did you want us to get shot?' He took in his flame-lit surroundings as he descended. 'So this is what they were after?'

'Yeah,' said Nina. 'A map of Central America, and beyond – all linked to the real world. Touch Earthbreaker to a point on the map, and *wham:* you get an earthquake in that place.'

'How is that possible?'

'Quantum physics, apparently,' said Eddie. 'Don't understand it myself – the only quantum things I know about are the old TV show and that crap James Bond film. But I'll roll with it.'

Mancillo reached the bottom of the stairs, surveying the miniature landscape. 'You really believe it works?'

'I do,' said Nina. 'I've seen it happen.'

'And he believes it as well.' He nudged Corazón, less than gently, with his foot. The cult leader was too weak to react with more than a groan. 'Where is the dagger, this . . . Earthbreaker?'

'I've got it,' Macy told him, holding up the green blade.

'And you are able to use it.' It was not a question. 'Show me.'

The demand was met by surprised silence. 'What?' Macy said, after a moment.

'Are you kidding me?' Nina objected, more forcefully. 'The whole point of our coming here was to *stop* it from being used! You test it, it'll cause an earthquake – there's no telling how much damage that might do.'

Mancillo was unmoved. 'There is only one way to find out.'

'No,' came a snarl from the ground. Corazón rolled painfully onto his side, glaring up at them. Macy hastily retreated behind Eddie. 'Only the Tekuni can use Earthbreaker. For anyone else, it is blasphemy! The Jaguar God will kill you! *I* will kill you! I have waited my whole life to claim Earthbreaker and to find the Underworld – you will not take them away from me now!'

The Guatemalan made a dismissive sound. 'Yes, I will.'

He drew a pistol and shot Corazón in the chest.

The sudden, *casual* nature of the act caught everyone by surprise. 'Jesus Christ!' shouted Eddie, holding Macy behind him as he sidestepped to shield Nina as well. Above, Rosamaria screamed, Diego yelling in shock.

'Holy shit!' was Nina's own response. 'What the hell are you doing?'

Mancillo didn't reply at first, shouting an order up the staircase. The remaining Kaibiles quickly appeared, herding the surviving cultists down into the chamber. 'I am doing my job, Professor Wilde. Protecting my country. From people like him,' a disdainful glance at Corazón's unmoving form, 'and anyone else who is a threat to it.' He turned back to the shivering Macy, still sheltering behind her father. 'Now,' he said, pointing at the dagger in her hand, 'show me what it can do.'

Nina also placed herself between the soldier and her daughter. 'Why do you need to see it?'

'Because if it really works . . . I can use it,' was Mancillo's blunt reply.

'For what?' Eddie asked suspiciously.

'To bring down my *government*.' The last word was said with a sneer.

Macy was shocked. 'Why?'

'They are weak, pathetic cowards, terrified of the drug gangs and the communist rebels and the foreign corporations buying everything we own, a piece at a time. They will give away the whole country if they are not stopped! But now . . . I *can* stop them.'

Nina stared at him in disbelief. 'So you're going to . . . what? Improvise a coup by causing an earthquake?'

Mancillo laughed, a short, patronising bark. 'I am not improvising anything! Why do you think the government sent me with you? They wanted me out of the way. I have been making plans with other senior officers for some time. The government do not know what we are doing – if they did, we would have been arrested. But they *suspect*. So they gave me and my men an insulting task and sent us to look for some legend, some nonsense. But . . .' he cast a hand across the glistening green map, 'it is real. They tried to get rid of me – but they have given me the perfect weapon to use against them! I only need to tell my friends to be ready, then when an earthquake hits Guatemala City, we strike in the confusion – and take control.' An unpleasant smile, which rapidly became a stern frown. 'If it does what you say.'

He stepped back, raising his gun and aiming it at Eddie. 'So I will ask you again, for the last time,' he said to Macy. 'Show me. Or your father dies.'

The soldiers reached the bottom of the steps, rounding the fallen Corazón. The cultists regarded their former leader with expressions ranging from crushed defeat to horror. Juarez left his men to guard their prisoners as he pointed his own weapon at the Englishman.

Macy gripped the back of Eddie's jacket. 'Dad!'

'It's all right, love,' Eddie said slowly, eyes flicking between the two gun muzzles. 'Stay calm. Nobody else needs to get hurt.'

'We can't let him start another quake!' Nina protested.

'For now, I only want a demonstration,' said Mancillo. 'Proof, in an isolated area.'

'And after that?'

He gave her a disdainful look – then, before anyone could react, lunged and struck Eddie's head with his gun. Eddie fell. Juarez quickly stepped closer, rifle aimed down at him.

Macy shrieked – but before she could run, Mancillo grabbed her wrist, bringing Earthbreaker between their faces. Nina started towards them, but he snapped up his gun. She flinched back. 'Come with me,' the major growled. He pulled Macy onto the map. Eddie tried to stand, but Juarez slammed him back down with a foot on his chest.

Mancillo strode across the carved landscape, searching for familiar landmarks. 'There,' he said, going to a thumb-high mountain near the coast of the mercury Pacific. 'We are here, at Tajumulco.' He crouched, bringing Macy with him as he pointed out the tallest peak. His finger moved towards another, fractionally smaller mountain to the north-west. 'So *that* must be Tacaná. It erupted recently, so nobody is allowed to climb it. There is no one there to be hurt.' He locked eyes with her. 'Use the dagger.'

Despite her fear, she shook her head. 'No.'

'Do you want your father to die? Use the dagger!'

She looked desperately back at her parents . . . then her shoulders slumped in surrender. Mancillo tapped the volcano on the map. 'Do it. Make an earthquake, there. Show me that this is real.'

Reluctantly, Macy turned Earthbreaker's point downwards. Mancillo kept hold of her as she lowered it towards the little peak. She felt the repulsive force grow stronger the nearer it came. Anger flared in the officer's eyes, and he closed his fingers painfully tight around her wrist until he realised she wasn't resisting – the map itself was forcing the blade away. 'Push it down,' he said, adding his own strength to hers. 'Do it! Now!'

She made a final effort – and the dagger made contact.

It felt as if she had been struck by lightning, a charge jolting every muscle in her body. She instinctively tried to pull away, but Mancillo held her in place, the power like ragged metal scraping along every nerve . . .

The sensation became too much, so much so that not even the soldier could stop her from jerking away. The connection broke, and she fell on her back, gasping. Mancillo stared down at her. 'Did it work? Did it—'

The ground shook beneath them.

Fear rose amongst the group at the staircase as a tremor rolled through the cavern. 'What have you *done*?' roared Mancillo. 'You've killed us all!'

For a moment Nina thought the same thing: that Macy had touched Earthbreaker to Tajumulco rather than Tacaná in a desperate attempt to stop his plan. But the vibration faded, and she realised what had happened. 'No!' she shouted, before the major could take out his fury on her daughter. 'That's the shock wave from the quake. Seismic waves travel faster than sound.' A second shudder rattled their surroundings, this one less intense, but longer.

Mancillo stared angrily at her, then called out an order to

Borrayo. He replied with a rapid '*Sí, jefe!*' and set off up the steps at a run.

'Where's he going?' Eddie asked. 'Putting money in the parking meter?'

'To the entrance,' said Mancillo. 'To see what has happened to the volcano.' He pulled Macy to her feet, taking the dagger, then brought her back to her family. 'Galarza, *míralos.*' Another soldier came to them. Juarez released Eddie at Mancillo's command, and the two Kaibiles backed away to begin an intense discussion. Galarza took Juarez's place, but at least allowed Eddie to stand.

'I'm sorry,' Macy whispered.

'For what?' said Nina.

'For giving in to him – for doing what he said.'

'You didn't do anything wrong,' her mother assured her. 'You were protecting your dad.'

'But now he knows that Earthbreaker works!' Tears appeared in Macy's eyes. 'And he'll make me use it again, on a city. Lots of people will die – and it'll be my fault!'

'It'll be *his* fault,' Eddie said firmly. 'But it's not going to come to that, okay? We'll get away from him.'

'How?' Macy demanded.

'I'm curious myself,' added Nina.

'Well, so am I,' said the Yorkshireman. 'But I'll let you know when I figure something out. Even if it's only half a second before it actually happens.'

'I'd prefer a *bit* more advance warning,' said Macy unhappily. But further discussion was curtailed by Galarza, who jabbed his rifle at them to signal for silence.

It took several minutes for Borrayo to return. Even with the death traps deactivated, he had still needed to negotiate the web of chains twice, and find a vantage point from where he could see Tacaná. But his excitement was immediately clear as he hurried down the stairs, shouting to his commander. 'The volcano erupted!' Macy translated for her parents. 'He says there's smoke and lava coming from it, and a big mushroom cloud going into the sky.'

'I'm not surprised,' said Nina. 'I can still feel it.' The tremors had continued the whole time, occasionally strong enough to dislodge small stones from the rocky ceiling high above. Some landed on the map, but most either fell into the pool at the bottom of the waterfall far below, or landed on the conical slope and skittered away before taking the plunge.

Borrayo reached Mancillo and Juarez, giving more details. Mancillo turned towards Nina. 'It really works,' he said in amazement, holding up the dagger. 'This knife – it really caused an earthquake, exactly where it was put on the map.'

He walked back across the jade landscape, squatting to examine a particular part. 'Guatemala City is here,' he said, tapping an upland plain. 'If I touch the dagger here, when Congress is in session . . .' He looked up at Eddie with a nasty smile. 'Just like in Britain, when Big Ben fell and killed most of your politicians. I wipe them out – then my friends take control.' He stood. 'Or I do it tonight, when they are all asleep – and bring their roofs down upon them. I only need to reach one of the villages in the valley, and find a telephone. The plan is already in place. I just have to choose a time.'

'We're not going to let you use our daughter to start a coup,' Nina told the major, holding Macy.

Mancillo returned, gesturing with the dagger. 'You do not have a choice. She obeys, or you and Chase die. It is that simple.' He turned to Juarez. 'Put them with the others. No, not the girl,' he added, as Galarza took hold of Macy. 'She stays with me.'

Juarez advanced on Eddie and Nina, gesturing with his gun. 'Go. Or I shoot you.' The couple reluctantly started to move, exchanging worried looks with Macy – then the lieutenant raised a hand, signalling Eddie to stop. He indicated his leather jacket. 'I said before, nice coat. I want it. Take it off.'

'Are you fucking serious?' said Eddie.

'You are lucky he does not want your ears,' said Mancillo with a callous half-smile. 'If you want to live? Give him your jacket.'

Eddie shook his head in disgust. 'It's wrecked anyway,' he said, shrugging off the garment—

And feeling something solid at the bottom of the left-hand pocket.

The flick knife he had confiscated from Macy.

He had forgotten it was there. The cultists had given him only a cursory search when the group was captured, looking for guns rather than anything smaller.

A split second of hesitation – then he slipped his hand into the opening, closing his fingers around the weapon. 'Here you go, then.' He offered the jacket to the Guatemalan.

Juarez took his left hand off his rifle to accept it—

Eddie whipped the knife from the pocket, flicking it open in a single rapid movement – and stabbing it up through Juarez's wrist.

The soldier yelled in pained shock as blood squirted from the entrance and exit wounds. Eddie threw the jacket at Galarza, who instinctively brought up his gun hand to deflect it away over the side of the map. Before anyone else could react, the Englishman grabbed Juarez, ducking behind him to yank up his impaled arm and press the knife's point to his throat. 'Let Macy go,' he growled. 'Now!'

Galarza recovered, looking to Mancillo for orders. The major shook his head. 'I'm serious,' said Eddie, pushing the blade's tip into his prisoner's neck hard enough to draw blood. 'Let her go, or I'll cut his fucking throat!'

The other Kaibiles spread out, moving away from the rest of their captives to aim their weapons at Eddie and Nina. But they didn't fire, also awaiting Mancillo's instructions. The remaining cultists stood in uncertain fear, not knowing what would happen.

Mancillo stared levelly back at Eddie . . . then smiled. 'If you are going to kill him, then kill him.'

'I'm not fucking joking,' said Eddie.

'Nor am I. And my men know that. They *accept* that.' The smile vanished, replaced by a snake-like coldness. 'This is why the Kaibiles are stronger than your SAS. On our first day in training, in hell, we are each given a puppy. We are told we must give it a name, care for it, protect it – love it. And then, the last thing we must do to prove we are ready to leave hell? We kill it. And eat it. I will never forget the shock in my animal's eyes, the look of betrayal, as I cut its throat.'

Macy gasped, appalled. 'The dog wasn't the animal,' she managed to say.

Mancillo ignored her. 'But I have no regrets, no guilt,' he went on, his eyes never leaving Eddie's. 'I did what I had to do to make me a man. We *all* did. We will do anything necessary to achieve victory, even if that means sacrificing one of us. Or all of us. Can you say that?'

'I can't,' Eddie rumbled. 'But then I'm not a fucking psychopath.'

'Nor am I. I am just a man who is willing to do what must be done. And that is why I will win.' He drew his gun again, aiming it at Macy. She froze, looking fearfully at Eddie. 'You will surrender, Chase. Because you will not risk anything happening to your daughter.'

'If you kill her, you won't be able to use Earthbreaker,' said Nina in desperation.

'I have no intention of killing her.' Mancillo let the words sink in – and Macy's parents draw their own conclusions about their meaning.

'You *bastard*,' Nina snarled.

Mancillo merely shrugged. 'Surrender,' he said to Eddie. 'Let him go. *Now.*'

Eddie took in the forces facing him. Four men, all armed. Even if he killed Juarez, the others would shoot him a moment later. But there had to be *something* he could do, some way to save his family—

'Dad,' said Macy, a new, imploring maturity to her voice. 'If you try anything, they'll kill you. Let him go. You need to find the right time to rescue me. But . . . I know you will.'

'He will not,' Mancillo said coldly. 'Juarez? *Estás preparado para morir por tu país?*'

Juarez stiffened. '*Sí,*' he rasped, the knife pressed against his larynx.

The major nodded. 'He will die for his country,' he told Eddie. 'For *me*. I will count to three. Release him. Or my men will shoot you, your wife – and them,' he added, gesturing at the other prisoners almost as an afterthought. Diego and Rosamaria reacted with shock. 'Whether you kill Juarez is up to you. One.'

'Dad,' Macy pleaded. 'They're going to kill you!'

'They're going to kill us anyway,' he replied.

'Two,' said Mancillo.

'Dad! Please, don't! I can't – I can't watch you die!'

Nina gripped her husband's shoulder. 'Eddie . . .'

He looked at Macy, realising that she might be the last thing he ever saw. Mancillo opened his mouth to say the final, fatal number—

A scream echoed through the cavern.

28

Everyone whirled – to see that Corazón was not dead.

The cult leader had risen unseen to his knees while all eyes were on Eddie and Mancillo. Crimson running from his chest wound, he let out an anguished, gurgling howl before vomiting a thick stream of liquid metal—

The startled Kaibiles opened fire as one.

A frenzied storm of bullets ripped into his body, gouts of blood bursting from his back as rounds tore through him. Mercury sprayed from his ruptured stomach as he fell backwards—

Eddie released the knife and swung an elbow up to crack Juarez on the back of his skull, sending him reeling into Galarza. 'Go!' he yelled, grabbing Nina – and rushing for the nearest edge of the map. Behind them, Diego pulled his mother with him in another desperate sprint.

The other Kaibiles were still firing into Corazón's spasming corpse. Only Mancillo saw the prisoners break loose. He spun as the cultists scattered, gun tracking Eddie—

Macy charged at him, ramming into his arm as he fired. The bullet cracked harmlessly away into the chamber's shadowy reaches. She turned to follow her parents—

Mancillo tackled her. She cried out as she hit the carved surface.

Nina looked back in alarm. 'Macy!'

Eddie pulled her onwards. 'He won't hurt her, he needs her!' He glanced back, seeing Galarza tug the knife from Juarez's arm – and Mancillo bringing his gun back up. *'Jump!'*

They reached the map's edge – and leapt off.

Mancillo fired again, but the round whipped over their heads. They thumped onto the sloping surface below . . .

And slid down it.

'Oh, fuck,' Eddie said, trying to slow his descent, but finding almost no grip on the polished surface. 'Maybe this wasn't such a good idea!'

A shout to one side; Nina saw Diego and Rosamaria hit the conical peak. Further away, a cultist made a flying leap, another man about to follow him over the edge—

Automatic weapons crackled. The man spun, bloody holes erupting across his body. He bowled limply downhill, rolling through an oil channel and erupting into flames. Someone else managed to reach the edge, mercury splashing under his feet as he veered into the metallic ocean to dodge gunfire.

But he was the last to escape. Another angry fusillade was followed by screams as the remaining cultists were cut down.

Nor had the Kaibiles given up. Mancillo bellowed commands. Eddie risked a brief look back, seeing soldiers appear at the map's edge. 'Down!' he said, dropping flat on his back. Nina followed suit as the Guatemalans opened fire. Rounds twanged off the slope around them. The tailmost cultist shrieked as a Kalashnikov's bullet shattered his shoulder – only for the cry to end sharply as another blasted a grapefruit-sized chunk of bone and brain from his skull.

More bullets snapped overhead. Eddie and Nina had made themselves harder targets by lying flat – but had also increased their speed. And a new danger lay ahead. They were nearing the bottom of the area that had been carved smooth; beyond, the surface was far rougher, with numerous jutting protrusions.

Nina was heading straight for one of them. She kicked at the slope to change her course, but it wasn't enough—

Eddie threw himself in front of her. He hit the chunk of

rock sideways-on – then Nina collided with him. The impact knocked them both breathless, sending them spinning down the incline.

The remaining cultist was less lucky. He rolled to avoid one ragged promontory – only to career into another hunk of stone below. The *crack* as his skull struck it was loud enough to echo across the cavern.

Winded, pained, Eddie forced his eyes open – and saw the bottom of the slope approaching fast. The flickering oil channels illuminated the chamber's far wall, the waterfall dropping from on high into the void below. But there was no way to stop – and even if there were, plunging into the unknown was probably the least-worst option. He and Nina gripped each other as they reached the edge—

And plummeted into darkness.

A second in free fall, two – then they hit cold water with stunning force.

A long moment of pain and disorientation, then Eddie recovered from the initial shock. Bubbles and froth churned around him. He extended his arms to stabilise himself and kicked upwards. Vague shapes shimmered above as he struggled towards the surface . . .

And broke through.

He drew in air, kicking to stay upright. A foul smell stung his nostrils. Part of the reason was obvious: lines of burning oil were running over the cliff edge more than sixty feet above, splashing down into the large pool and sending up greasy smoke as the fire was snuffed out. But the other cause was more insidious, more toxic. Heavier-than-air mercury vapour had sunk to the bottom of the chamber, building up above the water's surface.

'Nina?' he rasped, searching for her. She had landed with him – so where was she? 'Nina! Can you hear me?'

'Mr Chase?' Diego's breathless voice, behind Eddie. The

young man was supporting his mother thirty feet away. 'Are you okay?'

'Yeah, but I can't see Nina!' He spun in place, hunting for any sign of his wife—

Bubbles broke the rippling surface not far from him. He immediately dived to find their source. There was almost no light below, but he could hear something over the waterfall's constant rumble. Muffled moans, rising in pitch . . .

He descended, arms outstretched – and found Nina.

She was upright, struggling to ascend but making no headway. Eddie blindly swam deeper, guiding himself down her legs. Something had caught around one of her feet – a rope? He couldn't tell in the darkness. Her efforts to break free only pulled it tighter. He dropped downwards, tugging at the entangling object. His hands brushed more unidentifiable debris. The followers of the Jaguar God had once used the pool below their temple as a dumping ground – and now Nina was caught in it.

He pulled at her foot, working the binding over her heel. The task was made harder by her panicked movements, rising fear and diminishing air causing instinct to overpower reason. She would exhaust herself, draw in a breath that wasn't there, drown—

A final twist – and the restraint jerked free.

He kicked himself the right way up, his own feet thumping against unseen flotsam below, and helped her upwards. She breached the surface first, gasping. He followed, taking several deep breaths before being able to speak. 'You all right?'

'Yeah,' she managed to reply. 'Not dead. So doing okay.'

He looked up at the cliff, a near-vertical face sheared from the glistening green peak. 'We've got to get out of here before they find somewhere to shoot at us from.'

Nina looked around. 'How? I can't see a way up.'

'There must be an outflow channel.' Diego swam closer,

bringing Rosamaria with him. 'There's a waterfall, but the water level isn't rising.' He raised a hand to indicate darker bands across the chamber's rock wall. 'You can see how high it's gone during floods, but it's come back down to this level. The channel probably isn't far under the surface.'

'Where is it, though?' Nina asked.

Eddie spotted movement off in a corner, the water rippling without apparent cause. 'That must be it. Can everyone swim?'

Rosamaria spoke for the first time since escaping the carnage above. 'No, my leg hurts, and . . .' She trailed off, almost embarrassed. 'And I never learned how.'

'I'll help you, Mom,' said Diego. He started towards the disturbance, holding his mother's head above the surface. 'What about Macy? They've still got her!'

'She'll be okay as long as Mancillo needs her,' replied the Yorkshireman as he started swimming. 'So we've got to get her back before they reach a vehicle. How far away were you parked?'

'From the Underworld's entrance? About a kilometre. There's a Jeep and a bus; they're on an old track downhill from a little lake.'

'We need to get to them before Mancillo,' said Nina. 'If we drive to the nearest village, we can find a phone and warn the Guatemalan government about the coup.'

'Got to get out of here first,' Eddie noted. A current became discernible, heading towards the disturbance in the water.

'What if the outflow's too narrow for us to fit through?' Nina asked.

'I've done some cave diving,' Diego assured her. 'It'd have to be pretty wide to drain that much water quickly enough.' He gestured towards the waterfall. 'I'm more worried about how rough it is inside. If it's fast enough to pull us through and then we hit a jagged rock . . .'

'Yeah, thanks for that. I think I'd have been better off not knowing.'

'Nowt we can do about it now,' said Eddie, glancing back. A shout rolled across the cavern above, someone on a high ledge across from the map pointing down at them. 'If we don't go through it, we're going to get shot.'

'Can they hit us from that far away?' asked Rosamaria.

'They're special forces,' said Nina. 'They can probably hit us with a *knife* from that far away!'

The draw of the current was now impossible to mistake. The water's surface was no longer flat, instead bending downwards into a vortex at the cavern wall. Floating wood and vegetation carried into the chamber by the waterfall was now on its way out again, spiralling around the whirlpool's event horizon.

Eddie looked back at Diego. 'You're the expert at this. What do we do?'

The young man looked unhappy. 'I didn't say I was an expert. I just said I've been cave diving!'

'Oh, fucking great! Guess I'll have to figure it out, then.'

'I don't think there'll be much to figure,' said Nina. Another man, carrying a rifle, was now picking his way across the ledge. 'We've got to go through it.'

'Yeah,' her husband reluctantly agreed. 'Okay, take deep breaths, then follow me – and hopefully I'll see you all on the other side!'

He took in several rapid lungfuls of air, giving the ledge a last look – and seeing the gunman raise his weapon. 'Go!'

He held his breath – and dropped underwater as the crack of rifle fire echoed through the cavern.

The current had already been pulling at him strongly. Now, as he swam into it, it was as if he'd been snatched up by a tornado. The vortex sent him tumbling as he was dragged into the outflow. He'd intended to keep his arms extended to feel his way through, but instantly knew that would end with at least one broken bone. Instead he hunched up tightly, protecting his head as best he could – and hoping the others would realise they had to do the same—

He hit a wall, pain exploding through his elbow. Sharp stone sliced at his upper arm. Then he was whisked on, spinning around to slam against the floor. On and on he went, bashing against the channel's sides, the pressure on his lungs rising as his body burned through its reserves of oxygen . . .

Then suddenly he was flying.

A flash of panic: he was in free fall for the second time in minutes. Wind rushed through his wet clothing as he plummeted from the top of a waterfall. If the pool below was too shallow, he was dead—

Another hard splashdown – then he hit unyielding rock below the water.

The blow jarred agonisingly up through his spine. An involuntary yell was choked by a mouthful of water. He blew it out, then fought to bring himself back to the surface. The landing had been hard, but he had escaped injury – just. His lower back would probably be one massive bruise for the next several days, though.

If he survived that long.

He broke through the churning water. Where were the others?

The question was answered a moment later as he heard Nina's scream rise in pitch and volume. She splashed down behind him, and he swam to her as she resurfaced. 'Eddie!' she gasped, wiping water from her eyes. 'Eddie, are you here?'

'Yeah, I'm here, I'm okay,' he said. More splashes signalled the arrival of Diego and his mother. 'Are you all right?'

'I've hurt my leg again. Ow, shit!' she added as she tried to swim. 'Goddammit, that hurts.'

Eddie took hold of Nina and helped her to the bank, taking in their new surroundings. They had ended up in a pool at the base of a sheer rocky cliff, the waterfall gushing from near its top, jungle overhanging it. The threatened storm had arrived: it was now raining heavily, the sky dark with menacing clouds. Treetops whipped back and forth in the wind. 'At least we can't get any wetter,' he joked – then something floating nearby caught his eye. 'Ay up! Look what I've found.'

'You're kidding,' said Nina as he retrieved his leather jacket.

'Hey, don't knock it. At least we've still got some luck left.'

'So long as that wasn't the last of it,' she said as he brought her onto the muddy shore.

A shout from behind: 'Help!' They turned to see Diego struggling to hold Rosamaria above the surface. 'Help!' he cried again, near panic. 'She's been shot!'

Eddie gave Nina a conflicted look – Rosamaria had after all been directly responsible for everything that had happened on and in the mountain – but he knew what she wanted him to do without needing a word to be said. 'Fuck's sake,' he muttered, wading back into the pool. He swam to Diego, and together they brought his mother to the bank. 'Where was she hit?'

'Her arm, I think.'

Eddie examined her. A gash ran across her forehead from her uncontrolled journey through the outflow. One sleeve was torn; his fingertips became stained with red when he peeled open the material. Rosamaria flinched even in her barely conscious state. A round had ripped through her biceps from a high angle, clipping her torso as it exited. 'She's going to lose a lot of blood, fast, if we don't get a tourniquet on that arm.'

Diego fumbled at his clothing. 'Here – use my belt.' He handed it to Eddie.

Nina sat up, checking her own injuries. Her trousers were torn, a deep cut gouged into her thigh by a rock, but it was nothing compared to the other woman's wound. 'Will she be okay?'

'Need to get her to a hospital,' said Eddie, all business as he drew the belt tight around Rosamaria's upper arm. She squealed in pain. 'That's as much as I can do with what we've got.'

'There might be a first-aid kit in the Jeep,' said Diego. 'We're not far from it. We passed this waterfall on the way up.'

'Then we'd better get moving. Nina, can you walk?'

Nina struggled to stand, pain surging through numerous new bruises and cuts. But she stayed upright, pressing a hand against her thigh. 'Yeah.'

'Okay, me and Diego'll take Rosamaria.' The redhead didn't have the energy or inclination to correct his grammar. Eddie donned his sodden jacket, then the two men carefully lifted Rosamaria, supporting her between them. 'Which way?'

Diego gestured downhill. 'Over there.' They set off through the rain-swept jungle.

'Did you get them?' Mancillo called across the chamber.

The soldiers on the ledge shook their heads. 'I winged one of them,' replied Borrayo, the rifleman. 'They haven't come back up, though.'

'There must be a way out under the water. It's got to drain to *somewhere*.' The major thought for a moment, then: 'We need to get to the surface and find the cult's vehicles. If Wilde and the others get out, they'll go for them as well.'

'They'll have gotten out,' Macy told him defiantly. 'They'll find a phone, and tell the government what you're doing. Then your coup's over before it even starts, and you'll spend the rest of your life in jail – if you're lucky.'

He gave her a baleful look. 'You're a very obnoxious girl, did you know that? Typical American. But your mom and dad won't do anything – because I have *you*.' He grabbed her arm, far from gently. 'They know that if they try to stop me, I'll kill you.' Cruel amusement in his eyes as he glanced towards Juarez, who was tying a makeshift bandage torn from his clothing around his wounded wrist. He gave her a nasty leering grin. 'If you're lucky.'

'You bastard,' she replied, trying to mask her fear.

The soldiers from the ledge joined the others. Juarez finished binding his wound, and at Mancillo's command grabbed Macy firmly by her arm. Then the major led the group up the steps, beginning the journey to the jungle above.

29

Despite her injured leg, Nina was forced to act as pathfinder on the hike downhill. The torrential rain had turned the ground into sludgy mud, and anywhere not a quagmire was home to rocks and gnarled roots ready to trip the unwary. Eddie and Diego followed her, supporting the barely conscious Rosamaria.

Even with Nina picking out a relatively safe route, Diego still stumbled. His mother gasped as she bumped against him. 'Mom!' he said. 'Are you okay?'

She raised her head slightly. 'No, my arm – it hurts, but . . . I can't feel it, at the same time. That makes no sense . . .'

'We'll get you to a hospital,' he promised. 'It's not far to the Jeep now.'

'Oh, Diego,' she said in a tremulous sigh. 'What have I done? Ciro was mad, a murderer, but I believed him, I followed him – I loved him! All those things he did, and I helped him! What was I *thinking*?'

'It's okay, Mom. It's okay,' he said. 'You were in a bad place, and he took advantage of you. It wasn't your fault.'

'But it was! Nobody forced me to do all those terrible things. I was a part of it all. And I helped him find Earthbreaker, and the temple of Tekuazotl. All those people who died at Teotihuacán – it is all my fault!' She clenched her eyes shut, sobbing.

Nina felt some sympathy for the other archaeologist, but not yet enough to forgive her – and they had more immediate concerns. 'Let's get out of here and rescue Macy,' she said firmly. 'That's all I care about.'

'Same here,' said Eddie. 'How much further?'

Diego peered through the trees. 'Not far. As long as we keep going downhill, we can't miss the road.'

They continued their treacherous trek through the storm-lashed jungle.

Macy saw daylight ahead as her captors neared the Under-world's gate. It was much darker than when they'd first entered, however. The storm had arrived. 'We can't go out in that!' she protested.

Mancillo pushed her onwards. 'It's just rain. I've been in worse. I've fought in worse.'

She cringed as she passed through the threshold. Her clothing was soaked in moments. But the unpleasant sensation was forgotten as she looked ahead. A gap in the trees revealed the landscape beyond, the deluge reducing the hills almost to two-dimensional cut-outs. But there was one bright point of colour amongst the flat grey.

An orange glow, red and yellow flares flickering within it.

Mancillo halted. 'The volcano,' he said, impressed. 'The dagger really did start an eruption at Tacaná.' Earthbreaker now sat, somewhat awkwardly, in the sheath for his lost combat knife on his belt. He put a hand on it. 'It works. I can cause an earthquake, whenever I want . . .' He stared at the distant fire, falling into a contemplative silence as the ancient weapon's true power and potential became clear. Then, as if stung by Macy's disdainful glare, he snapped back to the present. 'All right,' he called to his men. 'Spread out and head downhill, double time. When we reach the road, find the vehicles.' His next command horrified Macy. 'If you see anyone, kill them!'

★ ★ ★

'There's the road!' Nina called. Through the incessant downpour, she spotted a muddy brown line cutting through the trees. She led Eddie, Diego and Rosamaria towards it.

'Where did you park?' the Yorkshireman asked. 'Off to the left, or the right?'

Diego searched for landmarks. 'The left, I think,' he said, spotting a large fallen tree beside the track to their right. 'I don't remember passing that.'

Nina angled leftwards towards the old mining road. They soon reached it. Walking became easier, but with less cover from the jungle canopy, the rain fell even more heavily. After a couple of miserable minutes, she saw colour through the trees ahead – a *lot* of colour. 'I think I can see the bus.'

'That's it,' Diego confirmed. 'Mom, we're almost there. Just hold on, okay?'

Rosamaria's reply was weak, tired. 'I'll try.'

'You can do it. We'll get you to a hospital.'

'And then to prison.' Resignation was clear in every weary word. Her son drew in a breath as if to give her reassurance, but could find nothing to say.

Nina neared the parked bus, also seeing a Jeep Wrangler. She checked inside the open-topped 4x4. 'No keys.'

Eddie assessed the vehicle. 'It's old enough for me to hot-wire.' He guided Diego and Rosamaria to the bus. 'Get her inside and sit her down until we're ready to go.'

Diego pushed at the bus's door; slightly to his surprise, it opened. He and Eddie helped her through the doorway to rest on the step, then the Yorkshireman went to the Jeep.

'How long will it take to start it?' Nina asked him.

'Depends if I can find any tools. I'll probably have to break the steering lock.' He climbed in and searched the cabin. The vehicle's owner turned out to have been prepared for any eventuality on Guatemala's rough roads; a bag under the front passenger seat contained assorted basic tools, including a screw-driver and a pair of multi-purpose pliers. 'These should do. It'll take a few minutes.' He used the screwdriver to prise off part of the steering column's plastic cover, exposing the ignition wiring. 'Keep an eye on the jungle,' he said, gesturing up the slope. 'I don't think it'll take Mancillo's lot long to catch up.'

Nina took up shelter under a nearby tree, watching nervously as he set to work.

Despite the slippery ground, Mancillo and his men descended at a rapid jog, traversing the tricky terrain with experienced ease. The only thing slowing them was Macy, who was both far less fleet-footed, and determined to help her parents escape. She tripped over a root – magnifying her genuine stumble into a full fall.

Mancillo stopped and nudged her forcefully with his boot. 'Get up. And stop wasting time.'

'I fell over!' she snapped. 'I'm not a fricking goat, I can't run over ground like this.'

'Then I'll shoot you in the leg and carry you. A bullet won't affect whether you can use the dagger, will it?' He drew his sidearm.

'All right, all right, I'm getting up!' said Macy, reluctantly rising.

'Good. Now keep moving.'

They set off again. It wasn't long before a shout came from the trees ahead.

One of the Kaibiles had reached the road.

Eddie worked fast, finding the three wires he needed to activate the ignition switch and using the pliers to cut them and strip off some insulation. He twisted the first two together, then bent the end of the third into a small hook and touched it experimentally against the others. A spark, and the starter motor turned over. He withdrew the wire and used the screwdriver to lever away a metal plate under the ignition system. It broke loose – and a spring popped out.

If he had done the job correctly, the steering lock would now be disengaged. He gave the wheel a half-turn. It moved freely. 'Okay, we're ready to go!' he shouted to Nina—

Another shout from not far away: a man's voice. 'Did you hear that?' said Nina, hurrying to the Jeep.

'I heard that,' he confirmed. 'Diego! Come on!' He ran to the bus as Nina clambered into the 4x4.

Diego brought Rosamaria out. Together they carried her to the Jeep and lifted her into the rear. She gasped in pain as her wounded arm bumped against the seat. Diego vaulted in beside her.

Eddie took the wheel. He hooked the third wire around the first two, crimping it with his thumb and forefinger. An electric shock made him flinch, but the engine started. 'Hold on,' he said, putting the Jeep into gear.

He drove forward, swinging into the undergrowth before sharply spinning the wheel in the opposite direction. The Jeep made a tight turn, barely clearing the trees on the track's far side as it came about. Eddie straightened out, increasing power. He checked the mirror. A running figure was visible on the track behind – carrying a rifle.

The man stopped running—

'Down!' Eddie barked, ducking. The others followed suit as the Kaibile opened fire. Rounds snapped past, some striking the Wrangler's rear. Diego yelped as one ripped through the top corner of his seat.

Eddie swerved the Jeep to make it a harder target until he was able to bring it behind a stand of trees. The gunfire stopped. 'Anyone hit?' The replies were all in the negative. 'Okay, they won't catch us in that bus even if they get it started.'

'What about Macy?' said Nina. 'They've still got her.'

'We might be able to set up an ambush at that bridge.'

'How? They've got guns, and we haven't.'

'Yeah, that's the bit I'm still working on.' He checked the mirror again. The bus was now out of sight. 'At least we're way ahead of 'em.'

Mancillo reached the bus at a run, hauling the protesting Macy. His four remaining men were already at the stationary vehicle. 'What happened?'

'They got away in a Jeep,' Juarez told him.

'Oh, gee,' said Macy, feeling a surge of hope. 'That's too bad.'

'They haven't escaped yet,' Mancillo growled. 'I remember seeing this road on the map back at base. Galarza, Juarez, get the bus started. Watch the girl – we need her. Borrayo, Porras, with me.'

'Where are we going, sir?' Borrayo asked.

Mancillo left the road and started down the hill at a run. 'We're taking a shortcut!'

Eddie slowed as the road dipped into a hairpin turn. 'How the hell did they get that bus around this?' he said as he eased the Wrangler through the tight bend.

'This is nothing,' said Diego. 'The bus drivers in this part of the world are crazy. They fly along narrow roads I wouldn't even want to take on foot.'

The Jeep made it around the turn. Eddie increased speed again, the 4x4 jolting along the rutted track. Even though the old mining road had straightened, he didn't dare risk going too fast. The windscreen wipers were swiping at full speed, but the rain was so heavy he could still hardly see. 'How far to the bridge?'

'I don't know. Mom and I landed on this side of it. I remember this bit, though. There's another hairpin, and then the

300

road runs quite close to a canyon, so the bridge can't be too far away.'

Nina looked back at Rosamaria. The other woman's face was tight with pain. 'Rosamaria, how are you managing?'

'Not good,' she replied. Her breathing was shallow and laboured. 'We are bumping so much, it is hurting.'

Diego took hold of her hand and drew her wounded arm away from the seat back. 'I'll hold onto you, Mom.'

She managed a faint smile. '*Siempre has sido un buen chico, Diego.*' He smiled back at the compliment, but the worry didn't leave his face.

'I can see the next turn,' said Eddie, slowing again. 'Once we're round it, we should be clear.'

Mancillo and his two men raced downhill, weaving between trees and hurdling broken branches. Through the rain he saw the brown line of the old road ahead – and heard an engine, getting louder.

He slowed – but the Jeep swept past before he had a chance to ready his gun, heading from left to right. If his memory of the map was accurate, it would soon reach the last leg of the switchback road.

'Down here!' he ordered, speeding up again and angling left. There was one final chance to intercept the fleeing vehicle. A glance right as he reached the muddy track. The Jeep was about two hundred metres away, brake lights aglow as it rounded a tight corner.

He looked ahead again as he re-entered the jungle. 'Get your weapons ready!'

Eddie guided the Wrangler through the looping bend. Even at low speed, the 4x4 threatened to slither sideways in the wet mud. But the track ahead appeared relatively straight for some distance.

To his right, the ground sloped down to the canyon Diego had mentioned.

Feeling more confident, he brought the Jeep to a steady fifty kilometres per hour. Not exactly hyperspeed, but given the conditions, as much as he was willing to risk. 'Any idea how long it'll take to reach the nearest village?' he asked.

'I don't know,' Diego said apologetically. 'Maybe a half-hour?'

'What about phones?' said Nina. 'Do they have cell service out here, or will it only be landlines?'

'Some places on the Mexican side of the border have cell towers, but I don't know about Guatemala—' His eyes went wide as he saw movement to their left. 'Shit, look out!'

Eddie spotted figures running downhill towards them. He immediately accelerated, passing them, but he knew they were armed. 'Get down!'

Nina dropped as far as she could into the footwell as gunfire erupted behind. Even though the Wrangler was now moving away from the soldiers, it was still well within rifle range. Shots whip-cracked past – then struck home as the shooters refined their aim. Lead struck metal, plastic, rubber—

And flesh.

Rosamaria lurched, blood from a ragged neck wound splattering the seats in front of her. But nobody had any time to react. The rear right tyre exploded, the Jeep slewing sharply around. Eddie fought to straighten out, braking hard, but the remaining wheels aquaplaned over the sludgy mud. The Wrangler crashed through the undergrowth along the right-hand side of the track . . .

Then slithered uncontrollably down the slope – towards the ravine below.

Low branches smashed the windscreen, showering Nina and Eddie with glass. Dangling vines and creepers whipped the Jeep's occupants as it bounded violently downhill. Eddie yanked the handbrake, trying to swing the vehicle into a tree – a hard stop now would be infinitely preferable to going over a cliff.

He was only half successful. The tail clipped the trunk, spinning the 4x4 violently around. It hurtled sidelong through the mud, picking up speed. 'Jump out!' Eddie yelled.

Nina scrambled from the lurching vehicle's side, landing with a splat in the slurry of dead foliage and running storm water. But she still wasn't safe. She clawed at the vegetation, trying to slow herself as she slid after the Jeep.

Eddie clambered over her empty seat to follow her. 'Diego!' he shouted. 'Get out!'

The young man looked back at him desperately. 'Not without Mom!'

A glance at Rosamaria told Eddie she wasn't going anywhere. A chunk had been blasted from her neck, which was running with blood from a ruptured artery. Without immediate surgery, she wouldn't survive – and there was absolutely no chance of her receiving any. 'She's gone!' The ravine loomed before them. '*Go!*'

He leapt from the Jeep, thumping down on the muddy hillside. If Diego didn't follow, he was as dead as his mother . . .

But his own survival took priority. He grabbed at ferns and vines as he slithered downhill. They snapped in his hands. The Jeep was acting like a plough, shredding the larger plants ahead of him. Behind him, Nina yelled a panicked obscenity as she also failed to halt her slide. He rolled, trying to bring himself clear of the vehicle's swathe through the jungle—

Another cry, this one from below as Diego made a hard landing. A moment later came a huge bang as the Wrangler hit a tree stump. It flipped over, bowling ever faster down the hill – and flew over the edge, Rosamaria still inside.

Eddie grabbed at the stump as he passed. He caught a protruding chunk of bark – which broke off in his hand. Diego yelled in fear as he neared the cliff. There was nothing Eddie could do to help him, still struggling to save himself—

A clutch of vines sprouted from the ground, wrapped parasitically around a tree teetering at the ravine's edge. He threw out his arms – catching one of the lianas. It instantly tore from the trunk . . .

But its root held.

Just.

A length of the creeper jerked from the ground, tendrils popping and ripping before the thickness of the tangled net beneath the soil caught it. His hands slipped along the wet vine, tearing away its leaves. He squeezed harder, slowing himself, then finally stopping – with both legs dangling over nothingness below.

He let out a shaky, relieved breath – then looked up. Where was Nina?

Coming right at him.

She collided with him – and the root ripped free. He grabbed her as they both slithered over the edge—

This time it was Nina who caught a creeper hanging over the ravine's side. Her own weight combined with Eddie's was too great for her to keep hold – but she arrested their fall for the split second he needed to seize another thick vine. They both jerked to a stop, swinging beneath the mass of roots overhanging the top of the precipice. Dirt and water fell on them from above.

Nina panted in fear, clutching at more vines. 'Jesus!' she said, scraping a boot against the cliff to find a shallow foothold. 'Are you okay? What about Rosamaria and Diego?'

'Rosamaria's dead,' was his blunt reply. 'Diego, I don't know.' He looked down. A swollen river rushed through the canyon over a hundred feet below, branches and other debris swept along by the current. The Jeep was a mangled wreck amongst the driftwood.

Something else floated beside it. Rosamaria was face-down in the water, limbs splayed limply as she was carried downstream. But where was her son?

A gasp not far away gave him his answer. He looked past Nina to find Diego straining to pull himself up a twisted knot of vines. The young Mexican looked up at them. 'Professor Wilde, Mr Chase – you made it!'

'You sound shocked,' Eddie replied.

'I'm shocked that any of us made it.' He stopped his ascent, a terrible thought coming to him. 'My mom . . . ?'

Eddie paused before replying. 'I'm sorry.'

'Oh . . .' Diego closed his eyes and leaned his head against the taut creepers. '*Mamá* . . .'

'Quiet, quiet,' Nina said urgently. 'Someone's coming!'

Voices reached them from above.

The Kaibiles.

30

Mancillo led the way down the slope. He could have sent his men to carry out the reconnaissance task, but this was one kill-count he wanted to do himself. 'Spread out,' he ordered his companions. 'If they managed to jump clear, find their tracks.' The soldiers moved to obey.

The Wrangler's path was easy to follow. It had ripped up a swathe of undergrowth on its journey downhill. Even though the route had been cleared, it was still far from easy to traverse. The ground was steep and perilously slippery, rivulets of rainwater gushing down it. He hopped from root to root, seeking out firm footing as he descended.

But despite the treacherous path, it didn't take him long to reach the bottom. At least one of his quarry had bailed out of the Jeep before it went over; the mark where they had landed was obvious. So was the weaving groove in the mud as they slid down to the edge – and over it.

He leaned out to look into the ravine below. Mud and stones fell away underfoot as his weight shifted; he withdrew slightly, supporting himself on a nearby tree. At first, he saw only drifting branches in the churning water below – then, looking downstream, the Jeep's battered rear end breaking through the surface. Where were its occupants?

There was one, still further away: the Mexican woman, Rendón. He watched her, rapidly judging that she was either unconscious or dead. In these conditions, the former would soon become the latter. What about the others? His gaze returned to

306

the river below. There was no shoreline, the swollen torrent breaking against rock. Nowhere for anyone to land – or hide.

He leaned forward again to look higher up the cliff—

A root snapped under his foot, clods of earth dropping away. Mancillo hurriedly withdrew. No sense risking his life, not now. He looked back downriver in the hope of spotting another body. But all he saw was Rendón as she was carried out of sight.

Not being able to confirm the other kills irked him. But even if Wilde, Chase and the boy had survived the fall, they would almost certainly be hurt – and they were in the middle of a jungle during a storm. On foot, there was no way they could reach even the nearest village before nightfall. By then, he would have made contact with his co-conspirators; maybe even have carried out his plan.

Even if they were still alive, they could do nothing to stop him.

Buoyed, he stepped back as the two other soldiers approached. 'Did you find anything?' he asked.

'No, sir,' Porras replied.

Borrayo also shook his head. 'No sign of anybody – and no tracks, either. They went with the Jeep.'

One last look back at the river, then Mancillo started back uphill. 'Let's get to the road.'

Nina and Eddie clung to the vines, listening to the activity above. At one point a foot appeared directly above them, dislodging dirt onto Eddie's head. They both pressed themselves against the cliff. If the soldier leaned out far enough to see past the over-hanging vegetation . . .

But he retreated. Another exchange, Mancillo talking to his men, then their footsteps faded.

Nina raised her head warily. 'Do you think it's safe to go up?' she whispered.

'Give it a minute,' Eddie replied. 'If they look back and see us, we're fucked.'

'What, even more than now?'

'We're not dead, but they think we are. That gives us *something*.'

'My mom's dead,' said Diego quietly. Nina turned to see him staring blankly at the rocky wall. 'She . . . God. I don't know what to do. I don't know what to *think*. Everything's . . .' His face tightened, lips trembling with barely contained emotion.

'Just hold on,' Nina told him. 'This will sound harsh, but don't think about it. Right now, we need to concentrate on surviving. We'll wait for the soldiers to go, then climb up – and rescue Macy.'

Anger flashed across Diego's face at her bluntness, but only for a moment. 'Okay,' he said. 'Okay. We'll find Macy. It's my fault this happened to her after all.'

'It's not your fault,' said Eddie, to Nina's – and Diego's – surprise. 'You didn't know what your mum had got into, not all of it.'

The young man nodded. 'I'll help you find her. But – I can't stop thinking about Mom,' he admitted, voice cracking. Tears joined the rainwater running down his face. 'How do I do it? How do I go on without . . .'

'You just do what's needed to stay alive,' said Nina sympathetically, 'and to protect the people who are still here. That's all you can do for now. Everything else has to wait until later.'

He forced his feelings back under control. 'Okay. I can do that. I can.' He looked back at Nina. 'It sounds like . . . you've been through this before.'

'I have,' she replied. 'Too many times.'

Eddie cocked his head at a new noise. 'Ay up. I can hear an engine.'

He cautiously pulled himself upwards until he could peer past the overhanging roots. Bright colours flickered through the trees above. 'It's the bus,' he told Nina and Diego. 'Give 'em a minute to get clear, then we'll climb up – and go after them.'

'What happened, sir?' asked Juarez, at the wheel, as the three dripping-wet soldiers boarded. 'Did you get them?'

Macy was in the seat immediately behind him, Galarza guarding her from across the aisle. Mancillo looked straight at her as he replied. 'They went over the cliff,' he said. 'They're all dead.'

He kept his eyes fixed on her, waiting for his words to sink in. It did not take long. 'They – no, no, they can't be,' Macy said, despair rising in her voice. 'They *can't* be!'

'They're dead,' the major repeated, turning away. 'Let's go.'

The bus set off. Mancillo sat directly behind Macy. He watched her impassively as she started to shudder, her body flinching with the effort of holding in her sobs.

'They're gone,' said Eddie as the bus passed out of sight. 'All right, let's get after them.'

He tightened his grip on the creepers, reaching down to take hold of Nina's free hand. She clasped it, and he raised her higher, letting her grab the vines above to pull herself up. She brought her knee over the lip of the cliff and dragged herself back onto solid ground. Once sure that she was safe, Eddie followed her up.

Diego had already made the ascent. He stared down into the canyon. His mother had been carried out of sight by the churning river. 'Are you okay?' asked Nina.

He didn't reply for a moment – then he started up the slope, jaw set. 'Yeah,' he said. 'Let's get those bastards.'

★ ★ ★

Macy barely registered the bus's bumpy journey. All she could think about was Mancillo's callous, dismissive words about her parents: *they're dead*. Her first reaction had been shock, followed by denial. They *couldn't* be! They'd been through so much before, but always survived, always came back to her . . .

But the Kaibiles' commander had appeared completely certain. Mancillo didn't seem someone to leave loose ends. If he believed that her parents, and Diego and his mother, were dead . . . they probably were.

And that was when she started to cry.

Even in her rising grief, she refused to let Mancillo or the other soldiers see it, turning her face away. She wouldn't give them the satisfaction of knowing that they'd beaten her, crushed her. She would stand up to them. She would resist. She wouldn't let them use her to kill potentially thousands of people. She wouldn't!

But deep down, she knew there was nothing she could do to stop them.

They had won.

She squeezed her eyes shut, feeling tears roll down her cheeks. Grief rose within her, a gnawing, terrible emptiness tearing at her soul. Only days before, she had felt the awful sensation of loss following her great-grandmother's funeral. Now it was back, amplified a thousandfold. The most important people in her life were gone. She would never see them again. Throat tightening, she shuddered, a cry of pain and anguish about to escape . . .

The bus braked hard. Unprepared, Macy almost slid from her seat. Mancillo rose, standing beside Juarez to look at what lay ahead.

The bridge.

It swayed in the storm, rain splashing from every rotten plank. Even inside the bus, the creaks of its support ropes could be heard over the wind and the pounding of raindrops on the roof. 'Fuck me!' said Juarez. 'We'll never get this thing across there!'

'They drove it over, we can drive it back,' Mancillo replied. 'Galarza, go check it.'

Juarez pushed the button to open the door. Galarza jumped out and went to the bridge, walking part-way across and examining the beams before returning. 'Some of the planks are broken,' he reported. 'But I think we can make it. We'll just have to take it very carefully.'

'You mean *I'll* have to,' Juarez said unhappily.

'You're our best driver,' said Mancillo. He addressed the two other soldiers. 'Borrayo! You act as guide. Go in front to keep the bus absolutely in the middle of the bridge, and watch out for broken planks.'

Borrayo took his cigarette from his mouth and blew out an aggrieved jet of smoke. 'Aw, *jefe*. I just lit up a new one.'

'You can be Minister of Tobacco after the coup,' Mancillo told him, with a faint smile. 'But before that can happen, we need to cross this bridge.' He pulled Macy up by her wrist. 'Okay, everyone else goes over on foot. Galarza, you guard her. Make sure she doesn't try anything.'

Galarza gave Macy a lazy, malevolent grin. 'Count on it.'

She tried to hide her fear behind a mask of disgust as Mancillo released her, Galarza taking hold instead to bring her off the bus. Rain hit her again. But her discomfort at being soaked was nothing to what she felt at the sight of the bridge. 'We can't get across that!' she said. 'It's rocking about so much, we'll fall off.'

'Or maybe you hope *we'll* fall off, eh?' said Galarza, not easing his hold. 'Move.'

Mancillo took the lead, the others forming a line behind him. He started across the bridge, following its centre line. The first few metres were easy enough, but as he moved further, it began to twist and tip alarmingly. He widened his stance, extending his arms for balance. 'We can do it,' he called back to the others. 'Just take it slow and steady. Spread out so we're not too close together.'

'You heard the man,' said Macy, when Galarza didn't release her. 'How about you let go of me?'

'I don't think so,' he replied. He turned his upper body to keep her at arm's length behind him. 'Try anything stupid, and I'll throw you over the side.'

Mancillo gave him a sharp look. 'We need her to use the dagger. Keep her alive!'

Galarza lowered his head at the criticism. 'Understood, sir.' He transferred his anger back upon his charge. 'All right, you little bitch. Walk.' He followed Mancillo, pulling Macy with him.

She forced away thoughts of her parents, focusing on the possibility of escape. If she kicked Galarza's feet from under him, or knocked him over the edge . . .

But they remained that: only thoughts. The chunky Porras took up position behind her, blocking any chance of retreat. And after only a few steps, she realised that merely staying on her own feet would be difficult enough. The planks were slippery, every step tricky as the bridge swayed in the wind. The shin-high guide ropes along each edge looked almost worse than useless as a safety measure. If anything, they seemed more likely to trip people right over the side.

Mancillo continued his advance, stepping carefully over weakened or broken wood. He was forced to stop at the halfway point as a strong gust hit, the whole deck twisting. Macy gasped, dropping low to grab a plank for support. Galarza staggered and almost fell. He swore loudly as he managed to catch himself. For a moment he lost his hold on Macy's arm, but before she could react, he grabbed her again. 'You stay there!' he snarled.

'That's what I'm trying to do!' she shot back. 'Dumbass,' she added in English.

312

Galarza might not have understood the word, but he knew the tone. 'Watch yourself,' he said, scowling. 'The boss needs you alive. He didn't say unhurt.'

'Ooh, a real tough guy, threatening a teenage girl,' said Macy – but the undisguised menace in his voice sent a chill through her.

The bridge slowly levelled out. 'We need to move faster,' said Mancillo. He set off again, increasing his pace despite the danger.

The group had to pause a couple more times as the deck rocked underfoot, but still made quick progress. Macy glanced down as she stepped over a gap where a broken plank had fallen away. The swollen river rushed past forty feet below. If she broke free and jumped over the side, the drop should be survivable, but there was enough debris in the water to hugely increase the odds of injury – and the low rumble of a waterfall downstream put paid to any further desperate ideas of escape.

Mancillo took the last few metres at a run to reach the far side. He turned with relief to urge the others on. Galarza followed him onto solid ground, Macy behind him. Porras cleared the crossing a few seconds later. The rain's intensity fell as they reached the cover of the trees along the track. 'All right,' said the major. 'Let's get the bus across. Galarza, watch her.'

The downpour was now so strong that the bridge's opposite end was half hidden in a grey haze. The bus was a blocky shape beyond, only its headlights standing out clearly. Mancillo waved, signalling for it to start its journey. Borrayo briefly blotted out one of the lights as he moved in front of the vehicle and cautiously backed onto the crossing. The bus, moving at slower than walking pace, gingerly followed him.

Macy watched as it crawled towards her. Borrayo occasionally waved his arms, telling the driver to steer left or right to keep the bus centred. Even holding a straight course, its weight was putting a dangerous strain on the old ropes. They were lashed around logs driven deep into the ground, but their tortured moans made her want to move clear – *well* clear. Her attempt to back away was rebuffed by a hard shove from Galarza. She gave him a poisonous glare, then turned back to the slow-motion spectacle.

The thunder of a waterfall echoing from the canyon almost drowned out Nina's laboured breathing. 'Slow down, slow down,' she rasped as she hurried after Eddie and Diego. 'I can't keep this up!'

Eddie slowed to let her draw level. 'We've got to keep going, love. If they get across the bridge, we'll never catch them – and we'll never get Macy back.'

'It can't be much further,' said Diego. 'We're past where Mom and I met Ciro and the others.'

Eddie took Nina's hand. 'You can do it. Just stick with me.'

'Okay,' she said, panting. 'God, I should have gone running with you and Macy all those times!'

They kept going. Before long, the track ahead curved towards the ravine – and Eddie pulled Nina to a halt. 'Diego! Slow down – I can hear the bus.'

They advanced at a cautious pace. One end of a rope bridge came into view past rocks and trees, the juddering snarl of a big diesel engine rolling across the canyon. Eddie led the others into the cover of roadside undergrowth.

He peered out. There was the bus, about a third of the way over the crossing. Black exhaust smoke spewed from its rear as it revved in low gear. The bridge juddered and swayed alarmingly. One of the Kaibiles was ahead of it, waving the driver forward at a snail's pace. 'Where's Macy?' Nina asked. 'God, if she's on the bus and it goes over—'

Eddie's gaze went to the bridge's far end. Rain-shrouded figures stood on the track beyond it. The bus's headlights picked out Mancillo, standing with hands on hips as he observed the crossing. Behind him . . . 'I see her,' he said with relief. 'She's on the other side.'

'Oh, thank God. But how are we going to reach her?'

The Yorkshireman looked back at the crawling vehicle. It was an old American school bus, painted in garish colours with a luggage rack on its roof. But one thing hadn't been altered: the rear emergency door . . . 'Wait here,' he said. 'I'm going to get her.'

'How?' Nina demanded.

'The usual way – just do stuff and hope it turns out all right!'

He dropped low and scurried to the bridge. The bus took up almost its entire width, barely enough room to get by on either side, and even then only by turning sideways. The man guiding it and the Kaibiles on the far side were all blocked from his view by the vehicle – which meant he was blocked from *their* view. The only person who might see him would be the driver, if he checked his mirrors, but he should be entirely occupied with keeping the bus from going over the side . . .

A last look back at Nina, then he ran onto the bridge.

His burst of speed didn't last long. Even with the bus weighing it down, the structure still swayed alarmingly in the wind, and the planks underfoot were slick with rain and rot. He slowed, planting each step carefully to find balance.

But he was still moving faster than the bus. It inched onwards, rear wheels slithering on wet wood. Eddie gained on it – then had to stop and brace himself as the deck tipped to the left. The bus jerked to a stop, air brakes hissing. The sudden jolt made the whole crossing shake. He held in an obscenity as he slipped sideways, jamming a heel against a cracked plank to support himself. The tilt worsened, the canyon upriver coming into view beyond the edge—

Mouldering wood splintered under Eddie's boot. He fell onto his side – and slithered towards the drop.

The flooded canyon opened out before him as he went over the edge—

He threw out an arm – catching the guide rope. He held in a cry, managing to bring up his other hand to clutch the line. He hung there for a moment, then dragged himself back up as the bridge started to tip back the other way.

A glance along its length. Nobody had seen him . . .

Juarez, knuckles white on the steering wheel, exhaled in relief as the bridge slowly rolled back towards level. He'd thought the bus was about to slide sideways. The pathetic little rope along the edge would do nothing to stop it from plunging into the ravine. He checked the side mirror to see how close he had come to disaster—

And saw a pair of legs scrabble up onto the crossing.

'What the fuck?' he gasped – before realising the truth. Someone had survived the Jeep's crash. He looked ahead. Borrayo was just regaining his footing. 'Hey! Hey!' Juarez shouted. 'Someone's still alive – they're behind the bus!'

Borrayo stared at him in incomprehension before cupping a hand to one ear. The wind and the ceaseless rattle of rain on the bus's hood were drowning him out. Juarez swore again, then slammed his hand on the horn and flashed the headlights to draw Mancillo's attention. 'Behind the bus!' he yelled again, opening the door so Borrayo could hear him. 'Someone's behind the bus!'

Macy saw Mancillo tense as the deck tipped sideways, only relaxing as it began to roll back. A close call, and the bus still had over half the crossing to traverse—

The horn suddenly blared, a rapid-fire tattoo – a warning. The headlights flared in accompaniment. Something was wrong. But the bus wasn't slipping, so what was happening?

Galarza pushed Macy forward and stood beside his

316

commander, raising a hand to shield his eyes from the rain as he stared across the bridge. 'What's the matt—'

Macy threw herself at him, driving an elbow into his sternum as hard as she could.

Her father's training had ensured that was enough to hurt even a grown man. Caught completely by surprise, Galarza gasped, lurching backwards. Macy burst into a run, snatching Earthbreaker from the startled Mancillo's holster as she went. She hared onto the bridge with the dagger tingling in her hand. Hope had given her the answer that the Kaibiles had missed: the driver had raised the alarm because someone had escaped from the Jeep before it went over the cliff.

Porras snapped up his rifle. He fired – as Mancillo swept his arm up beneath its barrel, sending the round skywards. 'No! Idiot! We need her alive! Bring her back!'

The abashed Porras shouldered his gun and ran onto the bridge after Macy.

31

Borrayo finally heard Juarez over the noise of the horn and the engine's clatter. 'There's someone on the bridge, behind the bus!'

The guide sidestepped to the bus's right side. Nobody in sight. He squatted to peer underneath it. Legs were silhouetted against the wet greyness behind. 'I see him!' He squeezed past the front wheel, then entered the vehicle and started for the rear door.

It opened before he was halfway to it.

Eddie slowly turned the emergency door's handle. The catch released with a clunk. He eased it open—

And saw a soldier advancing on him, drawing his sidearm.

'Whoa, fuck!' Eddie yelped. He dropped as the gun whipped up at him. A bullet struck the floor just above his head.

If he ran, he would be an easy target. Instead he scrambled under the bus's rear bumper. A shout, followed by thudding footsteps above – then the Kaibile jumped down onto the bridge after him.

'He's gone under the bus!' Borrayo warned from the rear door. 'Go forward!'

Juarez hesitated, not wanting to move the hulking vehicle without a guide, but then released the brake. The bus lurched backwards, rear wheels settling into a gap between planks. He eased his foot down on the accelerator—

The sweeping wipers briefly cleared the pounding rain – and he saw the girl running across the bridge towards him, pursued by one of his comrades.

Borrayo hurriedly retreated as the bus rolled back at him. The movement was far more terrifying from Eddie's position. A protruding part of the chassis swept barely an inch over his head. He flattened himself against the deck. The engine revved, the exhaust pipe rattling, and the vehicle moved forward again. Stinking exhaust fumes swirled underneath it.

The soldier overcame his alarm and squatted to look beneath the bus, gun ready—

The bridge rolled to the right like a ship on a heavy sea.

Borrayo swayed, feet slithering on the wet wood. He spread his legs wider, throwing out both arms to stabilise himself—

Lying flat, Eddie recovered first. He shoved himself out from under the bus's tail and kicked Borrayo's ankle. The Kaibile dropped hard on his side. His gun hand hit the planks, knocking the weapon from his grip. It skittered across the tilting bridge and disappeared over the side.

Eddie started to rise – but the younger man was faster. Borrayo kicked him in the chest, slamming him back against the bus.

Juarez braked hard as the bridge tipped. Without Borrayo to direct him, he could no longer tell if he was centred on the crossing. A glance through the open door revealed to his horror that the vehicle was almost touching the right-hand guide rope. The deck's roll worsened, the bus's weight pulling it over.

He gasped a fearful obscenity and turned left, applying power. The rear wheels slithered before finding grip – then the bus bounded into motion, swinging leftwards. He whirled the wheel back to straighten out, then braked again. Another violent stop – and the whole bridge bucked beneath him.

★ ★ ★

Macy yelped as the planks underfoot swayed like a demented fairground ride. She held out her arms for balance, almost skipping from one beam to the next.

The pursuing soldier was less agile and much heavier. He staggered as the bridge tilted, rifle swinging across his back – shifting his centre of gravity just enough to overbalance him.

One foot slipped – and he fell, slithering downwards. Before he knew it, his legs were already over the side. He grabbed in panic at the guide rope, catching it as he went underneath. The line snapped tight, leaving him dangling over the edge.

Ahead, Macy had also been pitched sideways. A flash of fright – then she dropped into a ball. The taut rope caught her body . . .

Jolting the line from Porras's grip.

The Guatemalan fell with a scream into the churning torrent below.

Mancillo's dismay at the loss of his man immediately turned to anger. He turned to Galarza. 'Go after her!' he roared. 'Get her!'

The soldier clenched his fists, then started back across the bridge.

The bus's forward lurch had dropped Eddie on his back behind it. But Borrayo couldn't press his attack as he struggled to stay upright. Eddie kicked at his legs and scrabbled away, grabbing the bus to pull himself up—

Intense pain sliced through his palm. He yelled, snatching his scalded hand off the exhaust pipe.

Borrayo leapt on him, pounding the air from his chest. Eddie clawed at the other man, but the Kaibile slammed a brutal punch into his face. He slumped, dazed.

Another punch – then Borrayo slid off. Eddie tried to catch

his breath, but one of his attacker's hands clamped around his throat—

The other forced his head towards the hot metal pipe.

The bridge tilted queasily back towards level. Macy set off again, nimbly navigating its centre line as it reeled beneath her. A glance back as she neared the stationary bus. Galarza was coming after her—

A plank broke under her foot.

She plunged through the gap as the wood fell away, too startled even to scream—

Her other leg hit the next beam, its ragged edge tearing her jeans and skinning her shin. Now she screamed. The impact momentarily slowed her, but then she dropped again, throwing out her arms in panicked instinct.

They slammed against the planks, jarring her to a stop. For a moment. Then she started to slide, her own weight pulling her downwards . . .

She was still holding Earthbreaker. She could drop it – but part of her mind had already made the opposite decision.

Use it.

She stabbed the dagger's point into the mouldering wood. A sodden creak, damp splinters breaking loose as it dug in . . . but it held. Macy gasped, hanging onto the ancient weapon's hilt as her other hand searched for grip. A louder crack as the old plank started to split under the pressure—

Her fingers found another beam's edge. She dug in her nails, stopping her fall.

But her legs still hung helplessly forty feet above the debris-filled maelstrom below.

The sight of Eddie brawling with Borrayo, and clearly not winning, filled Nina with fear – but that was nothing compared to her horror when she saw Macy plunge through the bridge. *'No!'* she cried—

Her daughter caught herself. Fear was driven aside by relief. But the new feeling vanished almost instantly. Through the rain she saw Galarza picking his way across. 'We've got to help her!' she said, running towards the bridge – to find to her surprise that Diego was already with her.

Juarez hurriedly checked his mirrors. He had brought the bus away from the right side of the deck, but the vehicle's long rear overhang meant its tail end now extended over the guide rope. He needed to straighten out . . .

He looked ahead – and saw the American girl not far away. She had fallen through a gap in the planks. Galarza was some way behind her. Porras had been chasing her – so where was he?

Appalled realisation. 'Little *bitch*,' he snarled. She had got his comrade – his friend – killed!

He released the brake and pressed the accelerator again, setting the bus rolling slowly but remorselessly towards her.

Eddie felt the heat from the exhaust pipe on his cheek. He strained to push himself away – but the Kaibile was stronger, driving him ever closer to the searing metal . . .

The engine roared – and the pipe juddered, spewing out dirty fumes as the bus started moving.

Eddie squeezed his eyes shut as hot, stinking exhaust whirled over his face. Holding his breath wasn't a problem – Borrayo's hand around his throat was doing that for him. The Kaibile himself took the full force of the searing diesel blast. He jerked back, clapping both hands to his burned, soot-blackened face.

The bus lumbered on, jolting over the planks. Now free, Eddie rolled clear of the exhaust plume and sat up. Borrayo knelt before him, clutching at his eyes—

Eddie drove a ferocious knuckle-punch into his unprotected throat.

The bridge shook beneath Macy. Not the storm's pounding, but a lower-frequency thumping, deep, getting stronger—

She looked up – and saw the bus snarling towards her, its heavy front tyres closing the distance one plank at a time.

Borrayo reeled from Eddie's punch, mouth gaping like a dying fish. The Englishman grabbed him, intending to throw him over the side, but in his own breathless state, he lacked the strength.

Instead he rolled backwards, using his own bodyweight to propel the Kaibile at the exhaust pipe. The end of the rusty metal tube impaled Borrayo through his open mouth, smashing teeth.

Eddie wasn't finished with him. He twisted, hammering an elbow into the back of the other man's skull. The razor-edged pipe punched through the back of Borrayo's throat. His jaw snapped convulsively shut. His cheeks blew outwards as his mouth filled with hot gas, jets of high-pressure fumes blasting through his nostrils—

The bus's engine stuttered, coughed – and stalled.

Macy fought to pull herself higher as the bus's broad wheels bore down upon her, nearer and nearer—

The vehicle's engine abruptly cut out.

She gasped in relief. Saved—

But the bus kept coming.

Juarez had no idea why the bus had stalled. Caught by surprise, he pushed the accelerator to no effect – then hurriedly did the same to the brake pedal. It felt spongy, only slowing him rather than stopping. Worse, the vehicle was drifting towards the bridge's right edge, and without the engine, the steering had no power assistance. He hauled at the wheel – then frantically pulled the air brake lever beside his seat.

'Shit,' Macy gasped as the bus rolled closer. 'Shit!' All she could see was the radiator grille, towering ever higher as it came to crush her—

A sharp hiss – and the vehicle juddered to a stop, its tyre barely two feet from her outstretched hand.

Breathing heavily, Eddie stood. Borrayo was still attached to the bus's exhaust, dragged behind it before the blowback of trapped gas stalled the engine. Thick black smoke boiled from his burned lips. 'Told you smoking's bad for your health,' the Yorkshireman said to the corpse.

'Eddie!' He turned to see Nina and Diego hurrying towards him. 'Macy's fallen through a hole!' his wife shouted. 'We've got to pull her up!'

Any thought of his various new injuries was instantly driven away. 'The driver's still in the bus,' he told them. 'I'll get him, you help her.'

He used Borrayo as a stepping stone to clamber through the emergency door. The dead man flopped to the planks as Nina and Diego started around the stalled vehicle's side.

Juarez pushed the button to restart the engine, praying that whatever had made it cut out wasn't terminal. Sickly chugs echoed through the bus . . . then with a strained clatter, it fired up. He experimentally turned the steering wheel, finding that the power assistance had been restored. He could bring the bus back onto a safer line.

He looked ahead. Galarza had stopped, holding the guide

rope as the bridge's swinging eased. The American girl was out of sight below the hood. Had he run her over? A glance in the mirrors to see if she had climbed up and gone past—

Two people were coming along the bus's right-hand side.

He drew his gun, ready to shoot them as they passed the open door – then caught more movement in his peripheral vision.

Eddie ran down the bus's aisle. The driver was raising a gun—

He hurled himself at the Kaibile, slamming him against the steering wheel. But Juarez immediately retaliated. An elbow pounded into Eddie's stomach. Already breathless, he gasped and reeled back. The soldier twisted to bring his gun arm around. Eddie grabbed his wrist with one hand, clawing at the gun with the other.

The two men struggled for supremacy. Eddie, standing, was in the better position, but had been weakened by the fight with Borrayo. Juarez strained to break loose – then stabbed his free hand at Eddie's eyes.

The Yorkshireman jerked back to protect his sight, but kept his grip. The Guatemalan was pulled sideways in the seat. He clutched at the first thing he found to support himself.

The air brake control.

The brakes released. A sharp hiss, and the bus jolted forward – angling to the right.

Nina and Diego, sidestepping alongside the bus, were almost at its open door when it suddenly lurched into motion. A wall of brightly painted metal pushed the redhead towards the edge. She gasped and grabbed at the bus's flank. A window above her was open, its upper pane lowered. Her fingers gripped its top.

But she was still being forced backwards, the guide rope driving harder and harder against her trapped calves.

★ ★ ★

Eddie heard Nina's cry of alarm. A brief glance, and he saw her clinging to a window – and the bridge's side getting ever closer through the open door.

He abandoned his attempt to get the gun. Instead he grabbed the air brake. The bus jolted to another abrupt halt, throwing both men forwards.

Nina lost her grip with one hand as the bus stopped sharply, swinging her outwards over the guide rope and the rushing river below. She flailed her arm, fingers finding only wet glass and metal as her other hand strained to take her weight—

Diego grabbed her.

He shoved her back against the bus. 'Lift your legs!' he said, using a foot to push the taut rope away from her. She pulled free. The bus was now right against the bridge's edge, leaving nowhere to walk, but she was almost at its open front door – and from there she could climb onto the hood.

She held onto the open windows and used the straining line almost like a tightrope to traverse the few feet to the door. Diego followed. Nina reached the door, with relief swinging herself inside – and reacting in shock as a gun swung towards her. 'Shit!' she gasped, ducking.

Eddie forced Juarez's hand upwards. 'Get Macy!' he said through gritted teeth. 'Don't worry about me, just get Macy!'

Nina backed away and scrambled up onto the hood. The rain-drenched metal felt as slippery as ice. She slithered along it on her backside to bring her legs down over the radiator grille.

Macy was a few feet ahead of the bus, using Earthbreaker as a piton to hold herself in place. But the mouldering wood around the ancient weapon was splitting and splintering. And beyond her, Galarza was still closing.

'I'm coming!' Nina called to her daughter. She dropped to the deck. Diego landed beside her, and the two of them started to haul the teenager up.

Galarza spotted Macy's rescuers. Despite the danger, he increased his pace across the swaying bridge.

Juarez was underneath Eddie, shoulder jammed against the steering wheel's spokes as the two men fought. The Yorkshire-man's left hand was still clamped around Juarez's right wrist. The Guatemalan tried to angle his weapon towards Eddie's head.

Eddie pushed it back as hard as he could – then made a sudden, unexpected move, hitting Juarez's temple with his elbow before chopping his forearm down onto his opponent's throat. The Kaibile struggled to break Eddie's hold, the wheel turning back to the left as he squirmed and kicked—

His thrashing foot hit the air brake lever.

'We've got you, honey, we've got you!' Nina told Macy as she and Diego strained to lift her. 'Stay with us, you're almost out—'

A loud hiss behind them – and the bus started moving.

It was an automatic, its gear selector still in drive. The engine had enough torque to set it into motion even while idling. The bus ground forward, barely exceeding a snail's pace . . . but even snails eventually reached their destination.

'Mom!' Macy cried as she saw the gaudy juggernaut crawl over another plank, closing the gap.

'I know, I know!' Nina replied, pulling harder. 'Diego, get her leg up—'

The young Mexican let go of her.

Macy shrieked as she dropped back into the hole. Nina took her daughter's weight, almost losing her hold. Earthbreaker's point rasped through the rotten wood, carving a groove before catching again.

Clinging to Macy, Nina was about to demand what the hell

Diego was doing – when she saw for herself. Galarza was now only twenty feet away. Diego had moved to intercept him.

Macy turned her head to see. 'Oh my God, Diego, no!' she cried. 'He'll kill you!'

'Professor Wilde, get her out!' Diego replied, not taking his eyes off the approaching soldier. 'I can handle him!'

Nina didn't believe that for a moment, but she could do nothing to stop him. She slid a leg forward for better leverage, then hauled at Macy again.

The bus rumbled relentlessly onwards, planks creaking beneath its tyres. It angled left, right front wheel curving towards the two women.

Diego blocked Galarza's path, fists raised. 'You want her?' he shouted over the rain. 'You'll have to come through me!'

Galarza regarded him with amused contempt. 'Okay,' he replied, for a moment not moving – then his right arm lashed out with the force of a cannon shell.

Diego jinked, whipping up his forearm to deflect the incoming blow—

The Kaibile's punch hit so hard that Diego's arm was slammed back against his face. The strike sent him staggering. He recovered – only for Galarza to attack him again.

This time, the Guatemalan's fist struck his head with nothing to lessen the impact. Diego's nose broke, lips splitting. Rain running red down his face, he reeled towards the bridge's side . . .

And caught the guide rope.

Steadying himself, he looked back at Macy, then faced the soldier again—

Galarza whipped out the flick knife that Eddie had used to stab Juarez – and drove its blade into the young man's chest. Macy screamed.

The Kaibile pulled the knife out. Blood spouted from the

wound. Diego staggered forward, feebly raising a hand to his chest . . . then crumpled to the deck.

Nina hauled harder at Macy as Galarza stepped over Diego and continued towards them. 'Macy, you've got to get up,' she said in desperation. Her daughter didn't move, gazing in horror at the fallen Mexican. 'Macy! I can't lift you on my own – you've got to *help me!*'

Macy looked up at her – then at the bus bearing down on them. She strained to pull herself higher, swinging one leg sideways to try to hook her foot over the edge of the gap. Earthbreaker gouged deeper into the wood.

A thud from the bus's front wheels as it lumbered over another plank. But Galarza reached the women first. He gave Nina a cruel grin, relishing his choices: how to kill them. Stab them, kick them off the bridge – or simply wait for the bus to crush them—

Diego staggered back to his feet – and with a scream, dived at him.

A heavy thud as he collided with the startled soldier. Both men toppled over the low guide rope. A last wide-eyed look at Macy – then Diego was gone.

Macy stared in horror at the empty space where he had just been. *'No!'*

32

Mancillo swore as Galarza and Diego fell into the maelstrom. One of his men, a Kaibile who had survived hell, had been taken down by an untrained civilian – a *boy!*

He broke into a run across the bridge, fury giving him balance on the swaying planks. If he had to do the job himself, so be it. He would get the girl and the dagger – and kill everybody else in his way.

The rattling clamour of the bus's engine behind Nina over-powered all other sounds. She pulled at Macy, but didn't have the strength to lift her alone. 'Macy, *please*,' she begged, 'get up, get *up* . . .'

Macy looked back at her, desperation in her eyes—

Her swinging heel caught against the plank.

She gasped – then levered herself upwards. Nina dragged her higher. The rotten wood under Earthbreaker's point disintegrated, jarring the dagger from Macy's hand. She clawed at the planks instead – and finally dragged herself from the hole.

Nina hauled her clear a split second before the bus reached the gap. It thumped to a sudden stop as its tyres dropped into the space between the planks, rear wheels slithering as they tried to push it onwards. Both women screamed as the deck tipped, threatening to pitch them over the edge. They grabbed the guide rope, clinging to it as the crossing swayed.

★ ★ ★

Eddie kept the pressure on Juarez's throat, feeling the Guatemalan straining to breathe. He shifted position, wedging one foot against a handrail – and pushed against it, driving himself down harder. Juarez choked—

The bus slammed to a halt, throwing them both forward. Eddie landed on his back at the top of the steps. Juarez hit the windscreen before dropping back to the floor – on top of Eddie. He ploughed an elbow into the Yorkshireman's stomach. Eddie convulsed, keeping hold of Juarez's gun arm, but his grip was now weakened.

Juarez took advantage. He punched Eddie in the face, twice, three times – then forced the gun towards him.

Nina scrambled up, heart racing. She and Macy were on the bus's right, level with its open door – and inside she saw Eddie still grappling with the driver. 'Eddie!' she cried. 'I've got Macy!'

'Get off the bridge!' Eddie shouted. 'Get Macy out of here!'

'Go on, go,' Nina told Macy, flattening herself against the bus so her daughter could squeeze past. 'I'll be right behind you.' She looked back as Macy cleared the doorway to see Mancillo approaching from the bridge's far side. 'Shit! Eddie, Mancillo's coming!'

Eddie grabbed the gun with his free hand. Juarez gripped it, trying to bend his fingers back. The weapon wavered as both men fought to overpower the other. 'Just go!'

Nina ducked below the line of fire, glancing back at Mancillo again – then spotting something else. Earthbreaker was under the bus, wedged between two planks. The gap was not quite wide enough for it to fall through – but with the bus still scrabbling for traction, it could be shaken loose at any moment.

She hesitated. If the dagger fell into the river, the chances of its ever being recovered and used to cause another deadly earthquake were almost zero.

Almost. Could she take that chance? And if Mancillo realised Earthbreaker was lost, he would have no reason to keep Macy alive . . .

Her decision was made in a moment. She reached under the shuddering bus, stretching out to grab the dagger. The unsettling tingle of power ran through her hand. She pulled it into the open and started after Macy.

Another worried glance through the door as she passed it—

Juarez saw her – and forced the gun downwards.

Nina dropped flat below the step. The gun roared, a bullet clanging off metal just above her head.

The gun bucked in Eddie's hand as it fired, scorching his skin – but he ignored the pain, his wife his only concern. He looked frantically down the steps to see if she had been hit—

His grip on Juarez's gun slackened in his moment of distraction. Only by a fraction – but it was enough.

Juarez released Eddie's hand and delivered another vicious punch to his face.

Nina crawled past the door, then rose, sidestepping along the bus's length. Ahead, Macy had already passed the rear wheels.

Behind, Mancillo was almost at the vehicle's front.

Juarez's punch left Eddie dizzied. Before he could recover, the other man pushed himself higher, using the leverage he'd gained to force the gun towards Eddie's head.

The Englishman struggled to push it away, but the barrel inched inexorably closer, Juarez's finger tight on the trigger—

Eddie twisted – and kicked the steering wheel.

His heel caught a spoke, spinning it sharply around – and the bus lurched as the front wheels turned. It rode up out of the gap and veered across the bridge.

The deck rolled alarmingly, left side dropping lower, and lower. The bus's front bumper hit the guide rope, stretching it . . .

And snapping it.

The bus slithered towards the edge. The two men thumped against the driver's seat as it tipped, the gun forgotten in the fear that they were about to plunge into the river—

The bridge's roll slowed, stopped . . . then it swayed forcefully back the way it had come.

Macy had just cleared the bus's rear end when it started to move. She grabbed the guide rope and clung on as the bridge tilted under her. Nina, only halfway along the vehicle, was less lucky. As the vehicle's front end angled to the left, its long overhanging tail swung outwards, blocking her path – and shoving her towards the side of the bridge.

Eddie felt the bus tip back to the right – pitching both men down the steps. He grabbed for a handrail—

And missed.

He and Juarez rolled through the open doorway together. Eddie hit the bridge's edge, the guide rope beneath him. A desperate lunge – and he snagged it with his left hand.

But he was already over the side, falling into the void—

The rope yanked taut. He jerked to a stop, pain exploding in his overstressed shoulder and fingers.

But he held on—

Juarez fell with him – clutching in panic at Eddie's jacket. He caught his right sleeve. The garment was snatched from Eddie's arm as Juarez fell – then pulled agonisingly tight over his other shoulder as the Guatemalan's plunge was suddenly arrested. Eddie screamed as his arm took both men's weight.

Above, his fingers slowly slipped from the wet rope.

★ ★ ★

The bus's tail continued to swing outwards. Nina jumped up to grab an open window pane before the rope could trap her legs. Earthbreaker fell onto a seat inside as she held on with both hands.

The bridge's wallowing roll reversed again, tipping back to the left. She scrambled upwards, toes kicking against the rear wheel arch. The bus was about to fall into the river. If she didn't get clear, she would be going with it. Where was Eddie? She turned her head to look for him—

Fear surged through her as Mancillo reached the bus. His gun came up—

Only the bridge's undulation kept her alive. The major had to grab the front wing for support as the deck tipped ever further over.

Nina's feet found the metal rub-rails along the bus's side. She used the extra traction to propel herself through the open window, landing heavily on the worn-out seat beyond.

Mancillo steadied himself, then rounded the bus's nose and pounded up the steps. A moment of surprise: the driver's seat was empty. But there was no time to wonder what had happened to Juarez. He saw the American woman two-thirds of the way down the cabin.

The rear door was open. He hurried down the aisle to make sure she never reached it.

Every inch of Eddie's left arm burned with pain. He felt muscle fibres stretch and tear under the combined weight of himself and Juarez, his joints threatening to break. His leather jacket was like a saw cutting into his trapezius, but he couldn't shrug it off without surrendering his grip.

And even that was rapidly fading. The bridge rocked, the two men swaying beneath it like a pendulum . . .

He looked down. The Kaibile still had the gun.

Their eyes met. Eddie knew instantly what Juarez was thinking: that his chances of survival were rapidly shrinking.

So he was going to take his adversary with him.

The gun rose. It didn't matter where Eddie was hit; the shock of impact would make him lose his hold. And at such close range, it would be impossible for Juarez to miss . . .

Some combination of desperation and anger drove the Yorkshireman into action. If he was going to die, it would be on his own terms, not some puppy-killing psycho's. He let out a roar of exertion as he bent his left arm to raise himself slightly higher – and swung his right up at the planks above. 'You want my jacket?' he snarled at Juarez. 'Fucking have it!'

His right hand caught the edge of the battered wood – as his left let go of the rope.

He fell for a split second – then yelled again as his right arm took his weight. For a moment Juarez was still suspended from his left shoulder . . .

Then Eddie twisted his arm downwards.

The jacket was whipped away as Juarez, still gripping the sleeve, plunged towards the furious waters below. In his shock, he didn't even think to shoot. All he managed was a scream – which ended with horrific suddenness as he hit a tree trunk sweeping downriver. A broken branch punched through his back and burst out of his chest. Then the log rolled over, the frothing rapids swallowing him.

Eddie watched the dead man disappear, then raised his aching arm to take hold of the bridge. He started to climb back up – only to find himself swinging towards its underside as the whole crossing tipped over.

Nina stood, grabbing the seat back for balance as the bus reeled beneath her. She looked for Eddie – but instead found Mancillo advancing on her. His gun snapped up. She threw herself back into cover on the seat, but knew he would reach her in moments—

The bus's left front wheel went over the edge of the bridge.

Its front axle landed hard on the creaking planks as the rear wheels pushed it inexorably onwards. The deck tipped crazily as more and more weight went to one side . . .

The vehicle slipped sideways – and went over the edge.

Nina screamed as it fell towards the river—

The front right wheel snagged on the broken guide rope, yanking it tight. The bus's back end swung downwards beneath it as the vehicle hung from the edge of the twisted bridge.

Nina was flung against the now-horizontal seat back. Mancillo, in the aisle, fared worse. The floor pitched away from under him, throwing him down the length of the bus towards the open rear door. He snatched at a seat as he hurtled past Nina – flicking himself sideways just enough to smash down on the rear window beside the doorway.

The bus's fall downwards flipped Eddie *upwards*, the deck's sudden roll throwing him over what was now the top of the twisted crossing. Still gripping the guide rope, he thudded against the planks – which had become more like a fence.

Breathing heavily, he peered downwards. The bus was almost directly below him, its headlights pinning him in their beams.

Macy had nearly reached the end of the bridge when it bucked beneath her, throwing her into the air. She landed hard on the rocking planks. The supporting ropes groaned, on the verge of snapping. She dragged herself forward, reaching muddy – yet blessedly solid – ground.

Panting in fear, she looked back. The bridge had been twisted almost into a helix by the weight of the bus hanging from it. The long vehicle swayed back and forth, its tail not far above the thundering waters. She couldn't see her mother, or Mancillo, but her father was clinging to the side – or rather, the top – of the battered deck.

'Dad!' she yelled. He responded, but she couldn't hear him over the noise of the storm. Slowly he started to clamber towards her.

Nina groggily raised her head. Her surroundings only added to her dizziness. The bus hung vertically, the ranks of seats now forming ladders. It swayed queasily as wind pounded the bridge above.

Even over the roar of racing water, she could hear ropes straining and overstressed metal moaning and creaking. It was a coin toss which would give way first: bridge or vehicle. The thought galvanised her. She was about two-thirds of the way down the cabin's length, the climb to the front over twenty feet. She started to clamber upwards—

Metal clattered on glass below. She looked down – and saw Mancillo splayed on a rear window beside the gaping door, retrieving his gun. He checked the weapon, then glanced up . . .

And saw her.

She threw herself back into cover as he fired. Bullets ripped through the seat backs below her. The multiple layers of wood and plastic and padding blocked the initial fusillade – but then he slid closer to the bus's ceiling for a better firing angle. A hole exploded through the seat by Nina's side. She shrieked as more rounds burst through the cushion—

The gunfire stopped. Was he climbing up after her, or just out of ammo? Nina gambled on the latter; the cultists had taken the soldiers' gear when they were captured. She peered down the aisle. He was indeed out of bullets, his pistol's slide locked back. She hurriedly resumed her awkward ascent.

Mancillo followed.

The Guatemalan was faster, using his longer limbs to haul himself upwards two seats at a time. Fighting panic, Nina climbed more quickly, passing the window where she had entered the bus—

Earthbreaker was still wedged down the side of the seat.

Stopping to recover the dagger would let Mancillo gain on her. But she couldn't allow him to take it – not while he might recapture Macy and force her to use the ancient weapon. Or force *Nina* to use it. Mancillo wasn't stupid; he might have realised that what the daughter could do, so could the mother . . .

She leaned across to grab the green stone blade. The action took only a moment – but Mancillo was now just a couple of seats below her.

She shoved the dagger into the side of her waistband and scrambled upwards. The major pursued, closing on his prey. Nina felt his hand brush one boot. She jerked away, still climbing – but he raised himself higher and caught her foot again—

She kicked her other leg down hard, catching his fingers. Mancillo grunted in pain, losing his hold.

Nina kept going. The open door was not far above. Mancillo recovered, shouting a Spanish obscenity at her before pursuing once more.

Two more seats to traverse, one – then she reached the steps, clambering onto the panel at their side and going to the opening.

Rain hit her face. The bus hung precariously from the swaying bridge. Above it, the deck rose vertically, twisted and weighed down by several tons of metal. Even if she got off the bus, she would have to climb along the wall of planks until they started to level out . . .

No choice. She eased herself outside, using the wing mirror to pull herself higher. Standing in the wheel arch, she took hold of the shivering rope—

A loud thump below. Mancillo had reached the door.

'Shit,' she gasped, using the front wheel as a step to climb onto the bus's nose. She felt the rope straining as the vehicle swayed in the wind. The line was already rough with broken strands; as she watched, another snapped.

Mancillo clambered out of the doorway. Nina struggled to climb the rope, pain in her injured arm and leg flaring again—

The Guatemalan's hand clamped around her ankle.

She cried out in fright as he pulled hard, trying to shake her loose. She kicked at him, but this time couldn't make solid contact.

Her fingers slithered down the sodden rope. Another kick at his hand – but it was intercepted. He now held both her legs, dragging her remorselessly back down. She gripped the rope as tightly as she could, but he was too strong. Her right hand slipped loose. She shrieked, flailing to regain her hold—

Something jabbed into her side.

Earthbreaker.

The dagger was still in her waistband, the point catching her as she struggled. She snatched it out with her right hand, slashing it at Mancillo—

No good. He was out of reach. But the pressure on her legs eased for a moment as he reacted to the unexpected attack . . .

And she realised she had one chance of survival.

She held the sharp blade against the creaking rope – and sawed at it.

Earthbreaker's edge was old, but not dull. Strands tore with a shrill ripping noise. Mancillo looked up in alarm. 'No, what are you doing?' he barked. 'You'll kill us both—'

More strands broke. The bus dropped sharply. Only by an inch, as the rope partially split, but that was enough to shake Mancillo's footing. One hand released Nina's leg as he instinctively threw it out to keep his balance—

The rope snapped.

The bus fell away towards the river. Mancillo kept his hold on Nina's ankle – for a moment. Then his fingers slipped from her wet boot and he plunged after it.

Nina shot upwards.

With the bus's weight gone, the bridge twanged like a bowstring back towards its normal position. Nina clung onto the rope as she was flipped helplessly over the thrashing deck. Planks broke loose, wooden missiles hurtling into the air.

Below her, the bus hit the river tail-first, the torrential current sweeping its back end downstream. It toppled like a felled tree, landing on its left side with a huge splash. Mancillo hit the right front wheel, bowling back inside through the doorway. Water exploded through the open windows, sweeping him down the aisle as the bus rolled upright.

Nina lost her hold on the rope. She shielded her face from flying wood as she tumbled across the planks towards the opposite edge of the bridge—

She hit the remaining guide rope. It yanked taut, stopping her. Relief—

Vanished as the rope broke.

She screamed as she toppled from the bridge and plummeted towards the river—

Only to smash down on the bus's roof as it swept past beneath her.

The impact hurt – but it was nothing compared to the fire erupting in her leg. She had landed on Earthbreaker, the dagger's blade driving deep into her right thigh. Another scream as she tugged the weapon out. Then she slumped onto her back, blood staining the muddy froth washing over her as the bus was carried away downriver.

33

Eddie finally traversed the twisted bridge far enough to stand upright on the deck. He hurried towards the mining track – only to be thrown off his feet as the entire structure kicked beneath him. A plank split with a sharp crack as he made a hard landing.

He pulled himself clear and looked back. The bus had finally fallen, the straining bridge levelling out. No sign of any of the Kaibiles – or Nina—

'Dad!'

A voice through the storm: Macy, standing in the mud at the bridge's end. 'Macy!' he said, going to her. They hugged tightly. 'Are you okay?'

'Yeah, I'm fine – but Mom's on the bus! Look!' She pointed downriver.

Eddie saw with shock that his wife was sprawled on the bus's roof as it was swept down the canyon. 'Buggeration and fuckery! Okay, Macy – get across the bridge. Find the main road and reach a village, call for help.'

'What are you going to do?' she asked.

'Catch the bus!'

He turned, about to run back over the bridge. Macy stopped him. 'No, Dad! No! You can't leave me here!'

He smiled at her. 'You can do it, love. I know you can – you're my girl, and there's nothing you can't handle. You get to somewhere safe. I'll go and help your mum.'

'Mom,' she corrected.

His smile widened. 'I love you. See you soon.' With that, he ran for the middle of the treacherous crossing.

The bus was already some way downstream. A quick glance to make sure no logs were rushing down the river behind him – then he leapt into the raging torrent.

Nina clung to the edge of the roof with one hand, Earthbreaker in her other. Water sprayed over her as the bus reeled through the waves. She looked along the canyon's sides, hoping to find some way ashore. But the sheer rocky walls hemmed her in. There was no way she could climb them, not with a wounded leg—

A metallic thud behind her. She turned – to see Mancillo dragging himself up from the open rear door. He reached the roof, pausing to catch his breath, then looked ahead, seeing her. A flash of surprise – then his face set into a vicious snarl as he advanced.

Nina crawled forward. Her leg wound flared as if burning metal had been thrust into it. Jaw clenched to hold in a scream, she pulled herself along. But Mancillo was gaining even as the bus lurched through the maelstrom. Water smashed against its side, spray blinding and choking her. By the time she recovered, he was on her—

He grabbed her injured leg.

The trapped scream finally escaped as he yanked at her, straining the torn muscle – then she lashed out with her other leg. Glancing hits on his hand, his arm—

Then a solid strike to his face.

His head snapped back as his front teeth broke. He lost his hold on her, spitting out blood. Nina shifted position. A hard enough kick might send him over the side—

A thunderous bang echoed through the metal as the bus hit something under the water.

Nina was almost thrown over the edge as the vehicle slewed around, now moving sidelong. She caught herself, but even so, both feet went into the swollen river. She flailed her uninjured leg, catching the luggage rack, then pushed against it, bringing her other leg out of the water—

Mancillo grabbed her again – this time seizing her left ankle.

A red-hot wire burned in her right thigh as she moved it. She couldn't kick him. The Guatemalan hauled himself closer, seeing the bloody wound – and smashing his fist against it.

The pain was so intense she almost passed out. She screamed—

The cry was choked off as he grabbed her by the throat.

His fingers dug into her neck. He hissed something in Spanish, but she couldn't hear it over the river's echoing roar. He raised his other fist to hit her wound again . . .

An electric tingle in her hand. Earthbreaker.

She swung her arm, driving the dagger at his neck—

He caught her wrist.

The blade's tip was barely an inch from his throat. Nina pushed as hard as she could to finish the attack, but he was too strong. He effortlessly forced her arm back down. His bloodied lips stretched into a malevolent smile as his grip on her throat tightened—

The smile vanished as he saw something ahead. A shocked bark of '*Mierda!*' – then suddenly the crushing pressure on her neck was gone. He jumped up and leapt from the bus into the water behind it.

Nina gasped, raising her head. Mancillo had been only seconds from claiming Earthbreaker. What had he spotted?

Fear filled her as she saw for herself.

A waterfall.

Utter terror drove her into motion, the pain in her leg all but forgotten. Mancillo was swimming for one of the cliffs. Still clutching the dagger, she turned towards the opposite bank and half dived, half fell into the river.

The force of the churning current sent her tumbling. She tried to swim, but couldn't even tell which way was up. Booming scrapes and bangs echoed through the water as the bus hit rocks at the edge of the falls – then suddenly the sound was gone as it went over, leaving only the thunder of the storm-swollen cascade.

Nina broke the surface, getting a brief glimpse of the cliff before a surge of froth washed over her. But that split second was enough to know she wouldn't make it. The current was too strong, sweeping her along too fast . . .

The river's relentless push was suddenly replaced by gravity's pull – and she fell.

She screamed again as she plummeted from the top of the sixty-foot drop—

Only to slam down on something just ten feet below.

The bus had gone over the waterfall sideways-on – and was now wedged between protruding rocks. Nina landed on a window on its left side, the glass smashing to leave her hanging through the broken pane.

Falling water pounded her. A screech of tearing steel, and the vehicle dropped several inches at its front. She looked through the deluge to see the hood bending upwards, shearing away as it ground against the rock. The sheer weight of water coming down would hammer the trapped vehicle loose at any moment.

She had to get off it before that happened. But how?

Vegetation on the rock, beyond the mangled hood. A small tree had managed to take root. If it could survive there, so could she, and wait for rescue—

Someone was already there.

Shock as she saw a man amongst the branches. Porras, his head tipped grotesquely backwards on a broken neck. His rifle dangled from his shoulder. Nina tried to lever herself free of the broken window. Her hips hung through the hole, upper body and lower legs supporting her. Her thigh wound blazed again when she moved. She used both hands to lift herself, trying to lighten the load on her other leg—

Her right hand hadn't been empty when she went into the water. Where was Earthbreaker?

She saw the stone dagger precariously caught on the lowest of the bus's three rub strips. Below it was smooth, brightly painted metal . . . then a fifty-foot fall.

It was only three feet from her. Within reach – if she could raise herself from the window.

The blade rattled as water splashed down around it. A sudden gush, or a piece of debris hitting it, and it would be dislodged. She pushed herself upwards. Shards of the broken window rasped against her. She carefully edged sideways, hand stretching out for the ancient weapon—

Mancillo smashed down onto the bus's side.

The impact shook Nina – and she dropped back into the hole, barely catching herself on her elbows. Glass stabbed into her back. Earthbreaker clattered along the rub strip, away from her – and closer to the Guatemalan.

Mancillo groaned in pain as he slumped onto his side. He squinted in momentary confusion . . . then saw Nina.

And the dagger.

Both combatants burst into motion at the same moment. Nina forced herself from the broken window as Mancillo rolled onto all fours and scrabbled towards Earthbreaker. She lunged for the weapon—

Mancillo reached it first.

He snatched it away, then stood, looming over her. 'You should have destroyed it,' he said over the roar of falling water. 'Now I win. And you *lose*.' His meaning was clear.

'If you kill me, you lose too,' Nina replied. The bus lurched, the front wing starting to rip from its frame. Mancillo wavered, but recovered his balance before she could take advantage. 'You don't have Macy – so you need me to make Earthbreaker work. You've got to keep me alive!'

A contemptuous shake of his head. 'The power is in your blood – so I will find someone else with the *same* blood. I may have to test a hundred, a thousand, a *million* people . . . but I *will* find them. But you will already be dead!'

Nina flinched as he drew back the dagger to stab her—

'Oh *fuuuuuuck!*'

A shout from above – and Eddie fell onto the bus behind Mancillo.

The driver's window cracked under the Yorkshireman's weight. Metal shrilled and tore again as the force of his landing jarred the bus's nose still lower down the treacherous rock.

Mancillo staggered as the vehicle shook, glancing back to locate the new threat—

Nina put all her strength into her uninjured leg – and leapt up at him. She grabbed his outstretched hand as they collided . . .

Driving the dagger into his stomach.

Mancillo let out a shocked grunt. He released Earthbreaker's hilt, looking down to see blood trickling from the wound – then the trickle became a gush as Nina yanked the dagger out and fell back to the bus's flank.

The Guatemalan staggered backwards, hands clutching at his ruptured abdomen—

Eddie whipped up both his legs – and rolled back as Mancillo toppled against his feet, flipping the Kaibile over him to land with a hard bang on the bus's nose. The vehicle rocked again, grinding another few inches downwards.

'Nina!' Eddie said, crawling towards her. 'Are you hurt?'

'Got stabbed in the leg,' she replied through clenched teeth.

He shot a furious look at Mancillo. 'That fucker!'

She decided not to tell him what had actually happened. 'We've got to get off here,' she said instead. 'This thing's going to fall any second.' Behind her husband, Mancillo had started to drag himself towards the outcrop with the tree.

Eddie peered over the bus's side. 'There's a pool down there, but there's rocks underneath us. We'll have to make a running jump to clear 'em.'

Nina turned to show him her bloodied thigh. 'I'm not running anywhere!'

'I'll give you a hand.' He braced his feet, then squatted to lift her—

Her breath froze in her throat.

She'd thought Mancillo was trying to reach solid ground on the outcrop. But now she saw his real goal. He stretched out a hand towards Porras's dangling body, grabbing his rifle by its barrel and pulling it from the dead man's shoulder.

Then he turned, flipping the weapon into firing position—

Eddie's back was to the Kaibile. No time to warn him, or jump from the bus . . .

Earthbreaker was still in her hand.

She acted on the thought before it fully struck her conscious mind. Her arm whipped around, hurling the dagger at Mancillo—

It thunked into his chest.

He reeled back with an expression as much of utter disbelief as pain. But he didn't fall, staggering against the protruding rock.

Then his gun came up again.

Eddie had by now realised something was wrong. He grabbed Nina tightly by the waist and swept her around, making a flying leap from the roof's edge as Mancillo pulled the trigger—

Tortured metal let out a final shriek – and the battered vehicle's front end ripped apart.

The bumper and hood tore away, the bus's nose swinging downwards as its tail end remained briefly caught on the other outcrop. Then it broke loose and plummeted towards the rocks below.

Mancillo fell screaming ahead of it, rifle blazing uselessly. He smashed down on a rock at the waterfall's foot, bones shattering and organs bursting from his ruptured body – then the bus pounded down on him like a colossal hammer.

Nina and Eddie splashed down in the pool a few metres clear of the plunging juggernaut – but didn't escape the fall unharmed. Eddie hit the surface with his wife on top of him. He dropped through the churning water – and struck his ankle hard on a large jagged stone below. A cry escaped his mouth in a burst of bubbles. Then the swirling current carried them both away from the falls.

Nina surfaced, drawing in a panicked breath before clutching Eddie, supporting his head above the waves. 'What happened? Are you okay?'

'No,' he gasped, grimacing. 'Hit my leg. Think I've broken my ankle.'

The turbulence subsided as they moved further from the waterfall. Nina looked around to find the nearest bank – and check they were not about to be swept away once more. Luckily, while the pool had overflowed in the storm, with the roots of many nearby trees now in the water, the outflow was fairly broad and somewhat more gentle than the torrent above. 'Over there,' she said, turning as best she could with her one useable leg.

They made slow and painful progress towards shore. Finally they brushed over mud and roots, crawling the last few metres. Eddie slumped against a tree. 'Oh, buggeration,' he groaned, carefully extending his right leg. 'Yeah, that's fucked.'

Nina pulled herself alongside him, pressing a palm against her leg wound. 'You want me to take off your boot?'

He shook his head. 'Probably the only thing keeping it attached. I won't be running with Macy for a couple of months.'

'Macy!' Nina said in alarm. 'Did she—'

'She's okay,' Eddie told her. She exhaled in relief. 'I told her to find the nearest village and get help.'

'How long will that take?' His only answer was an uncomfortable shrug. 'I guess we're here for a while, then.'

'Yeah. At least we won't die of thirst.' They both shared a strained laugh as the rain fell around them. 'What happened to Mancillo? I didn't see, he was behind me.'

'He wanted Earthbreaker,' she replied. 'So I gave it to him. Between the ribs.'

Eddie nodded in appreciation. 'You got him with a throwing knife? Nice.'

'I've been with you for a long time. I guess I've picked up some tips.'

He chuckled. 'What about the dagger? Where is it?'

'Still in him, as far as I know. Somewhere under that.' She gestured towards the bus's wreckage, a mangled mass of multicoloured metal half visible in the spray at the waterfall's foot.

'So he literally caught the bus.'

She managed a faint laugh. 'Yeah. With his face.'

Eddie chuckled, but said nothing else in his exhaustion. Nina completely understood. They sat together in silence, watching as the storm rolled by.

Nina jerked awake. Darkness surrounded her. For a moment she was confused, not knowing where she was, then she registered the waterfall's rumble. It was less loud than before. The storm had passed, only a light rain plinking into the nearby pool. But that wasn't the sound that had awoken her—

A voice, not far away.

'Eddie,' she said, nudging her husband. 'Eddie! I heard someone!'

He didn't respond. For one terrible moment, she feared he was dead, that he had succumbed to his injuries while she was unconscious . . . then he shifted with a pained grunt. 'Where?'

'I'm not sure. Downriver, I think.' She sat upright, pain coursing through her leg. Her hand was stuck to her thigh with dried blood; a good thing, perversely, as it would have kept the jungle insects from doing their worst to the wound. She peered into the dark. 'Hello?' she cried, in a voice that sounded laughably weak. 'Hello! Can anyone hear me?'

Nothing but the patter of rain . . . then the voice returned: a man, calling out in Spanish. A flashlight beam cut through the trees near the flowing river. 'Over here!' she shouted. 'Hey, hey! Help! *Ayuda!* Over here!'

The beam turned in her direction. Beyond it, other lights did the same. 'They're coming,' she gasped in relief. 'They've found us.'

It took a few minutes for the approaching group to reach them. But Nina identified one of them before they arrived. 'Mom?' came a familiar voice. 'Dad? Are you there, are you all right?'

'We're here, love,' Eddie replied. He gripped Nina's hand, adding in a tired whisper: 'Thank God she's okay.'

Nina squeezed it back. 'I know.' She raised her voice again. 'Macy, we're here!'

The lights swept over the bank, soon finding them. Several men in grubby clothing squelched through the mud to the couple – and in their midst was Macy. She hurried past the other new arrivals to embrace her parents. 'Oh my God, oh my God! You're both okay!'

'Wouldn't go that far,' Eddie said with a strained smile. 'Hope your mates have got stretchers, 'cause we're not walking anywhere.'

Macy quickly spoke to the rescuers in Spanish, getting a

positive response. 'They do,' she said. 'They're from a village a couple of kilometres away. They'll carry you back to the road – they've got a truck.'

'How did you find us?' Nina asked.

Macy's face became sombre. 'Some bodies were recovered downstream. Rosamaria, one of the soldiers . . . and Diego.' Her voice caught as she said his name. 'They were already about to search for where they'd come from when I got to the village. I've never run so hard in my life,' she added.

Eddie put a hand on her shoulder. 'I'm proud of you, love. You did great.'

'You really did,' said Nina, beaming.

One of the rescuers spoke, a question. 'What did he say?' asked Eddie.

Macy translated. 'He wants to know if there's anybody else they need to look for.'

Nina and Eddie exchanged glances, eyes flicking towards the smashed bus, shrouded by darkness and water. 'No,' Nina said firmly. 'Everyone else is dead. There's nothing here.'

Macy gave her a small, understanding nod before relaying her words to the locals. They assembled makeshift stretchers, lifting Nina and Eddie aboard. Then they began the laborious journey back through the jungle, leaving the last remnants of the doomed expedition behind.

Epilogue

New York City

One Month Later

Macy entered Nina's study to find her mother sitting contemplatively at her computer, gazing not at the screen but something far beyond it. 'Mom? You okay?'

Nina blinked, emerging from her reverie. 'Yeah, yeah. I had an email from Oswald Seretse at the IHA. The Guatemalans sent an archaeological team to survey the Underworld, so he arranged for someone to check out the waterfall where you found us. Surreptitiously; he didn't let the Guatemalan government know what they were really looking for.'

'Which was?'

'Earthbreaker.'

Macy tensed. 'Did they find it?'

'That's the thing,' Nina told her. 'They didn't. They found the wreck of the bus, and Mancillo's body, or what was left of it. But no dagger.'

Her daughter's eyes widened in alarm. 'So somebody else found it?'

'Not necessarily. It might have been washed away downriver, or just ended up somewhere under the waterfall. There was a lot of debris coming over it in the storm.'

'But you don't know for sure.'

'No.'

'Is that bad?'

Nina closed her laptop. 'I guess we'll find out if Central America gets hit by a lot of earthquakes.'

'Not funny.'

'You see me laughing?' She stood, pausing as she realised she had done so without any pain – or even instinctively bracing for it. 'Oh, hey. I think my leg's pretty much recovered.'

'Too bad Dad can't say the same.' Eddie still wore an orthopaedic boot to protect his healing ankle.

'He'll get there.' Nina was about to exit when she noticed that Macy wore a faintly pensive expression. 'Was there something you wanted, honey?'

Her daughter hesitated before answering. 'Yeah. I . . . I was thinking about the other Macy. The one you named me after.'

Nina mentally prepared for a fight – but there was no anger or hostility in Macy's tone. 'What would you like to know?' she asked softly.

'Do you have any pictures of her?'

She nodded. 'Are you sure you want to see them?'

'Yes.'

'Okay.' She took a box of photographs from a drawer. 'I'm sure there are some in here . . .' The past flicked before her eyes as she thumbed through the pictures inside, faces long gone reappearing with flashes of memory, and emotion. 'Here.'

She took out a photo. Macy Sharif stood with her in Egypt, smiling for the camera. Her namesake regarded the image for a long moment. 'Wow. She's really beautiful.'

'She was, yes,' said Nina. 'But so are you.'

Macy smiled. 'It's okay. I don't feel threatened, or competitive. I understand why you named me after her now. She must have been someone special.'

'She was. Just like you.'

Mother and daughter shared another smile. 'Thanks, Mom,' said Macy, gently squeezing Nina's hand.

They both turned at the sound of thudding footsteps. 'Ay up,' said Eddie, leaning on the door frame to take the weight off his polycarbonate boot. 'What are you two doing?'

'We're looking at some old photos,' Nina told him. 'What's up?'

'Just wanted to see my family, that's all. Got bored of staring at my phone.'

Macy grinned. 'It helps if you turn it on, Dad. I know these new-fangled gadgets are really hard for old people to operate . . .' Eddie's elderly phone had finally given up the ghost after its trip down the river, forcing him to buy a replacement.

'Tchah! Everything I've been through in my life, and it all led to this: a sarcastic child.'

'She's not too bad,' said Nina, amused. 'Oh, I was just telling her that my leg feels okay.' She flexed it experimentally; there was not even any residual discomfort. 'How about yours?'

Eddie shifted his footing. 'Still hurts if I put pressure on it. Nowhere near as much as it did, but it'll probably be another couple of weeks before I can take this thing off.'

'Oh, man,' said Macy, shaking her head. 'It's getting kinda boring going training on my own. None of my friends want to do it with me – they're all wimps.'

'I'll come with you,' said Nina.

Macy gave her a surprised look. 'Really?'

'I need to get back into shape. Hell, running around in the jungle proved that I *really* need to. And as long as I start out nice and gentle, it should help my leg strengthen up.'

A moment of internal debate, then: 'Okay,' Macy said. 'I'll go easy on you. But not *too* easy,' she quickly added.

'Have you ever?' Nina asked.

Macy laughed. 'When do you want to go?'

'Might as well make the most of now.'

'Okay. Okay! Let's do it.' Macy almost skipped to the door. 'I'll go get changed. What are you going to wear? Your wardrobe's not exactly bursting with Spandex.'

'I've tried to convince her . . .' said Eddie, smirking.

'Eddie,' Nina chided, but with humour. 'I'm sure I've got something useable.'

Macy nodded. 'Okay. You get changed, and I'll meet you at the door.' She passed Eddie, excited to get started.

Her father watched her go, then turned back to Nina. 'She's a good lass, isn't she?'

'Of course she is,' said Nina, kissing him. 'She's my daughter.'

Twenty minutes later, Nina and Macy stood on the bank of Conservatory Water in Central Park. 'Okay,' said Macy, 'we'll start off easy, like you wanted. The distance around the pond's about three hundred metres. Can you manage that?'

Nina regarded the path around the oval lake. 'I think so. As long as you don't go too fast.'

'Don't worry, I'm not going to race you.' A wry smile – with just a hint of apology behind it. 'I know I don't need to compete with you.'

'And I don't with you,' Nina replied. 'Come on then. Let's do it together.'

They smiled at each other, then set off side by side on their journey.

A man on a bench near the boathouse watched them go. He was middle-aged, hair a thin and messy pale ginger thatch, with the yellowed fingers of a smoker – and the edgy tension of one denied his addiction by New York City's strict anti-smoking laws, which prohibited tobacco products inside Central Park. He waited for the two women to reach the lake's far side, then made a phone call.

'It's me,' he said, in a weary and gravelly Scottish accent. 'The one I've been watching? She's a prospect.' He tapped an irritated foot at the reply. 'Well, obviously I'll keep an eye on her. That *is* my job, after all. I followed her to Mexico; would have gone to Guatemala too, if the bloody airport hadn't been closed to civilian flights. But I'm sure her being in both countries right when they had their little *disturbances* wasn't a coincidence. Especially with what we already know about her past.'

He listened as the person on the other end of the line spoke again. 'Aye, I know it's far too soon to make a move yet. But give it a bit of time. I think she might be who we're after.'

A last look across the lake at the running women, then he stood up and set off into the great city.